• *OTHER BOOKS BY* **B.V. LARSON:** •

HAVEN SERIES

AMBER MAGIC

SKY MAGIC

SHADOW MAGIC

DRAGON MAGIC

BLOOD MAGIC

DEATH MAGIC

STAR FORCE SERIES

SWARM

EXTINCTION

REBELLION

CONQUEST

OTHER SF BOOKS

SHIFTING

VELOCITY

• *Visit* **BVLarson.com** *for more information.* •

TECHNOMANCER

UNSPEAKABLE THINGS: BOOK ONE

Published by 47North
P.O. Box 400818
Las Vegas, NV 89140

ISBN-13: 9781612182322
ISBN-10: 1612182321

TECHNO-
UNSPEAKABLE THINGS: BOOK ONE
MANCER

B. V. LARSON

47N⬥RTH

1

I slowly became aware of my surroundings. I felt groggy and I knew I must have been drugged—probably for pain. I was lying in a bed. I knew I was in a hospital room, but I had no idea how I had come to be here. There was a TV mounted high on the wall in front of me, blaring with late-night infomercials. The TV tried in vain to sell me waffle irons, jewelry, and exercise equipment. Attractive, almost frantic people tried to get me to pick up the phone and call *right now*. The bluish, flickering light from the TV screen provided most of the illumination in the room. The door was closed and the curtains were drawn around my bed. Apparently I rated a single occupancy, as the bed to my left was empty.

I searched my foggy brain for information, but I found precious little there. I had names for all the furniture around me, and I understood the function of each item. But I did not know my own name.

Much of what we are exists in the mysterious realm called memory. Our identities reside there. Without memories, what are we? Virtually nothing. Since I had no memories, I decided to investigate my surroundings and build some new ones.

I stirred under my sheets and felt sharp, stabbing pains. I noticed an intravenous drip line taped to my wrist. I curled my lip at the IV. Here was the source of the drug fogging my brain. I thought vaguely of pulling out the needle, but it seemed like too much effort. I reached out, kinked the clear plastic tube that ran to the sliver of steel in my arm, and pinched it. The flow stopped.

I waited for several minutes, lying there and gathering my thoughts. I felt like sleeping again, but stubbornly refused to let my mind fade away. I knew if I did, that IV line would open and the fluid would run into my veins.

After a while, my mind began to clear. Carefully, I lifted away the sheet over my legs and inspected the damage. My parts were all there, but there was a hard cast on my right leg below the knee. I was pretty well mangled. I saw staples, sutures, dark scabs, and even glassy spots where they'd used glue to hold my flesh together. The scabs flaked away at my touch, revealing fresh, pink skin growing underneath. How long had I been here?

Still pinching the IV drip line, I forced myself into a sitting position. The world swam for a moment, then steadied. I noticed that someone had brought me a flower. I spotted it to my right on a tiny table. I turned my stiff neck from side to side, but didn't see a phone in the room, or any sign of clothing more significant than the flannel smock I was wearing.

I looked at the flower again. Someone must have placed it there, either out of concern or kindness. Maybe it meant

I had at least one friend in the world who cared. I tried to remember friends, relatives. I drew a blank. As the implications sank in, I began to worry. How much of my mind had I lost? Would it come back in time?

I looked at the flower one more time, seeking solace. Whoever had brought it, they must have done so a long while ago, because it was dead. The flower wasn't a red rose—which would have left me hopeful of a romantic interest. It wasn't pink, yellow, or even white. In fact, it wasn't even a rose. It was a chrysanthemum. A big purple one. It had sagged over, its frilly head growing too heavy for the stalk as it expired. Dipping down like a weeping mourner, each of its long thin petals was tipped with crinkly brown.

I stared at the dead flower in its cloudy vase of green glass. How long would it take for a flower to die like that? Three days? A week? Somewhere in between, I guessed. In any case, the inescapable conclusion was that I'd been lying here in this hospital bed for quite some time.

There was a tiny note on the chrysanthemum, tied around its neck like a collar. It was written on folded purple paper and said: *Hope you feel better—Holly.* I wondered who the hell Holly was, but my mind produced no answers. Maybe she was the woman who had hit me and landed me here. Maybe she hoped I would lighten the lawsuit if she did the courtesy of sending me a flower. If so, she was in for a surprise.

By this time, I'd grown tired of pinching the IV line. I untaped the needle from my wrist, wincing as the adhesives plucked out fifty or so hairs from my arm. I found a box of tissues and wadded up a stack of them before pulling out the needle. It didn't hurt much, but the blood flowed. I pressed the tissues against my wrist and muttered curses.

I got up at last and staggered around my bed in widening circles. My mind was still fuzzy, but it was clearing up fast. The cast on my right leg made walking difficult. I stretched painfully, and some of the stiffness left my body as I did so. I found a paper inside a plastic sheath hanging from the foot of my bed. Inside were a few printed facts. My name was Quentin Draith. It seemed like an odd name, but it did ring a bell. The rest of the sheet was a list of stats: blood gas numbers, dates, operations. I'd been here for ten days.

The door rattled. Some dark instinct within me caused me to release the paper in its plastic sheath and let it fall back into place. I flopped back, painfully, onto the bed. There was no time to pull up the sheets, so I didn't bother. I did conceal the dangling IV line, however.

I didn't move as the door swung quietly open. A figure stood there, watching. I opened one eye to a slit in the dimly lit room, and I watched her in return. The nurse had a fresh IV bag in her hand. The clear liquid inside gleamed in the light from the corridor behind her.

I had a hazy memory of someone coming in and changing that little bag of drugs now and then, whenever I showed signs of life. Perhaps this nurse was the culprit. I did my best to simulate deep sleep. I let my head loll on the pillow as convincingly as I could, even though it hurt to do so. The nurse hesitated for a long while, then finally closed the door quietly and left.

My eyes snapped open again and roved the room. For ten days they'd been drugging me, keeping me in this helpless state. How long did they plan to continue? Although I could not recall the details, I had the impression that my personal history was not one filled with happy events. I didn't like depending on the kindness of strangers.

I stood up again and dragged my leg to the door. I leaned heavily on the door when I got there. The window had security wire embedded in it, forming a pattern of diamonds. I peered out of the small, rectangular pane of glass into the quiet corridor beyond.

I tried the handle, applying gentle pressure to make sure it opened quietly. It only went down half an inch before it stopped dead. I looked down and rattled it gently. I realized with a cold feeling that I'd been locked in. I tried the bathroom door next, but that was locked as well.

I looked around the room with wide, staring eyes. A trickle of sweat went down the back of my neck. I hobbled back to my bed, dragging a leg that remained encased in a fiberglass cast. I was already thinking of escape, but the leg cast would make such a thing difficult, if not impossible.

I was uncertain what to do next. I tried to take stock of my situation. I was being drugged on a regular basis, which could be excusable immediately after an accident, but not a week later. I was locked in my room as well. What was going on?

I searched the room. All the basics were there: TV, water bottle, bedpan—but no phone. No windows to the outside world either. Digging in the bed on a hunch, I discovered something. A photograph lay tucked under the pillow. I had a vague memory of placing it there. But why?

I took a moment to examine the image. It was old, from the days before people printed such things in their homes. A young woman and a baby were tightly framed in the shot, plus most of a man wearing a white T-shirt. I couldn't see his face, because he apparently had taken the picture himself by extending out his arm and trying to capture the entire family. He'd missed and cut off his own head above the chin. There was little else in the photo, as the people were too close to the camera and filled the frame.

I examined the photo, flipping it over and searching for a date. There was nothing. I didn't recognize the people, and that upset me. Was this my mother? Was I the baby? I really didn't know. The thought was disturbing because I'd so clearly made an effort to keep possession of the picture. Some previous version of me had considered it valuable. I took it with me, determined to hold on to it. I trusted the wisdom of my past self more than anyone in this place.

A new fear filled me as I pondered my situation further. What if I had awakened like this many times, only to be drugged back into sleep and forgetfulness? I knew there were plenty of modern anesthetics used by paramedics that erased traumatic memories from victims. Was such a drug being administered in my case? If so, why?

I frowned and decided to take matters into my own hands. I recomposed myself upon the bed and waited in approximately the same position I had been when the nurse had last looked in on me.

It didn't take long. Less than ten minutes later, she was at the door again, peering in. This time, she didn't retreat. She stepped inside, having obviously decided to freshen my drugs whether the old bag was empty or not. She was Hispanic, about thirty years old, and good-looking. Her brunette hair was cut short, but remained feminine. Her eyes were a reddish-gold rather than brown.

As she approached, my eyes snapped open.

"What can I do for you?" I asked.

"Oh, hello…," she said. "I have to adjust your medication."

I revealed the needle and the tube connected to it. The plastic tube drooped and the needle at the tip gleamed. "You mean this?"

"You pulled it out?"

"Apparently."

She sighed. "We're going to have to put that back into a fresh vein now."

"I don't think so."

"Don't be difficult, Mr. Draith."

"I'm known for being difficult," I said, feeling in my bones it was true.

She licked her lips and eyed me for a moment. She took the old bag down from the hook over my bed. She examined it critically. "How long ago did you...? Your medication is dangerously low. You may be suffering from withdrawal symptoms."

"Withdrawal? It's far too early for that. What is that stuff you've been pumping into me, anyway?"

"The doctor does not appreciate this kind of—"

"Send him around then. I want to talk to him anyway."

"*She* won't be back until the morning shift."

I nodded. "Good enough, but tell her to hurry. I'll be checking out today."

"What?" she asked, shaking her head. "That's impossible. You've got seven broken bones and there was internal bleeding. I can't understand how you're able to sit up."

"I always heal fast," I said. For some reason, I could remember that detail of my previous life.

"Mr. Draith, your lack of cooperation is not appreciated. I have a hard enough job here without this nonsense. I have a fresh needle, and we're going to start this line again now."

"Sorry," I said, shaking my head.

"Are you afraid of needles or something?"

"I'm only afraid of what people can put into them."

I stared into her face, and she looked troubled for a moment. I took the time to read her name tag.

"Miranda," I said. "Don't get yourself into more trouble than you're already in."

Her eyes widened, then narrowed again. She moved her hands quickly, and I should have seen it coming, but I didn't. She reached up and pressed a call button over my head. I moved to grab her wrist, but halted. What was done was done. I knitted my fingers behind my head and leaned back against the headboard.

"You shouldn't have done that," I said.

I watched her lip-glossed mouth tighten. "You're going to have your medication, Mr. Draith," she said.

I gave her a confident smile in return. "We'll see."

The nurse left without another word. I stared at her as she exited the room, but I was too worried to enjoy the view. After she was gone, I wondered if I'd been a fool. Maybe I should have taken her hostage. The trouble was, I didn't think it would work. I had no weapons—I didn't even have clothes.

The next face to appear at the rectangular window was much less to my liking. Made all of harsh angles and beetling brows, the orderly had muscles that jumped in his cheek as he peered in at me. He rattled the door and opened it, watching me warily. I lay on the bed as before, seemingly relaxed and unconcerned.

He was dressed in ugly surgical green. He looked like a TV wrestler, and his face was acne-scarred. He stepped inside with the attitude of a man stepping into a tiger cage. I could have looked at his name tag, but I didn't care to know his name. I simply stared at him, smiling with my mouth but not my eyes.

He let the door click behind him. Instead of needles, he had a tangle of black straps in his hands. The straps had a number of clips like those used on backpacks. There were two blue circles of thick cloth as well. Those, I imagined, were to go around my wrists. My heart accelerated in my chest.

"All right, Mr. Draith, give me your wrists," he said.

"How much do they pay you for this?" I asked.

That threw him for a moment. He blinked at me. "What?"

"Keeping people drugged against their will. Illegally restraining patients—that sort of thing? I bet you have a long list of felonies on your sheet working here. They must pay you better than they pay the doctors."

The orderly took two uncertain steps toward me and grimaced. "We've got ways of dealing with uncooperative patients such as you. There's no crime in it."

"All right then," I said, sitting up. I lifted my bare wrists toward him. "Let's do this."

His eyes flicked from my face to my arms, which didn't bulge with a power-lifter's biceps but were reasonably athletic. He took another step forward, his frown relaxing a fraction. "I'm glad you have come to your senses, Mr. Draith. I certainly didn't look forward to having to wrestle with you. The nurse thought you were going to be a problem."

I let him put one hand on my wrist before I made my move. My other hand stabbed up, thrusting two stiff fingers into the larynx. I pulled the blow slightly, using enough force to stun but not to break the delicate bones of the throat and possibly kill him.

He choked in shock and dropped the tangle of restraints. His free hand groped for his throat.

I took the opportunity to give him a hard kick. Lower leg casts are really only useful for one thing: turning your foot into a club. My fiberglass-covered foot connected with the orderly's gut. Aiming really wasn't difficult; his knees had flexed in reaction to the pain in his throat, and he'd lined himself up with my foot perfectly. I couldn't miss. He went down with a woofing sound.

"You're right," he said a few moments later while sitting on the floor. "They don't pay me enough."

"I need my clothes," I said. "I'm checking out early."

The orderly recovered somewhat, and I saw rage in his face. I'd hoped to have knocked all the fight out of him by now, but I could see I'd failed.

"Fuck you, man," he said, his voice rasping. He attempted to rise.

His left hand came up with a small canister. I knocked it down before he could spray me. Pepper spray, garden variety. Somehow, he managed to get some of it on his own forearms, and he howled about that. Still, he didn't stop coming at me. I could tell if he got the upper hand, he wouldn't stop with strapping me into bed. He'd keep going.

I felt a little bad for him as I repeatedly bashed his head with my cast and fists. In the end, I took his clothes when he lay sprawled on the floor. If I'd had my wallet handy I would have left him a tip. He was a dedicated man.

I took a card key from his belt. When the corridor outside looked empty, I popped open the lock.

I ran into the night nurse at the desk down the hall. It was Miranda, the same woman who'd sent the orderly in after me. She did a double take that was almost comical. By the time she realized who I was, it was too late for her.

She reached for something under the desk, but I twisted it out of her grasp before she had the safety off. It was a .32 automatic, a compact but deadly weapon. I didn't aim it at her face, not wanting to be rude, but kept it between us. I leaned over her desk and talked to her in a low, earnest voice.

"Is this whole place armed to the teeth?" I asked.

"We have a lot of dangerous patients here," she explained, glaring at me and rubbing her right wrist. "We take in all the psychos the police drop off at night." She looked at me pointedly as she said this.

I shrugged. "So, was I brought in under arrest?"

"No."

"Then who paid you off? Who gave the order to keep sticking me with these drugs and keep me drooling?"

Miranda looked worried for a moment. Maybe, for the first time, she realized she might be the criminal here, not me. She shook her head slowly.

"I don't know what you're talking about. We just follow Dr. Meng's orders. You were dropped off, like any other crazy off the Strip. The orders were a little odd…"

"You don't say?" I asked. I helped myself to a handful of Halloween candy I found in a bowl on the counter. It was slightly stale, but now that I was off my medication, my stomach was working again and I was getting hungry.

"Did you kill Ron?" she asked, her eyes widening as she examined the surgical greens I was wearing, no doubt noting the dark stains and the name tag.

I glanced down at myself. "Is that his name? No, he's just having a nap."

Miranda glared at me. "What do you want?" she asked.

"Let's see, kidnapping, unlawful restraint, illegal use of prescription drugs…oh, and let's not forget about assault. I would say five to ten years each in the federal pen should do it."

She swallowed. "I was just doing my job."

"Is that why you went for a gun under your desk rather than calling the cops?"

"I'm not in charge here. I follow my employer's orders."

I smiled. "Not a novel defense. But I'll accept it. Just cut this cast off me and take me to your leader, the honorable Dr. Meng."

"She won't be down until—"

I cut her off, pointing with the black barrel of her pistol at the clock on her wall. It read five thirty.

"Shift change at six?" I asked. "Things are pretty quiet around here. I've never seen such a quiet hospital at night."

"We're private, and Sunset isn't exactly a hospital. It's a sanatorium."

I nodded slowly. That explained all the safety glass and the lack of external windows in my room.

"I get it. When does the good Dr. Meng get to work?"

Miranda chewed her lip. "Six," she said.

"We have just enough time then. Cut this thing off me."

Miranda got up and led the way. I humped along close behind her, expecting a trick, but she didn't try anything. We went into an exam room and she produced a small circular saw built for the precise purpose of cutting off fiberglass casts. I sat up on the exam table and threw my leg onto it. I kept the pistol lying on my belly with my hand on top of it.

She pointed at my toes, which I could see in the brightly lit room were fairly purple. "Are you sure about this?" she asked. "The fracture is only about a week old."

"That's long enough," I said, hoping that it was. I didn't feel much pain inside that cast. I would have liked to leave it on to be certain, but I knew I couldn't run with that thing. Of course, if I cracked the bone again I would be crippled. I breathed through my teeth as she began sawing.

It didn't take long. When she'd made the cut, I reached out and cracked the cast wide open with my hands. Inside the fiberglass and cotton, my leg was pale and crisscrossed with black sutures. I lifted my leg out and placed it gently on the floor. I leaned down with increasing weight. It tingled, but it held.

"See?" I said.

"I can't understand how you can walk on it. And there were more fractures, ribs mostly."

"Don't worry about it," I said. "Now, take me to the doctor's office. We'll wait there."

Miranda looked at me uncertainly. "What do you intend to do?"

"Find out what the hell is going on—starting with why I'm here."

Dr. Meng's office was totally unlike the rest of the sanatorium I'd seen thus far. There were expensive paintings, a high wall of real books in a cherry wood bookcase and thickly padded chairs of shiny leather. I sat myself behind the cherry wood desk and threw my sickly looking leg on top of it, knocking aside a tablet computer, an elaborate phone, and a cup bristling with gold pens.

"Nice setup," I said, looking around.

"I've got to go back to my station now," Miranda said, taking a step toward the door.

I shook my head. "No way."

She halted, looking at me sidelong. "If I'm away for much longer, someone will notice and come looking for me."

"They won't come in here."

She hesitated. "Well, what about Ron? I need to give him first aid at least."

"Ron's asleep and doesn't care about that right now."

Her shoulders slumped as she realized I wasn't letting her go. I still had the pistol in my hand, aimed at the ceiling.

"You really are a bastard. Has anyone ever told you that?" she asked.

I reflected on it for a moment, but couldn't recall. "Probably," I admitted. I picked up Dr. Meng's tablet computer and pecked at it.

"Pull my records up on this thing, will you?" I asked.

"Do I have any choice?"

"We always have choices," I said, waving the pistol in the air a little.

The nurse tapped at the screen angrily and shoved it back at me. She looked at the clock nervously. It was ten minutes to six.

"I see," I said, studying my own record. I was determined to recall details. There weren't many; apparently I was as blank a slate to these people as I was to myself. There was no prior address, no employer listed, and no primary care physician. No relatives were in the records either. There was only a list of injuries and operations, followed by a link to a billing record. I tapped at that, but was blocked by another password.

"Sign me in so I can read my billing records, please," I said.

Miranda shook her head. "Sorry. I don't have the password for that."

I believed her, and since it was almost time for the infamous Dr. Meng to make her entrance, I figured it didn't matter much anyway.

"What's Dr. Meng like?" I asked.

Miranda smiled prettily, but I thought I saw something mean behind that smile. "She's tough," she said.

I frowned at her, not liking the way she looked at me. It was as if she thought revenge was near, and it was going to be sweet.

3

Dr. Meng arrived in a whirlwind of energy at precisely 6:03 a.m. She was a small Asian woman with short black hair and flashing eyes. She appeared much younger than I had expected for a doctor in a management position at an institution like this one. Late thirties, if I had to guess. She wore the traditional white lab coat over professional-looking clothing. She didn't seem to notice me at first, despite the fact I still had an injured leg thrown over her desk and a pistol in my hand.

"There you are, nurse," Dr. Meng said in irritation. "Why are you in my office and away from your station?"

Miranda made a silent sweep of her hand, indicating me. Dr. Meng followed her gesture and curled her lip upon seeing me. She walked quickly into the room and began picking up the objects I'd knocked onto the floor. She moved with rapid, irritable motions.

"You've made quite a mess," she said.

"I have a few questions for you, Doctor."

Meng straightened and looked at me with her head cocked to one side. "I'm not really surprised to find you out of your room and pestering my staff. You always were a rude guest, Draith."

It was my turn to frown. "Have I been here before?" I asked, reluctantly giving away that I had amnesia. I figured it was a secret I couldn't keep forever anyway. If she knew me and I didn't remember her, faking it was going to be quite hard. I had the faint hope she was a friend of some kind, but I didn't get the feeling that our prior relationship was cordial. There was no warmth in her toward me, no friendly greeting.

She put her hands on her hips and tilted her head farther. Then, she slowly nodded. "If you are who you appear to be, then it must have been the accident."

*If you are who you appear to be...*I wondered about that statement, but I decided to file it away until later.

"I want to ask you about the medication I've been receiving," I said. "Did you prescribe it?"

"Of course. But I hadn't intended you to lose more than the unpleasant memory of your recent trauma."

"You might have overdone it, in that case. What were you covering up?"

"Did you really wish to remember a car accident? Aren't such unpleasant, frightening events best deleted?"

I glared at her. "I certainly don't think that was your decision to make."

Meng chuckled. "Who else then? This is my domain, after all, Draith."

There was something in her face, something predatory. It was as if *she* held the gun and not I. She didn't seem perturbed by the fact I was armed. I wasn't pointing the gun at her, but a normal person would have been eyeing the weapon with concern. Instead, she had the attitude of a principal sternly rebuking an errant student.

"I'll be getting back to my station, Dr. Meng," Miranda said quietly.

Dr. Meng nodded. She still wore that confident, bemused expression and continued to gaze at me. I thought about waving my gun around and ordering Miranda to stay put, but somehow, it didn't seem worth it. No one appeared interested in calling the cops. They didn't seem to know quite what to do with me, but they didn't actually fear me. It was disturbing.

"Could you take your foot off my desk, Draith?" Dr. Meng asked. "I believe you've leaked some lymph fluids on my blotter."

With a sigh, I eased my foot off the desk and put it down beside its twin. In a way, it was a relief. They both ached, but the one on the desk had begun to throb.

"Why don't you just tell me what all this is about?" I asked. "Start with the beginning. How did I get here and why have you been holding me?"

Meng stared at me for a moment, then laughed loudly. She shook her head. "I'm not here to help you nose around, Draith! Have you forgotten *everything*?"

I leaned back and tried to look confident. I had a flash of memory then, something I knew was a snippet of my real past. I remembered buying her a drink in a bar. It had been a strange place full of strange people. I grabbed hold of the memory before it could fade away and tried to make the most of it that I could.

"Of course not," I said. "I remember buying you a drink once—not long ago."

Meng shook her head. "You're wrong. That was a long time ago, in a distant place."

I didn't argue, having no way to judge the honesty of her words. I did note that she seemed mollified, however. She didn't know how severely my mind had been erased. That was just how I wanted things.

She took something out of her pocket, a metal object. She placed it upon the desktop between us with a mysterious air. It was bronze in color and looked well aged. Staring at it, I realized it was a statuette of a woman with wings raised in midflight.

Dr. Meng was studying me, watching my reaction closely. "What do you think of that, Quentin?" she asked, using my first name for the first time. "How does it make you feel?"

I flicked my eyes up to meet hers, then looked at the statuette again. I shrugged, feeling nothing special. "I thought the Maltese Falcon was supposed to be black."

She glared at me and moved her hand toward the thing, as if to snatch it up again in a fury. I felt as if I'd insulted a religious icon of hers. Perhaps I had.

"Fine," she snapped. "Your resistance is high—but that's not an excuse for rudeness."

"Um, why don't you tell me what it is?"

"It's a hood ornament," she said. "The rarest of them. Found right here, on this scrap of land where they built this sanatorium."

"Uh-huh," I said, trying to sound impressed. It looked like a hunk of old bronze to me. It would serve fairly well as a paperweight, but appeared likely to fall over if bumped.

"We think Harriet Frishmuth sculpted it around 1920. She did a lot of these, and due to the stamp, we know it was forged at the Gorham Foundry in Providence…"

"Look," I said, tapping my fingers on her desk, "I'm sure this antique is worth thousands, but I don't see—"

"Always you play the fool," she snapped, cutting me off. She picked up the statuette and eyed it closely. "It's worth millions, billions—perhaps more. It's priceless, like all of its kind."

My eyebrows were riding high in disbelief. "Billions? For part of an old car?"

"Not just any old car. It came from here, at this crux point. It was probably mounted on an automobile that moldered away in the barn of some desert rat before they developed the area. I'm not sure why it became a local nexus—but it did."

I let out a sigh of breath. She had used a long list of terms that meant nothing to me. I was having difficulty buying anything she was hinting at. "OK," I said. "So what exactly does it do?"

She released a puff of air, a tiny snort. "It rules this place. Or rather I do, as I'm attuned to it. Have you forgotten everything?"

"Show me," I said.

Meng laughed. "A rare request indeed. Most people I meet in this office beg for mercy when I reveal the artifact—not a demonstration. But I'm going to take a chance on you, Draith. I'm going to assume you are who you appear to be, and not some copy from another place. I'm going to lie for you. I'm going to tell my associates you escaped."

"I did escape."

"No, not just from your room. In this fiction, you've escaped *me*. You've slipped from my grasp and vanished from my domain entirely."

Her domain? I thought, but I didn't ask more.

"This is a daring step for a person in my position, Draith. I'm not like you. When I take silver for a job, I stick to it. I'm not a wandering rogue. I have a reputation and a home."

I had the vague feeling I was being insulted, but I shrugged and waited for her to continue.

"First, you will need better clothing," she said, pressing a button on her desk. I'd not noticed it before. It was recessed into the wood itself.

I shifted in my chair, concerned. Had she activated a silent alarm, fitted in with all kinds of bullshit meant to put me off my guard? I wasn't sure, but if it was, it was too late to do anything about it. I leaned back, letting my pistol rest on her desk, and tried to appear calm and in control.

"I would be happy with whatever clothes I came in with," I said.

She shook her head. "I'm afraid they were cut away and destroyed. We kept some of Tony's things, however. They were in better shape and there was one item we were looking for."

We? I thought. Yet another reference to an out-of-sight cabal of allies. I was determined to remember that *we* and find out who they were. I wondered about this person she called Tony. The way she mentioned him, it seemed she assumed I knew who she was talking about.

"What happened to Tony?" I asked.

"Killed," Meng said without a hint of concern. "In the same accident that brought you to us."

"Did you know him?"

"Of course I did. Everyone knew Tony. You were his friend, Draith. Pull it together, man. You must remember something."

I narrowed my eyes toward her. She didn't have much of a bedside manner. She was telling me my friend was dead, but without a note of compassion. If I could have remembered the man, I was sure I'd have been upset.

Miranda showed up, apparently having been summoned by the button in Dr. Meng's desk. The good doctor ordered her to get Tony's things. Miranda quickly returned with a plastic bag. There wasn't much inside. Mostly, it consisted of a black overcoat with a few lumps in the pockets. I shrugged it on.

"That's all?" Dr. Meng asked the nurse. "Disappointing."

"He wasn't wearing this at the time of the event, milady," Miranda said. "The coat was in the backseat. Everything he had on at the moment of death has been...lost."

Milady? I couldn't hide my wide eyes when I heard that. It sounded to me like their relationship went deeper than the professional norm.

I cleared my throat. "It will cover these green scrubs, at least," I said. I took this opportunity to slip the photograph I'd found under my pillow out of my scrubs and into a pocket.

I decided I would play along with these two. I wanted a clean break from this place. If I could get out of here without further weirdness, I'd be happy.

"What do you want me to do, exactly?" I asked.

"I want you to go out there and do what you do best. I know there are strange things happening in the Community, and I know you've been trying to investigate them. Keep doing it. Keep pestering and sniffing about like a stray dog at a butcher's shop. If you find anything interesting, come tell me about it. Find out what happened to Tony. I liked him—even if he was a petty thief."

All this talk of my being a mongrel and a loser who consorted with more of the same finally annoyed me. I waved the pistol around. "I don't understand your attitude. I've got the gun."

"You do?" she asked.

I felt a tingling in my hand. My eyes snapped to my fingers, which were still curled around a ghostly trigger. There was no pistol visible in my hand, however. There was nothing there at all. The freaky thing was I still felt the weight of it, for a fraction of a second. But then that was gone too, and I was left clutching air. The gun had vanished.

"How did you do that?" I asked, feeling my first real thread of fear. Up until that moment, I'd taken all her hints as a big mind game, perhaps meant to talk me into giving myself up. She was, after all, a brain doctor.

"Like this," she said, and she smiled at me more broadly.

I eyed her teeth, and they grew in my sight until they were big and white like the infamous grin of the Cheshire Cat. At the same time, the rest of the room that surrounded us faded. For a split second, it was just me and that grin in our own private universe. The rest of reality was a gray-white nothing, like an old TV tuned to static air.

I tried to shout, but there was no sound. I felt my throat quiver, but that was all. The next sensation I had was that of falling briefly, followed by a hard landing on unforgiving, rippled concrete—a set of stairs that came up and hit me in the ass. I tumbled forward with a series of mild pain explosions. Fortunately, I only had about three of those hard steps to roll down. At the bottom, I picked myself up and felt for newly broken bones. There were only bruises.

I had fallen into an emergency stairwell. It was a big, echoing place, where everything was gray-painted steel tubing and stained cement. Above me a sole fluorescent tube in a wire cage illuminated the scene with harsh, blue-white light.

A single dark object sat upon the steps. It was the .32 automatic Dr. Meng had caused to vanish from my hand before she had made me vanish after it. I snatched it up and put it into my coat pocket.

I faced the emergency exit at the bottom of the stairs. Above me the stairs wound upward, switching back and forth into the distance. I reached out and pushed the panic bar on the emergency door and hobbled outside.

A whining alarm sounded. It wasn't very loud, but it was irritating. I walked away, limping as I went, and pulled my overcoat around myself to cover the surgical greens I'd stolen. The gun weighed down the right pocket, causing it to bang into my thigh as I limped along.

I was on a sidewalk, stained and deserted. The sun had recently risen and the early morning light was diffused through clouds. I looked up and down the street, then behind me. The Sunset Sanatorium rose high, built entirely with ugly square blocks of concrete. It looked like a fortress, and the top of it was complete with a tall square tower. Free at last, I had no plans to return to this freaky place. I wanted to put some distance between me and Meng's prison.

I limped down the street and took the first turn I could. I didn't look back again.

One thing I remembered was the city. The streets of Las Vegas felt familiar; they felt like home. They called this place Sin City. Viewed from a distance in the dark, it was a glittering mass of lights that rose from the desert floor a hundred miles from everywhere. Once, it had been a lonely rest stop on highways between Los Angeles and the rest of the world, but it had grown and gathered its own followers. Most of these followers sought fame, fortune, and decadence. But my town was waning now, eclipsed by online gambling, online porn, and economic decay. It had taken a turn for the worse. For all of that, it was a unique city, and I felt at ease here.

After I'd turned a few random corners and avoided several sets of staring eyes, I paused, leaning against a chain-link fence surrounding a boarded-up gas station. The rusty links rattled and pushed back against me like bedsprings.

I felt a little off balance. I wondered how many days it had been since I'd eaten solid food.

I took stock of things. As it stood, I was apparently destitute and not overly loved by those who knew me. I had no close relatives—no mom I could call and pester for a loan. I methodically searched the pockets of Tony's coat. I found the pistol where I'd put it, in the right front pocket, but underneath that was a pair of sunglasses. I pulled them out and eyed them. They were black plastic and appeared to be of little value. I shoved the sunglasses away and forgot about them. I kept digging and found a set of keys next. These had far greater possibilities. I examined them closely to see what they might open. The keys had few distinguishing characteristics. There were several that could have been for any door in town, standard house keys. There was a large car key, however, and a keyless remote to go with it. I eyed the key in the dawn light until I made out a Cadillac emblem. *Great*, I thought. All I had to do now was roam the city parking lots, pressing the unlock button, until either a car beeped or the batteries in the remote ran out.

I slipped the keys back into a pocket, and found something even more interesting in the inside breast pocket. A wallet. I waited until no one was staring at me before I looked inside. Eighty-three dollars and a few pieces of plastic. There was a pack of business cards describing Tony Montoro, the manager of a bar called the Pole Dance Palace. Seeing the cards made me chuckle and provided me with a brief glimpse of memory. I saw a bar built around a circular stage and a lively crowd of drunks sitting at tables. The card had an address. I committed the address to memory and slipped the wallet back out of sight. Had I been a regular there? Not knowing gave me a strange feeling.

When I reached the boulevard, I was able to flag down a taxi. I had it haul me a few miles uptown and drop me off at an all-night diner that was close to Tony's joint. I didn't want to pull right up to the door, and I didn't want to wait any longer for a meal, so a diner seemed like a good compromise.

I ordered black boiled coffee and a plate of eggs Benedict. I knew somehow when I saw the picture on the menu that the dish was a favorite of mine after recovering from a rough night. The waitress raised one eyebrow, but took the order wordlessly and swished away. When the food came, I ate all of it. My stomach rolled slightly when I was done, but I kept it down. What I needed now was sleep, but my instincts told me this was not the time to lie down and check out.

I washed up in the bathroom and spotted a clock on the way out. It was 8:00 a.m. I paid with a twenty and left the place feeling considerably better. I fished the pair of sunglasses out of Tony's pockets and stepped into the growing glare outside. The desert sun was over the buildings now, and painfully bright. The streets had been populated mostly by garbage trucks when I had entered the restaurant, but now a fair number of pedestrians had appeared. I kept my coat pulled tightly over my stolen medical garb and managed to look normal enough. Still, I received a number of wary stares from passersby, which I stoically ignored.

I reached the address on Tony's card without incident and went around to the back. It was off the Strip by a few blocks, but it was close enough to get some of the traffic. Hanging over the alley entrance was a single security camera. I waved at it briefly, figuring Tony wouldn't be reviewing the footage from the grave. I dug out the keys and tried each one. The third key rattled, then clicked. The door swung open a fraction with a shriek of unoiled hinges.

"Who are you?" a voice asked.

I whirled, knowing the action would make me look all the more guilty, but I was unable to help myself. A woman stood some twenty feet away. She was young and pretty, but she had experienced, suspicious eyes. She wore a short leather jacket and a short leather skirt—all black. I would have stared at her shapely legs on a different day, but I was in a suspicious mood. I eyed her hands for weapons—or strange little statues. Neither was apparent.

"I'm a friend of Tony's," I said, looking back into her blue eyes.

Her face changed from narrow-eyed suspicion to an expression of surprise and recognition.

"Oh," she said, taking a step back. "That's his coat, isn't it?"

I nodded. "And these are his sunglasses," I said, pulling them off and putting them away.

She watched my hands as I folded the arms of the sunglasses and tucked them into a pocket.

"Are you handling his affairs?" she asked.

"I've been asked to look into things here, yes."

"Sorry, I didn't know," she said. "I'll come back later then."

"Wait a second," I said as she began to walk quickly away. "Do I know you?"

She hesitated. "I don't think so."

I pushed the door the rest of the way open, causing it to squeak louder. The interior was dark and smelled of cigarettes and spilled beer.

"If you want to come in and have a look around," I said, "you're welcome to join me."

She paused, clearly uncertain. I could read worry in her eyes now. Worry and indecision.

"Why are you here?" I asked her conversationally.

"I—I came to pick up my last check."

I nodded. "No one around at this time in the morning, eh? I'm not surprised. Strip joints aren't usually known for their breakfast specials."

She shrugged. "It's been closed since the accident."

I nodded, thinking to myself she must want that check pretty badly. The place had been closed for days, yet she was here first thing in the morning. But I kept the thought to myself. I suspected she recognized me, and I hoped she knew some details about my situation.

She took two hesitant steps toward me.

"You want to come in and see if he cut your check?" I asked.

After a moment of further soul-searching, she said, "OK."

"What's your name?"

"Wildfire."

"No, not your stage name."

She flashed me a resigned look. "Holly," she said.

I thought about the note I'd seen on the dead flower when I'd first awakened. It had been signed Holly, and I didn't believe in coincidences. I did, however, believe in playing my cards carefully, so I smiled at her reassuringly.

I walked into the gloomy interior and waited. After about seven seconds, I finally heard her clacking heels. She followed me into the place and let the door groan and click behind her. I approved. It seemed she didn't want anyone discovering us inside either.

"Where are the light switches?" I asked.

"I'll just open some of the blinds," she said quickly.

"OK."

I watched as she walked deftly around the tables, each of which was circled by a huddle of pushed-in chairs. I could tell she knew the layout of the place well, which made her story about having worked here more believable. She twisted the blinds open a crack here and there. There was just enough light to see our surroundings. The sunbeams glowed with golden motes of floating dust. Clearly, she didn't want anyone seeing us inside. I realized then that she didn't have any more right to be in here than I did.

I wandered around behind the bar until I found a door marked OFFICE in tiny gold letters. I tried the handle. This one was locked too. I produced the jingling set of keys again and rattled them one after another in the lock.

Suddenly, Holly was right there, very close behind me. I could feel her body heat and her breath on my shoulder. I glanced back, mildly amused.

"You really want that check, don't you?"

"Hard to pay the rent without it."

Our eyes met, and I could see right away she had some bad habits. She had more to pay for than rent. I turned back to the lock and worked it harder. The key seemed stuck.

"Let me try," she said.

"I think I've got it," I said, but another thirty seconds of jiggling proved I didn't. I hit the door with the heel of my hand. It felt quite solid.

"Try the sunglasses," she said in a quiet voice, almost a whisper.

I stared at her. "What?"

"Put them on. Tony always did when he came back here."

I snorted, but thought *what the hell* and put them on. I jiggled the knob one more time. The door popped open at long last.

I took off the glasses and frowned at them. There was no way they could have helped me open the door. All they did, as far as I could see, was make the gloomy bar two shades darker. I looked at her.

"Are you trying to tell me that these sunglasses...?"

Holly shook her head. "I'm not trying to tell you any-thing, Mr. Draith."

She pushed past me into the office before I could ask her how she knew my name. She had never asked me what it was. I noticed her attitude had changed. She seemed much more confident in my presence now. Perhaps she'd meas-ured me and marked me down as harmless.

I followed her into the office. The interior was acrid with stale cigar smoke. A full ashtray sat on the desktop, brimming with ashes and thick cigar stubs. The ashtray was smooth, thick glass shaped like a clamshell. The glass had a faintly green color to it, and I figured it was a refugee from the last century, when ashtrays decorated everyone's coffee table.

We both took a look around. I found papers, receipts, bills. No checks or cash. Nothing of any real interest.

"The safe is down here," Holly said, kicking away a dirty scrap of carpet with a rubber backing.

A round metal door with a recessed combination dial was planted in the floor. The floor felt very flat even if you stepped on the dial.

Holly sucked in her lips, and looked at me. She made a brief, hurry-up gesture in my direction.

"What?" I asked. "I don't know the combination."

She rolled her eyes and put out her hand.

"What?" I asked again, feeling as if everyone at the party was in on some secrets—but no one had bothered to tell me anything.

"The sunglasses," she said, still holding out her hand.

I stared at her, then at the safe. I knelt beside the safe, and she knelt beside me. I reached down and gave the handle a twist. It didn't budge. I let my hand fall away. I took the sunglasses out of my pocket, but I didn't put them on.

"Are you telling me that if I put these things on, I'll know the combination?" I asked.

Holly shrugged and shook her head. "I don't know. All I know is—it will open."

I rubbed my chin for a moment. I took out the sunglasses and eyed them with alarm. What was I playing with? Could these plastic shades do something…strange? I recalled the way Meng's hood ornament had tossed me out the back door of her sanatorium.

For a moment, as I stared at them, I found the sunglasses threatening. A cold ripple ran through my nervous system. I knew it was silly. The lock on the office door had been a fluke. This woman was as crazy as the rest of them. But back at the sanatorium that pistol *had* vanished from my hand—and I *had* been transported and dropped onto a set of cement stairs.

Sometimes, when a man's world shifts under his feet, it causes paranoia. I had experienced these odd events stoically, if suspiciously. I'd played along up until now, assuming some logical explanation would eventually present itself. Perhaps I'd been experiencing side effects from days on heavy drugs. But now it was different, because I was being asked to actively participate in this particular impossibility.

"This can't be real," I said.

"You know it is."

I looked at her. "How do you know me?"

Holly appeared incredulous. "Your picture is on your blog," she said.

"Blog?"

"Draith's Weird Stuff," she said. "You post photos of creepy things every week. You're an underground hit, you must know that."

I smiled weakly. "I didn't realize."

"You should be the one explaining this crazy crap to me. I never believed in any of it until I began seeing it with my own eyes. I thought you must be trying to sell health supplements and dating sites on your blog, so you made it all up. Now, I know you were telling the truth. Don't you believe your own stories?"

"Um," I said, having no recollection of having written articles about the supernatural. "I suppose it's different when you are staring them in the face."

Holly nodded. "OK. I guess I can understand that. But you should at least try, don't you think?"

I nodded, then lifted the sunglasses to my face. I paused.

"Open it!" she urged.

I stared at her. "No," I said.

"What?"

"You want this safe open more than I do. But I'm not going to do it. Not until you tell me your story."

Holly made a sound as if she were strangling. "What can I tell you that you don't already know?"

"Start with how you know me. Besides reading about me online."

"That night," she said, looking down at her hands. "The night Tony died. You were in the accident."

"You remember any details?"

"He almost ran me over with his Cadillac."

I took out Tony's wallet and eyed the photograph on the driver's license. I'd never taken the time to look at it before. Light brown hair, swept to the side. A single earring gleamed beside a crooked smile. So that was Tony. There was some familiarity to the tiny square headshot. I recalled liking him.

"I don't remember the accident," I said. "There were head injuries."

"I'm not surprised about that," she said. "I'm surprised you made it at all. I can hardly believe you are walking and talking. When I first saw you, you scared me. You were really messed up after the wreck. You were ejected and broken up. That was less than two weeks ago."

"Tell me about it."

"Look," she said. "I'll tell you all about it. I swear. But you have to open this frigging safe before we get caught in here."

I realized she had a point. "You promise?"

"I said so."

I nodded and turned back to the round, flat door of the safe in the floor. We were both down on our knees. I had no idea what the combination was. None at all. I gave the dial an experimental spin and tugged at the handle. Then I spun it in the opposite direction and tried the handle again. It didn't even click or rattle. It was like tugging on a lamppost. The handle didn't even move fractionally. Nothing.

"What the hell are you doing?" Holly hissed.

"If this works, I want it to be a clear test. I don't want to be telling myself afterward that it opened only because the combination had already been dialed and all I had to do was twist the handle."

Holly made a sound of exasperation.

I took a deep breath and put on the sunglasses. I didn't *feel* any different with them on. But the room did look darker, just as it should have. I reached down and tugged the handle.

I hadn't really expected that it would open right away. I had expected that I would have to give the dial a spin or two first. Maybe the dial would click itself into precisely the right spot when I spun it at random. But that wasn't how it happened. It was easier than that. The handle twisted and I heard a clinking sound.

"I think it's open," I whispered.

"No shit," Holly said. "Lift the door up, man."

"What if there's something bad in there?"

She looked at me as if I was crazy. "Like what?"

"I don't know." I felt a chill. A creepy feeling, as if I had just invoked an unknown power. I didn't like the sensation. It was exciting, but also frightening.

Sighing loudly, Holly placed her hands over mine and tried to force my hand to lift the door open. I resisted, and the door stayed closed. She wasn't very strong. She made a sound of vexation and sat back on her haunches.

"What's wrong now?" she asked.

"I wasn't ready yet."

She crossed her arms, waiting. After another few seconds, I faced my demons and yanked the door open.

Holly whooped. She shoved her hand deeply into the safe and pulled out three wads of money. They were thick packets of twenties, hundreds of them in each wad, folded over once and wrapped neatly with thick blue rubber bands.

I reached out and took one of the wads from her. She frowned, but then shrugged. I hefted the wad in my palm. Three thousand, I figured. Maybe four.

"For expenses, Tony," I said aloud to no one. "We'll call this full payment for investigating your death."

"I'll call it severance pay," Holly added. She reached back into the safe with a grin on her face. I grabbed her shoulder and pulled her back.

She gave an irritated squeak and slapped my hand away. I looked into the safe. There was more money in there. A lot of it. I slammed the safe closed and spun the dial.

"What the hell?" Holly exclaimed. She stood up and grabbed at my sleeve. "Are you crazy, Draith?"

"It's not ours. Not all of it."

"What are you talking about?"

"There are other girls who need to get paid. Maybe Tony had heirs too."

Holly shook her head. "I never figured you for a do-gooder."

"I didn't figure you for a thief either," I lied.

She slapped at me, but I caught her wrist. I stood up, still holding her wrist so she couldn't slap me again.

"Two wads of cash are all you're getting. I'm sure that is more than you were owed."

Holly seemed to get hold of herself then. She heaved a sigh. "Yeah. I'm sorry. I just got a little carried away."

"Sure. I understand."

She shoved the cash into her purse and headed out. I followed. She pushed open the back door a fraction, then paused to look back at me.

"What are you going to do now?" she asked.

I shrugged. "I don't know. I guess I'll find a hotel. I need some sleep."

She nodded. "Yeah, I can see that. You could use some fresh clothes too. Say, you want to come to my place? I'll let you get some sleep and borrow some of my ex-boyfriend's clothes. He was about your size."

I thought about it. Was this real consideration or something else? "I don't know," I said. "But thanks a lot for the offer."

Her lips cinched tight. I wasn't sure if it was because I wasn't cooperating with a sneaky plan of hers, or if I had insulted her somehow.

"I'm not going to try to take them, you know," she said hotly.

"What? The money?"

"The sunglasses."

I eyed her for a second. Right then, it occurred to me that sunglasses that let you open vaults were quite valuable. Priceless, maybe.

"People are going to be looking for you," Holly said. "Do you understand that? You can't use Tony's plastic. You shouldn't even be in his clothes, or showing off those sunglasses."

I nodded. "Maybe you're right," I said. "Let's go to your place."

Holly twisted her lips and made a face at me. I pretended not to notice.

"You can tell me the story you promised while we walk," I said.

Neither of us had a car, and it was a long walk. Holly began to talk. Somehow it turned into more than the story of the accident. She told me everything. At least, I thought she did.

When she was done, everything was a lot clearer.

5

Holly Jensen had started off her career in the city as a dealer. Her job mostly consisted of flipping out cards when smoking, vodka-drinking men said "hit me" at the blackjack table. She learned to charm them with her pretty smile and thus garner tips. The job had gone well for a year or so, until she'd been fired for palming a few extra chips that had not been intended as tips. Those cameras and mirrors and the assholes that sat behind them didn't miss a trick, as she put it.

Fortunately, there were others on the casino strip who wanted her. She'd moved on down to the Lucky Seven, a big horseshoe-shaped building that flowed with twinkling green lights each night. The twin towers of the horseshoe were filled with hotel patrons while the base of the U-shaped building was a giant casino. Behind the casino was what they called a "show palace." The palace had once hosted comedy acts and singers from both coasts and had been filled with high rollers who kept gold on their wrists and in their mouths. After the turn of the century, the show palace had decomposed into something that resembled a giant titty bar.

The bosses at the show palace wore too-tight suits and experienced leers. They gave her a job on the chorus line. She had a face they constantly referred to as "sweet" and legs that made them stare. She'd blushed hard when she had gone topless for the first time, feeling ridiculous in an outfit constructed of rhinestones, sequins, and feathers, all built upon a soft bedrock of black nylon. But she'd done it, and she'd kicked and strutted her way onto the stage.

Holly didn't mind the dancing, after the initial shock of baring her breasts in public. She'd always kept in shape and found the job easier than dealing cards for hours on end. At least it went by faster.

But trouble quickly came again. This time, it was a murder that interrupted her life. There had been a growing number of strange killings in town. When they weren't talking about boyfriends, bragging about big tips or snaking each other with gossip, the showgirls talked about little else. One rumor that made her a little sicker than the others was the story of a tourist from Boston. According to the coroner, he'd fallen from twenty stories up and pulverized every bone in his body—but somehow he'd landed in his own hotel room. They'd found him splattered on the bathroom floor. She'd discounted the story as too incredible to believe.

Then came the night Holly found Lavita, a showgirl who claimed to be from Jamaica, but who was rumored to really be from Houston. Holly found Lavita dressed in her sequins and feathers, facedown under the makeup table. Holly described her as resembling a roadkill pheasant, with her tail feathers pluming up from her head and butt.

Holly made the mistake of turning her over, thinking maybe she could help. There was blood everywhere, and Holly should have known Lavita was dead, but she had to check anyway.

It was horrible. Face smashed in, the front of her body flattened as if she'd been crushed in a trash compactor—but only the front of her. Holly let go of the body as if she'd been stung, but instead of flopping back down into the pool of blood, the corpse had rolled slowly over onto its back in a grotesque, boneless fashion.

By this time, Holly was screaming her head off. Cooling blood ran down her fingertips. She'd thought of the man from Boston who had apparently fallen from a great height onto a bathroom floor. This was similar, if not quite the same. People soon flooded the room and asked her questions she couldn't answer. The police talked to her at length, but she had nothing useful for them. They stared at her with hard-eyed irritation. The killings were freaking them out, she thought. Like mean dogs, they had turned their fear into anger and suspicion.

The rest of the dancers had shunned Holly after that. Somehow, finding her there with blood on her face, having obviously disturbed the corpse, had put her into the untouchable category. She learned then what it must have been like to be declared the village witch when the crops failed.

When new girls came to audition, the bosses treated Holly like old meat. She'd pushed away their grasping hands on many occasions and she thought they'd come to accept she wasn't going to go for that kind of thing…but she was wrong. When the new girls were hired, no one had a kind word for the girl who had found Lavita. They dropped her off the list. After less than two months as a showgirl, she was back on the street again.

Her next job took longer to land. Money was tightening up around town as it headed into the cooling, windy period that passed for autumn in the desert. Her rent money came due and she found herself hiding in a dark apartment, listening to hammering and threats from outside her door until her landlord gave up and stomped away, muttering curses. She knew eviction was coming, as relentlessly as the desert winds.

Holly had headed down to the end of the Strip that night—to the seedy side—then walked a few blocks away from the boulevard. There she found bars with patrons who didn't want to be identified. The streets were dimmer, as every other pale orange sodium-vapor streetlight had been knocked out. She walked into the first strip club she found, which turned out to be Tony's place. She found the Pole Dance Palace discouraging, but she was desperate. The establishment specialized in something called "friction dancing," and after a ten-minute audition followed by a five-minute training, she found herself out on the floor.

Friction dancing was just what it sounded like and she was having a hard time with it until another of the girls grabbed her by the arm on her break.

"Here," the older girl had said, pushing a black ovoid pill into Holly's palm. "Try this. It makes things easier."

Holly dry-swallowed the pill without looking at it or thinking about it. She didn't want to think at all. After that, the night slid by and at quitting time she had over a hundred in tips alone. Four nights later she paid up her rent. The future had brightened.

Before two months had passed, however, she was hooked on cocaine and pills and when the next month's rent came due, she didn't have it again. Her habits ate money like a hungry flame.

Tony Montoro had finally fired her on a Tuesday night.

"Come back if you clean up, doll," he said with a serious face.

Holly understood they were kind words. In truth, perhaps the first ones she'd heard in a long time. Walking the streets again, she eyed the girls who walked there with her. They had glazed eyes and painted faces. No one had heels less than three inches high.

Holly opened her purse and sucked in all the special medications she had left inside it. When there was nothing left but makeup, she felt a little better and a little worse at the same time.

An hour later she was still wandering the streets. By this time, she had decided to turn things around—to go into business for herself. She needed more money, she needed it fast, and she needed it easy. She knew how attractive young ladies in Las Vegas made things like that happen. She had to turn a trick. She'd had a number of bad boyfriends that had made her feel like a hooker, but she'd never really been one. Maybe this was the night to take that last step.

Holly eyed the other streetwalkers, but didn't want to try her first play with witnesses nearby. She didn't want the pros to laugh at her. She stumbled down a street that was darker than the rest and waited until a big car came cruising along with two men in it. The car was weaving a bit, and she figured they were probably as high as she was. She glimpsed the passenger's face. He didn't look too old or too ugly. She flagged them down.

To her surprise, the car swerved toward her. After a stunned second in the headlights, she scrambled to move out of the way. The car's engine revved high, as if the driver were flooring it. Did they want to kill her? Shock melted into fear.

The front tires twisted, throwing the car into a half spin. Sliding sideways, it hit the curb and flipped over. She threw herself out of the way, but what really saved her was a lamppost. The car plowed into it, sliding on its back.

It was then that Holly recognized the car. It was purple and black. Made long ago when cars were heavier and longer and full of thick steel. It was Tony's Cadillac.

Holly got to her feet, shaking. She took quivering steps forward. Was Tony trying to kill her now?

The passenger had been ejected and was lying on the sidewalk, motionless. The driver caught her attention first, however. It was Tony himself, the man in the silver suit who had fired her only an hour ago. He crawled out of his window. The jagged safety glass cut his hands but he kept crawling slowly, relentlessly.

She walked close and stood over him. "Are you crazy, Tony?" she asked.

Tony rolled up his eyes to look at her, and she saw *sand* burbling from his mouth. She thought at first it was vomit, but then she realized it really was *sand*. Some of it was wet and dark, but as more gushed out, it turned dry and seemed endless. It gushed from him as he lay there at her feet shivering and dying.

The sand inside him was *dry*, she thought. Didn't that mean there had to be an awful lot of it? Didn't that mean it had to be fresh? It wasn't possible. His eyes were open. They were bulging and every red capillary stood out on the round whites. He appeared to be just as surprised at his death as she was to witness it.

At this point, I touched her shoulder. We both stopped walking. I looked into her face, frowning. She didn't have the look of a liar, which I found very disturbing considering the insane nature of her story. She had the look of someone who was remembering something traumatic. She was staring at the street, lost.

I told myself I shouldn't doubt her. After all, hadn't I just encountered some very strange people at the sanatorium? Wasn't I using sunglasses as universal lock picks? How could I doubt Holly after what I'd seen?

"How could he have been filled with *sand?*" I asked.

She shrugged, shaking her head. "I don't know. I just remember staring down in a daze. I didn't even scream. Being mildly high helped."

I started walking again. She joined me. "Am I in this story?" I asked.

"Yeah, I was getting to you."

"Keep talking," I said. "It's just getting good."

She went on.

Tony was so full of sand, she said, that his belly looked distended with it. She backed away from the bizarre sight. She wanted to comfort him, but she could not. She was so stunned and horrified by what she saw—something that could not be.

When Tony had finally stopped squirming and lay still, she remembered the second man and stepped around the car to where I lay.

"You were a crumpled lump on the concrete," she told me. "Really, I can't understand how you are walking next to me now. You were in worse shape than Tony—but you weren't choking out sand. You had a lot of cuts and bruises and your leg was twisted at an impossible angle."

"What did you do?" I asked.

"I made sure you were breathing," she said. "After that, I thought I recognized you. I knelt beside you and realized who you were. It took me a minute or so, but I remembered your picture from your blog, which I'd spent some time reading when I was trying to understand Lavita's murder."

"Did you call the cops?"

Holly flicked her eyes downward, to the street. "I didn't have to. Someone else did. There were others around, everyone had a phone. The cops showed up pretty fast. I'd say they were patrolling just a block or two away when they got the call."

I nodded. It was the kind of territory cops liked to cruise through. "So," I said, glancing at her. "You took off, right?"

Holly squirmed uncomfortably. "Well, look. I was high, trying to turn my first trick, and had just witnessed my second freaky murder of the season. Wouldn't you be walking away fast?"

"I guess I might."

"OK then. You have to understand, Draith, it wasn't about you or Tony. The cops are edgy these days. They don't like whatever it is that's going on in this town. Out on these streets at two in the morning, nobody wants to meet up with the law."

Holly suddenly stopped walking. "This is the spot," she said.

I halted in surprise. I looked around. There was the lamppost. It hadn't been sheared off, but there was a big gouge in the paint and a dent at the base. I could see white lines scratched into the concrete where the metal roof of the sliding car had scarred it.

"You got away from the cops and walked home then?" I asked. I walked around the lamppost, but didn't get any special memories from the location.

"No, it was already too late for that. There was a cruiser coming up behind me, I heard the engine purring. There were more cars behind that first one too. I could hear them, but I didn't dare glance back. Flashing blue and red lights washed all over these walls."

I looked at her, surprised. "More than one car, that fast?"

"Yeah. There were no sirens, just flashers, engines, and radios that buzzed with the voices of dispatchers. They always come in packs, you know?" Holly reflected. "Lately, they like to come in overwhelming numbers, like sharks scenting blood."

"They questioned you?"

"They did more than that. They took me in. The cops in this town are bastards, Quentin. I think they've all gone bad."

I nodded thoughtfully. I doubted I'd ever meet a stripper who was in love with the law. But I didn't press her further, as I had heard enough. She had certainly kept up her part of the bargain.

All the rest of the way to her place, I thought about Holly's incredible story. People inexplicably smashed to pulp. Tony Montoro's body being filled with sand. She had found Tony and me on the sidewalk and watched Tony die. I wouldn't have believed a word of it if I hadn't just been transported across a building and opened a safe with what appeared to be a magical pair of sunglasses.

Eventually, Holly pointed at a sagging apartment complex from the middle of the last century. "My place is on the second floor," she said.

As we walked up the cement steps, I asked, "Did you leave me a flower?"

Holly shrugged. "Yeah. I went to Memorial Hospital to find out if Tony made it after the police let me go. He didn't. They said you were alive, but hadn't had any visitors. I felt sorry for you."

"So...you bought me a geranium at the gift shop?"

She looked embarrassed.

"Thanks for the thought. But I didn't wake up at Memorial. I woke up in the Sunset Sanatorium under the gentle care of Dr. Meng."

I was hoping she would react to that name, but her face was a blank.

"Maybe they transferred you after patching you up," she offered.

At the top of the stairs, she opened the door without any mystical help from me. I followed her inside and accepted a beer while she told me some of her theories about what was happening to the city.

According to Holly, everyone working on the Strip talked about the decay of the city, wondering about the cause. Some blamed online gambling, or soaring unemployment, or the city's famously high crime rate. Holly had a less complex answer: in her opinion, the city had "moved on." It had gone from one century to the next and changed in character as inevitably as people did while they wended their ways through life. She believed a new presence had formed in the midst of the crumbling casinos. Something had replaced the old source of energy and vibrancy. Just as the city had once grown out of the desert sands like a mushroom.

"The economy has fallen apart in Vegas, just as it has everywhere else," I said, unwilling to see something more sinister.

"I think it's more than that," she said.

"We used to have people flowing here, bringing their millions in gambling money," she said, "but now this new source of energy has brought worse things."

I thought about what she was suggesting. That a new kind of life force had come to the city. That this new attraction wasn't as wholesome as a natural drive toward sex and greed.

"Sometimes, when enough sinning is done in single place," she said, "I think it attracts the attention of *bad things.*"

"What kind of bad things?" I asked her.

Holly caught the smile I'd tried to suppress and glared at me. "Imagine *you* being the skeptic. You should read your own blog, Draith."

"I suppose I should, but tell me what you mean, anyway."

She went on to describe a frightening scenario. In her imagination, strange shadows were being drawn to this spot like insects gathering around a flickering bulb at night. This had all started years ago, she believed. There had been stories…small things at first. People disappeared, but that was not unusual, especially in Vegas. Soon, the disappearances had turned into outright murders—weird ones. These weren't just simple gangland killings—there had always been people beaten to death with baseball bats, shot and left for dead on the Strip, hookers found in garbage cans— no, this was worse than all that. These crimes were…disturbing, unusual, even *bizarre.*

"It's almost as if the city is under—I don't know, some kind of attack, I guess," she said.

"From demons, aliens, or evil scientists?"

"You write about this stuff, and you are making fun of me?"

"Sorry," I said.

We talked on in this vein for another hour. At last we finished our drinks, and I had grown very weary. She let me have the sole bed in the place. She wasn't tired. She went out into the living room where she had a computer and spent her time on the web. I heard her moving all around the apartment when the door was closed down to a crack. She was probably hiding cash here and there, squirreling it away so no one intruder could get all of it. As I was passing out, she left, telling me she had a few bills to pay.

"Take care of yourself," I slurred.

She looked surprised, like no one had said that to her in a long time.

6

I awoke with a start from a dream about a world full of cement walls and shadowy people who resisted illumination despite the harsh glare of fluorescent lights. The shadowy people talked to me, but I could not make out what they were saying.

It was dark again. I'd slept the entire day away. I got up with a bone-weary groan. I wondered why sleeping for great lengths of time made a man's body more sore than when he lay down.

I felt around for the sunglasses, the gun, and the wad of cash. They were all still there. I was happy about that. I'd taken a chance with Holly, and it had paid off. Or maybe she was too happy with all the money I'd helped gather for her to rob me right off. But I knew her kind. If she ever ran out of cash, that was when she would become dangerous.

After a quick shower and shampoo, which left me smelling overpoweringly fruity, I roamed the tiny apartment. I couldn't help but smirk when I found a few crumpled twenties stuffed inside the sugar jar and three more tucked underneath the plastic silverware tray. I left them there and made myself coffee.

The fridge had next to nothing in it. I unhappily spooned some orange crème yogurt out of a plastic cup and chewed on a stick of celery filled with peanut butter. It was skinny-chick food, but better than nothing.

I spent the next hour on her computer. I found my own blog quickly. The content startled me. Was I a wack-job, a con man, or a person haunted by the bizarre? Murders, disappearances, and equally alarming reappearances of missing persons were listed. The stories presented were told in a flatfooted, matter-of-fact style. One stood out among them to me, a recent entry.

Heath Anderson was a mild-mannered street person known to this author. He was found in a downtown alley off Garces Ave., burning to death. Covered in flames, the man remained lucid and smiling. Even as the victim's skin curled, he explained that the fire didn't hurt. A group of onlookers including myself gathered to help or simply to watch. We tried to splash water on him and beat at the flames, to no avail. The man smiled until the end when he slumped down into a heap indistinguishable from a pile of ash. He remained calm throughout, even gesturing for the crowd to relax. It is unknown if Anderson had relations in the area.

A photo accompanied the entry. I saw a pile of gray ash mounded up against a sooty brick wall. A single item stood untouched in the middle of the remains: a gleaming metal flask. I supposed no one had had the guts to steal it.

Holly came back with a bag of groceries an hour later and froze when she saw me sitting there on the couch.

"You're still here," she said.

I looked up. "I'm sorry. I haven't been awake long. I should have cleared out."

"No," she said. "No, no—that's cool. Did you get some coffee?"

I tipped my mug as evidence that I had.

"I didn't mean…" she began. "Never mind. I didn't mean I wanted you out right away. You just seemed like the kind of guy who would take off while I was out."

I nodded slowly. "I hear you. I'll be leaving soon, don't worry."

She sighed. "I'm sorry. Where are you going to go?"

"First, I'm going to check out my own home."

"You found out where it is?"

"Whatever is left of my brain can still work the web. I live at the northeastern edge. Not too far from here."

"What about after that?"

"I'm going to hit the police station in the morning," I said.

Holly recoiled slightly. "That's not a good idea, Quentin."

My eyes slid to her face. When had I moved up from "Mr. Draith" to "Quentin"? Sleeping all day at a girl's apartment had some benefits, I supposed.

"I'm not in love with the law," I said. "But they have the facts concerning Tony's death and my own involvement in the accident."

Holly shook her head. "Uh-uh. They only have what they want to have."

"What's that?"

"A monopoly on cracking heads in this town, for one thing. And they want to keep it that way."

I frowned. "What does that mean?"

"Pray you don't find out."

I stared at her for a second. "You didn't tell me every-thing you know, did you?"

She laughed. "No. And you should be glad I didn't, for both our sakes. Just listen to me and keep out of the police station. It's not like it used to be."

I eyed her speculatively. It was easy to see a casual user, a girl who was hooked on nightlife and recreational drugs. She'd gone as far as she could working with the good genet-ics that had made her attractive. She had managed her resources to their best effect in order to fund her habits. No one living her lifestyle sent people to talk to policemen. Maybe her worry was a simple underlying fear I would grow a big mouth and talk about magically opening safes full of cash...and how we had helped ourselves to it.

"Don't worry about me," I said, standing up.

She looked me over. "Let me at least get you some clothes that don't scream *freak in a raincoat.*"

I smiled and let her lead me to a cluster of paper bags that stood behind an army of strappy shoes in her closet. Each bag was full of neatly folded clothes, which seemed odd, but I quickly figured out each bag had been left behind by a different boyfriend at one point or another. She had a variety of sizes and soon managed to outfit me in jeans, a dress shirt, and a navy blue hoodie. The pants were a bit loose, so she handed me a belt. For shoes, I had my choice. I went with black running shoes. They looked good and wouldn't slow me down if I needed to move fast.

I checked my legs out, squeezing with my hands. Before I had slept and showered, they had been sore and I'd had a noticeable limp. Now, they felt fresh and only slightly stiff. I really did appear to heal fast, just as I'd told the nurse back at the sanatorium.

"Thanks," I told her, and I meant it.

"It's the least I can do," she said.

Holly followed me to the door. I stepped out onto a concrete walkway.

I turned around and looked at her. "Can I come back to call on you sometime?"

She smiled and kissed me lightly on the cheek. It felt good.

"You can," she said. "But don't bring trouble, OK?"

I shook my head. "No promises in that department."

I left her then and headed down the stairs. Experimentally, I took two at a time. It hurt my knees, so I slowed down and leaned on the rail. There was no reason to push things.

I looked back at her once and saw her standing above me, bent over the rail and watching me. Then I left the courtyard and headed out onto the street.

I pulled my hood over my hair and headed into the northern districts. People were less likely to mess with you when they couldn't see your face. It was a bad neighborhood that had once been middle-class. Everyone I passed was either a predator or a victim—I found it easy to pick out one from the other. Each eyed me, calculating which category I was in just as I did the same to them. As we passed by one another, people invariably took a step or so to the side—a respectful acknowledgment that I didn't look like a mark. I often did the same, signaling I wasn't dangerous at the moment. But my silence, my hood, and my lack of expression gave the impression I *could* be dangerous under the right circumstances.

I knew something was wrong before I reached my house. I suppose it was the smoky smell in the air. The stink grew and grew until I stopped dead on the sidewalk. My place... was gone.

7

I knew what my house must have looked like—even if I couldn't remember it. Every house on the block looked more or less the same. They were all mid-1900s stucco boxes. There were rows of flip-up garage doors, blandly painted walls coated in spiderwebs, and yards full of weeds. Some yards had degenerated into pure crabgrass and dried-out trees. Others lawns had taken the final step, reverting to the purity of the desert sands from whence they'd come. Water was expensive in the city, and not everyone could afford to water their patch of land.

My house was on the right, the third from the corner. There wasn't much *house* left, however. Looking at the devastation, my first thought was that it must have burned down, although it looked more thoroughly destroyed than a burnt house should. All that stucco and the old brick fireplace—something should have survived. Instead, it reminded me of a bomb crater. Only the farthest corner of the garage stood, a sooty finger of concrete and charcoaled two-by-fours.

Getting over my shock, I walked with quiet care among the silent eddies of ash. Had I left the stove on when I'd gone to talk to Tony? Had I owned a pet that had accidentally tipped over a source of combustion? I didn't think the answer was so mundane. It was hard to believe fate alone had dealt me such a hard blow. Call me distrustful, but this went beyond an accident or even arson. Someone had demolished my house in hopes of destroying whatever it was I had discovered. Possibly, the same somebody had tried to kill me more than once.

As I looked around the place, I began to think maybe Dr. Meng had done me a favor by keeping me on ice at her institution. What if someone had killed Tony, but meant to kill us both? Or maybe they'd really been targeting *me* all along. I didn't like the idea.

I trudged around the ruins in the dark, looking for clues. When I finally found something interesting, I was greatly surprised by the nature of it.

There was a trembling movement in the ashes. I froze, staring. I suspected it was a cat, but what kind of an idiot animal would be caught playing in this mess at midnight? Perhaps a rat, then, I thought. This faint hope propelled me to take a step closer to the shivering pile of ashes, then a second and a third.

I stood over a lump covered in the black ashes that I calculated were the cremated remains of my living room furniture. The lump shivered again as I watched it. All I had to do, I knew, was reach out with a toe and tap the thing at my feet—but I hesitated.

The wind sighed in the trees around me. Distantly, a siren wailed out in the direction of the boulevard. I could hear TV voices floating out of a neighbor's window from somewhere nearby. I stared at the lump and waited for it to shiver again. It did nothing. I willed the thing at my feet to reveal itself without my having to act upon it.

Then I began to feel something on my face as I stared at the thing. I felt *heat*. This spot, alone among the fifteen hundred-odd square feet of ash and debris, was still hot. The heat spread to my exposed hands. As I stood there, I felt the burning sensation intensify upon the legs of my pants and sensed it sinking into my shoes as well. Did it come from the shivering thing before me? I wasn't sure.

Still staring, I reached out my foot and touched the lump with the toe of my shoe. It was hard, heavy, and solid. I felt it tremble. It was as if I had nudged a vibrating bowling ball covered in sodden ashes.

I yanked my foot away and lifted the other, planning to beat a stealthy retreat. It was too late, however. Whatever was crouching in the middle of my home, I'd awakened it.

The thing unfolded itself. Ash dribbled away and it grew taller as I watched. Still, it was barely a foot in height—make that eighteen inches now. I almost bolted, but kept watching. Maybe that was my curse, my weakness. I felt an overwhelming urge to investigate this oddity, rather than to flee from it. I knew in a flash of remembrance I'd faced alien things like this before and failed to run from them when any sane man would have.

The unfolding thing rotated a part of itself to look up at what had nudged it. To me, it now resembled a bulky worm made of lava rock, with a head section that rose up to regard me. The sensation of emanating heat grew ever more intense and its eyes met mine—eyes of blue flame on stalks of blackened, porous stone. It did not run from me, but instead straightened and slid forward very slowly. It stared at me with curiosity—or was that hunger?

I saw it clearly now, despite the fact it was not illuminated by a streetlamp or neighbor's security light. The thing glowed faintly with the color of dying coals. The creature seemed weak, almost pitiful. I sensed it might have become aggressive in a moment of strength. But for now it only eyed me curiously and approached very slowly.

"You're a crazy bastard, Draith," said a voice. "Just like they said."

My head jerked toward the voice. A man stood on the sidewalk. He lit a cigarette and continued to watch me from a safe distance. His cigarette glowed orange, but the rest of him stood in shadow. I could tell from his voice and bearing he was a plainclothes cop.

I looked back toward the thing at my feet. It raised a stony appendage in my direction, moving lazily, tiredly. It reached toward my feet. I took a step backward. The thing stirred itself like a tired old man and rippled in weary pursuit.

The cop on the sidewalk chuckled around his cigarette. "It *still* wants to get you. Talk about dedication! Ninety percent dead and almost burnt out, but it *still* goes for you."

I took another step back, then a third. The thing at my feet looked up at me reproachfully, but with exhausted determination, it squirmed its form closer. As it moved, I heard a faint sound like that of two bricks grinding against one another.

"What is it?" I asked the man on the sidewalk.

The man ignored my question. "Do you know how long I've waited for you to come back? I've endured long days on this stakeout. My back is sore from sitting in my car for so damned many hours. You owe me, Draith."

"I take it you want to investigate this obvious case of arson?" I asked. Maybe Holly had been right and the cops weren't going to be helpful.

"Ha," said the cop. "Yeah, right. Come out of there, man. Nice and easy. Do you know I had no idea that thing was still alive? It must have smelled you or something and woke up again."

"What put it to sleep?"

"The water from the fire hoses, I figure. It likes fire; cold seems to mess it up. But how the hell do I know? You're the expert on freaky shit like this. Don't you read your own blog? Get over here, Draith. You're under arrest."

I backed away from the thing, which still pursued me in relentless slow motion. I tried not to stumble in the ashes and debris. I didn't want to turn my back on it, suspecting it might leap upon me in that moment. When I crossed onto the scorched yard, I turned toward the cop.

The cop had stepped closer while I retreated from the thing in the ashes. He pressed his car remote and the headlights flashed. I caught a glimpse of him then. He was a little taller than I was, with an athletic build, and I guessed him to be about forty. He wore a gray blazer over a yellow dress shirt. His gray slacks were as nondescript as the rest of his clothing, intended to make him blend into any crowd. His face had strong features, with a thick brow ridge and a large chin. His eyes and hair were dark.

"Come on," he said, waving me toward his car. "Get in. I'm taking you downtown."

"Let's see your badge first," I said. I took out my sunglasses and slipped them on. I figured I might need them. Then I reached into my pocket and touched my gun. That was a mistake.

"Here's my badge," he said, flashing a shield in his wallet. "Detective Jay McKesson, Las Vegas Metro. And here's my gun."

McKesson hit me in the face with his pistol. I went down to one knee. I'd been suckered, and a burst of anger boiled up inside me.

"I should leave you here," the man said, standing over me. "That thing will come close eventually and burn you. One more freaky death for one more freak."

"What was that for?" I asked, rubbing my cheekbone. It didn't feel cracked, but it did feel numb.

"Making me wait. And because you're armed and dangerous. Everyone says so. Just like that thing you summoned up to burn down your own house for the insurance money. You're not going to collect, you know. Not on my watch."

While he talked, I put my sunglasses back on and climbed slowly back up to my feet. I was surprised the sunglasses didn't seem damaged.

"Turn around and put your hands behind your back," he said.

McKesson kept his gun on me. He clicked on the cuffs, then spun me around to face him. "Not so tough in bracelets, are you, Draith? They never are."

I didn't answer. He holstered his gun and gave me a tight smile.

"Shades? You're wearing shades at night? Are you trying to be cool?"

I still didn't answer. Inside I was boiling, but I bided my time.

The creature made a sound then. This was something new. We both glanced toward it. The slug had crossed the border of what had once been the concrete slab foundation of my house. It had squirmed its way into the flowerbeds and then out onto the open lawn. At that point it had made a squeaking, bubbling hiss, a sound that was both unpleasant and alien. Like hot coals dropped into a bucket of water, the hissing continued as it approached us with painful slowness. I thought perhaps the grasses it crawled over stung it. The greenery twisted and blackened at the creature's approach and it left behind a trail of scorched earth.

When McKesson turned his attention back to me, he realized I'd freed myself. It had been easy. I just twisted my wrists and the cuffs fell apart. I was sure he was willing to go for me, but then he felt my .32 automatic under his chin and froze at the cold touch.

"Surprise," I said.

McKesson eyed the cuffs that dangled from my wrists. The right bracelet hung open. With the sunglasses on, there had only been a rippling sensation of resistance that quickly gave way. It was as if the lock had turned to rubber. I'd hoped it would work that way, and it had.

"You don't want to do this, Draith," he said quietly.

"Do you always arrest people by pistol-whipping them?"

"Only murdering scum like you."

I stared at him for a second. This was the first I'd heard I was a murderer. The scary part was, for all I knew he was right. I decided to bluff it through.

"Am I a suspect, then? In what murder?"

"You're a perp in one case and a suspect in a dozen more," he said. His eyes strayed toward the thing that still approached us with agonizing slowness. A crawling slug of hot, molten stone.

I pressed the short barrel of my .32 automatic into the flesh of his throat and took his gun out of his hand. I turned him around, but kept the two of us face-to-face. The stone slug was now behind him, still crawling across my lawn, leaving a blackened trail as it came. McKesson's eyes widened, showing the glistening whites. He flicked his gaze this way and that, breathing harder, but he couldn't see the thing that crawled closer with infinite slowness behind him.

"You know what it's going to do when it gets to you, don't you?" I asked. "I have a feeling a man's legs will broil nicely, from its point of view."

"You won't be able to control it if it gets to a source of fuel," the detective said. "It'll get you too."

"What source of fuel?"

"My body fat."

I peered at him, suspecting bullshit, but there was no hint of a lie there. I felt vaguely disgusted. I dared a glance over his shoulder. The thing had passed over its first plastic-headed sprinkler. A wisp of steam rose up. The slug made an unhappy, mewling sound. It slowed down a fraction more, probably from contacting a source of cold water. McKesson didn't know that, though.

"What the hell is it doing?" he demanded.

"It's eyeing your haunches and speeding up."

"You've got my gun, just run for it. I'll catch up to you later."

"If I'm a killer, why shouldn't I knock off one more?"

"You haven't killed any cops yet. If you had, there would have been five of us waiting for you to show up out here."

I glanced back behind him, faking a startled look. I pulled him forward by the shirt collar, keeping the gun under his chin. He stumbled forward.

"What?" he asked.

"It was just getting a little close. But I'm not done with you yet."

McKesson was breathing harder and sweating now. "Ask me something then, asshole."

"Ah, ah—I prefer Mr. Draith."

"Yeah, OK," he said, glaring. "Mr. Draith."

My cheekbone was throbbing and I thought about making him call me sir. But I decided not to waste any more time.

"Hard, fast questions; hard, fast answers. Any bullshit and I push you a step back."

"Ask then, dammit."

"What the hell is that thing that's about to crawl up your calf?" I asked. "How can a rock move?"

"Do I look like a frigging scientist? It's just a living piece of flaming rock. Some call it a lava slug."

"Are they always this slow?"

"Only when firemen accidentally spray them with hoses."

"How do you know so much?" I asked. "Do you keep them for pets?"

"Not me."

"You just burn down houses by planting them?"

"Not me either," he said, his teeth clenched.

"Who, then?"

Detective McKesson shrugged. "People. The Community."

I recalled Dr. Meng using that term. *The Community.* "Give me a name, a place."

"You know a couple of names already."

I pulled him suddenly toward me again, forcing him to take two stumbling steps toward the sidewalk. He came with me, alarmed.

"Oops," I said.

"What?" he asked quickly.

"It almost got you," I lied. The creature was still a good distance away. It was definitely going slower now that it traveled over cool grass and earth rather than the ashes of my house. "How about you and me getting into your car and getting out of here?"

"You're letting me take you in? Good choice, Draith. You might get a plea out of this."

"No, Jay," I said, "I'm going to let you keep answering questions in a different environment. I'm keeping both the guns."

McKesson tried again to look through the back of his head. I had to give him credit: if it had been physically possible, he would have managed it right then.

"Kidnapping?" he asked. "Maybe you *were* innocent, but you are stacking up real felonies right now."

"You burned my house down by putting some kind of alien rock in it and then waited until I got home, at which point you smashed me in the face," I said. "Can you understand why I'm not in a trusting mood?"

McKesson stared at me and read my eyes. I stared back flatly.

"OK," he said. "I'll drive. I can't stand another second with that thing behind me."

We climbed into his car and drove off together. He didn't snap on the lights until we'd reached the corner.

"Where are you driving?" I asked. I still had the pistol out, but it was resting in my lap now. I kept my hand on the grip and my finger on the trigger. Occasionally, I caught his eyes flashing down to look at it, then away again.

"There's a place I know where we can talk," McKesson said.

"Your station or a coffee shop?"

"A twenty-four-hour place with good pie."

"All right."

The detective relaxed a fraction. Maybe he thought we had some kind of bond going.

"You going to put that thing away?" he asked me.

"No," I said. "Not yet. I've got plenty of questions. Such as what murder you suspect me of having committed."

"Good idea," he said brightly. His mood and demeanor shifted. "Let's assume for the moment you are innocent. We can help each other out."

I glanced at him. "How?"

"Let's pool what we know. How did Tony's murder go down?"

I shook my head. "I really only know what I heard from an eyewitness. I was in the passenger seat, we crashed, and he apparently choked to death in a freak accident."

"Ha!" McKesson exclaimed. "Come on. You were there. You know what happened to him."

I eyed him. "I can't remember the accident. I was hauled off to the hospital too, remember?"

"Useless." McKesson sighed, shaking his head and rubbing his chin. "Totally useless. I got more out of the whore who found you on the sidewalk."

I looked at McKesson suddenly, deciding I didn't like him much. Clearly he was talking about Holly. Was he the one she was afraid of now? I frowned, increasingly annoyed. "What about this exchange of info? What happened to my house? What happened to Tony? What do *you* know?"

McKesson shrugged disinterestedly. "Not enough. Tony Montoro was a small-time thief who ran a strip joint to launder his money. He died mysteriously on the night of the twenty-seventh with a gut full of sand."

"Sand? You mean like actual sand?"

"Yeah, sand. We live in a desert, you know. His gut was full of sand. His lungs too. He suffocated, exploding with the stuff."

I nodded. That matched with Holly's story. It was freakish indeed. What a way to go. I wondered how long you would remain conscious. A minute? Longer? I wasn't sure.

We pulled into a parking lot.

"This is the place," McKesson said. "You want to give me back my gun?"

I eyed him. "We're not best friends yet," I said. "You never even told me what I was accused of."

"We going in, or what?" he asked.

I eyed the place. It looked like a dump, but sometimes these cheap little hole-in-the-wall places had the best food. Cops always seemed to find places like that.

"Are you still planning to arrest me?" I asked.

"Eventually," he said.

"How about tonight?"

"Are you buying?"

I thought about it. "Yeah," I said.

McKesson sighed. "All right. You've got the gun, and you're not my biggest problem tonight. We can call a truce. You forget about the slap and don't talk about the loose cuffs. I'll pretend you got by me. We'll sort it out later. But I can't promise I won't be coming after you tomorrow."

I thought about the offer. Even as far as it went, I wasn't sure it was genuine. But I needed some kind of ally. I figured I could always slip his cuffs again, or get out of his car, as long as I had the sunglasses. He didn't seem to understand their power yet. I decided to risk it.

"You've got a deal," I said, and I put the gun away.

McKesson got out of the car and walked into the place as if we were old friends. Had he read me so well that he knew I wouldn't take off running? Was he just swaggering and overconfident? Was all of this some kind of elaborate con job? I really wasn't sure. He left me wondering what to do next.

The place looked like a dump inside. Ugly old wallpaper with small images of banana splits, hamburgers, and frying pans was everywhere. The seats had rips in them showing yellowed foam rubber.

We sat across from one another in a booth and ordered pie. His was lemon meringue. Mine was coconut cream. He was right—the pie was excellent. Unsurprisingly, it was also cheap.

The waitress recognized McKesson and knew he was a cop. The coffee was free and she refilled it whenever it was halfway down. I smiled at the arrangement. This was a cop hangout, a business with an inexpensive security plan in place.

"You still haven't told me what I'm suspected of doing," I said when my pie had been reduced to crumbs.

"All of it," he said. "You've been in or around a dozen strange murders. With this last case you were in the guy's car at the time. When the showgirl fell from a hundred feet into her own dressing room, you were in the hallway outside. When the bum exploded into flames and burned happily to ashes, you were there, snapping pictures for your blog. The list goes on."

I thought about his list. I hadn't realized I'd been present at these crime scenes. I didn't doubt McKesson, however. Strange events seemed to occur in my vicinity. I couldn't deny that.

"I'm not a killer," I said.

"I don't believe you."

I frowned. Was I a killer? I supposed I might have pulled a trigger or two in my lifetime. The gun had felt natural in my hand. I knew how to use it, where to place it. The thought was disturbing. Was I one of those guys who woke up happy and forgetful after every psychotic killing?

"Maybe ignorance truly is bliss," I said, frowning into my coffee. "But I'm more determined than ever to figure out what the hell is going on in this town. No one seems to know everything, but everyone I meet seems to know more than I do. And we all have one thing in common: we are all paranoid."

McKesson laughed. "You've got that right, Draith."

"You have a family, Detective?"

"No. You?"

"I don't think so."

McKesson nodded. "Let me clue you in there: you're right. You don't. I would have been sitting at your momma's place, if you had one. I mean, what kind of perp comes back to their burned-down house a week later? It was a long shot."

"Why didn't you look for me at the sanatorium?"

He shook his head and snorted. "No one goes into that place—not if they want to come back out."

I didn't reply to that. I was too busy thinking about Dr. Meng and her odd staff. The halls were quiet, and the rooms were windowless. It was a weird, dangerous place. I didn't want to go back there, although I knew I might have to.

"So what else have you got for me?" McKesson asked.

"You give me more first," I said, bluffing.

McKesson shook his head. "No way. I've told you too much as it is." He leaned forward and gave me an intense stare. "But this isn't over between us. We have a truce right now, tonight, but don't think that makes us tight. When the time comes, I'll do what I've got to do. Just so we understand each other."

I nodded and sipped my coffee calmly.

"Right," I said. "I hear you. And just so *you* know, I'm not your typical, terrified perp on the run. I'm in this to find out what the hell happened to me—what the hell is happening to my hometown. And I'll go right through anyone who gets in my way."

McKesson studied me for a second, then leaned back, smiling and checking out the waitresses. He nodded. "The funny thing is, you and I want the same thing."

"Wait a second," I said. "Does that mean you are going to let me dig into this? Without harassment? Like you said, we are on the same mission."

McKesson stared at me. "Maybe. For a day or two. That's all I can do. We all have our masters, you know."

I thought about Dr. Meng, and I wondered if he had someone like that behind him—some member of the "Community," as they liked to call themselves, who pulled his strings.

I nodded finally. "I understand."

"You know what you are, Draith?" he said, looking me in the eye. "You're what they call a *hound*. A bloodhound who finds things. The Community uses your type, because most of them are stuck in one place in order to hold onto their power. Do you understand any of that?"

"Yeah," I said. And I thought that I truly had begun to understand. These people who called themselves a Community had *domains*. Dr. Meng had explained that. She had also indicated I was a fringe member, a minor person-age barely worthy of note in this community of important people. I suspected I was looked upon the way celebrities might look upon a lifelong member of the paparazzi. I was a face they'd grown to recognize among what they otherwise considered to be a crowd of gawking vermin.

"I get it, all right," I said. "You and I are both hired hands. Meng called me a rogue."

"Exactly," he said.

"Do rogues work together?"

"Sometimes—or sometimes we kill each other."

"We came close to doing both tonight," I said. "Who are you working for then?"

"Myself."

I snorted. "Liar."

"Do *you* work for Meng?" he demanded.

I shook my head. "She gave me a hand—sort of. But I'm not her servant."

"So, you understand my position then."

I looked at him. "OK. You aren't a power player, but you *are* a player. Is that what you are saying?"

"Yeah."

"So just give me the name, then. Who else wanted Tony murdered? Who is on the top of your suspect list?"

McKesson looked around as if the walls themselves were listening. Maybe they were.

"No names," he whispered. "But I'll give you a place: The Lucky Seven. You might just find somebody interesting there—dressed in white."

"OK," I said. "Thanks."

"Now you give *me* something," he said, putting out a hand and making tickling motions in the air. "My gun."

I shrugged. "Don't have it."

McKesson looked like he wanted to lunge at me from across the table. "Just taking it from me was your sixth felony by my count."

"You've got a fair number of them racked up yourself," I said, enjoying the process of baiting him for a change. I saw his face grow purple. I knew he couldn't go back to the station having lost his gun and his suspect. He would be humiliated.

I put up a flat palm to halt his next tirade. "Calm down. I left it in the car. Before you ask, your cuffs are there too."

The detective showed me his teeth and gave a tiny snort, nodding. "Smooth," he said. He stood up then and fished inside his coat. I thought for a second he was pulling out a twenty to pay for the meal after all. I was disappointed when he threw down a business card with his name and cell number on it. "If you ever feel like turning yourself in, or you have a wild flash of returning memories, give me a call, Draith," he said.

As he left, I called out after him, "You want to know how to find me?"

"I'll find you," he said, pausing at the door. "All I have to do is follow the trail of bodies."

I paid the tab with Tony's folded twenties and walked out soon afterward. Somehow, I didn't feel relieved in the slightest after my encounter with the law. I now understood much more thoroughly why Holly had told me to avoid them. Still, I had made a connection. McKesson and I had met, sized each other up, and both lived through the experience.

What the hell, I thought. For all I knew, it would blossom into a wonderful friendship. Somehow, however, I doubted it.

9

I wandered the Strip for an hour or so, thinking hard. There were tourists and palm trees everywhere. The tourists seemed to fit the scene. I tried to recall if the city had always had so many palm trees, but couldn't. Maybe they were more noticeable because they were moving. Their fronds waved and rattled in the cool autumn winds.

I'd learned a lot about what was going on in this town, and some of it was very hard to believe. I did believe it, however. My acceptance of the situation taught me something about myself. I decided that this had to be one of my personality traits, or based upon a personal philosophy. I knew I believed in playing the cards life dealt me, rather than whining or dreaming about a better hand. I was a pragmatic person. I didn't believe in witches or aliens—but if you plunked one down in front of me and it performed as advertised, I would change my mind on the spot. Maybe that sort of flexibility had allowed me to survive in this tough city full of strange people, things, and events.

As best I could sum up the whole situation, I was caught up in the center of a struggle between powerful people. They called themselves "The Community" and they were a distrustful, secretive bunch. I was reminded of the organized crime families that had run this city in the past, when this was the center of vice in the nation. In recent years, with the spread of vice into the diffuse online environment, their power had faded somewhat. Something new and possibly worse had come here in their place.

This new power was based, as far as I understood it, on objects or locations. They performed various tricks, such as Tony's sunglasses making metals soft and flexible. I supposed Meng's object, that hood ornament, gave her the power to teleport people here and there. I could see how useful that could be. Being able to open a lock was one thing, being able to pop a rival into a room with no exit was quite a bit more powerful. Meng had indicated, however, that her object worked within a domain. I suspected that meant it would only work in and around the sanatorium.

Tony's sunglasses seemed to be different. They had worked at different spots around the city. Looking back on our conversation, I had to surmise that Meng had decided to let me go with the sunglasses to snoop around for her. Perhaps during our interview, while I sat there smugly with my pistol, she had really been deciding my fate. Maybe it had been within her power to instantly kill me. If she could have sent me anywhere, she could have popped me ten floors up into the air and dropped me onto the concrete. Or, maybe she could have put me into a sewage tank full of bubbling liquid far below the earth to drown. Instant death had been facing me, and I had been blissfully clueless. I guessed she had given me the sunglasses and let me go so I could use them to gather information. So far, they had been a significant help.

After encountering two of these powers, I had to wonder what else was out there. I'd seen evidence of more strange effects. That lava slug that had burned my house had come from somewhere. And Tony had been filled with sand while driving along the street—that could have been Meng, but the street was nowhere near the sanatorium. What about the bum in the painless flames? What about the rest of the dead?

Vegas casinos never close—at least they don't these days. In the middle of the night, you can walk in and throw your money down. When red-eyed wanderers stagger in and gamble their credit cards over the limit, they always find a smiling dealer to take their money. Even at 3:00 a.m. on a Tuesday morning. Coincidentally, it was six minutes after the third hour of Tuesday when I reached the Lucky Seven.

The casino was huge, but it was mostly deserted. Only a few of the massive salons full of gaming tables and one-armed bandits were still lit and operational. The others were sectioned off with green velvet ropes. Vacuums with headlights worked the carpets in those quiet zones, where the lights were turned down to a dim, flickering blue-gray.

I eyed the tables and the patrons. They were unremarkable for the most part. The gamblers looked liked they'd been in their clothes too long. The dealers and security looked like they were bored and waiting for the night to be over. The only spot with any real life to it was a high-stakes blackjack table at the far end. I saw the little sign that listed the minimum bet at a hundred dollars. I winced at the thought, but walked in that direction anyway.

The most interesting person at the table was a young bride, still in her white wedding dress. Even if McKesson hadn't given me a hint about who I was looking for, she would have stood out like a lighthouse on a dark shore. She looked about thirty and held herself with perfect posture. Her medium-length blonde hair flipped up where it touched her shoulders. I looked for the ring and the groom, in that order. The ring was there, but the groom wasn't. Strange, and intriguing.

I bought some chips with Tony's money, then sat at the table one seat down from the bride. We played six hands, with me betting the minimum each time. I lost each round until the fourth, by which time I was sweating. When I finally won a hand, I let out a deep sigh. The bride glanced at me, and I smiled back at her. She stared for a moment, expressionlessly. Her fingers had those classic French nails—white crescents of polish on every tip.

I proceeded to lose two more hands. It was about then I noticed the bride had never lost. She had a mound of chips in front of her—mostly hundreds and five hundreds. I tried not to stare, but it was hard. I rubbed my eyes, calculating that with my terrible luck, I was going to have to make another trip back to Tony's soon.

The guy between the bride and me folded up his tent on the next hand. He'd been losing hard too. He threw his cards in disgust, swilled a drink, and slammed down the glass with a thump. Muttering something about "bullshit" and "freaks," he left the casino and stepped out into the dark streets. I looked after him. Two hands later, everyone at the table was gone except for me, the bride, and the dealer, a Hispanic-looking fellow who was frowning. His mustache seemed to droop farther with every hand he dealt the bride.

She was unbeatable. I knew that couldn't last long, and I was right. About hand number fifteen, a short guy in an expensive suit and an embarrassing comb-over came to the table and quietly spoke with the dealer. He was a pit boss, I knew. It occurred to me that as much as I'd forgotten the personal details of my past, I still knew the casinos well. Pit bosses were floor managers who watched the games for cheats and made decisions on whether to take outlandish bets. For the most part, they were there to make sure the casino didn't lose too much money. I knew, for instance, that the moment the pit boss showed up, every camera in the place was recording our every move.

With the pit boss watching, the bride pushed forward fifteen hundred dollars in chips. I wasn't good at reading women, but I knew this one was angry. Her mouth was small and tight and her eyes were staring at the two men, daring them to reject her bet and close down the table. After a glance of approval, the dealer took the bet and dealt himself a twenty-one right off. The house took her chips, and the dealer looked relieved.

The pit boss wandered off, and I took the opportunity to say a quiet word to the bride. "You know," I said, "gambling in an emotional moment isn't always the best way to win."

"Emotions are all I have left," she replied without looking at me.

I turned my attention to the dealer next. "Can I side bet on her?" I asked.

He nodded to an area of the table outlined in lime green. I pushed three hundred into the box and the dealer stared at those chips for a second. Resignedly, he dealt out the cards.

The bride and I won, but I was the only one there who was smiling. I lost my own hand, but I'd put only the minimum on that. I did the same play on the next hand, and the next. I had all my money back by that time and a little bit more.

The pit boss came back after a couple more hands and closed the table. I was up by about a thousand bucks by then, so I didn't care. The bride got a bucket for her chips and headed for the cash-out window. I followed.

"Thanks for letting me ride your luck," I said.

"It wasn't luck," she replied in a wooden voice.

"I know."

She looked at me then, for the first time. "You work for the casinos, don't you? You're the first security man. The pit boss was the second."

I shook my head. "No. I'm Quentin Draith."

I held out my hand, but she ignored it. "Jenna Townsend," she said.

"I don't work here, and I doubt I ever will now. They hate me too, because I took their money."

Jenna cashed out her chips. I did the same, but I bought a small bucket of silver dollars. She turned away, but I called to her.

"Mrs. Townsend? You want to mess with this casino in a new way?"

She froze, then turned back toward me, staring.

"I don't know what problem you have with them, or how you did what you did, but I can add some pain for them tonight."

"How?" she asked. Her eyes were intense, hungry.

I rattled my paper bucket of silver. It jingled and thudded. "Come with me to the dollar slots."

She followed me, as did a dozen cameras and sets of eyes, I suspected. I felt a bit nervous pulling this, like I'd stumbled onto part of the late-night terrors going on in this city, but I wasn't even sure of that. Maybe she was just angry because the hotel dry cleaners had put a burn mark in her expensive dress.

I had a hunch it was more than that, however, so I took a chance. I went to the biggest, gaudiest dollar-slot machine in the place and put five coins into it. Then I reached into my breast pocket and drew out Tony Montoro's sunglasses. I put them on my face.

Jenna frowned at me. "What are you doing?"

"Pull the handle," I said. "Now."

She licked her lips, looking around briefly. Then she did it.

There was a strange sound. It wasn't right—anyone who heard it would have known that. The handle snapped down, but instead of stopping at the usual spot, at about a forty-five degree angle, it kept going. It came down to a ninety, then past that so it aimed at the carpet. It didn't go back up again.

I sucked in air through my teeth. I half expected coins to come gushing out, but they didn't. What happened was worse. The dials on the face of the machine spun, showing fruit—*why was it always fruit?* Bananas, cherries, bells, and WIN signs flashed by. But they spun on and on too long, and before they were done, the rightmost dial came off its tracks like a wheel coming off a bike. A quick, sharp shrieking sound came out of the machine once, then it quit moving altogether.

I tucked away my sunglasses and stepped away from the machine. Jenna Townsend, her mouth hanging open, stepped after me. The slot machine gave a death rattle that sounded like gears grinding in an old stick-shift truck. A few defeated coins pissed out into the silver tray underneath the monster.

"What the hell did you do?" she asked in an excited whisper.

"Probably ten grand in damage," I said.

"How did you do it?"

I shrugged and smiled. "Wait a second, *you* pulled the handle. You must have focused all your rage into that one yank."

Jenna shook her head. "You're risking your life, do you know that? I don't even know you."

"I'm Quentin Draith. I thought I mentioned that."

"Draith? Do you run that blog full of crazy stuff online?"

"The same," I said. "E-mail me sometime."

She eyed me with suspicion. "I don't know what kind of game you're playing."

"Slots. You want to keep going? Or are you done wrecking this place?"

"No," she said. "I'm not done."

"Before we do any more damage, can you tell me why you're so angry?"

"It's my husband," she said. That dead tone had returned to her voice. "He's gone. They say he just went someplace, but I know what happened. This place ate him."

Ate him? The words rang in my mind. I nodded slowly, thinking of Dr. Meng. Maybe such a thing could happen. Maybe this woman wasn't as crazy as she sounded.

"Want to tell me how you did that trick at the table?" I asked.

"You want to tell me how you did yours?"

"All right," I said. "I made the guts of that machine turn into rubber. The metal went soft, and when you pulled the arm it twisted out of place and broke."

She blinked at me, shaking her head. "OK then," she said. "You did tell me first. I—uh-oh."

I followed her gaze over my own shoulder. The pit boss was coming. He had two chunky members of the Lucky Seven security brigade behind him. Left with little choice, I decided to bluff it through.

"Can I help you?" I asked, meeting his charge head-on.

His face was red and his eyes were bulging. They reminded me of boiled eggs with blue yolks.

"You broke that machine, you freak," he said. His breath came out in puffs.

"Don't worry about it," I said, "this thing has to be under some kind of warranty."

"You two are coming with us."

The bride and I were taken by the arm, but she shook free.

"I'm going to start screaming," she said.

"All right," the pit boss said, putting up his hands. I could see the wheels turning behind his boiled-egg eyes. He didn't want any part of manhandling a lovely, screaming bride across the floor. Some asshole was sure to take a vid with his cell and it would be all over the Internet by noon. "You get out now, lady, and stay out. You are banned from this casino for life. Albert, take her to the door and get her into a cab."

"Just a second," I said, and I pushed the bucket of jingling dollars into her hands.

"What's this for?" she asked.

"Your room number. Tell me."

"Eighteen-eleven," she said.

I pointed to the bucket of coins. "Be careful with that. You can give it back to me later."

Jenna gave me a quizzical look, but they led us in two opposite directions after that. I kept glancing over my shoulder at her. She was pretty, but that wasn't my only concern.

I'd put my .32 automatic in that bucket, sloshing around with the silver dollars. I watched to see if she would blow it and pull it out. She didn't. If she'd noticed the gun, she was playing it cool.

They took me to a pair of double doors that swished shut behind me. I had the feeling they weren't going to pay my cab fare when they were done with me.

10

Once we were through the doors marked "Private," the beefy guy in the too-tight security uniform tried to twist my arm behind my back. I yanked my hand away. I could have probably taken him with a surprise elbow to the throat, but I held back. After all, my little display had been intended to get the attention of the management, not just to impress Jenna Townsend.

"You gentlemen may not know who you are dealing with," I said.

The pit boss smirked at me. "You're a rock star, right? No, maybe an Arab sheik?"

I shook my head. "I'm part of the Community, and I've come to talk to your boss."

His eyes narrowed. I took the time to read his name tag. Bernard Kinley. I figured people probably called him Bernie.

"You're full of shit," Bernie said. "I knew it the moment I laid eyes on you. I don't know what you were pulling back there at the blackjack table—but I do know you broke our most expensive slot machine. I don't even know how the fuck you did that."

"I guess they don't build them like they used to, Bernie."

This remark didn't improve his mood. He put his left hand up to stop the security guard and used his right to put a finger into my face. I thought about grabbing, twisting, and breaking it—somehow I knew I could. But again, that wasn't my purpose in coming here.

"In the old days we would have worked you over and put you out in the alley with the cats and bums. You know that?"

"Yeah," I said, "lawyers and cameras have ruined everyone's good time."

Bernie snorted and we all started walking again. "You are one funny, crazy son of a bitch. You want to see the boss? OK, fine. He's probably still awake. But you should be careful what you wish for, Draith."

It was my turn to be surprised. I should have known they would have ID'd me by now. Casinos were paranoid places full of cameras, computers, and unsmiling security types. Money, booze, and lowlifes mixed in every casino, making a volatile brew. They knew who I was all right. Maybe they knew more about me than I did.

We came to a private elevator. We rode up at least thirty floors in silence. When the elevator dinged and the doors opened, I knew I was in a private region of the hotel. There was a lobby outside a single closed door. The burgundy carpets were rich, thick, and framed with green borders. Bernie and his henchman led me to the door and paused. There was a camera dome over the door, with one of those pricey infrared units spinning around inside. The pit boss had the security goon search me. I'd given my gun to the bride, so they didn't find much except my wad of cash, which they left alone.

Bernie ran a card through the door slider, then touched his thumb to a pad, which glowed green after a few seconds. I was impressed by the heavy security.

The door swung open silently. The interior was black. I blinked and squinted inside.

The two men gave me a push, propelling me into the room. The pit boss laughed, which broke into a coughing fit. He put his fist to his mouth and hacked. He sounded like a smoker in his last decade of life.

"Any last words of advice for me, Bernie?" I asked as the door swung shut between us.

He grinned unpleasantly. "Too late for that, funny guy."

The door closed, and all sound shut out with it. The walls seemed to suck up any hint of vibration, like a soft, fresh coat of snow in a forest.

Not liking this situation at all, I pulled out my sunglasses and put them on. I felt for an opening mechanism and found it. The door was locked. I twisted the handle and felt the gears fight for a moment before going rubbery and beginning to give way.

"Very impressive," said a sonorous voice in the dark. It was male and authoritative.

Startled, I turned toward the voice, taking off my sunglasses and putting them in my breast pocket. I could make out a figure in the dark room. There was about as much light as a movie theater with a black screen, but my eyes were slowly adjusting. Runners of LED lights ran under the furniture along the floor and around the ceiling, providing just enough soft illumination to see outlines once my eyes were used to it.

"I'm Quentin Draith," I said, trying to sound nonchalant. I peered at the seated man. It didn't look like a monster. I decided to ask a dumb question. "Can we turn the lights on in here?"

The man with the musical voice chuckled. "No. That would not be wise for either of us."

I detected a slight accent, European most likely. Maybe Russian. I blinked in the blackness, wondering where to take the conversation and why we were in the dark. Was the guy an albino or a vampire or embarrassingly deformed? Did he have the senses of a bat and a gun on me, enjoying a private joke? I decided to play along. I could see the furniture in the room now as dim outlines. I took a step forward, felt the back of a leather chair, and took a seat without asking.

"You have what my relatives would have called pig balls, Draith," my host said.

"Pig balls?"

"Have you ever been to a hog farm? Boars have very large equipment, you know. The size of cantaloupes. Did you know that, Mr. Draith?"

"I can't say that I did."

"They do, take my word for it," he said. "They are quite impressive creatures. As are you."

"Thanks," I said, never being one to turn away a compliment. "You are doing a nice job with the intimidation routine as well. But what do you find so impressive?"

"Tony's trick. I knew he had one, but I did not know it was the sunglasses. He stole from me several times in the past, did you know?"

I paused. "No, I didn't know that." Inwardly, I cursed myself. I'd used the sunglasses right in front of him. Now he knew what object I had, and how it worked.

"Did you come here to steal from me?"

"No, I came to ask you what happened to Tony."

"Ah," said the man. He stirred and moved in the darkness, rustling. I heard the clinking of ice in a glass.

"May I ask your name, sir?"

"I am Rostok, but people here call me the Ukrainian."

Better and better, I thought with a hint of despair. I felt myself yearning for the good old days of Italian mobsters. At least they kept the lights on.

"Mr. Rostok, sir," I began, "now that I've met you, I would ask you for information. For the good of the entire Community, can you shed light upon the recent killings?"

A rumbling sound began. For a moment, I was alarmed, then I realized he was laughing. "Shed light, he says! Funny! Pig balls, I tell you! Is it not so, Ezzie?"

"He's got big ones, all right," said a strange voice to my right.

My head snapped toward the voice of a third party I'd been unaware of until that moment. There was *something* there, but I couldn't see it. Something that didn't sit in a chair, but was gathered into a pyramid formation. It was almost in the pose of a sitting person, but I had the feeling it was a coil of flesh on the floor. Perhaps it was a giant cobra. Whatever it was, it was not human in shape. I felt rather than saw the shadow rearrange itself. It was an abyss that sucked in light even in that dim room.

"Allow me to introduce you, Draith," Rostok said. "This is a very new member of the Community. This is Esmeralda. She is here for purposes I will explain shortly."

My mouth had gone dry. Up until that moment, I'd been maintaining my cool. But now I'd been faced with something that could not be human. Meeting it in the pitch-dark made it worse.

I steeled myself against panic. I felt a great urge to run to the door and fling it open. Was that what they wanted? Was that the trigger that would allow the feasting to commence? I forced myself to sit back and put up a brave front. I was sure they could see in this darkness better than I could. They could probably read my shocked expression. I reshaped my features even as the thing reshuffled its odd body. When it moved, I heard a grinding sound, as if stones rubbed stones. I also felt a slight warmth as it passed nearby in the dark.

"Nice to meet you, Esmeralda," I said. I was surprised my voice didn't squeak, but it didn't.

"I want to taste him," said the shadow called Ezzie. "He makes me curious."

I compressed my lips into a tense line. Again, I thought of bolting, but I suspected it wouldn't do any good.

"Did I mention who sent me?" I asked, deciding it was time to do what little name-dropping I could. "Dr. Meng asked me to find out what happened to Tony Montoro."

I realized, of course, that Rostok could be the very person I was searching for. He certainly seemed stranger than anyone else I'd yet run into. If he was in the habit of feeding people to this thing called Ezzie, which I was sitting next to, that would explain a lot right there.

"You see?" Rostok said to Ezzie, leaning forward in his chair. The leather creaked, and I got the impression he was a big man. "He stays right on target. He does not quake and shit himself. So many others have failed inside their minds when they first meet Ezzie."

I supposed I was being complimented, but I didn't trust myself to speak right then, so I kept quiet, waiting for an answer.

"I'm cold," complained Ezzie.

"I will do an unusual thing," Rostok said, ignoring her. His outline shifted. I thought I saw him lift a thick finger into the air and point at the ceiling as he talked. "I will talk of the things you ask about. I will give you a message to take back to the others who suspect me."

"I'm listening," I said.

"I'm hungry," said Ezzie.

"You are annoying," Rostok snapped. "Shut up."

Ezzie twisted parts of herself in the darkness and squirmed irritably. But she did shut up.

"You have asked about Tony Montoro. I have told you that he stole from me. I can see how others who know this might believe I took revenge upon him. But I did not kill this man."

"Who then? And how?"

"Do you know how to kill a thing like Ezzie?" he asked.

"No. I don't even know what she is."

"She is a person from another place that mixes with this place. She has stepped through from another of the spheres."

"Spheres? You mean planets?"

"Not exactly. Imagine a dozen shapes all slowly spinning like soap bubbles. Imagine them touching one another, adhering to one another."

"Different worlds then?"

"Ah—more like different *existences*. Occasionally, the rules in these places are different."

"The rules?" I asked. "You mean the rules that govern our physical world?"

"Yes. In one, the sky may be metal. In another, time may run backward. That sort of thing is rare, however. I've never seen a place like that myself."

I stared at him in the dark room. "All right," I said. "Then Ezzie is from one of these places, am I right?"

"Yes."

"And where did the groom go, the man Jenna Townsend told me vanished from her hotel room. She said this hotel *ate* him."

The big Ukrainian slouched back into his chair. "She is probably right. I do not command my own hotel these days. Things come and go as they please."

I glanced toward Ezzie. "This is your power, isn't it, Rostok? You can open up doors to other—existences."

"Yes," he said. "But only to one place. I can do other things as well—but only here at the Lucky Seven."

I thought about that. He could summon monsters in this hotel. I had to wonder what he had summoned here to make himself rich and powerful. What horrible secrets these walls must hold.

Rostok went on explaining the situation while I pondered the implications.

"In a way, that is the power of all the objects, all the domains," he said. "They each connect to other places where the rules are different. Your sunglasses, I believe, connect to a place where metals are soft like rubber. From them the rules of that place leak and change their surroundings."

"You said you've changed your mind about me. What else can you tell me?"

"I've said too much to a person of your low status. You have no domain. You know almost nothing about us. You have no history with us, Draith."

"Then make me a player," I said.

"It is not so easy. I can't simply declare such a thing. We are like a family of spiteful people. We fight amongst ourselves, but still we have a certain level of respect for one another. You are an outsider. A wandering rogue with a minor item—barely worthy of notice by the Community. But the killer must think you are a threat, because you have been close to many deaths."

"Can you give me another name, then, another suggestion?"

Rostok muttered and shook himself. "No. But I will give you your freedom. Go."

"I'm cold and hungry," said Ezzie.

Rostok chuckled as I stood up to leave. "Stay away from my gambling machines, Draith. Or I will feed you to Ezzie. Your fat will warm her."

This last statement startled me. Could Ezzie be a larger version of the thing that had burned down my house? The thought was disturbing. I headed to the door and it slid open at my approach.

I was sorely tempted, but I didn't look back at the strange pair in the room. I was fairly certain I didn't want to see what either one of them looked like. Not even in the half-light.

11

I couldn't leave a lead dangling, not when Rostov had left me in the dark—literally—and Jenna Townsend was a big lead. Besides, she had my gun. I left the casino and walked into the hotel that bordered it. I walked to the front desk and requested a courtesy phone. Jenna answered quickly. "Robert?"

"No, it's Quentin," I said. "What are you doing?"

"Packing," she said. Disappointment was evident in her voice.

"Do you want me to come up there?"

She hesitated. "You left a gun in that bucket, you know."

"Yeah, I know."

"When I found it I freaked out."

"Sorry," I said. "I've got some information."

"About my husband?"

"Maybe."

She hesitated again. I was very strange—as strangers went—and it was late at night.

"Come up," she said finally. "Room eighteen eleven."

I hung up and headed for the elevators. I felt a bit shitty, as I didn't really have a lead on her lost groom. I had only a foggy idea of what might have happened to him—something like Ezzie. I consoled myself with the idea it was all for a good cause. People were dying and vanishing. Maybe I couldn't get Jenna's husband back, but her tragedy and my experiences were almost certainly related. If I could figure out what was going on, maybe I could help both of us. I was sure of one thing: she was the only lead I had.

Jenna wasn't in her wedding dress when she opened the door, but her beauty remained. She had changed out of her white satin into blue jeans and black boots. Her jeans hugged her body in all the right places and dragged my eyes downward. I knew it was rude to ogle her—she was a bride or possibly a recent widow—but I couldn't help myself.

"What do you know?" she asked at the door.

"Can I come in?"

She hesitated, then turned around and walked back into her room. I caught the heavy door before it could shut and followed her. We both sat in hotel chairs around a hotel table and faced each other. I looked around the place, noticing it was a full suite. There was a half-sized fridge and a king-sized bed. The bed wasn't in the shape of a heart—but the Jacuzzi was. I could just see it through the archway leading into the bathroom. It would have been worth a joke if it hadn't been further evidence of her tragic circumstances. I looked back at her and hoped the poor bastard she had married had at least gotten to enjoy his wedding night.

Jenna reached down and pulled up a rattling bucket of coins. She pushed them toward me, sliding them over the table.

"I suppose you are waiting to get this back. It's all there, you can count it."

"I trust you," I said. I took the pistol out of the bucket and put it into my pocket.

She shook her head. "Well, that makes one of us. Why did you give me that gun, anyway?"

"I didn't want them to have me arrested. You can't carry a pistol into a casino, and I don't have a permit for it, in any case."

Jenna eyed me warily. "Why the hell are you doing this? How did you get caught up in my life? I'm not going to give you anything—if that's what you're hoping for."

"Did you get a chance to look me up on the Internet?"

"Yeah. The crackpot website. Stories about monsters and stuff."

"That's all real," I said. "You told me yourself that your husband vanished. Where did it happen?"

She pointed toward the bathroom. "In there, just last night. He was wearing his tux still. We'd just gotten back from the wedding. No family. I wish now we'd flown out my mom, but we didn't. She's a pain—it just comes naturally to her. So we got married in private, and dressed up all the way for the pictures. I wanted to send them home and make it look real to everyone back there."

I thought about asking her where "back there" was, but it didn't really matter. Besides, she was gushing now, telling me her story all at once. I didn't want to interrupt and slow her down. I wanted to hear it all.

Jenna stood up and headed with halting steps toward the bathroom. I followed her discreetly. It was as if she didn't even see me. "Right here, see this scorch mark on the floor?" she asked. "That's the spot where it touched down."

"Touched down?"

"Yeah. A weird thing—a small, quiet tornado. But it wasn't windy, really. It was as if part of the room itself was twisting—as if the colors and shapes were all bending and blending. I don't know. It was like this spot touched some other spot in another place. Two places blurred together. The air moved and rippled like water going down a drain."

"OK," I said, trying to envision it. "Did something come through, or go out?"

"Just Robert. He was here one second, and then the room shifted around him and warped as that tornado shape began to form around him. I was sitting on the bed, adjusting my shoes. I was still in my wedding dress. We were going to make love in these rentals—you know, for a memory."

"Sure," I said, thinking that Robert had been thoroughly ripped off. I wasn't sure if he was dead or not, but he certainly hadn't gotten the chance to bed his bride, just as I had suspected. The thought made me angry for some reason, even though I'd never met the guy.

"He had the strangest look on his face. It hurts me, just to think about it. He tried to shout something at me, I think, but the sound was muffled, as if he was already behind a door or a wall. Then he was sucked away as if that quiet tornado had *inhaled* him."

"Was anything left behind? Besides the scorch mark?"

"Yeah. This one shoe."

She showed it to me. It was black, shiny. Polished with that permanent glossy surface that never seems to fade. The shoe was size eleven and would have fit my left foot, should I have been inclined to try it. I turned it this way and that, but didn't see anything on it that indicated exposure to heat or stress. The laces weren't twisted. The heel wasn't melted. Nothing.

Jenna kept talking, telling me about her panic, her tears, and the police. They'd thought she was crazy. A jilted bride with a wild, made-up story aimed at getting them to chase down her man who had obviously changed his mind and taken off on her. She claimed the hotel staff had been less dismissive. They'd looked worried, rather than embarrassed.

"I could tell they knew something," she said. "I could tell they had seen this before, or something like it. That's when I changed."

"Changed?"

"From crying and scared to angry."

I nodded. "So you went down to the casino and set out to screw them."

"Right."

I stared at her for a moment. The emotion in her face was obvious and I'd seen enough over the last day or two. I bought her story.

"Well," I said. "For what it's worth, I believe you."

I then proceeded to tell her about my house, and the freaky thing that had burned it down. I mentioned McKesson along the way.

"McKesson?" she asked.

"Yeah, that was his name."

She walked over to the dresser drawers and picked up a card. She handed it to me. It was Detective Jay McKesson's card. Las Vegas Metro.

I stared at it. "Same guy."

"He knows more than he's letting on. It can't be a coincidence."

"I'm not sure what his game is," I said, "but I do think he's trying to figure out what is going on here, just as we are."

"You told me you had information on my husband. What have you got?"

"I said it might be related. Now, I think it is. We have two strange events in different places. The same detective was investigating both, and he sent me here, to you, connecting the two."

"That's not much," she complained.

"I know," I said. Then I told her about Tony. I told her how he'd died in the car with me, and how I'd ended up in the hospital.

She stared, and I realized there were tears welling up in her eyes.

"Robert's dead," she said with certainty. "I know it now, with all these horrible things happening. I'd hoped he would just turn up somewhere, wandering the streets or the desert highways. I don't think it's going to happen that way."

"We really can't know for sure," I said. I wanted to tell her not to give up hope, but I didn't think I should. I'd calculated the odds and figured she was probably right.

Her head went down, her hands came up. She was racked with quiet sobs. I wanted to comfort her, but I didn't really know her. I didn't want to touch her and have her get the wrong idea. So I stood there awkwardly and muttered soothing things.

Jenna surprised me by stepping close and putting her cheek against my chest. I waited until her hands touched my sides before I gently reached up and patted her back. I stroked her hair once, then stopped myself. The scent of her perfumed body was in my face, and I felt myself attracted to her, and I began to feel protective.

"We'll figure this out," I said. "I promise."

And I meant it.

12

Jenna pulled herself together after a few minutes. She went back to the small table and chairs and sat down. I called room service and ordered cola, coffee, and beer. I wasn't sure which one she would want, but I figured I would drink whatever she rejected.

She was a tough young woman. Instead of falling apart, she'd taken action and tried to get back at the casino and find out what she could about her husband's odd disappearance. I just had one question left: how had she won over and over again at cards?

Normally, I would have just assumed it was all luck. But she'd gone down to that casino on a mission, full of rage. That indicated she *knew* she was going to win. I had a suspicion how that could be true, but I sat in the chair next to her waiting for her to compose herself. Jenna's blonde hair circled her face, which was red with emotion.

"What are you thinking?" she demanded suddenly. "Do I look silly to you?"

"Not at all."

"Do you do this kind of thing often? Comfort grieving widows after they watch the bridal suite swallow their husbands? Does it help your blogging somehow, is that it?"

I almost laughed, but I knew it was the wrong move. "You are the first," I said.

"Where do we go from here then?"

I frowned slightly, trying to figure an easy way to ask her about her luck at cards without seeming greedy and crass. I was saved by a knock on the door. I got up to let the bellhop in.

He looked surprised, and eyed me with a wide stare that lingered about a second too long. Maybe he thought I was the amazing Mr. Robert Townsend returned from the void. Then he noticed the tears still streaking Jenna's face and hurried to put a silver tray loaded with drinks on the dresser. I gave him a few bucks and let the door slam behind him.

"That's just great," Jenna said after he'd left.

"What?"

"I'm sure he's hurrying off to tell someone there is some guy in the crazy lady's room."

I shrugged. "They don't matter. They aren't going to find him in the lobby."

Jenna winced at my words. I realized instantly that saying anything about not finding Robert wasn't going to improve her mood.

"If he does turn up as suddenly and mysteriously as he vanished," I said, "he'll find his way back to you."

"How can you be so sure?"

"Well, if you were my wife, I'd find my way home."

She frowned and took the coffee. I took the cue and drank the Pepsi.

"Look, there's something I'd like to ask you about—if you are willing."

"No promises—but name it."

"How did you get so lucky at cards?"

Her expression changed. Her eyes closed halfway. It was a guarded look. She didn't answer right away. "I'll tell you, if you tell me first."

"Tell you what?"

"Come on. Tell me again, how did you wreck that big slot machine?"

"Oh, that," I said. "I turned the metal gears inside to rubber, then I twisted up its guts when I pulled the handle all the way down."

She stared at me. "What did you use?"

Right then, I knew she had an object. She would have asked *how* I'd done it otherwise. She knew these effects were managed with the help of a focusing object.

"I played this game as a kid," I said. "You show me yours first."

She smiled despite herself. In a flash of my true memory, I recalled a girlfriend once telling me I was so funny I could make a corpse laugh. I wasn't sure at this point whether that was a compliment or not. I couldn't recall the girlfriend's face, but I could hear her voice.

"What's wrong?" she said.

"I was just remembering something," I said. She was leaning on the table with her elbows now. The tears were gone, but her face was a little puffy and her makeup had run. I saw she was looking down at her hands, toying with her wedding ring.

"It's the ring, isn't it?" I asked quietly.

"Dammit," she said, slipping her hand under the table.

"Don't worry, I'm not going to take it or tell anyone."

"Robert told me never to let anyone know about it. No one. And he told me never to abuse it the way I did at the casino. I'm an idiot. These places have lists, you know. They won't let me walk in the door if I get on those lists."

I nodded slowly. They did have lists. Once you were marked as a card-counter or some other kind of cheat, they hustled you back out the second you walked in—whether they knew how you did it or not.

"How does it work?" I asked.

"He told me not to tell anyone anything."

"I understand, but I already know most of it, and we're supposed to be exchanging information."

She chewed her lip. Her hand and the ring were under the table. "You know what I've got. You show me yours now."

I held back the funny responses that bubbled into my mind. I slowly reached into my pocket and took out Tony Montoro's sunglasses. I laid them on the table.

Jenna scoffed, looking at them. "They're plastic," she said. "That can't be one of the objects."

"Why not?"

She leaned back and crossed her arms under her breasts. She frowned at me. "You've been full of crap this entire time, haven't you? You don't really know anything, do you? You had me going."

"Look," I said. "These are Tony's glasses, the guy I told you about. His object."

Her head tilted suspiciously. Her eyes were narrow, calculating. "You are supposed to run that blog—but you don't know crap about what you're writing about, do you?"

"I suppose not. Now, clue me in."

She shook her head and lifted the ring back into my sight. "See this?" she said, showing me the thin gold loop with a single marquis-cut diamond in the setting. "You can't break this. You can't break any of the objects."

I blinked at her, then looked down toward my pathetic plastic sunglasses. "Can you mark them up?" I asked.

"No. Not according to Robert."

"Hmm," I said. I got up and went into her bathroom.

"What are you doing?" she called after me.

I came back in a moment with a pair of gold-plated nail clippers.

"Those are mine," she snapped.

"I'm not selling them online," I said. "I'm going to conduct an experiment."

"Oh," she said, catching on.

I sat at the table, took the sunglasses, and tried to snip the tip off one of the arms. I clipped at the final hockey-stick-shaped hook that went over the ear. I couldn't do it, however. It was as if I were trying to cut into a sheet of steel. After a bit of grunting and squeezing, I gave up.

"Not a mark," I said.

"Let me try," she said. After I handed over the sunglasses and the clippers, I felt a twinge of worry as she went at them. She couldn't mark them either. Not even a crease.

"I didn't think plastic could be unbreakable," she said, staring at them in defeat.

"Talk to me about the process. Why do these things exist?"

Jenna shook her head. "I don't know much—just what Robert told me. At some point—back in the sixties, I think, these objects were made. Some say they are still being made today, but less often. This one looks newer than most. Once they become objects, they can't be damaged."

"What if you put them into acid or a volcano?"

"According to Robert," she said, shaking her head, "nothing happens."

I retrieved my sunglasses and tucked them away. She slid her hand back off the table, hiding her ring again. So much for building trust.

"OK," I said, "how does yours work?"

"I don't know that. I only know what the ring does."

"Can you give me a hint, then?"

"Well, it just makes you lucky. Whatever you want tends to happen."

My eyebrows shot up. Right away, I was wondering why Robert had vanished. Was that what she wanted to happen? I didn't voice the thought, but she caught the look in my eye.

"No!" she said. "It wasn't like that! It only works with things that are very close—it has a short range. And you have to be thinking about what you want—and most importantly, it only changes small, physical things. Like dice or cards."

I nodded. "Sounds useful in Vegas."

"Right. But not if you overdo it. There's one other critical thing. The bad side. The ring makes others around you have *bad* luck."

"Ah, I see. That's why I was losing so badly, hand after hand."

"Sorry," she said.

"No problem. I started betting on you and made all the money back."

"You also alerted security. Now, tell me the story of these sunglasses."

I did so, as best I understood them.

"What's the downside?" she asked when I was finished.

I shrugged. "As far as I know, there isn't one."

She stared at me and shook her head slowly. "There's always a downside. Robert told me that in no uncertain terms."

Frowning, I took out the sunglasses and rotated them slowly with my fingers. I wondered what evil these were doing without my knowledge. I supposed it couldn't be too bad, like giving me cancer or something. Tony had seemed to live life fully enough—at least up until its abrupt ending.

I decided to try not to overuse them, all the same.

13

I'd gotten as much out of Jenna as I could, and it didn't make sense for me to stay, not with her stretching out semi-provocatively on the king-sized bed while she drank coffee. Besides, I had things to do, and she was devoted to that hotel room, still convinced Robert might come back or call her—if he wasn't dead.

"Thanks for helping out, and for being a gentleman about it," she said as I left, and that made me feel good. She'd promised to stay put and I'd promised I would report back if I found out anything.

I called a cab, shelled out a twenty from my thick roll of bills, and got a ride to an all-night convenience store. It took me three stops, but I finally found one with disposable phones. I felt eyes on me as I entered the store, but put it down to nerves.

The convenience store was typical of its breed, but, typical of Las Vegas, had lottery tickets in unusual abundance and variety. There was a slot machine in the store, an old one that let you play draw poker for a quarter. I smiled at that. People would pay money to play a repetitive card game against a computer—as long as they thought they had a chance of winning money. Gambling was a powerful incentive.

I located the phones, called "dealer phones" on the street, near the poker machine and pulled one off the rack. No point in trying to get a real cell phone. I had the feeling I wasn't going to impress anyone with my burned-down house and lack of identification at a cell phone store.

That's when a casual glance toward the cloudy front window sent a chill through me. *A shadow, quickly moving away.* I was definitely being followed. The question was, who was doing the following? Cops? Rostok's goons? Bill collectors? I had no idea, but despite the fact the streets were nearly empty at dawn, I'd been seeing that same blue Buick at every store I went to.

Rather than heading back out to the street, I asked the kid behind the counter if he had a bathroom.

"It's only for employees," he said. He was a tall kid with the triple whammy of braces, glasses, and acne.

"I'm gonna puke. Long night."

He looked at me unhappily. I still had some healing cuts on my face and I had been up all night long. I looked the part of a sick tourist who'd overdone it in Sin City.

"All right," he said, sighing. "There's a key hanging behind that little sign beside the door."

I walked toward the back without thanking him. I'd heard a door crumping closed outside. Apparently, my stalker felt I'd taken too long in here. I ignored the bathroom and the key, and instead put on Tony's shades. I twisted the stockroom's locked door handle. The door rattled, groaned, and then opened. I walked inside and let it click shut behind me. One bad thing, I realized, was I couldn't lock the door again behind me. The shades got me through locked doors, but they opened them for everyone else too. Not ideal when being pursued.

I found the exit that led into the alley behind the place, threw the door open, and stood to one side of it. I snapped off the lights, stepped behind the open door, and froze. I waited there, barely breathing.

It took a full minute. This guy wasn't too bright, I surmised. Eventually, he found his way into the stockroom. I peeped around the edge of the door with one eye. The glare from outside hid me from the intruder's point of view. I didn't recognize the face, because I didn't see one. He had a mask on. My heart thudded when I saw his hands. There was blood on them, and they held a dark object. A gun? Was he really here to rob this place, or to get rid of me?

I stared at his hands and the object in them. Yes, it was a gun. But that wasn't why I kept staring for an extra second or so. It was that hand. It was gray, and it had ridges on the back of it. No—they were more like spurs. Curved, bladelike hooks that resembled tiny shark fins.

I stayed behind the door while he trotted past and out into the alley. I imagined him out there—whatever he was—looking around in confusion. He didn't say anything, not even muttered curses. I pushed the door quietly shut behind him. The door clicked and he was locked out, as I hadn't used the sunglasses on this one. Like most alley doors at the back of convenience stores, it locked automatically when you closed it.

He didn't make a sound. He didn't say a word. I'd expected cursing, but I didn't get any. The door handle rattled vigorously, however. When he gave up on that, an odd, spitting sound erupted. He must have had a silencer. I'd been ready for him to shoot through the door and hadn't stood in front of it. Bullets punched holes through the steel, leaving three white circles of light.

I ran back out into the store. I found the kid who'd been nice enough to let me into his bathroom. He was lying in a bloody pool. I sighed and frowned. I hadn't meant for that to happen. I touched his neck and felt a thready pulse. He might make it. I called emergency as I left, dropping the phone I'd bought into a trashcan after I reported the shooting. I took a fresh phone off the rack. The cops would be hunting for the one I used to call in the shooting, and I'd already answered enough of McKesson's questions.

The alley didn't open up anywhere close to this store, which left the gunman outside a long run around half the block to get back here. Deciding I had a bit of time, I grabbed a box cutter from the counter and sank the right front tire on the blue Buick. Then I got back into the cab, which had been patiently waiting for me out front. I'd been feeding the driver twenties as we drove around town, and cabbies were like stray cats when you fed them twenties.

The driver wasn't happy with me when I climbed back into his cab, however. "No way, man," he told me. "I saw what you did in my mirror. That tire is going all the way down. Get out and walk."

I thought about pulling my gun on him, but he'd never done me any harm. If it came to that, I would rather shoot it out with the asshole in the alley. So I tried cash instead.

"Two hundred bucks, two miles," I said, "but decide fast."

"Crazy mother," he muttered, then gunned the cab.

I gave the driver Holly's address and we were flying down the street in seconds. I figured if I'd been followed from the casino hotel, Holly's place was safer. As we left, I sank down in the backseat, looking this way and that for the gunman, who had to be truly pissed by now after his little jog around the block. But I didn't see him.

A few minutes later, I stood on Holly's doorstep in the pink glow of dawn, the cab hauling ass away behind me. I'd asked the cabby to wait, but I couldn't blame him. He knew trouble when he saw it.

I tapped on the door and waited. After half a minute, I did it again. Still nothing.

After the fourth set of knocks, I put on my sunglasses and twisted the knob, which squeaked as the lock relented. I let myself in.

"You've got balls," Holly said, standing inside in a long pink T-shirt and little else.

"People keep telling me that," I said, smirking. I could tell she'd heard my knocks, checked the peephole, and decided to take a pass. I didn't hold it against her. After a long night, I probably looked like hell.

She had a tattoo on her bare thigh I hadn't noticed before. It looked like a hummingbird hovering around a flower. Right then, I thought I wouldn't mind watching her pole-dance. It must be quite a show.

"What are you doing back here?" she asked. "At frigging daybreak, no less?"

"Sorry," I said, "but I've got new information and I was wondering if I could crash here. I'm dead tired."

"Get a room. You've got the cash."

"Hotels in this town want plastic."

"Not the crappy ones."

"OK," I said. "I shouldn't have come."

Holly stared, then shook her head, sighing. "OK, you might as well come in, since you have already turned my lock into Jell-O."

"It will turn back, as long as the lock hasn't been twisted to an impossible position," I said.

"I know that."

After ten more seconds of hesitation, she finally stepped out of the way and let me in. I sank onto her couch with a sigh.

"Look," she said, standing over me with her fists on her hips, "we both have Tony's money, and we had a nice chat yesterday. But we aren't roomies. You got that?"

"Yeah." It was a good pose for her, so I admired the view.

"What did you do, anyway, kill somebody?" she asked after staring at me suspiciously for a few long seconds.

I squirmed a little. I must have had that kind of look on me, the look of a hunted, worried man who was grateful to be in a relatively safe place. I had to wonder how often she'd seen it before.

"I don't think so," I said.

Holly began rubbing her temples. "I don't believe this," she said.

"You got any beer?" I asked, knowing that she did.

She got me the beer and slammed it down on the coffee table. "You're like one of those bums my mom used to let move in with us," she complained. "I never should have fed you."

I chuckled. I drank the beer and ate the open bag of chips she tossed onto the couch beside me a minute later. The beer was lite and a little warm. The chips were half-stale, but I was hungry. After a breakfast of champions, I fell asleep on her couch.

Coming to her place and crashing was becoming a habit—one I didn't half mind.

I woke up to the sound of a ringing phone. It wasn't a traditional ring, nor was it a traditional phone. It was a cell phone, and as I blearily opened my eyes, I saw it was buzzing on the coffee table.

I groaned into a sitting position and reached for it. Holly showed up and snatched it away.

"It's mine," she said.

I shrugged, leaned back, and stretched. I looked for a clock and found one on the TV set, which decorated one wall of the apartment. It was four thirty in the afternoon. I'd been out for a long time.

"Hello? What?"

I looked at her curiously. She stared back.

"I don't believe this," she said. She handed me the phone. "It's for you."

I took the phone and looked at it dubiously. Who knew I was staying with Holly? I wasn't happy that *anyone* knew I was here. My last unknown contact had fired three rounds through a door to kill me. I thought about waving the phone away, but she'd already blown it by handing it to me.

I put the phone to my cheek. "Hello?"

"Draith? It's McKesson."

"Of course it is. How'd you know I was with Holly?"

"You were both at the Tony Montoro event. Call it a lucky guess."

I frowned at his use of the term *event* to describe a murder. "What do you want?" I asked.

"Were you at the liquor store this morning?"

I hesitated. I kicked myself for that hesitation. "What liquor store?"

"That's a confession in my book. The kid lived, in case you wanted to know."

"I didn't shoot anyone."

"Yeah, it was the wrong caliber. I checked. Besides, the kid said it wasn't you, it was some freak chasing you."

"What do you know about the freak?" I asked.

"I know he wanted to kill you."

"I figured that much, but why?"

"Because you are still alive. I think the subtle attempts they've made haven't worked, so they've stepped it up, going for a more direct approach."

I thought about that for a moment. It sounded like I was in trouble, not just unlucky. How many times could one person be in the wrong place at the wrong time?

"You've been holding out on me, Jay," I said.

He laughed. "What about you? After a full day of nosing around and stirring up trouble all over town, you never even called."

"I was getting around to it," I lied.

"Let's meet and talk."

"We're talking now," I pointed out. "Where did that freak come from?"

It was his turn to hesitate. "Where all this crap comes from. Another place."

I decided to drop some names to jolt him a little. "You mean out of another existence? That's what Rostok called it."

"You've met Rostok?"

"And Ezzie too."

He fell silent.

"You there, McKesson?"

"That explains some things," he said. "You've gotten in deeper faster than I thought you would."

"Give me something I can use, then. Share some real information."

"All right," he said. "You want to see what we're up against? I'm on the way to a disturbance right now. Get a ride and come out to Henderson."

He gave me an address. I hung up and looked to my left. Holly was sitting there on the couch, staring at me like an irritable cat.

"Your tail is lashing," I said.

"What's up?"

"I need to get to Henderson."

"I told you to steer clear of the cops. Now they are calling my cell looking for you. This is bullshit."

"At least you know I didn't kill anyone. They would have done more than just call if I had."

"Am I coming with you?" she asked.

"Can I bum a shower and a ride?"

Holly heaved a sigh and rolled her eyes. "I just bought a car. How did you know that?"

"I didn't," I said. "Tony's money?"

"Shut up about that."

In the end, I got the shower and the ride. Thirty minutes later, we were driving down Interstate 515 to Henderson, a suburb south of Vegas. Her car was far from new. It was a nondescript Ford from a better decade. The seats were cloth and mine had a rip that kept scratching my right arm. The ride was free, so I didn't complain.

The address was in a pricey neighborhood full of McMansions. I had Holly stop at a drive-through to let me get some instant food before we went up into the hilltop neighborhoods. We finally rolled up to the wrought-iron front gates and watched them swing open automatically. I was still chewing.

Holly hung her head out the driver's window and stared at the camera that had swiveled to watch us. She didn't drive into the open gates. She let the car sit there, idling.

"Are you sure this is the place?" she asked dubiously. I could tell she didn't feel comfortable in a rich neighborhood.

I pointed through the windshield up the driveway. There was a fountain circled by concrete and a single, featureless sedan. There were two other cop cars there as well.

"That's McKesson's car, isn't it?" I asked.

"I guess so," she said. "Why don't you just walk up there? I'll wait in the car."

I looked at her, swallowing the last of my breakfast. "What did they do to you?"

"It's not what they did. They were—threatening."

"Did they say something? Or did you just get a bad feeling?"

"A little of both. They know about the objects, Draith. Be careful. They might even know about Tony's sunglasses. The only reason you still have them is because they are hoping you will lead them to more players—more objects."

I stared at her for a moment. "Are you sure about that?"

"Yeah."

"According to your logic, I must walk in there. Being nosy is the only reason I'm still breathing. Now isn't the time to turn chicken and disappoint them."

She shrugged. "I guess not. Be careful."

"OK. If you change your mind, come up after me."

"I won't," she said.

I got out of the car and walked up the driveway. I had the feeling I was walking into the lion's den, but I'd felt that way before. I knew somehow the sensation was part of my regular life, even before the accident. I supposed one couldn't be an investigator of actual paranormal events without being stubbornly determined about it. Normal people would have long since run off and sought counseling.

Before I reached the door, three police officers wearing rubber gloves walked out and got into the cars. Two were uniforms, one was a woman with wild hair, normal dress, and rubber gloves. They glanced at me but said nothing. They spoke quietly among themselves and then drove off. It looked like an investigation team to me. I steeled myself, expecting to see something unpleasant inside.

McKesson met me at the door, which was an elaborate affair of iron-bound wood and cut glass. The door alone must have cost ten grand. I marveled at it as I followed him inside. The entry was gray-white marble tiles—the real stuff, not something made of vinyl or polished cement. Yellow plastic crime scene tape was all over the place, but it had been pushed aside.

The mansion was two stories and clearly built in a better day when people in this part of the country were richer and crazier. There were cupolas with Greek statues stationed under soft recessed lights, a grand spiraling stairway that would have caused a southern belle to swoon, and a huge saltwater fish tank that filled one curved wall between the kitchen and the dining room.

I walked toward the fish tank first, noting the glass was cracked. The tank was half-full of cloudy water. Inside, a few exotic fish floated on their sides.

"That looks expensive," I said.

"It *was* expensive. Must be a thousand bucks worth of sushi in there."

"Who owned this place?"

"Some dot-com guy who lost his bank account over it. They rented it out to some people who called us about a week ago. We found the place like this. Never found the residents."

I looked at him sharply. "A week? About when I had my accident?"

"Same night," McKesson said, returning my stare.

"Why'd you bring me here?"

He pointed at the fish tank, and I looked at the dead fish. There were lights inside the tank, making it a bright point in an otherwise dim room.

"What?" I asked. "Do you want me to scoop out the dead ones?"

McKesson snorted and flipped a switch at the base of the tank. The lights inside it went out. I could see through the tank now. There was a darkened kitchen beyond. Three islands could be seen in the kitchen—it was big enough to run a restaurant.

I frowned, noticing dark shapes laid out upon the counters and overflowing the sinks.

"Are those body parts?" I asked.

"Yeah. But they aren't human."

I felt a chill. I didn't want to walk back there into the kitchen. Not if it was full of chopped up monsters.

"Not—*things* either," McKesson said, reading my mind. "They are animals. Someone bought out a butcher shop. Sides of beef, legs of lamb, ham hocks, and at least ten buckets of lard. They even cut up a fifteen-pound turkey."

"What the hell for?"

"Now you know why you're here. They're cultists of some kind. These events always attract them like beetles to a corpse. Don't you specialize in investigating this sort of thing?"

"I specialize in unexplainable events," I said. "Not loonies with knives."

McKesson rubbed his chin and shook his head. "You know, a couple of years ago I would have agreed with you. I would have dismissed these people as freaks with a collective mental problem. But if you do something like this and it *works*—I mean it really has a measurable effect on our physical world—can they really be dismissed as crazy? Like a thief or a robber, they are doing something with a purpose. A bad purpose, but a purpose nonetheless. They aren't simply deluded."

I stared at him for a second. I wasn't sure if he was apologizing for these freaks or having some kind of philosophical episode. Either way, I didn't have any answers for him, so I just shook my head.

"Is that it?" I asked.

"No, there's more downstairs."

McKesson led the way past the kitchen to a dark stairwell leading down. I glanced to my right, where stacks of meats were spread all over the granite counters. I squinted in the gloom. Were those catch basins lining the counters? Had they defrosted the meats and caught the juices? Why?

Shaking my head, I followed him down a narrow stairway. As wide and grand as the stairs were leading up from the marble entry, this stairway was ignoble, dingy, and dimly lit. The steps were made of wood planks rather than ringing tiles. Our shoes scraped and the planks creaked as we descended.

The cellar had a single purpose: to store wine bottles. Unlike the kitchen above, the cellar wasn't trashed. I fully expected a cluster of candles and a pentagram painted with old, brown bloodstains. I found neither, however. The center of the cellar was clear, with the wine-laden shelves shoved back against the walls. On the cement tiles there were only two things: a scorch mark and a single, severed finger. It was grayish in color.

I stopped following McKesson when I reached the bottom of the creaking steps and spotted the finger. That was close enough for me. I recalled distinctly Jenna's tale of a warping of space in her suite's bathroom. Could this have been a similar phenomenon?

McKesson turned back, saw me lingering at the stairs, and chuckled. "Don't worry," he said. "This finger's pointing days are over."

"Do you know how it got there?"

"Not a clue." He stepped in front of it and squatted, staring down. He obscured the finger from my view, which was just fine with me.

"Why did you guys leave it there?" I asked, taking a step or two forward despite my misgivings. My eyes were roaming the cellar for other oddities. "Couldn't you just take pictures and put it in a baggie or something?"

"Normally, that would be the procedure," he admitted. "But this isn't a normal finger."

I frowned at his back. "Because it's gray? Isn't that normal for an old, dead digit?"

He shook his head and looked back over his shoulder. "It's pretty fresh, they tell me. Maybe less than a day old."

"A day?" I asked. "You mean it just appeared recently? After you came to check this place out?"

"Yeah."

"Was the scorch mark there before?"

"All week."

"But not the finger."

"You're catching on."

I hesitated. "Does it have a spur-like growth on the back of it?" I asked.

That comment brought him to his feet. He turned toward me with a hand on his gun. It was the same weapon I'd taken off him the night we'd met.

"How did you know about that?" he asked.

I told him about the man who'd chased me out of the convenience store. He'd had strange gray hands like that.

McKesson took his hand off his gun. "So—a stranger came through and somehow lost his finger doing it. And he immediately tried to assassinate you. At least, that's what you're claiming."

"I guess so. Unless there is more than one of them around. I didn't see a missing finger on the man I encountered."

The detective was frowning and thinking hard. "It's not supposed to work this way," he said.

"What do you mean by that?"

"When these disturbances, confluences, intersections—whatever you want to call them—when they open up, they're like small natural storms. Things might wander in and out, but beings aren't supposed to purposefully come through into our existence."

Into our existence? I thought. But I didn't ask him what he was talking about. The meaning was plain enough, if disturbing. I didn't want him to think too much about what he was divulging. I desperately needed information.

"That's what happened to Robert Townsend, isn't it?" I asked. "He went through one of these openings."

McKesson looked at me. "The newlywed guy? Yeah, I think so. Now, let's get some air. This place is stifling."

15

Detective McKesson and I left the stucco mansion and walked outside. It was early evening now, and the cool breezes felt good on my face. McKesson checked his watch. It was gold and old-fashioned, with hair-thin metal hands that ticked over the face.

That watch reminded me I had a question for McKesson. "How are these objects made?" I asked, trying to sound nonchalant.

He laughed. "I thought I was the detective."

"Come on," I said. "It can't be critical information."

"I don't know how they're made."

"I think you do," I said.

He gave me a sidelong glance, then gestured down to the street. "Your ride took off on you."

I turned and took a step down the driveway. I squinted westward, into the dying sun. It was about to fall behind the Spring Mountains. There, at the bottom of the driveway, was the open gate. Holly's car was gone. My mouth twisted in disappointment.

"Don't even think about begging for a ride," he said. "I'm not leaving here just yet."

"Why not?"

"I'm waiting for something to happen." He lit a cigarette and we watched the sun go down.

I thought about McKesson. He always seemed to know where and when something was going to happen.

"You want me to stay for—whatever happens?" I asked.

"Up to you. I'm not going anywhere." McKesson checked his watch again as he puffed on his cigarette.

"Will it come after dark?"

He shrugged. "Maybe. These events usually do."

Just what kind of detective was this guy? Who the hell did this kind of work? I knew he always seemed to show up at events, as he called them. But how did he learn about them so quickly? And how come he was alone, with no army of police backing him up?

I followed his gaze out toward the Spring Mountains. The rocky range ran along the west side of Las Vegas to the California border.

I glanced back at McKesson. The man was a black hole of information. He sucked it all up, and gave back as little as possible. If we were just going to stand there anyway, staring at the mountains, I decided to start guessing and see if I could figure out some of his secrets.

"Can I see that watch?" I asked, putting out my hand.

McKesson ignored my hand. "No," he said.

"Is that real gold? Not many people wear watches these days, you know. I just use my cell phone when I want to know the time."

He glanced at me with unfriendly eyes and took one last drag on his cigarette before stamping it out on the porch. "Maybe you should start walking after all," he said.

"Don't want me around anymore, huh?"

"You can stay, if you want to see what happens next. But I'd prefer it if you were quiet. I'm trying to think, here."

"Why did you bring me in the first place?"

"To verify that one of the Gray Men had taken a shot at you at the convenience store. You identified the finger. That's why I brought you. Now I'm convinced."

The Gray Men, I thought. I didn't like the sound of them. I especially didn't like the indication that there were a number of them around. After all, they appeared to want me dead.

McKesson checked his watch yet again, and I glanced at it sidelong. I tried to read the dial, but couldn't. I frowned. Both the hands were pointing in the same direction. The big minute hand was directly on top of the smaller hour hand. I frowned further as I noticed even the second hand was piled up on top of the other two. All three hands pointed at the mansion behind us.

"I get it," I said. "The watch points toward these events— maybe before they happen? That's how you always get there first, isn't it?"

McKesson flashed me a dangerous look. When he spoke, it was in a lower, more menacing voice than I'd heard from him since we'd first met at my burned-down house. "Don't even go there, Draith. People kill for their objects. Even to keep the details secret."

I realized he was probably just another rogue with a weak object, like me. "OK, OK," I said, backing down. "So, what do we do next?"

"We go back down to the cellar and wait for something to happen."

By the time the vortex showed up, I'd almost forgotten why we were down there. It was about one hour shy of midnight, and I'd consumed most of a bottle of very expensive French wine. McKesson had taken only a single glass. He sat at the bottom of the stairs like a bulldog whose master had died on him. He didn't budge, but kept eyeing the scorch mark and the finger that lay nearby. The hands of his old gold watch kept shivering and pointing toward the spot, and he seemed to have a lot of faith in that watch.

I'd found him a poor conversationalist over the preceding hours. He seemed to have had series of broken relationships, and he'd given up on women except for the occasional casual hookup when he felt the urge. He drank, smoked, and used recreational drugs now and then—but not while working. Because the man had only one focus in his life: his investigative work. He'd doggedly followed these freaky events around the metro area for the last couple of years. Each month, they'd gotten more dramatic and disturbing. Somehow, he'd gotten himself assigned to handling these impossible cases. After sitting in this spooky, echoing mansion for hours, I could see why no one else wanted the job.

I'd investigated the various vintages during the long hours and marveled at the expensive bottles. Most of the racks were empty, but there were a large number of dusty bottles still present.

The anomaly didn't take shape exactly over the scorch mark; instead, it appeared atop the Gray Man's severed finger. It didn't look like a swirl of dust as I'd expected. It was more of a bending of light and mind. It reminded me of a heat shimmer on a desert highway, seen close-up.

"Whoa," I said, taking a step backward among the wine racks. "There's something happening, Detective."

His gun was already out. I followed his lead and drew my .32 automatic.

The vortex was much closer to the stairway—a good five feet closer—than either of us had expected. Part of the stairway was, in fact, merged with the twisting of space, if that's what it was. More than anything else, this fact worried me. I felt my heart pound as I realized there was no way out of this cellar if things went badly. The only way past was to walk through the edge of the warped region. I could tell that if I ran up the stairs, I would be forced to touch the border of that blurred area. I had no intention of doing so.

"Is something coming out?" I shouted, although the vortex really didn't make that much noise. There was as odd sound…a susurration like that of a distant train or a breeze moving through the treetops of a forest.

McKesson peered into the blurred region. "I see something," he said. "It's growing bigger—closer."

I stared into the space and I could see what he was talking about. Something loomed inside that region. I realized we were looking through the vortex into another place. The image was still blurred, as if seen through churning water or rippling smoke. A shadow approached. I wondered about the scene I was peering at. Was it a city street on the other side? I couldn't tell.

The approaching shadow loomed larger. If that shadow was a creature, it was massive, the size of a great white shark. Cold concrete pressed against my back. I held my gun in both hands. I wished now I'd called Holly and asked her to return and pick me up. I should never have stayed here.

The shadow slowed, and as I watched, it spit out more shadows from its sides. Four of them—no, it was at least six.

It took a moment for me to register what I must be seeing. Realization came with a tiny fraction of relief. I wasn't witnessing a monster spawning young. The original looming shadow was a truck or tank. It wasn't a single living thing. But it had been full of smaller shapes, and now they approached us in a rush.

Without hesitation, they began to step through into our world. It took them several seconds to make the crossing. I stared as they grew ever more distinct. At first, I thought they were human, but as the figures stopped rippling like open flame they coalesced into what I now knew to be Gray Men.

McKesson fired first. He didn't cry out a warning or a challenge. He didn't say anything at all. The first Gray Man didn't even get his weapon up, which appeared to be a strange, shotgun-like device. There was a stock and a handle at his end, and a muzzle that pointed in our general direction. But unlike a shotgun, the device had a circular disk of dark metal built into the middle of it and a bulb at the business end instead of an open barrel. I was reminded of an old-fashioned Thompson submachine gun. Whatever it was, he handled it like a weapon.

McKesson put three rounds in him. The Gray Man never even pulled the trigger. He sagged down and I almost felt sorry for him, ambushed like that. I wondered right then, for the first time, if I was helping to start a strange new war.

"Shoot them the second they look solid," McKesson shouted at me. "It takes them a bit to get their bodies to operate properly after they come through."

The second and third came through together, but these guys knew the score, I could tell. They had their weapons up and were firing even as they unblurred and formed into solid masses before my eyes. Gouts of blue light flashed out—no, it wasn't *light*, exactly. It was some kind of ice-cold plasma. It was as if they fired glowing, smoky gushes of frozen flame. The shelf full of wine bottles beside me came apart at the touch of this released energy. Century-old bottles were frozen solid, but others that were only touched by the plasma popped and drenched me in freezing wine. The smoky cold liquid burned my head and back. I howled in pain.

McKesson returned fire, and I joined him. The stairway took another hit from the blue plasma, splintering the wooden steps and icing them over instantly. The Gray Men weren't able to aim properly the moment they stepped through, but they damn sure could pull their triggers.

We cut the two down in a fusillade of shots. I fired four times, putting two rounds into each of the alien men. My cheeks and back were burning in streaks from the supercooled wine. Broken green glass rested on my head and my scalp was cut under my hair. I didn't dare do so much as reach up and wipe away the blood. We were in a fight for our lives, and there were a number of dark shapes still on the other side.

But then the Gray Men stopped coming for a while. Instead, they hung back in a growing cluster. They regarded us. I wondered briefly how they saw us, how we might look to them from their side. Three shadows on the far side stared at us, two defenders on the home front. They knew we had the advantage. If I could have heard their thoughts, I was sure they weren't wishing us well.

"Can they shoot through?"

"Neither side can," McKesson said. "Only slow-moving objects can pass through."

"What if they push a bomb into the room with us?"

"Then we're screwed," he said.

I swallowed but kept my gun trained on the shimmering forms. "What are they doing?"

"Probably hoping we'll come through to their side."

After a minute or so of hesitation, they must have decided we weren't dumb enough to walk into their weapons. They merged again with the big, dark blur, which I was now convinced was some kind of vehicle. For a second, I thought they might try to crash through the opening and pile out of it on our side—but they didn't. They drove away and disappeared.

McKesson got up from his crouch, holding his pistol out in front of him. He walked forward cautiously to the three bodies that were piled up and bleeding on the concrete floor. I noticed for the first time that although their blood was indeed red, it was darker than our blood. Almost black. It seemed thicker too, like a tarry substance. I supposed my own blood might look like that after it had lain there and dried to a thick and sticky puddle.

He gave each of the Gray Men a hard kick in the ribs. One stirred, but was clearly helpless. He aimed his pistol at its head.

"Don't," I said. "We need them alive, don't we? Questions? Information? The government has to get involved in this, right?"

McKesson glanced at me and snorted, as if I still didn't get it. But he didn't shoot the wounded enemy. Instead, he kicked away the weapon in the man's spurred hands, knocking it back into the twisting space from which it had come. It slid over the concrete, then with a transition of sound, slid away into another place.

"Help me out," he said, bending down and grunting as he picked up one of the bodies.

I stepped forward, disgusted and breathing hard. "What are we going to do with them?"

"We're tossing them back onto their side."

"Why?"

"Just do it. Trust me. There's no point questioning any of them."

I decided after all I'd seen I had to trust him. I helped him, and we picked up each of the men, one at a time, and gave them the old heave-ho back into their world. We did the same with their weapons. When we were done, I saw the twisted space fade, becoming solid again. The floor was even and smooth and no longer rippled like a mountain stream.

"Why the hell did we do that?" I asked. "Is it some kind of honor thing with them?"

"We did that to get rid of the evidence."

I stared at him. "What the hell for? Shouldn't we be calling Washington or something? Does the Pentagon know about this?"

"I don't know, and I don't care. The Community handles those decisions, and I handle what they don't want to touch."

McKesson walked to the rows of wine bottles. He picked out a dusty green bottle of burgundy and broke the top off with the butt of his gun. He lifted the bottle and tipped it, letting it flow into his face without touching his lips to the jagged glass. He guzzled the wine, pouring it from the broken neck down his throat. When he was done, he tossed the bottle down and let it smash on the floor.

As he did this, I watched the blurred region of space fade to nothing. There wasn't much left on the floor of the cellar. Just a big puddle of alien blood, much of it frozen.

The finger was still there, however, at the edge of the blood puddle. I thought I had a new theory on how that finger had gotten there. Perhaps the previous tenants had come down here with their knives and their odd sacrifices.

Maybe when the Gray Men had come through, the cultists had used one of their knives to remove an invader's finger. I had to wonder if the cultists had been taken captive to the far side for their troubles. What had I gotten myself into?

"We have to tell somebody about this," I said, staring at the scene in disbelief.

"What do you think my job *is*, you idiot?" McKesson snarled at me. He wiped his mouth on his sleeve. "I don't investigate these things—I cover them up!"

16

McKesson climbed up the damaged stairs, leaving me in the cellar. "I'm calling in backup from my car," he said. "Don't go anywhere. We'll have to make an official statement."

"Official statement? You mean a work of fiction, don't you?"

He didn't answer. He left me staring at the mess in the cellar. Half the wine racks and a section of the stairway were wrecked. The cellar was full of a strange stink—a mixed smell of blood, wine, and expended gunpowder.

I picked up one of the bottles, noticing that it was cracked and the contents had leaked out. I picked up a second bottle, which was intact. At first I'd been hunting for another drink, but after I saw the dates on the bottles, I lost my nerve. These bottles must have cost a thousand dollars each. Shaking my head, I walked to the center of what had, moments ago, been a desperate gun battle. I still had a bottle in each hand, but was uncertain what I planned to do with them.

There was the finger, still lying on the floor. I realized that it was the only solid piece of physical evidence proving the Gray Men had ever been here. One look at that finger would convince anyone it hadn't come from a normal human hand. The fingernail was purplish with an iridescent shine to it, like a pearl. The shark's-tooth spur on the joint was the same unusual color. I supposed the Gray Men grew these spurs the way we grew fingernails and toenails.

I paused, staring at the dead, alien finger. An idea slowly formed in my mind. I didn't like the idea very much, but I acted upon it anyway.

I gazed up the stairs toward where McKesson had disappeared. Then I looked down at the finger again. It was the only solid piece of proof left—but McKesson was sure to make it vanish before the night was over. They would spray down the concrete and wash away the syrupy blood. The finger would go into a jar or a bottle and vanish somewhere on the way to police headquarters.

I stooped quickly and used a broken bottle as a scoop. I chased it with the intact bottle, and after a few moments that made me grimace, I had shoved the thing into the broken bottle. I straightened and it fell against the glass with a tiny thump.

I mounted the stairs with the finger resting in the broken glass bottle. I heard McKesson walking back toward me. I thought of a hundred excuses, but I felt sure he wouldn't fall for any of them. I needed a hiding place for my prize, and I needed it fast. I thought about just dumping the finger into my pocket, but he might well search me if he noticed it was missing. I had to make him believe it had vanished in midst of all the action. I looked around, and saw that the stairs themselves might work. I found a split area of wood and slid the broken bottle inside. It clinked once, then lay quiet.

I marched up the stairs with the other bottle in hand.

"What are you doing with that?"

"It's a souvenir," I said, grinning.

He snorted and led the way back up. I followed him. He never searched me, but he didn't leave me alone in the cellar either. I figured I would have to come back for it at a later date. Uniforms arrived and worked on the place. They weren't taking pictures and bagging things, they were cleaning up. They eyed me unhappily.

After a half hour I was released. I used my cell to call a cab, which drove me to a gun shop first so I could confirm what I thought was likely—I had a gun permit already, and it applied to any weapon. I still needed more ammo, though, after the encounter with the Gray Men, and I picked up enough for an entire war. I wasn't taking any chances.

Then I had the cab drop me off at the Lucky Seven so I could check up on Jenna Townsend. I still had the intact wine bottle with me. I took the elevator up and tapped on Jenna's door. I had to tap a second time. Finally, the door clicked open a crack. She regarded me from the crack with a single, critical eye.

"Are you drunk?" she asked.

"Not exactly," I said.

"You smell like a gallon of cheap wine."

"I'm offended," I said. "It's very expensive wine." I held the bottle up for her inspection.

"Chateau Ausone?" she asked. "Bottled in nineteen twenty-six? Are you kidding me?"

"It's the real deal."

She let me in after that. She was wearing a tank top and jersey-knit shorts. I admired her while she gathered two clean glasses from the bathroom. I opened the bottle and poured carefully.

"Was it insanely expensive?" she asked.

"The wine?" I asked, shrugging. "It was on sale."

Jenna shook her pretty head disbelievingly, but she took her glass. I tried mine and found it tart but drinkable.

"Is this some kind of apology?" she asked.

"For what?"

"For not calling me."

"I didn't know we were that close."

She laughed and savored her wine. I took off my coat and went to use her bathroom. When I returned, I saw she had my pistol in her hands. She was inspecting it critically.

"Um," I said, "is there a problem?"

She sniffed the gun barrel. "This thing has been fired. Did you kill someone?"

I tilted my head quizzically. Holly had asked me a similar question. Jenna had gone as far as digging the gun out of my pocket to have a sniff. How did these women come to suspect these things?

"When was I voted 'most likely to commit murder'?" I demanded.

"When you showed up late looking banged-up, scared, and soaked in fine wine."

Women never liked it when you wandered back to them late at night smelling of booze.

"Can't you just drink your wine?" I asked.

"Did you do something awful, or not?"

"Sort of," I said.

Jenna frowned and pulled her legs up onto her chair with her.

"Sort of?" she asked, hugging her knees and looking over them at me. "What the hell do you mean, *sort of?* How do you *sort of* kill somebody?"

"When you're not sure the victim was a person in the first place," I said. "I mean, when you aren't sure they qualify as human."

Now I had her full attention. I gave her the story then, leaving out the part about stealing the finger. She was particularly interested in my description of McKesson's watch.

"That's how he's been doing it," she said. She rested her chin on her knees and stared at nothing intently. "He always knows where one of these doorways is going to open."

"Yeah," I said, "but apparently he doesn't know exactly when. This time they showed up hours after he'd been given the clue."

"Still, it's a great power to have. My wedding ring looks unimportant by comparison."

"Well, his watch hasn't paid any hotel bills."

She put her hand on my wrist while I poured a fresh glass of wine. I looked at her in surprise.

"I want that watch," she said.

I studied her face. "It might not tell you where to find Robert," I said.

"It's better than sitting here, doing nothing. If I'd been swallowed by the tornado, I'm sure Robert would be risking everything to find me."

I nodded, distracted by her fine legs. Maybe he would.

"Will you help me get that watch, Draith?" she asked.

"He's got a gun and a badge, you know," I said. "He's got a police force backing him up. Maybe other organizations, as well."

She sipped her wine. "I know."

I yawned. It had been a long night. "What about your plan to camp out here until Robert returns?"

"McKesson isn't here. He's never even called or questioned me since that first night. I think he's following the watch. That means there is no way this spot will open up again soon. I'm wasting my time, while Robert is—someplace else. I'm haunted by the idea he's screaming my name right now."

"What could you do, even if you had the watch? Even if you found the next connection point? Would you jump through into the unknown?"

Jenna hesitated, biting her lip. "I would if you went with me."

I shook my head. "You haven't seen these guys—if Robert is even in the same place. McKesson indicated there are several possible places that might connect with our world."

Defeated, Jenna studied her hands. I figured she was about to start crying. I'm a sucker for that, so I stood up and took a step toward the door. "I suppose I should go for now. I'll call you."

"Don't go," she said.

"I need to find a place to sleep."

She flashed her eyes at me, then looked down again. "Stay here."

I looked sidelong at the king-sized bed. It was inviting. There wasn't a couch in the room, so I supposed she meant I could lie down there.

"Um," I said, "OK, I guess."

She nodded, not looking at me. She got up slowly and headed for the bathroom. "I'll be out in a minute," she said.

I removed my coat and put the gun and phone on the nightstand. I stretched out on the bed and as soon as my head hit the pillow, I saw a few swirling half dreams. I thought to myself that the gun battle had combined with the wine and really exhausted me.

I felt a hand touch my cheek, and snapped awake.

Jenna was there, kneeling on the bed beside me. She had nothing on but a gauzy, see-through nightgown. It was pink and made of sheer silk. When my eyes focused, they were drawn inexorably to her breasts, which filled out the nightie perfectly. My mouth and eyes opened wide.

She smiled at me with trembling lips. A single tear wet her left eye. "Is this what you wanted?" she murmured.

I realized immediately that there had been a gross misunderstanding. She had thought I needed convincing in order to help her find her husband. I was surprised and uncertain as to how to handle the situation—so I did it badly.

"Hold on," I said, scooting backward and lifting myself into a sitting position. "I didn't mean—you're a married woman, Jenna."

Her eyes searched mine in surprise. She quickly realized her mistake and crossed her arms over her breasts. She turned away, embarrassed.

"I'm sorry," she snapped. "It was a misunderstanding."

"No, no, no," I said, giving my head a shake. I tried to wake my mind up, to get a coherent thought out of myself. I knew a bad moment like this could ruin everything with a girl. I frowned at myself for having such ideas. I reminded myself she was a desperate bride, not a pickup from a bar, and I didn't know anything about her past relationships with men.

I sighed and patted her knee clumsily. "All right," I said. "I'll give it a try."

Her eyes slid back to my face. "You'll try to get the watch for me?"

"Yeah," I said, "or find Robert some other way. Why not?"

She thanked me with a quiet kiss on the forehead. I heaved another sigh. How did I get into these things? I was a sucker, I thought. There wasn't any other explanation.

Jenna slid into the bed next to me and we turned out the lights. We lay there quietly without touching each other. The bed was big, but I could still sense her presence nearby in the darkness. I listened to her breathing until it became slow and even.

I thought about the sexy, see-through nightie she was wearing. It must have been meant for Robert. That poor bastard was really missing out.

Falling asleep again was hard to do, but I managed it eventually.

17

The next day, I treated Jenna to breakfast—even though it was early afternoon by then. In return, she treated me to a small shopping spree. I had very little in the way of personal possessions. She dragged me from store to store in the clothing level of the mall that adjoined the hotel lobby. I'd soon dressed myself in a random fashion. I chose a baseball cap that was essentially an advertisement for the Lucky Seven, a T-shirt with a cactus on it, and a pair of gray slacks.

"That's not going to work," she said, eyeing me critically. "That's just not acceptable."

"I like the hat," I offered. "It will make me fit in as a tourist."

She laughed quietly at me and dragged me back into the stores. I soon found myself wearing jeans, a hoodie, and running shoes.

"This looks like what I got from—I mean, it looks like the outfit I came in with," I said. I'd almost brought up Holly, but decided I didn't want to answer any questions about her right now. When she had asked anything about what I'd been up to, I said I'd spent my nights hanging out with McKesson—which was technically true. But I'd spent the *days* sleeping on a stripper's couch. Somehow, I figured that detail wouldn't uplift Jenna's opinion of me. How strange it was to be drifting from place to place—mostly from one woman's borrowed bed to another. At some point I needed to find a place of my own. And some memories.

"At least this outfit is new and doesn't reek of wine," she said. "Besides, it suits you. You aren't going to pass for a tourist anyway—you look a little too dangerous. But this outfit will let you blend in, which will make our mission easier."

I eyed myself in a mirror, thinking about what she said. Apparently, I appeared somewhat thuggish in her opinion. I saw short dark hair and dark, serious eyes. I was average in height, but with broad shoulders and a strong chin. I needed a shave. I pulled the hood up experimentally. I had to admit, I looked like I might rob the store. As if to confirm it, the Asian woman who ran the small clothing place stared at me with a clear mixture of worry and suspicion. I put the hood back down, smiled, and paid with Tony's money. As I did every time I spent his cash, I promised silently to learn the truth of his death.

Next, I bought a new bag to carry all my new stuff. It was made of soft black leather, and I slung it over my shoulder. The smell of the fresh leather was pleasant. It brought back vague memories of plane trips and hotel rooms. I had the feeling I'd traveled a lot in my lifetime—I just couldn't recall the details.

Jenna kept talking about our mission, meaning the removal of McKesson's watch. I was still uncertain about that part of her plan. I could see the value of having the watch to find her husband, but McKesson wasn't going to give it up without a fight. I was still hoping we could use it to find her missing groom, but preferably with the detective's cooperation. I hoped she didn't notice my reluctance in the matter. I had promised her I would help get the watch—but that had been under duress. Men were liable to say anything when faced with breasts after midnight. "How are you going to do it?" she asked me finally when we'd left the last store. In addition to the clothes, I now had a full shaving kit with all the essentials. After a few days of being homeless, I was looking forward to brushing my teeth with an actual toothbrush.

"Do what?" I asked.

"Do you think he ever takes it off?" she whispered. "Can we get it from his nightstand?"

I stared at her for a moment. "I figured we would just put a gun in his face and take it," I said.

She looked horrified. "Let's not try that."

I shook my head bemusedly as I led the way to the elevators. I had been joking about a stickup, but she hadn't picked up on that. She kept scheming on the way back up to the eighteenth floor.

Halfway down the hall to her room, I paused and put a hand up. She stopped talking in midsentence, looking around with wide eyes.

"Is someone listening?" she asked.

I pointed to the door handle. The tag we'd used to summon the maid service had fallen off and lay on the carpet. It was tucked half under the door. It had clearly been knocked loose and dropped as someone entered. The maid would have hung it back on the door handle, so I was suspicious. I pointed to it and leaned close to her ear.

"Someone is in the room," I whispered.

Jenna stared at me and shook her head. I stepped to the adjacent door and tapped on it. There was no answer. I slipped on my sunglasses.

I felt her hand on my shoulder. "Are you sure?" she whispered.

"No, but I'm suspicious enough to *make* sure," I said.

The sunglasses worked, as always. I twisted the locked door open. It gave way with the steady application of pressure, causing only a small clicking sound. I pushed it open. No one was in the room. The bed was made and the room looked vacant. The two of us slipped inside.

"Is this what life is like for you?" Jenna breathed. "I have to admit, it's exciting—if a little crazy."

"It's been wild lately," I agreed. I headed to the balcony, threw the door open, and stepped outside.

There was the small matter of making an eight-foot leap to the next balcony, with a hundred-and-fifty-foot drop under my feet. I hesitated as the dry winds gusted up and made my hair ruffle.

"Come over here and give me a bit of luck," I said to Jenna.

She slipped on her wedding ring. "You're crazy. I don't think it will work on something as large as a jumping person."

"Maybe it's all psychological," I said, "but I want your blessing anyway."

Jenna obliged by touching my shoulder with the ring firmly on her finger. I felt a sickening wrench in my belly as I jumped. I landed and wobbled for a moment, struggling to lever myself over the railing. The uncontrollable surge of adrenalin gave me an instant headache. Every part of my body strained to get away from the open space below me. My feet and teeth ached in a moment of near panic.

Then I was over the rail and safe. I got to my feet and turned back to Jenna, who had watched everything closely.

"Go out and make noise in the hallway," I told her. "Find a maid and start an argument or something."

Jenna nodded and disappeared. I waited about a minute, and then tried the sliding glass door. It was locked, of course. The sunglasses were soon out and on my face again. A moment later, the door clacked quietly and slid open.

I had my gun in my hand and I steeled myself. I nudged open those thick blackout curtains every hotel had, and peeked inside.

The room was dark. I knew I was letting in too much light. I stepped inside and tucked the curtains behind me.

There was a figure standing at the door with a gun of his own. He was using the peephole to observe the hallway, where I could hear Jenna shouting about something.

With my pistol aimed at his back, I flipped on the lights. "Drop your gun," I said in an officious, coplike voice. The man turned, lowering his weapon, but not quite letting go of it. We regarded one another in surprise and recognition. It was Bernard Kinley, the pit boss I'd met a few nights ago in the casino. He was as short, bald, and angry as ever.

"How'd you get in here, you cock-sucker?" Bernie hissed at me. His expensive suit was rumpled and his embarrassing comb-over had puffed up in the center like shark fin. I almost smiled at his bulging eyes and angry stare.

"Good to see you too, Bernie," I said evenly. I kept my pistol leveled on his chest and walked slowly closer to him.

"You're some kind of freak like the rest of them, aren't you?"

"Listen, this conversation is really uplifting, but aren't you supposed to be watching for card-counters or something downstairs?"

He glared at me, his eyes narrowing to a squint. "Not anymore. You did something to piss off the boss. Now I'm on permanent suspension."

"That's rough," I said without a hint of sympathy. "Is that why you're here? For revenge?"

Bernie's eyes swept the room. "I was looking for the girl, not you."

"Murder?" I asked. "I had you down as more of the petty-theft type."

"What? No, I wanted a piece of her luck. I've never seen anything like it. Did you know she went and did that same trick in three other casinos yesterday?"

It was my turn to stare at him for a second. I hadn't known that. No wonder she'd become so easy with her money.

"She's gotten smarter about it too," he said. "She hits the tables, different games. Only works them for about ten minutes, then moves on. Then after a big win, she loses for an hour—just a little cash at a time, giving back about ten percent of what she took off the house. Then she leaves. But we pit bosses talk, you know. When we see something going on, we talk, and we've been watching her, house to house."

My little Jenna, I thought. I was proud of her. She had learned a new game quickly. In fact, she had learned it so well she had been smart enough to tell no one about it. Not even me. But I knew the casinos still didn't like to lose.

"If you told everyone in town that she's a cheat, why are they still letting her play?" I asked.

Bernie smiled. "I'm not that dumb. I want to know the trick. So I told them she lost big at the Lucky Seven. She hasn't won enough in the other places to get kicked out. But I figure she's taken in fifty grand or so over the last few days."

"Not murder," I said, nodding. "You're a thief."

"I don't want her money, just her secret," he snapped. "And she's been stealing from the casinos anyway—somehow."

"That gives you every right to sit in here with a gun in the dark, does it?" I asked dryly.

"You're in here too, armed just like me."

"Yes, but I was invited. Now drop the gun or I drop you. Which is it?"

He finally let his weapon thump down onto the carpet. I decided that Jenna had spent long enough in the hallway. I pulled out my cell and told her it was OK to come in. She did so, and was startled to see our friend the pit boss. After she found out what he was doing in her room, she became angry.

I waved away her threats and recriminations after a while. "Bernie, please take a seat over here."

Bernie moved with ill grace, sitting in a padded armchair. It was the sort of thing they often had in nice hotel rooms. It was upholstered with a busy green print of washable microfiber. It would be a pity to put a bullet hole in it.

"You should really flip on the safety," Bernie complained as I kept my pistol aimed at him.

"I feel safer with it flipped off."

Jenna sat on the bed and watched him with slit-like, glaring eyes. "I'm calling the police," she said.

I waved for her to stop. "Wait just a minute."

"Yeah," Bernie said nervously. "There's no need for that."

"Let's talk, Mr. Kinley," I said. "Here's a scenario for you: a disgruntled, recently disciplined employee turns up armed inside the room of a lovely female guest. In order to get into her room, he must have used a keycard he's no longer authorized to possess. What's more interesting is that the female guest has recently lost her husband in that same room."

"That's not what I—" Bernie sputtered, interrupting.

"Let me finish painting this picture for you," I said, pressing onward. "The ex-employee blathers about supernatural gambling powers and revenge. He claims the guest has cheated the casino—but he himself has recently told other witnesses the opposite."

"Who are you going to tell that crap to, Draith?" Bernie asked me. "Oh yes, I know your name. I know you are wanted for murder as well. I doubt anyone is going to take your word in this fabrication."

"They certainly won't take yours either," I said. "But our lovely bride is very believable, isn't she? Her man is missing, and you definitely are involved somehow."

Bernie slid his eyes to her, then back to me. He looked defeated. I thought that Jenna rather liked playing the part of the lovely female guest. Either that, or she was enjoying Bernie's discomfort, which was now obvious.

"The question for us is whether to shoot you and put together a cover story," I said, "or to perform a citizen's arrest and call the police."

"Shoot me? Why the hell would you do that?"

"What if we had a system to make a vast amount of money off the casinos? A system that is so perfect, it compelled you to come in here and risk everything, just because you suspected we had it. Wouldn't we want to protect that?"

Bernie was sweating now. He slid his eyes from one face to the next. Neither of us smiled. "You two are in this together," he said. "You were working the con from that very first night I saw you at the blackjack tables."

"What you need to be thinking about is your own skin," I told him. "You need to bargain with us to keep it intact."

Bernie snorted. "What have I got to bargain with?"

"Information."

"What information?"

"About Rostok," I said. "Your former boss. And about something called Ezzie."

Bernie looked more than surprised now. He looked positively sick.

"I'm not talking about my employer," Bernie said. He crossed his arms above his ample belly.

"Jenna, use your cell to take a picture of our good friend," I said.

She did so, and he scowled at us.

"I don't know what you think you're doing, but I can't talk about that stuff," he said. "If I do, I'm a dead man."

"You're a dead man anyway if you don't."

Bernie looked at me and twisted his lips. "You talk big, but I don't think you have the balls for a murder, one right here in this hotel room."

"Well I do," Jenna said. "You pushed your way in here and I had no choice. It was self-defense."

Bernie licked his lips, eyeing her with concern. But I could tell he still wasn't going to talk.

"Quite right, Jenna," I said, "but we don't have to do the killing. We'll simply spread rumors. I know several people in the Community. Dr. Meng, and the rest. You were in Rostok's confidence, Mr. Kinley. You were fired, so you blabbed. Everything I know I'll relate to everyone I see, putting your name down as the source. Actually, it will be quite helpful. I can cover my own tracks using your name. They'll believe everything I've learned came from you. That allows me to safely cover my real sources."

He was sweating again. "What do you know? Probably nothing."

I put the gun down on the table. "You're free to go," I said.

"What?" Jenna said in protest.

I put my hand up. "He's worth more to us alive than dead. We've got the perfect fall guy. We don't even have to feel bad about it, as he moved on us first."

"Wait a minute," Bernie said. "The Community doesn't like people with big mouths."

"Oh, I know all about that, friend."

Bernie sat there, staring at us for a second, his eyes flicking back and forth. I could tell he was thinking hard. Jenna had joined in my act now. I could tell she had figured out my plan. She picked up her cell and tapped at it.

"What are you doing?" he asked.

"I'm broadcasting your picture," she said. "You want to take another shot while hugging me or something? No—I guess not."

"Who are you going to send it to?" he asked, still trying to look disinterested and failing badly.

"Detective McKesson, for one," Jenna said.

Bernie's face reddened further, although I would have thought it impossible just a moment before. "That rat bastard?" he asked. "He's a rogue, just like you. Figures you are working with him."

"Are you talking or am I sending?" Jenna asked. Her finger was poised over the face of her cell phone, ready to tap the send button.

"We probably know most of it anyway," I told him.

"Just tell us about your ex-boss," said Jenna. "About the murders. About all the strange stuff going on lately."

"If I tell you what I know, it won't leave this room?"

"Not with your name on any of it," I assured him.

"And all of this break-in stuff is forgotten?"

"Right," Jenna said.

He let out a long sigh. "I don't know much," he said.

Then he began to talk, and it turned out he knew plenty.

18

Bernie Kinley's words painted a strange picture. He had worked for Rostok, a man who was a recluse—who never left the twin towers of the Lucky Seven. Rostok was a Ukrainian immigrant who'd come from a tough criminal background from Kiev. Some said he was ex-KGB, or ex-military. No one knew for sure, but he'd come to Vegas and worked his way up quickly in casino security. He'd built a reputation for predictable brutality. No one wanted to cross him. About a dozen years ago, he'd gone from managing security to managing the casino itself. Then he'd somehow grown rich enough or frightening enough to purchase the entire enterprise. There were tales of disappearances and horrible deaths associated with the man, but nothing had been proven by anyone. There were never any credible witnesses—when there were witnesses at all.

At some point over the last decade, Rostok himself had disappeared from the public eye. Very few had seen his face since then. There was a rumor that held that he had been disfigured in some way. People hinted this was the reason he kept the lights off on the rare occasions when he did meet with people.

"How does McKesson fit into all of this?" I asked.

Bernie shrugged. "He's the cleanup man for the Community. He puts an official face on anything that goes—wrong."

"You mean when something bad happens? For example, when a creature like Ezzie gets loose?"

Bernie stared at me. "I've never seen Ezzie. It's some kind of pet of his, or…"

"Or what?" I asked. "Pets don't usually talk. I heard Ezzie talk."

"I don't know," Bernie said. "I've heard theories. People tell stories. Some say she's a mentally defective relative of his from Russia."

I snorted. "I think she's from farther away than that."

Bernie shook his head. "I really can't help you on that topic."

I believed him, but pressed for more. Oftentimes people knew things they didn't think were important. "Have you heard stories about fires?" I asked.

"Fires?"

"In rooms, maybe. People burning up mysteriously?"

He nodded slowly. "Yeah. We've had a couple of cases like that. Sometimes we find scorch marks or little piles of ash. McKesson told me once it was something called *spontaneous combustion*, and that it probably meant the hotel had wiring problems. That guy is so full of shit."

"Scorch marks?" I asked. "Like the one in Jenna's bathroom?"

"Yeah. We thought, at first, when Mrs. Townsend claimed her husband had vanished, it was one of those events. We were even more worried when we learned McKesson was involved."

"Does McKesson have a good record of figuring these things out?" Jenna asked.

Bernie laughed unpleasantly. "He's got a *perfect* record. He *never* figures out a damned thing. At least, nothing that he ever shares with the rest of us."

Jenna didn't look happy with that answer. I could understand why. She'd hoped the police were on her side and were going to help locate her lost Robert. As it appeared now, that was the furthest thing from anyone's mind.

"So when McKesson showed up, you knew you had one of those special cases, right?" I asked. "Did you suspect Rostok's involvement right away?"

Bernie shook his head. "No, not really. Your husband was nothing special to us, Mrs. Townsend. He didn't do anything to make us notice him. When people had vanished before, they were always clear enemies of Rostok."

"So why did he do it this time?" I asked him.

Bernie shook his head again. "I don't think that he did anything. I think that's why he let you go. He's not sure what's going on. He asked you to check around, didn't he?"

I nodded, but didn't elaborate.

We talked for a while longer, but that was all the ex-pit boss had for me. He really didn't know all that much, but he had confirmed a number of my suspicions. I decided I needed to start talking to more members of the Community. They might be in a mood to cooperate now that I had further evidence someone was moving among their domains, stirring things up.

After Bernie left, I told Jenna she couldn't stay here any longer. She was easily convinced. One man showing up with a gun to steal her ring was one too many. I helped her pack up her things. Tears glistened on her cheeks as she folded her wedding dress.

"I was supposed to return this," she said. "It's a rental. But I haven't been able to get myself to do it yet."

"We've got to find another place for you to stay."

"I know," she said, "but it feels like I'm giving up on Robert."

"You aren't. I'm not giving up on Tony either. I'm not giving up on any of them. I'm going to keep digging."

She hugged me, and I tried not to enjoy the feel of her body up against mine. I smelled the hotel shampoo in her hair.

Before she let go of me, my phone rang in my pocket. She pulled away so I could answer. She went back to packing, but I could tell she was listening while I answered my cell.

"Hello?" I said.

"Draith?" It was Holly's voice. "Come to my place—right now, will you? I need help."

"Um," I hesitated. I glanced over at Jenna.

"You need to leave, don't you?" Jenna asked.

"Who's with you?" Holly asked in my ear. "Where are you, Draith?"

"I'll be right there," I said to Holly. I hung up before she could say anything else.

Jenna stared at me. Was there a new hurt in her eyes?

"I've got to—" I began.

"It's all right," Jenna said quickly. "Really. I understand—just go."

"I'll be back. We have a lot to do together."

"I know you'll come back," she said.

I left her then, feeling awkward. I considered leaving my gun with her, but I figured the odds were higher I would need it than she would.

As I walked out, I could feel her eyes on my back, but I didn't turn around.

By the time I climbed out of the taxi and ran up the concrete steps to Holly's apartment, it was too late. Her door was a kicked-in mass of splintered wood. I pulled out my gun.

A woman backed out of the apartment, looking confused. I almost shot her, but managed to stop myself. She didn't seem dangerous, just disoriented. She saw me and gave a little whooping cry of alarm.

I slid the pistol back into my pocket, hoping she hadn't seen it in the fading light, quickly checked the apartment, and came back out. The woman was leaning up against the wall.

"Where's Holly?" I asked.

"Who are you?"

"A friend of Holly's."

"I'm the manager. She's had a lot of men over here, but none of them ever kicked in one of my doors until now." She stared at me suspiciously, and I realized she thought I had broken down the door.

She wasn't someone who dressed up for work. She wore crimson sweatpants and a sweater shirt, but they weren't quite the same shade of crimson. The shirt was covered in sequins in the shape of a rainbow. I walked past her and peered inside again, looking for signs of struggle. There weren't any, other than the kicked-in door.

"When did this happen?" I asked. "Did you hear anything?"

"Yeah, I heard my door split open."

"Did you see anything—anyone?"

The landlady had her fists on her hips. She eyed me critically, but must have seen my concern. She relaxed and frowned.

"I guess you didn't do it, then," she said.

"No, ma'am, but I think Holly is in trouble. Tell me what you can."

"There was a bright light," the landlady said. "Down in the space between the buildings. I saw that, then heard some hammering on her door. When I came outside, the door was kicked in and she was gone."

I pushed past her again and skipped down the steps two at a time. The breezeway between the buildings had scorch marks, not only on the concrete walkway, but on both the bordering stucco walls as well. I imagined the scene then. The air had warped here, letting someone come through. Probably, it was one of the Gray Men. Maybe they'd been looking for me, and my trail had led them here. They'd gone up the steps to her apartment, kicked in the door and…

And what? I didn't know what had happened next. She had called me in a panic. Maybe she'd been followed home. Maybe she'd heard or seen the warping of the air.

"Damn it," I said. My words rang from the walls of the breezeway. The landlady peeped around the corner behind me, but she kept quiet.

I looked everywhere in the complex over the next few minutes, but found nothing. I'd made a new friend, and I'd lost her. Maybe that's why no one had come forward since I'd escaped the sanatorium, claiming to be my close friend or relative. Maybe they were all gone.

"Draith?" called a man's voice from behind me.

I turned around slowly. It was McKesson.

19

I told McKesson the few details I knew about Holly's disappearance. When I was finished, he yawned. I glared at him. He'd made clucking sounds of concern and asked a lot of questions, but none of them were about Holly. He wanted to know how many witnesses there were, what they had seen and heard. I knew he was forming up a mental list, compiling a report on this incident. How big was the exposure? Could it be contained?

From his point of view, there was no problem. No real witnesses, no residual effects or evidence. Just a few strange words from a landlady who was more worried about who was going to fix her door than about her tenant. I came to understand that no one was going to be overly concerned about the disappearance of an unemployed stripper.

"Look," I said to McKesson, stepping close to have few intense, private words. "Forget about the event. That's minor, and you are in the clear there. Now, I'm asking you to do the rest of your job—find Holly."

McKesson sighed. "Oh, it's like that, is it? Doing more than sleeping on her couch?"

I didn't bother to deny his suggestion. It didn't matter if Holly and I had slept together—even though we hadn't, I still wanted her back.

"She's missing," I said, "and you know better than anyone what might have happened to her."

"Look, Draith, we aren't about to call out the bloodhounds and helicopters on this case. This isn't a junior high kid with perfect grades. She had a history with drugs. People like Holly vanish every day on these streets just because they want to. She might be skipping out on her rent. She could be anywhere."

I glared at him until I could speak without shouting. "You can't keep the Gray Men out of here, you know. You can't keep them a secret forever either. They are getting more and more bold. They are stepping into and out of our world as they please. Doesn't that worry you?"

I had his attention now. "Yeah," he admitted. "It does."

"We had a gun battle in that mini-mansion in Henderson. What about the next time? What if they had been inside that place when we got there, a dozen of them or a hundred? Armed with weapons we can't face?"

"This isn't an invasion, Draith."

"How can you be so sure?"

McKesson smiled wearily. "It's not like that. They come for their own odd reasons. They're more like mobsters than soldiers from a hostile nation."

"You've talked to them?"

"You just have to trust me concerning their motivations."

"All right," I said. "But something is up. You know that as well as I do."

McKesson looked thoughtful. "This is something that you can't help me with. I would tell you to stay clear entirely, but I don't think you can now."

I stared at him. "Are you saying we have people going through to *their* side as well?"

McKesson laughed. "There you go, thinking big again. Thinking of Pentagon boys and agents with perfect teeth and black belts. It's nothing so formal. We have our Community, they have their equivalent powers. We've had a truce for a long time, but—"

I cut him off. "A truce? How long?"

"Since the eighties, I guess," he said. He eyed me as if worried he'd said too much. Finally, he shrugged. "Since the tests ended."

I narrowed my eyes. "What tests?" I wanted to ask, but suddenly, McKesson leaned away.

I stepped forward and tried to look over his shoulder. He jabbed at me with his elbow, pushing me back. I came forward and grabbed his arm. I wrapped both my arms around his wrist and pulled his hand toward me.

We both stared at his wristwatch. The hands were moving, all three of them, all swinging around to point west.

"Something's coming, isn't it?" I asked. "Something is opening up. Is it close to us?"

McKesson had his hand on his pistol. "Let go of my arm," he said, speaking each word with slow precision.

I let him go. He glared at me for a second, then relaxed. "I've shot men for less, you know," he said.

"I'm sure you have."

"There is something coming," he said. "And yes, it will be close."

I looked toward the west and I began walking that way, the direction the hands on his watch had indicated. McKesson made a sound of exasperation and followed me. It was dark now. The pale orange sodium lights flickered into life, illuminating the streets and the apartment complex.

"You should keep your nose out of this one, Draith. We have rules in place."

"Rules?" I asked. "Since when are there rules in this game?"

"They aren't written down. But we have a mutual understanding. Like two dogs growling at each other on either side of a fence. As long as we don't mess with each other, there is peace. But the minute one dog digs a fresh hole and sticks his snout into the other's territory—well, all bets are off."

We were out in the alley now, behind the apartments. There wasn't much here other than dumpsters with green chipped paint and a few discarded, moldering couches.

I saw something there, a bright spot in the alleyway. I figured it was the final gasp of the dying day, a last sunbeam not blocked by trees or buildings. But I was wrong. McKesson headed for the bright spot and I followed. There was something slowly twisting in the alleyway. A shimmer in the air. It affected only a small area this time. It was just a crack.

I realized in wonder that the light I was seeing wasn't from our own sun. It was from somewhere else. The small, vertical warp in the air had let through light from another time or place—or both.

I paused there, studying it. McKesson stood beside me.

"A second one?" I whispered. "So close?"

"It's an echo," he said. "A smaller variety of rip in space. It happens sometimes when they force one through. Have you ever pushed your finger through a sheet of paper? It never makes a perfect hole, you know. There are always splits, folds, and tears."

I took a step toward it, then another.

"What the hell are you doing?" McKesson said behind me. "Be careful, man. You can't go stepping out through an echo, they aren't stable."

"Does this lead to the home of the Gray Men?" I asked him.

"I don't know—probably. They are the ones fooling around at the moment."

I stepped forward again. Three fast steps. I didn't want to give myself or McKesson time to think.

"What the hell?" shouted McKesson, angry now. "You can't step out! Get back here or I'll have to drop you, Draith."

I looked back over my shoulder. I felt strange. The twisting air around me was hot. It felt like my body was charged with static—as though a rainstorm were blowing up and filling the air with electricity. McKesson was close behind me. He'd followed me to the very border of the anomaly.

"What do you care where I go?" I asked.

"It could be seen as a breach."

"Unwritten rules again?" I asked. "They seem to break them at will."

"Our side does too, but I don't."

I took a step away from him, and he reached for me. His hand grabbed up a wad of my sweatshirt. In his other hand I saw something that looked like a black, wriggling fish. I figured it was his gun. It was like being at the bottom of a swimming pool and looking up at someone standing on the edge. His image wavered and distorted even at this close range. I could see him, but his face was twisted and almost unrecognizable. His voice was reaching my ears with much less distortion, however. Sights were more disrupted than sounds.

I can be impulsive at times. It's a personality flaw to which I freely admit, something I figure must have gotten me into a lot of trouble in my hazy past. I also don't like being grabbed. I didn't reach for his gun, or my own. I didn't want to give him a good excuse to shoot me. Instead, I pulled his hand off my shoulder with both of mine.

"Get off me," I said.

McKesson was much too slow to catch on. As I held his wrist, I pulled off his watch and tossed it into the rip.

When he realized what I'd done, I thought he really was going to shoot me. He did a very good impression of rage. There was a lot of cursing. The gun was in my face, close enough to make out the black circle of the muzzle despite the blurring.

"Settle down," I said. "All we have to do is step inside, grab it, and bring it back."

"It doesn't always work that way, moron," he said. "I said I was going to blow you away if you didn't listen. If I do it now and push your sorry sack into this echo, no one will ever know. Do you realize that? There won't even be any blood."

"If you come with me instead, we'll get the watch back together," I offered.

McKesson hesitated, and then serenaded me with a fresh stream of curses. I peered ahead into the rip. Was the unstable opening getting smaller? It seemed that way to me. I wondered what would happen if this rip between existences closed while I stood halfway in and out of it. I knew it couldn't be anything good.

"Are we going to go get your watch, or not?" I asked. "I think the echo is getting smaller."

Instead of answering, he shoved me through ahead of him, with his gun pressed against the back of my head.

I stood in the open desert, with mountains in most directions, stark and timeless. The apartment complex was
gone. The alley was gone. Las Vegas was gone. I was surrounded by sifting sands, spiny trees, flowering weeds, and
other desert vegetation. I held my breath for a second,
worried the air here might be different. But the temperature of the night, the look of the sky—it all seemed normal
enough.

   Then I looked up. The night was falling, darkening the
east. The first stars were popping out—but they were *wrong*.
I knew that, without picking any particular constellations.
That gave me a chill, but it was the red disk on the eastern horizon that really upset me. It was a moon, but not
our moon. It was a small, reddish circle of light. It was as if
Mars were hanging up there in the east. And that wasn't all,
because the moon wasn't alone. It had a nearby companion:
a thin crescent of bone-white.

"We're lucky," McKesson said. "The rip is still here on this side."

"Isn't it always?" I asked, staring fixedly at the moons. I'd spotted another moon. It was high and small to the north. I couldn't even be sure it was a moon. It could have been a companion planet or star. Whatever it was, it was clear proof I wasn't in Nevada anymore.

"No," McKesson said. "Sometimes these rips are one-way."

I spun around slowly, trying to take in the entire alien sky. Up until this point, I hadn't really believed there was another place behind these distortions—that I could step through a shimmering rip in space and instantly be some-place else.

"Seen enough?" asked McKesson. He was walking across the sands and kicking at a tumbleweed. "Did you throw the watch this far out?"

"I'm not sure," I said, not even looking at him. I was too busy staring at everything around me. "So, this is it? Just a spot in the desert?"

"This place is pretty similar to our world. But don't be fooled, there are always differences."

"I can see that. There are at least three moons here. But essentially this is our Nevada desert without the city."

"Look south," he said, waving his hand vaguely.

I gazed in the direction he'd indicated. I squinted, real-izing a structure stood there. It had looked like a mountain formation, but as I studied it, I came to understand it wasn't natural. It was a stack of cubes. I swallowed, tasting grit.

"Is that some kind of building?" I asked, my voice hushed.

"That's their kind of city. They build them like stacks of bricks. Very neat and orderly. No sprawl."

As I watched, I saw a grouping of lights flash and move away from the jumbled mountain of cubes and rectangles. It had to be a vehicle of some kind.

"Why don't they light up the exterior of their city?"

"I don't know," he said. "They don't seem to like windows. Why don't you go ask them?"

I realized, staring at their strange habitat, that I was the alien here. I was the green man who'd mysteriously appeared in the wilderness. If I approached them, I doubted things would go well. I continued to stare at the dark structure while I questioned McKesson further.

"How many places like this have you been to?"

He shrugged. "None. They are all different."

"Give me a number," I said. Somehow, I really wanted to know how many worlds I was dealing with.

"Hard to know," he said. "Sometimes, I can't tell if they are the same place or not. I mean, if you visited Earth and walked on Antarctica's ice, then later visited the Outback of Australia, would you think you'd seen one world or two?"

"How many have you visited—best guess?"

"Maybe a half dozen. But I know there are more of them. Some people think there are an infinite number of places like this. They are supposedly alternate realities, or versions of our own universe spun around a little bit. I have no idea, but don't like stepping out somewhere unknown without good reason. They are freaky—and dangerous."

Stepping out. I realized he'd used that term before. I looked at the surrounding desert floor. It didn't look overly strange to me, not at the moment. Only the sky hinted I was far from home.

In the distance, in the direction I assumed was to the west of us, the sun had dipped below the horizon. It was getting darker by the minute, the mountains just shadows now. They looked more or less like the mountains that had always surrounded Las Vegas. As close as I could figure, this was what Vegas would have looked like a century ago, before people had decided to build a city on the sand. Apparently, the Gray Men weren't as crazy as we were.

"Found it," said McKesson. He held the watch up like a trophy. "You really owe me, Draith. Thanks for all the help."

"Sorry, I was just so stunned."

McKesson pushed past me moodily. He walked back into the rip, as he'd called it. I watched his wavering form shimmer away to nothing. I peered at the rip—was it smaller than before? Or did it simply look smaller on this side than it had from home? I didn't know which it was, but the thought that it might be vanishing made my heart leap in my chest.

McKesson was gone. I couldn't even see him on the far side. I felt an immediate, soul-wrenching sense of loneliness. You can't really feel alone until you are standing on unknown, alien soil with the only way home fading away nearby. I couldn't withstand that feeling for long. A minute later I stood in the alley with him. I could see the anomaly was indeed shrinking. It was only a shimmer over the asphalt now. Barely noticeable unless you walked right up to it.

"You took your time," he said.

"It seemed pretty safe."

"It wasn't," he told me. "Things are different in those places. That one is pretty normal looking, but sometimes they are *very* different. Different people, different physics, even."

"What do you mean? Like lower gravity? Thicker air?"

"Worse than that," he said. "They aren't exactly different planets, they are different—I don't know. Different *existences*, the Community people say. Different versions of our world."

He'd started walking toward the street, and I followed him. I had McKesson talking now, and I didn't want to let him go. I eyed his watch, which was back on his wrist again. I'd missed my chance to bring it back to Jenna. I wasn't sure how I could manage to steal it now without killing the man. The more time I spent with him, the less I wanted to do that. McKesson was anything but a friend, but he was dedicated to patrolling these strange phenomena, and I wasn't sure his methods were the wrong ones. Did our world really want to know what he was doing and why? Physicists didn't like being wrong any more than the rest of us. If I went around talking about these vortexes, even with some evidence, I was unlikely to be met with enthusiasm and praise. Sometimes people just believed what they wanted to believe.

"Damn," McKesson said, stopping in the breezeway.

I walked up behind him and saw what he was talking about. Holly's landlady lay sprawled on the concrete. He stooped over her, checking her neck for a pulse.

"Is she alive?" I asked.

He shook his head.

"You think it was the Gray Men?"

"Nah," he said. "No marks on her. Heart attack, most likely. She was the nosy type. She probably followed us and saw us walk into thin air in the alley. The shock must have killed her."

He bent down with a grunt and attempted some half-hearted CPR. He pushed down rhythmically on the landlady's sequin-covered shirt. It rasped under the touch of his hands. She showed no signs of reviving. I was glad I wasn't the one in medical trouble. McKesson wasn't the nurturing type.

"We've got to call an ambulance," I said.

McKesson gave a heavy sigh. "Yeah, but I'll be filling out paperwork until Tuesday if I do it. You call it in, will you?"

I grimaced but pulled out my throwaway phone and made the anonymous emergency call. McKesson gave up after a few minutes of CPR. He shooed away passersby, which were few, by flashing his badge and telling them help was on the way.

"You haven't asked me yet why I did it," I said.

"Did what?"

"Threw your watch in there."

"Oh, that," he chuckled. "I know why you did it. You couldn't stand it any longer. A man like you—you're a bundle of curiosity. You've been investigating these things for years, and like the proverbial cat, you aren't going to stop until you're dead. Of course you wanted to see what was on the other side."

"What was it like for you? The first time you stepped out of our world?"

"Bad. I wandered into a bad place while checking out a murder. I was assigned to homicide originally, you know. But when I got back home, I became a department of one. Now I'm in charge of investigating freaky stuff like this. I don't have an official title or assignment. Everyone at the department knows they are supposed to call me when some really weird shit happens. It used to be once a month, maybe. Lately, it's been happening every day."

"Bad how?" I asked.

"What?"

"The world you walked into first. You said it was bad. What was it like?"

McKesson stopped and looked at me with guarded eyes. "All glaring, blue-white light. Like heaven maybe, except hot and uncomfortable. I think I might have gone mad out there, if I'd stayed much longer. The ground was reflective, like ground glass or diamond dust."

"Sounds enchanting."

He snorted. "It might have been with goggles and a gallon of sunscreen. What was really upsetting was the rip itself. It wasn't in the same location on the other side, you see. That happens sometimes. I had to travel for miles across—I don't even know how to describe it. The place was like an endless beach of blinding tiny mirrors. I came back with a severe sunburn. Radiation burns, the docs told me. My own primary care physician reported me to some Department of Energy people, suspecting I'd been playing with unshielded uranium or a similar substance. Maybe they still think that. I'll get skin cancer in another decade, they told me. Sometimes, when I wake up, I taste metal in my mouth and my bones ache…and I know why."

I hadn't considered the possibility of a radiation dose. I decided to change the topic.

"What about these Gray Men?" I asked. "They're coming through at will now, killing people in weird ways. Have they always been able to do that?"

"That's all new. Usually, we get some kind of beast wandering through—not people like us."

"Beast? You mean like a monster?"

McKesson shook his head. "No rubber suits. Just their idea of animals, I suppose. Natural enough on their side. I mean, if you opened a path to another time on Earth, you might get dinosaurs trotting out of it, right? Is a dinosaur a monster, or just another animal?"

"I suppose that depends on whether or not you're selected for dinner."

The ambulance showed up a few minutes later. McKesson waved them toward the landlady. He gave them the impression he was a cop arriving on the scene and I was the discovering witness. When the paramedics were busy going through the motions with the corpse, he beckoned to me. I followed him. Together we walked out to his car, which was parked out on the street.

"We can take off," McKesson said. "The old lady is their problem now."

I found myself glancing over my shoulder at the dead woman in the breezeway. I wondered if I would end up like that someday. Maybe it would happen in an alien desert under three strange moons.

McKesson climbed into his car and pressed the lock button, just in case I got any ideas about climbing in with him.

"Now disappear quick," he said, "or you'll be stuck when a patrol car shows up."

I didn't disappear. Instead, I leaned near his driver's-side window and kept talking. "We didn't find Holly."

"She's gone, and I have to get going too. My best advice is to forget about her."

"I can't do that."

McKesson checked his watch. "I've got to go."

"What? Are you late for a wedding or something?"

He twisted his lips. "Police business," he said.

"Just show me your watch for one second."

He made no move to do so. In fact, he scooted his sleeve down over his watch, so I couldn't see it at all. At that moment, I became certain he was heading to the site of yet another event.

"You've detected another rip, haven't you? Somewhere else?"

McKesson shook his head and stared through his windshield. He put on his seatbelt.

"You might want to step back, sir," he said out of the side of his mouth. "I don't want to run over your toes."

I had no idea where McKesson might go next, but Holly's apartment was clearly a dead end now. I recalled that when searching for a kidnap victim, the odds of finding them were the highest in the first half hour after the crime. If McKesson knew of another rip showing up, I wanted to be there to check it out. It was the only lead I had.

"Come on," I said. "I'll listen. I'll even follow your rules this time."

"I don't need a partner, Draith."

"These things are appearing all around me anyway. You're going to end up coming back to wherever I am. Why not let me check them out with you?"

For some reason, that argument got through to McKesson. Maybe because it was true. He hit the unlock button and I ran around the car, half expecting him to pull away before I could get to the passenger door. He didn't. I climbed in, and we drove off together down the dark streets.

21

McKesson and I drove through the city, following his watch. It pointed downtown, and after circling around the southern end of the Strip a few times, he and I looked up. Our eyes met. We'd both figured it out at the same time.

"Why the Lucky Seven, again?" McKesson groaned. "Rostok's going to be pissed."

"Will he come out and scold you?"

"No, he never comes out of his domain. Most of them don't. He's like a spider in there. But he has plenty of goons to do his complaining for him."

Thinking of Bernie Kinley, I had to agree. That man definitely qualified for classification as a "goon." I craned my neck out the passenger window and stared up at the towers. They formed two oblong shapes, thrusting upward side by side, looking like a giant tuning fork aimed at the sky. At night, the building was more attractive. I liked the way the walls ran with green lights.

McKesson parked his car, and we crossed the asphalt toward the eastern tower. I thought about the location of other recent rips. I could see a pattern.

"They're chasing me, aren't they?" I asked.

"The Gray Men? Maybe."

"No, not maybe. I was at Holly's place yesterday. About a dozen hours after I left, they kicked in her door. Now they are popping up at the towers, where I spent most of today. They are one step behind me."

He turned his head to look at me. "You think a rip is going to open in Mrs. Townsend's room again?"

I nodded. "A strong possibility. Only Jenna's not there—I moved her, fortunately. She should be safe."

McKesson began to trot. "If we get there first, they won't be able to come through," he said.

I ran after him, and we raced to the elevators. McKesson paused to call their security. Two unsmiling men showed up and handed the detective a keycard pass without comment. They followed us up to the eighteenth floor, but stayed in the elevator lobby. I could tell they were annoyed. I recalled Bernie telling me that they preferred to handle security issues on their own, but they clearly had their orders to cooperate with McKesson.

We entered Jenna's old room just as the space inside began to warp. I saw right away there was going to be a problem: the warping had begun in the region of the sliding glass door. The slider and the curtains were rippling. I heard the glass rattle and shiver, as if there were a storm outside.

McKesson gave a nasty laugh when he saw it. "If they don't pay attention and come through into that, this is going to be great."

It wasn't great. A figure stepped through, wearing normal clothing. A hood covered his face. His hands were covered by black leather gloves with the fingers cut away. Those fingers weren't gray, I realized with a shock.

The moment the figure was firmly in the room, the sheet of glass that formed the sliding door exploded in a gush of blood. Stricken, the man staggered and pitched onto the table where Jenna and I had consumed a bottle of century-old wine the night before. He quivered and died, his body winged by blades of glass and shreds of fabric from the curtains.

"You missed, buddy," McKesson said to the corpse. He nudged the body until it slipped off the table onto the carpet. "What the hell is this? A frat boy?"

I inspected the dead man, grimacing. We were clearly not dealing with a Gray Man. He was quite human. He had a growth of black beard, cut short and bristling. His hazel eyes stared up at the ceiling above us. There were strange tattoos on his neck that looked like tentacles trying to crawl up out of his shirt.

"Damned amateurs," McKesson grumbled. "How the hell did he step out to wherever he was and then get back here again?"

I peered into the smoky space that filled the balcony. I couldn't see much. It was dark on both sides of the opening. The darkness, plus a lack of caution, had killed our suspect.

"I'm going through," I said.

"Are you crazy?"

"Yeah, but I have to take a look. Someone is sending rips through wherever I've just been. Holly might have been taken by this guy—or his friends."

"You are stepping out again for a stripper?" he asked. "On a maybe?"

"No one else is coming through to our side. Maybe there is no one else over there. Or maybe there is and I'll find out who's trying to kill me. Clearly, it's not just the Gray Men who are involved in all this."

"Whatever happened to following my lead?"

"Look, they're going to keep trying for me. Are you coming or not?"

McKesson shook his head. "Hell no," he said. "But you go ahead. When they tear you up and toss you back, I'll put a bullet in your brain out of compassion."

"Thanks a lot," I said, and I stepped out.

The far side was pitch black, but I could tell I wasn't out in the open desert this time. I was in a room of some kind. The sounds were different, as were the smells and the temperature of the air. All the purring background city sounds had vanished. It was cooler now. The air seemed still and dank. Disoriented and fearful, I dug out my cell phone and used the pale blue radiance from its screen to illuminate the room around me. I knew I could be literally anywhere—but so far I didn't sense anything dangerous.

I took a step or two forward, feeling my way. My eyes were still adjusting a moment later when I heard a heavy *whump* sound behind me as if something had been thrown. I whirled with my .32 automatic in my hand, held my fire as I looked down to see a man-shaped form had slumped behind me onto the floor, right where I'd appeared a moment earlier.

It wasn't moving. I kicked it over onto its back. Then I knew.

It was the dead guy with the glass in his chest. McKesson must have tossed him through the opening after me, erasing evidence as usual.

"McKesson, you bastard," I muttered.

"Who's there?" called a quiet voice. A female voice.

I turned slowly. I could see more now, as my eyes had gotten used to the gloom. I walked toward the voice with my gun out. I held the cell phone up, but it went into sleep mode. I fumbled with it, and when it lit up again, I saw her.

Holly was sitting on the floor. She was shackled to a structure of some kind. I took two steps more toward her, and she squirmed in fear.

"It's me, Holly," I whispered. "Quentin Draith."

"Get me out of here before they come back," she hissed at me.

"Who are they? The Gray Men?"

"I don't think so. They're some kind of freaks. They like to cut up meat. I think they'll cut us up too, if we stay here."

The cultists, I thought to myself. I used the sunglasses to remove her bonds and helped her to her feet. I saw the place where she had been sitting. There was a row of shackles there, indicating the spot had been used to chain people up before this. I saw one other object, and squatted down to pick it up. It was a shoe. A black, brightly polished shoe. I looked it over carefully.

"What the hell are you doing?" Holly demanded.

"I think I know who this belongs to," I said, holding up the shoe. "Robert Townsend."

"Who the hell cares about a shoe?"

"Just carry it for me, OK?"

Holly did it, but she clearly thought I was crazy. I didn't care. If that shoe matched the one Jenna had packed up, it was worth carrying out of this hole.

I led her back toward the spot where I'd come into this place. I took a moment to look around. Clearly, we were underground. There were drains in the concrete floor, and they looked as though they'd drained away years' worth of blood.

I soon found the spot where I'd stepped into this place. The body of the man I'd seen come into the hotel room a moment ago was there, cooling on the floor. But I didn't see the vortex.

"How do we get out of here?" Holly asked.

"It was right here," I said, feeling around in front of me like a blind man. The cell phone kept going to sleep every few seconds, casting us into total darkness. I shook and cursed it every time.

"What was here?"

"Do you know this guy?" I asked.

"What?"

I toed the body at our feet and aimed the light down toward it. Holly gave a little whoop of fear.

"He might be one of the guys who grabbed me out of my apartment," she said. "Did you kill him?"

"No, he killed himself. But when you saw him a minute ago, didn't he step into a smoky region? An area that looked like a heat shimmer?"

I brought the cell light to her face. She looked terrified and baffled at the same time. "I haven't seen him since I was dragged here," she said.

Then I finally got it. Hadn't McKesson said they'd "missed"? Well, maybe they'd screwed up in more ways than one. There was no rip down here for me to find. This spot was a one-way chute from the hotel room to this dungeon. I had stepped through, and McKesson had tossed the body through after me, but there was no way back. The pathway the cultist had used to enter the hotel room started someplace else.

"What's wrong?" whispered Holly.

"The anomaly opened in two different spots. Each of the doorways was effectively one-way. That's probably why when I looked through, I couldn't see the other side."

"What the hell are you talking about?"

"I was in a hotel room. The hotel room can send things through to us here, but the starting point where the cultists are coming from is in some third location."

Holly stared at me with big, scared eyes. "Just get me out of here," she said.

I imagined McKesson at the far end, keeping his gun trained on the spot where I'd vanished. I wondered how long he would wait for me or something else to come through. I doubted he'd step out to look for me. That wasn't his style. He'd watch the shimmer until it vanished, then shrug and go have a drink. I doubted he would even tell anyone how I'd disappeared.

"You came to find me, didn't you?" Holly asked.

I nodded and put my arm around her. She hugged me in return. We were in an unknown dungeon—possibly in another version of our universe. A dead man lay at my feet, and he doubtlessly had friends somewhere nearby. We were in their stronghold, with no clear path of escape.

In short, we were screwed.

22

We searched the dungeon and eventually found two exits. One was a normal door, but the second was hidden and looked like part of the wall. I listened carefully at the normal door. I heard nothing on the far side other than the sighing of wind and possibly street sounds. The door was quiet and felt cool to the touch. The air that seeped beneath it smelled of the outdoors.

I moved to the hidden door. I could hear the sounds of voices from beyond it—possibly having an argument. I slipped on my sunglasses and put my fingers on the handle.

"Are you crazy?" hissed Holly, tugging at my arm.

"We have to find the other rip," I said. "We have to jump back through it before it closes."

"I don't know what you're talking about, but there are crazies behind that door."

"I've got a gun."

"What if they don't care?" she asked. "Look, let's just try the other door first."

I hesitated. She could be right, but I was afraid the pathway to the hotel room might close soon. Then we would be left with finding a new way home. Maybe we were on our Earth, maybe we weren't.

I decided it was worth giving Holly's choice a chance. I stepped up to the first door and the sunglasses worked like a charm. Metal squeaked as if the door hadn't been used much, but it swung open. Leaves blew in over my feet, giving me the immediate impression of a normal Earth environment. Beyond the door, we found concrete steps that led upward and a night sky beyond. I closed the door behind me, knowing it would lock itself again in a few minutes when the metal hardened again. I'd been gentle with it.

I moved up the stairway with Holly close behind. I paused at the top, looking around. What I saw filled me with relief: trees and a cinder-block fence. There was the stucco wall of a large building behind me. The sky was lit with the pale radiance of earthly streetlights. I now felt certain we were on our home world—or were we? McKesson had indicated there were many worlds, and some looked a lot more like home than others.

We were inside some kind of compound or large yard, so we followed the walls to the left, looking for an exit. I passed windows that were closed, but showed very normal-looking blinds behind the glass. Everything was the right size and shape. We reached a walkway of concrete and came out to the front of what was now clearly a large house—and then I knew the truth.

I recognized that front yard. I knew the dry fountain, the large circular drive and the powered iron gates out front.

I was in Henderson, Nevada, on the grounds of the mini-mansion McKesson and I had investigated few nights earlier. Things rapidly clicked into place. Holly had mentioned crazy people who liked to cut up meat. It appeared that they hadn't all vanished into the unknown. I'd run into them again. The cellar Holly and I had escaped had to be close to the wine cellar where McKesson and I had fought the Gray Men. Perhaps the hidden door even led to the wine cellar.

Ironically, I was disoriented. I'd been so certain I was in some other place. The last time I'd gone through a rip there had been extra moons and a dozen other differences. I'd been left expecting strange vehicles and cities built of cubes...

I wasn't out of danger, but I could walk home, or hail a cab, or call McKesson, or—suddenly, I realized I'd been an idiot. I took out the cell phone I'd been using for a flashlight. The batteries were low, but I had two bars of service. I shook my head. The next time I stepped out to an unknown place, I would check my cell first to know instantly if I was still home or in Neverland.

"Great," said Holly in my ear. "Now, let's get the hell out of here before someone comes looking for me. They are going to find the body of their friend down in that cellar and see that I'm missing."

I took her to the street. We got there without incident. I walked her downhill to a corner that looked perfectly normal. Insects buzzed and a bat flew overhead, snatching them from the air.

"Let's go get something to eat and a place to stay," she said, holding onto my arm. "I want to get as far from here as I can."

I had to admit she was making excellent suggestions. But I wasn't done here yet. "Let's walk to the nearest public place."

I took her to a quickie-mart at the bottom of the hill. The guy behind the counter smiled with bad teeth.

"Disappear," I told her. "I'll call you later. I have to go back and get something."

"You're going back up *there*?" she asked, her tone indicating she thought I was crazy.

"Yeah," I said. "I'm finally close to these guys, and I want information."

Holly searched my eyes. She must have seen I wasn't going to change my mind. She gave me a sudden, hard kiss on the lips. I smiled.

"Thanks for coming to get me," she said. "If you live, I'll owe you a big one."

I paused for a moment, wondering what "a big one" might be.

"Give me your cell," she demanded, holding out her hand.

I shrugged and handed it over. She could call a cab if she had to.

We parted ways and I went back to the big house at the end of the darkest street in the neighborhood. I watched the yard with my gun in my hand until I was sure no one was around. Then I walked up to the front door and opened it. The lock gave way without a problem.

I smiled to myself, thinking of Holly's kiss and how I was beginning to like locks. They gave the opposition a false sense of security. As far as I was concerned, the entire world should lock up and go for a long trip. It would make my life easier.

The cut-up meats were mostly gone now from the kitchen. There were, however, some fresh bloodstains at the cellar door. I heard voices from below. They weren't arguing or singing, now. They were chanting—speaking words in unison. I headed down the steps, trying to remember which ones creaked the loudest.

Quand il jette en dansant son bruit vif et moqueur,
Ce monde rayonnant de métal et de pierre

The words sounded like French to me. I didn't understand all of it, but I must have taken a French class at some point, because I picked out something about dancing, stone, and metal. I crept down three steps more. I could feel the sweat sprout from my body.

There they were: I could see them kneeling in a circle around a shimmer in the air. The rip was almost gone. Could they have created it by themselves? Was that even possible? Were these cultists—of all the cultists in the vast world—the only ones truly capable of functioning witchcraft?

I reached the sixth step down, and I bent slowly to slip my hand under the wooden plank I stood upon. At first, I couldn't find what I was looking for. I squatted and reached deeper. My fingers touched the bottle. McKesson had always been very thorough, but this was one detail he'd missed. I'd not bothered to explain it to Holly, but I'd come back for the Gray Man's dead finger. I wanted hard evidence. If I took this finger to the right people, I knew they would have to take notice. Or, at the very least, it could give me a bargaining chip with McKesson.

Et pour la déranger du rocher de cristal
Où, calme et solitaire, elle s'était assise.

Something about loneliness and rock crystals. On my haunches with the bottle in my hand, I was better able to see the cultists. There were eight of them, both men and women. They weren't wearing any special robes or anything like that. They had on normal clothing, but they were all sitting around the shimmering rip in the air with their heads bowed. One man had a leather-bound book in his lap and seemed to be leading the prayer, or chant, or spell—whatever it was. None of them had weapons in their hands.

Then I noticed the blood in their midst. There was a lot of it, and it all pooled up underneath the rip they had encircled. The cellar was gently sloped to that point, where as I recalled there had been a drain before. Now the drain was covered, preventing the blood from escaping. It certainly did look as if they had summoned the rip that shivered and twisted.

It was right about then that I dropped the finger. I don't have a reason why it happened. I just tipped the bottle a little too far and it fell right out and thumped down the steps one at a time to roll out onto the floor of the cellar.

I wouldn't have thought a finger could make all that much noise, but this one did. To me, it sounded like a stone dropped into a quiet well—over and over again as it struck each step.

I'm not sure who was more surprised, me or the cultists.

23

I trained my gun on the group. Their looks of surprise changed to glares. I walked down the steps with as much swagger as I could muster. Thinking fast, I came up with a lie and ran with it. It wasn't great, but it was all I had.

"All right," I said. "That's about enough chanting, people. Do you know this house is bank-owned? You are all trespassing and my partner is walking the rest of the uniforms in here right now."

The cultists, getting over their initial shock, stopped looking at me when their leader spoke up. At that point, every one of their eyes fixed upon him.

The leader looked at the woman seated to his left. "Abigail?" he said questioningly. He was a lanky fellow with sandy-blond hair that hung from his head in a long, thin mop. His nose was long and his eyes were large and dark. All ten of his fingers were weighed down by thick rings.

"He lies," Abigail said. "There's no one else near."

As I watched him, he closed the old leather-bound book, which had a gold-printed title. I took the opportunity to read the title: *Flowers of Evil*, it read, in both English and French.

"Yet, here he is," he said, "and therefore you have failed to warn us. It was your responsibility to prevent intrusions."

Abigail was a thin woman who sat next to the leader. She looked like a housewife who gardened all Saturday and played bunco on Tuesday nights. She had curly black hair, blood-red nails, and a worried expression. Maybe in this group, failure resulted in a loss of blood.

While most of them stared at Abigail, I walked down to the bottom of the steps and scooped up the gray finger. It felt hard and leathery in my hand. I shoved it into a pocket and straightened, vaguely disgusted. I told myself to man up and have a nightmare about dead body parts later. Now was not the time to be squeamish.

"He could not have gotten through," Abigail said to the leader. "Not unless he has power, or he stepped through a portal close by."

The lead cultist lifted his gaze to me again. "Do you have power?" he asked me seriously.

I stared at them. They didn't seem to be afraid of my gun. This worried me. The last time I'd confronted someone with this same weapon and gotten a disinterested response, I'd been tossed out of the sanatorium by Dr. Meng.

"Are you part of the Community?" I asked, deciding to name-drop and behave as calmly as they did.

The question got a strong reaction out of them. "*No*," came the powerful response from several throats. They stared at me with eyes that glittered, reflecting the glimmering rip in space they encircled.

"We are a group of—friends," the leader said. "We have no domains to rule. We are rogues, as I suspect you yourself are."

I nodded. "Yeah," I said. "A group of people with minor powers who've banded together, is that it?"

The left half of the leader's face smiled. "Not so *minor*," he said. "Strong enough to open pathways like this one." He gestured toward the vortex, and I nodded, impressed despite myself. Tearing a hole in the universe to go someplace you wished—I had to admit that was much cooler than Tony's sunglasses.

"Well, it's been nice meeting you," I said. "As one rogue to a group of comrades, I have to go now. I have responsibilities."

This caused a general twitter of humor to escape the circle. The leader lifted a hand and the group fell silent. They stared at me with shining eyes. I sensed a dark anticipation, so I knew it was time to do something.

I stepped forward to the edge of their circle. It was time to take a chance. If these guys were anything like Meng, they weren't bluffing. They could prevent my leaving, and I supposed I wouldn't be able to gun them down before they attacked me somehow.

They looked at me curiously, as if wondering what this intruder would do next. I smiled at them and put my gun into my pocket.

"The truth now," I said. "I'm convinced you are the group I've heard of. You are the people they whisper of in the shadows. I've come here to join you, if you will have me. Will you allow me to sit in your circle?"

Another round of mirth swept them. The leader did not laugh at me, however. He lifted his hands and gestured for the circle to part. I stepped forward and now stood in their midst.

"You can indeed be of use," the leader said. "Unfortunately, your power is too weak to sit among us. We do need fuel, however, and you can serve well in that regard."

"Fuel?" I asked. "For what?"

He indicated the shimmering region in the middle of the room. "Our fire is waning. Soon, it will go dim and die completely. We have to keep this flame alive, as one of our members has stepped out and is overdue."

I realized he was talking about the man I'd watched die in the hotel room. Apparently, these guys didn't know he was dead, and that I'd come from the same hotel room. They didn't know the pathway they had opened had split on their end, which had allowed me to get into their cellar. I decided not to enlighten them.

"Ah, I understand," I said.

Each member of the circle reached under his or her right leg and lifted a knife. Each knife was the same—a slightly curved affair with a wicked point. I seriously considered shooting them, but I figured that even if I did kill several, the rest might be crazy enough to keep coming. Either that, or my gun wouldn't stop them. Judging that the safest move was a quick exit, I strode forward toward the rip. It was the only way to get out before they could fall upon me.

The cultists took action. One older woman to my right, with thick glasses and a bad perm, lifted a rag doll and shook it. A blast of heat passed around me—but only dried my skin of sweat. She looked shocked.

A man to my left also moved. He wore a workman's set of grimy coveralls. He lifted a small ball-peen hammer in one hand. He looked like a mechanic. He made a striking motion in the air with the small hammer. I felt a puff of air pass by me as he did so. The woman with the rag doll screeched and fell backward, knocked flat. Her head bled and she didn't move.

"I couldn't have missed!" the mechanic in the coveralls shouted.

My right shoe splashed into the pool of blood they surrounded. I was moving into the swirling region of space that separated this place from the hotel room. A young girl who could not have been more than fourteen made one last attempt to stop me. She had long, pale arms as thin as a child's. Her arms and her steel flashed as she cut me with her blade and scored a nick in the back of my calf. I was glad she hadn't been closer, and I was glad the others had tried to use their powers on me rather than simply stabbing me as I passed by. If that girl had slashed a half inch deeper, I would have been hamstrung. The pain was intense.

"Killer!" the schoolgirl cried after me. It was the last word I heard from any of them. They all vanished, to be replaced more familiar surroundings. I was back inside the Lucky Seven. Judging by the shattered glass and blood on the floor, I knew I was in the same room where Jenna and I had spent a night together. The dead cultist was still gone, as was Detective McKesson.

Hissing with pain, I quickly tended to the sliced meat of my calf muscle. Fresh blood dribbled down my leg onto the carpet—which had already been soaked by the first cultist I'd met that night.

Someone stepped through space after me. He was blurry, but I thought I recognized that long, lank hair. It was the cult leader, and I was surprised to see him. I hadn't figured any of them would have the balls to follow me. Even working their little tricks together, they'd not managed to nail me—a fact that had left me relieved but baffled. I pulled my gun and aimed it at him, figuring I could blast him the second he walked into full view. Just like the Gray Men, he should be vulnerable the moment he came fully into this place. Whatever his trick was, I didn't think he would have time to pull it off.

He stood there, not quite coming out into the room. I stared and aimed at him, my finger twitching on the trigger. I didn't want to blink and give him a moment's advantage. I wondered if he was waiting for more of his crew to come through to offer support. If they all stepped through the rip together, they might be able take me. But it would cost them.

More figures did not appear, however. The lead cultist spread his hands wide. Was this some kind of gesture requesting a truce? I laughed and aimed my gun at his gut. He wasn't going to trick me so easily.

In response, he took out his gently curved blade and dropped it. I didn't see where it landed, it could have been anywhere on their side or mine. I had a thought then: if he stepped backward, would he go back to the cellar, or someplace else? His little rip was shrinking and dying in color like a cooling fire. Did they really feed these things with blood? I didn't know, but I supposed anything was possible.

The figure gestured to me, signaling that I should put away my weapon as he had done. I raised my free hand, extended my middle finger, and gave him a gesture of my own. I waved it around so he was able to see it, even if I was a shimmering ghost to him.

Finally, he decided to chance it. He spread his hands widely apart. Slowly, he stepped forward into my space.

I snarled as he entered the room. I almost fired—it was a close thing. Part of me urged my finger to squeeze the trigger, but it was hard to do. In the end, I found I couldn't shoot a man in the gut when his hands were up. I'd not seen him make any moves at me, or I would have done it anyway. Whatever his power was, I had no evidence that it was violent in nature. But I remained guarded. These people were anything but friendly.

When he had stopped shimmering and could speak, he found the muzzle of my .32 auto in his face. This time, to my gratification, he looked worried. He didn't have a gang of faithful minions surrounding him now.

"We've not been properly introduced," he said.

I had to give it to him, he was smooth. Smoother than I would have been with a gun in my face. My lips had curled away from my teeth, and I must have resembled a snarling dog. I was angry, and my leg was still bleeding. I was in a dangerous mood.

"Give me your name, then," I said. "I'll have them carve it into your headstone."

"Thomas Gilling," he said evenly. "And yours?"

"Quentin Draith."

Gilling nodded, then made a gesture of recognition, lifting a finger into the air and opening his mouth into an "O." My trigger finger tightened in paranoia, but he didn't seem to notice.

"Draith," he said. "Ah yes! The blogger! I know you now."

"You've read my stuff?"

Gilling nodded. His demeanor had changed a great deal. He seemed almost affable, despite my gun barrel, which never wavered from his face.

"I thought your columns were nonsensical originally, you understand," he said. "But I followed your bits and dribblings. You actually helped me make my initial contacts among the fringe of the Community. People with minor objects and other hangers-on."

"Glad I could help," I said bemusedly. "Now, if you don't want to die, I suggest you step back through."

Gilling looked back over his shoulder toward the rip. "Almost too late for that. I really must apologize. When you asked to join us, I didn't take you seriously. I didn't think you could possibly have the kind of power you demonstrated back there."

I almost said "what power?" like an idiot. I barely managed to stop myself in time. Realizing I needed to seem as cool and powerful as possible, I didn't confess my ignorance. Instead, I nodded as if I completely understood whatever it was he was hinting at.

"Quite impressive," he continued, watching me. "You were immune to both a sonic attack and a thermal projection."

"You mean the hammer and the rag doll, right?"

"Ahem," he said, as if I'd soiled myself. "Naturally."

"Yeah," I said. "I can be hard to take out."

"Quite," Gilling said. "But I'll tell you what really impressed me, what made me come after you for more information. The knife *did* strike home, didn't it?"

I took a half step back just in case he was planning another test. My pistol twitched in my hand.

Gilling made a calming gesture. "Again, let me apologize. We behaved abominably. You are possibly the most powerful rogue I've ever met."

I frowned at him. "How do you figure that?"

His hands spread wide again. This guy really liked to talk with his hands.

"Don't be modest," he said. "You resisted the powers of three others. No one there could touch you, I'd wager. Rheinman's blast went right by you and hit Caroline. That was quite a shock for us. I knew that it couldn't be something as simple as a shielding force that cocooned you, preventing harm. No, if it had been that, you wouldn't have been vulnerable to Fiona's knife."

"You mean the kid who slashed me?"

"Yes. After you stepped out, she held her blade aloft to show the rest of us it was stained with your essence. I inspected her blade immediately. That was the moment I became intrigued. I had to follow you."

"What for?" I asked.

"Why—to offer you membership in my coven," Gilling said. "After all, you did say you wished to join us, didn't you?"

I wasn't sure if I should be flattered or violently pissed. The cultists might or might not be murderers, but I was certain they had stabbed me.

"What's happened to you people?" I asked, honestly confused. "You look like normal enough individuals—housewives, schoolkids, laborers. How could you turn into a group that sits around in a circle and *bleeds* things?"

"May I sit down?" Gilling asked, as politely as always.

I gestured toward the chairs around the table. The shimmer in the midst of the sliding glass door had turned into an orangey glimmer. I suspected it was about to go out. It reminded me of a fire, just as Gilling had suggested.

"Your question has merit," he said. "Let me ask you how you have fared since you came into contact with these objects of power. Have you killed anyone?"

I opened my mouth to retort with a harsh no, but the word died in my throat. I recalled the Gray Men I'd met in the cellar with McKesson. They may not have been officially human, but in my book they counted for something.

"Nothing human," I said. "And only in self-defense."

"Commendable," Gilling said, nodding. "So the man you killed in this room attacked you?"

"Who?"

"Hugo was his name. He used to work for me—before you killed him."

I realized, then, who he meant. I frowned. There was blood and glass everywhere underfoot. The body was gone, but there was clear evidence of foul play at the very table Gilling had sat beside.

"Oh, you mean your cultist friend. We didn't kill him. He came through and—he landed badly. You see your rip? It formed right in the middle of the sliding glass door. When he stepped through…"

Gilling turned his head and inspected the scene. The torn curtain luffed in a breeze and the balcony was revealed.

"Ah," he said, nodding with regret. "I failed him. My aim is admittedly still poor."

I thought about what his words meant. *He* was the one who had opened the pathway from the mansion to this hotel room. That was *his* power, and it was an impressive one. I could immediately see why he was the leader of his group. My eyes drifted down toward his rings. I couldn't help myself. It had to be one of them. Why else would he wear so many? I supposed he wore them all to hide the one that mattered.

Gilling caught the direction of my gaze. A faint smile played over his thin red lips. "So, you have not yet taken a human life."

"The night is young," I snapped.

"Tell me, Mr. Draith, what would you do if someone tried to steal your objects from you?"

Objects? I thought. As far as I knew, I had only the sunglasses. Still, his question made me think. I'd come to feel strongly possessive of the sunglasses. I *would* fight to keep them—that much I was sure of.

"I suppose I would fight to keep what's mine," I admitted.

A long, thin finger flew upward and he waggled it at me. "Exactly!" he said. "I would expect no less. They are so magical—so captivating. They become like a part of us. The bond will grow ever stronger, you'll find. They are unique, priceless, and irreplaceable. The things you can do with them will define who you are. In time, they will become your beloved children."

I rubbed my chin with the back of my hand. I didn't like where this conversation was going. He was trying to prove to me that greed and fascination could take over my mind.

"OK," I said. "These powerful objects tend to make people do bad things out of greed and possessiveness. I get that. Still, you guys are a bit beyond the pale. I mean, bleeding animals and chanting bad French poetry in a circle? What's that all about? Are you wannabe witches or what?"

Gilling chuckled. "Hardly. We do not perform actual magic in the traditional sense. We call ourselves *technomancers*. We perform magic with advanced technology."

I blinked at him.

"Let me explain," he said. "To someone from the time of the American Revolution, a television set or the Internet would be magical. They could not understand how it worked, even if they could learn how to use it. You and I are in a similar situation. These objects do what they do because of principles of physics we don't understand—there are rules and reasons, but we simply don't know them. Therefore, they might as well be magical in nature."

I thought about that for a second, but knew he was still dodging my actual questions. "You still haven't explained the blood and the book."

"Both are functional. The power I have, as I'm sure you have guessed by now, is to open pathways through space."

"Yes, I've run into quite a number of them lately."

"I require organic material to light these fires," he said.

"Fires?" I asked.

"Do you know what flame truly is, Mr. Draith?"

I thought about it and decided honesty was the best policy. I shook my head.

"It's a body of incandescent gas. It requires a source of intense heat to begin burning, and then a supply of fuel to continue the chemical reaction. These rips in space are similar in nature: they don't last forever without some substance to keep them going. I am able to create the spark that starts the reaction, that's all."

"And you use *blood* for fuel? Why not wood or tap water?"

"I'm not exactly sure why, but most substances don't work. Recall what I said about utilizing technology one does not fully understand—in this way, we are like most computer users. We can read our e-mail, but have no comprehension of the complex process by which it actually appears on the screen."

"All right," I said. "So only blood fuels your power? That makes you some kind of vampire."

"We don't use that term," Gilling said stiffly.

"I'm not surprised."

Gilling pursed his lips for a moment in irritation before continuing. "Once these openings in space start burning, only organic fuels seem to work. Blood happens to be a very convenient, efficient source of fuel. We tried store-bought meats, both cooked and raw. They couldn't sustain the reaction. Freshly killed animals do marginally better, but only for short periods. A significant flow of warm blood, however, has moved us into a new realm of power!"

His eyes lit up as he spoke. I found his manner disturbing. The pistol in my hand, which I'd let dangle while we talked, perked up seemingly of its own volition. Some part of my mind had decided the world might be a better place if this man were dead. But I didn't shoot him. Instead, I asked him another question.

"And the poetry?"

"Oh, that. Again, functional. It helps me keep my mind focused as I maintain the opening. I have to think about where I want it to go while I set my fire, you see. If I'm distracted, I make mistakes—poor Hugo."

Indeed, I thought, staring at the table where a man had died earlier this eve, his torso merged with a sheet of glass. *Poor Hugo.* It was very different now, thinking of these people as individuals, as people who were caught up in a new kind of science humanity had never met up with before.

I had a thought then…what if we had discovered these things before? At a previous point in history?

"Gilling," I said, "do you think the witches of the past— do you think they might have discovered something like this?"

"Undoubtedly," he said. "Keep thinking about it. You've just uncovered the source of little men from other worlds. The truth behind both ghosts and goblins. All the things we've sought to erase from our consciousness with the clear light of modern science."

"So, you're saying our science simply isn't sufficiently advanced to understand these things yet?"

"Correct. And what a society doesn't understand it rejects and labels as heresy. Welcome to the ranks of the heretics, Mr. Draith."

He smiled at me, but I didn't smile back. He'd given me a lot to think about, and I didn't like most of it. I tried to remember my immediate goals. I wanted to know who was killing people I came in contact with and why. I wouldn't mind learning about my past life either—regaining my lost memories one way or another. Barring that, I'd settle for finding out how I'd lost them and who was responsible.

"Is your cult—excuse me, *coven*, responsible for the mysterious murders around town?"

Gilling licked those bright red lips. "There have been a few regrettable deaths," he said. "Hugo is a case in point. Others have sought to steal our objects. We thought you were one of those, an attacker."

I told him of my persecution, of the inevitable demise of those who came near me. He listened closely and his frown grew as I went on.

"We've been aware of the deaths. But our purpose has been experimentation and greater understanding. We've not engaged in any kind of assaults upon individuals."

For some reason, I thought he might be telling the truth. For one thing, the rift I'd stepped through before had led to the world of the Gray Men, not the basement of a ring of cultists. On my list of suspects, the Gray Men had moved up a notch, despite the shady nature of the cultists. I decided to proceed on another topic.

Gilling raised a hand to stop me. "This conversation seems more like an interrogation, Mr. Draith," he said. "Let me understand our relationship. Are you interested in joining us or not?"

"You kidnapped my friend Holly and manacled her in your dungeon. You were going to kill her. Why would I want to join you?" Beginning to wonder if he was trying to delay me, I figured it was high time I checked up on Holly and Jenna.

"She's not as innocent as she seems, Draith."

"Really?" I asked, but his words didn't really surprise me. I knew she was a thief and was quite capable of lying.

"We had good reason to pursue her, let me leave it at that—but she was awaiting questioning, not murder. Think about it: why would we want to bleed humans when less problematic sources of fuel are so abundant? Now, I really must insist—" Gilling said, moving to rise.

"One last question," I said. "Do you know Robert Townsend?"

Gilling opened his mouth, then paused. He sat down again. He tilted his head to one side, glancing around what had been Robert Townsend's hotel room. I knew he had sent Hugo here, which indicated there was some connection to Jenna and her missing husband.

Finally, he leaned forward conspiratorially. "Yes, I do. Have you seen him—lately?"

I shook my head. "I'm looking for him too."

Gilling nodded slowly. "He's a slippery fellow."

My eyes narrowed. Was he lying? I'd found Robert's shoe in his dungeon. Had he killed him in that dungeon?

"Are you telling me Robert was a member of your group?"

"Yes," Gilling said, turning around in his chair and closing his eyes.

Had Robert Townsend really stepped out on his newlywed wife on purpose? It seemed odd, as he'd left behind his lucky ring. In support of the self-styled technomancer's claims, however, I'd found a shoe, not a body. One other thing had been bothering me about Jenna's story: these rips, when they appeared, had never consumed anyone. You could step into them, but they didn't drag you in. That was further evidence that Robert had left purposefully.

Suddenly, a wink of light blossomed around Gilling. I pointed my gun at Gilling and almost fired, but I realized that he was already a blur of flesh and clothing in a ripple of space. I stepped to the edge of the rip and his flaring outline. "Come back out of there!" I shouted.

He lifted his hand one more time. Was he giving me the finger or waving at me? I wasn't sure, but after a second, he stepped away and disappeared. I stood behind in the room, cursing. If I followed him, I had no idea what I was walking into. Damn.

The rip closed and I examined the spot where it had been. There was a handy pool of blood on that exact spot, provided by the dead man named Hugo. I nodded to myself. He'd sat at the table, very close to the blood, on purpose. He was thus able to leave at will.

Shaking my head, I left the room and the Lucky Seven. I needed to see Jenna, but first I had to find Holly. I had too many women in my life right now.

25

I had given Holly my cell, so I didn't have an easy way to call her. Pay phones had long ago been ripped out of the lobby of the Lucky Seven and other casinos. Anyone they wanted to do business with could use the hotel room phones or their own cells. Anyone who didn't have a room or a cell, they figured, could get the hell out.

So instead I walked down the Strip to another big casino hotel. I needed a shower and a bed, not to mention a way to call Holly. I had money to pay for a room, but I didn't want anyone knowing my location. My eyes slid around the lobby in paranoia. Someone had made numerous attempts to find me and probably to kill me. Knowing a thing like that makes a paranoid person such as myself...even more paranoid. As for the Gray Men, I didn't know how they were tracking me, but I didn't want to make it any easier for them.

Coming up with a plan, I walked to the front desk. The clerk was perky despite the time of night. The palm trees in the vibrantly lit atrium behind her were motionless. I wondered how they kept plants from dying in there—I couldn't see an obvious source of sunlight.

"Do you have any rooms available?" I asked the perky clerk.

"We sure do! Weekend or not, the hotel is half-empty," she said.

I nodded. "I'll find out what the rest of my party wants to do," I said. "We just drove in."

"OK!"

I left her and walked to the elevators. Hotel security ran their eyes over me. I didn't look back, but instead walked with purpose. Security was supposed to make sure street people didn't get into the hotel. I knew they would assume I had checked in and was now heading up to my room.

I got off on the twenty-second floor and tapped on a door. A bleary-eyed man told me to piss off. I did as he requested, saying I'd forgotten the last digit of my room number. The second try resulted in a woman's voice suggesting I ask at the front desk. She wisely didn't open the door.

At the third door my knock went unanswered. I tried it twice more, with long waits in between. With my heart pounding in my chest, I put on my sunglasses and forced the lock. I slipped inside, finding the king-sized bed neatly made and smelling of fresh sheets. I stretched out on the bed with a sigh and considered a shower, but reached for the phone instead. I was glad they didn't have a computer system disconnecting the phones when not in use. Some hotels had such systems. I tapped in my cell number and Holly answered on the second purring ring.

"Draith?"

"Yeah," I said. "Are you OK?"

"Yes. How about you?"

"I'm alive," I said. "Where are you?"

"I had a cab drop me off at my apartment complex, but I got into my car and left. I was too scared to go up there."

"Did you see someone?"

"No, but the neighbors told me Sherri was dead."

"Who?"

"My landlady."

"Oh, right. Sorry about that."

"She was a witch, you know, but I never wished her dead."

I was quiet for a few seconds. "You don't mean—like an actual *witch*, do you?"

Holly laughed. "No, not like that."

"So, you're out driving around?" I asked.

"Yeah."

"I've got a new room. You can come stay the night if you want."

It was her turn to pause. "Yes, I'd like that. Thanks, Quentin."

"No thanks necessary. I owe you several nights' lodging."

She laughed, and after I gave her the room number, she promised to come right over.

I heaved myself up and took a shower. By the time I came out rubbing a towel against my head, I heard a tapping at the door. I checked the peephole and let Holly in.

She ran her eyes over me once, then frowned. "You're pretty scarred up," she said.

I nodded. "Thanks for noticing. The cuts have healed, but they still turn red after an application of hot water."

Holly reached out and ran a finger over one ridged spot on my flat stomach. I recoiled slightly in pain. She pulled away.

"Sorry," she said, then she pushed past me.

I followed her inside and finished drying my hair. When I came out of the bathroom, she had poured us two glasses of clear liquid.

I smiled. "That's not water, is it?"

She walked close and gave me mine. She smiled up at me. I could see now why Tony had hired her. It wasn't just for her dancer's legs. Her smile was entrancing.

"I raided the minibar," she said. "Hope you don't mind."

"Not at all."

"We need ice. I'll go get it."

I sipped at my drink. It was straight vodka. I made a face, then rummaged until I found a vial of orange juice or something that would pass for the real thing.

Holly took a long time coming back with that ice bucket. I muttered to myself about justifiable paranoia and I pulled on my jeans. I made sure my .32 automatic was in the front pocket.

While I waited I wondered if she would come back with someone who wanted to kill me. Could this be a setup? Was Holly an innocent bystander I'd gotten into trouble—or was she part of the trouble disguised as an innocent?

It was a disturbing thought that I tried to dislodge. I blamed Gilling. That guy was a crazy snake. He had put thoughts in my head, possibly seeking to pry me apart from one of the only living friends I had.

I tried to look cool when the tap came at the door again. I looked through the peephole. No Gray Men. No cultists. There was no one there but Holly.

I opened it and let her back inside. I checked the hallway after she came in. Empty.

"Sorry," she said, dropping cubes into our glasses. "I had to go down a floor to find ice."

"I see." I took my automatic out of my pocket and put it on the dresser. When I turned around again, she was staring at it.

"You didn't trust me," she said.

"What? No," I said, "I was getting ready to go look for you."

That made her beam again. It was a glib lie, but it had worked. She found the orange juice and put a dollop in her glass as well. We stirred our drinks and sipped them. She told me how scared she'd been in the cab, and how the cabbie had been eating her up with his eyes and asking her an annoying barrage of questions at the same time. I nodded and listened. I didn't talk about Gilling and his accusations. I figured I could save that for later or try to figure out if there was any truth in it in some other fashion. He had called her a thief, and I knew from experience he had a point there. It indicated he did really know something about her.

The second drink was gin and tonic water. For the third round, we moved on to a junior-sized bottle of merlot. I figured if we drank everything in the minibar, I was going to be sick in the morning, but I was beginning not to care.

Holly jumped on me after the merlot. Honestly, I was surprised. She straddled me while I slouched back in an uncomfortable chair. I hadn't even noticed she'd taken off her jeans at some point. Her legs were warm and strong. Her panties were silky against my thighs. When had I removed my own pants? I recalled us talking about comfort and now…

The kissing and touching began in earnest. Soon I wasn't thinking anymore. At one point, I pushed her off and held her up in the air for a moment with our faces inches apart. She didn't weigh much and she didn't squirm, so I kept holding her up. We studied each other's faces.

"Why the sudden interest?" I asked.

"More paranoia? Have you forgotten I was chained in a cellar, and you came to get me? You risked everything."

I thought to myself that I'd really lucked into finding her, but there was no way I was going to tell her that. I stared at her for a few seconds longer, then finally relented. After all, a man has to make the most of his opportunities. We made love a time or two and fell asleep at dawn. By noon the next day, I had to work hard to shoo Holly out of the room.

"What?" she asked, fooling with her hair. "Are you out of cash already? I can pay for the room if I have to."

I finally explained that *no one* had paid for the room and we had to get the hell out before someone figured out this detail.

Holly looked around the room and giggled. "You crazy bastard. I've pulled a lot of moves in my life, but this is a new one. It's exciting. *You* are exciting, Quentin."

I hustled her out of the room before she could tempt me back to the disheveled bed. Foreign maids were the only people we met in the hallways as we left. They glanced at us with blank expressions. Did they know? I decided it no longer mattered if they did.

It was on the way down to the lobby that my phone rang. My cell was still in Holly's purse. She pulled it out, and I reached for it. She ignored my hand with an impish grin and answered the call.

"Hello?" she asked, then paused. Her grin faded. "Well, who's this?" Another pause. The grin was gone now, replaced with a twist of her lips. "Yeah, he's right here." She handed me the phone.

I took it, looking at Holly quizzically.

"It's Jenna somebody," she told me.

I felt a jolt of embarrassment. She looked at me with her eyes narrowed. I sighed. I supposed these two were bound to come into contact eventually.

I took the phone. "Jenna?"

"Mr. Draith?" she said. Her voice sounded cold.

"Yeah, I…" I began. I made a small move to turn away from Holly. It was automatic, but it was also a mistake. In an elevator, privacy really isn't possible.

Jenna was telling me something in my ear, something about where she was and needing me to come by. I finally caught on.

"You're all right?" I asked. "I'm staying in a different hotel now. Yeah."

I noticed Holly's expression had shifted from a smile to a glare by this point. It had happened amazingly fast.

"Sorry," Holly said. "Let me off, I'll give you two some privacy." She reached out and used both hands to push every button on the face of the elevator panel. The bell dinged and she got out on the sixth floor.

I pressed the cell to my chest to block the sound. "Come on, Holly," I said as she flounced out. "Give me a break."

"You should have told me you had a girlfriend before I made a fool of myself," she hissed.

"I don't have a girlfriend—she's more of a client."

"That's not what *she* thinks," Holly said. "I heard her voice change when I answered your phone. I know men, Draith. You can't bullshit me. Don't even try."

"She's married, Holly."

"Oh, that's even better!" she said. She tossed her head, sending her hair flying, and marched away. When she reached the hallway, she stopped because there was no place else to go. There were long lines of hotel rooms on both sides of the elevator lobby, but no exits. She looked back and gave me the finger.

Part of me wanted to follow her and make a long series of apologies. Maybe that was what she expected. Instead, I decided to let her cool off for now. After all, I hadn't cheated on her. We'd only gotten together the night before.

When the elevator dinged, I let the doors close and I rode down to the lobby. Thanks to Holly, I stopped on every floor. I barely listened to Jenna, who was still talking in my ear. I rubbed my face and told her to meet me in my hotel restaurant for lunch. I was starving, and I was pretty sure I was lightly hung over.

26

Eggs Benedict. Here I was again, eating food that made most people feel worse when they'd had a rough night. But as usual, it worked for me and I felt better. I was already wondering where Holly had gone. I figured she would be safe enough now and she would get over things eventually. She had my number and could call me when she wanted to.

Jenna came to the restaurant with my black leather bag of stuff. She stood at an impersonal distance, put the bag on the floor, and slid it toward me with her toe. I wasn't a big believer in body language, but this didn't look good. I waved for her to sit down.

"I don't know, I've really got to—" she began.

"I found the other shoe," I said.

Jenna stared at me for a second, then slid into the chair across from me. Her expression shifted from wariness to intense interest. "Robert's shoe? Tell me everything."

I had no intention of telling her *everything*, but I did give her the essential information. I told her I'd found a portal like the one she said had sucked up Robert, and there was evidence a friend of mine had been taken through it. I'd followed that friend, rescued her from some strange people, and found Robert's shoe in the same location. I edited out what Holly and I had done all night long in our stolen hotel room after I'd rescued her.

"So, he might be alive?" Jenna asked.

I nodded. "I didn't find anything showing he *wasn't* alive. But I didn't find him either."

"Still, it's something," she said. She reached out her hand to pat mine where it rested on the table. "Thanks, Quentin."

"No problem," I said, eating the last of my brunch. While I chewed, I used the time to do some hard thinking. What should I say next? I could tell her more—about the cultists and their use of blood. But that would only panic her.

I realized she'd been talking while I was thinking. I tuned back in as I sipped fresh coffee. One cream, no sugar.

"Being an instant widow hasn't softened anyone toward me—except for you, of course," Jenna told me.

"What do you mean?"

"I keep getting these messages from the quickie chapel where we were married. I suppose they want to sell me more pictures, or bill me for something."

"Messages?" I asked. "Have you listened to any of them?"

Jenna shook her head. "I just can't face any of it. I can't imagine how women hold up when their husbands die on them—arranging for the funeral and all of that. I suppose having years to prepare yourself mentally would help. But I can't deal with it. I know I should, but I've been avoiding reality. I suppose I'm slightly mental in this regard."

I frowned at her. "No, I can understand your reaction. I'm sure it was a shock."

She dug in her purse and came up with an envelope. She pushed it across the table toward me. "Here's one of their letters," she said.

"They've been sending you mail too?" I asked. I took the letter and glanced at the return address. *White Rose Weddings*, it read. The envelope was business-sized and looked like a bill. I tore it open.

Jenna gave a tiny gasp and looked upset. I didn't look up. What had she expected me to do? Ignore it? She was going to have to face up to this one. I unfolded the letter inside and read it quickly. It wasn't happy news. My eyes flicked up to meet hers.

"Well?" she asked. "You might as well tell me, since you've gone and read it."

"Um, I'm not sure what to say. It's not good news."

She reached for the letter, but I slid it away.

"Jenna," I said. "Let's go somewhere else to talk about this."

"What the hell is wrong with you?" she demanded, becoming angry now. "It's *my* letter."

I sighed. "It says you're not legally married."

"What are you talking about?" she asked. Her face was full of mixed emotions, mostly shock.

I swallowed, unable to think of any way to get out of telling her. If I just handed her the letter, would that be better than hearing the truth from a friend? I didn't think it would be.

"It says Robert signed with a false name. That the license and the certificate aren't legal. They've been trying to contact you to come back and clear things up."

I explained the situation in a hushed voice and she began to quietly sob. People around us gave me dirty looks. I'm sure they all figured I was breaking her heart. I folded the letter and slipped it into my back pocket while she wasn't looking. The note gave details she didn't need to hear. Robert had signed as Harry Houdini. The people at the White Rose hadn't found this amusing. I figured Jenna wouldn't find it amusing either, so I made the letter disappear. Not only had she been jilted, the guy clearly thought it was funny. I wasn't even sure Robert Townsend was his real name.

I paid the check and walked her toward the elevators.

"Are you OK, Jenna?" I asked.

She didn't answer me. The elevator dinged and two couples stepped out. Their conversation halted as they saw the two of us. Jenna had her hands over her face and was shaking with suppressed sobs. The two men looked uncomfortable and tried to avoid staring, but they did frown. The women glared at me quickly, then looked away. I realized I had a bag over my shoulder, heightening the image that I was in the act of dumping her. Jenna made no move to get onto the elevator despite the fact I had my hand holding it open.

"Should I leave you alone?" I asked.

"Come up with me. I have more to tell you."

I nodded and guided her, lightly touching her elbow. She finally stepped into the elevator, and when the doors slid shut in front of me, I felt a wave of relief. When we reached her room, I headed for her minibar and made her a drink. She took it wordlessly.

"Remember when I told you about how it happened? About how Robert vanished? I left out some things. I changed some details."

"Why?"

"Because the details made it sound more like Robert was leaving me. And I didn't want it to sound that way. I knew if it did, the police would ignore the case. Once I had the story in my mind I stuck to it, even with you. I didn't think it would matter. I didn't think the details would stop you from finding him."

"So, he didn't get sucked into a rift?"

"Well, he did go into it and vanish," she said, "but he wasn't sucked up by it. He stepped into the shimmering, burning air, talking to me about how cool it looked. He didn't seem scared at all."

"And the shoe?"

Jenna looked a little embarrassed. "I ripped it off his foot. I thought maybe it was pulling him in, somehow mesmerizing him. He wasn't acting like himself. So I went after him and grabbed his left foot. His shoe came off...he yanked it away from me."

I nodded, rubbing my temples. *What a bastard.* It was one thing to take off on her—but for Townsend to not even call and let her know he was still alive? I was convinced now that Robert Townsend, or Houdini, or whoever he was, still breathed somewhere. He had quite a sense of humor, our friend Robert. I intended to discuss it with him when I got the chance.

"He seemed possessed. I thought I was helping."

I wanted to apologize for my sex, but I figured it was bad timing. I didn't need to associate myself with this cad in her mind.

"Love requires trust, Jenna," I said. "Don't let this man ruin your life."

"As of right now, he's done just that," she said.

I looked at her, hearing a new tone in her voice. She was angry now. I saw a look on her face that reminded me of the Jenna I'd first met down in the casino. I recalled she was willing to do anything to get vengeance then. Now, I supposed she was doubly dangerous. If I were Robert, I wouldn't come near her again. It occurred to me that perhaps he knew about her smoldering temper. Maybe that's why he'd bailed out on her in such a cowardly fashion. I also wondered what else she might have lied about.

I had a sudden thought. "What about the ring?" I asked. "Do you still have it?"

"Yeah," she said, lifting it up.

I stared at her. "If he was such a bastard, why would he leave you his ring?" I asked.

As I watched, she held up her hand and removed the ring. She reached out her hand toward me. "You should take it. I don't want it now."

I had to admit, I was sorely tempted. I reached out my hand, my eyes widening, delighted with the power they saw in her fine palm. But I controlled myself. I reflected that these unique objects *did* fill a person with greed, just as Gilling had said.

Instead of taking her ring, I closed her fingers over it. My hand gently encompassed her smaller fist. "If he did leave it by accident," I said, "then he's out there somewhere, kicking himself. What better way to get back at him? You have the one thing he truly loves."

Jenna brightened a fraction. Her tears had stopped now, and she looked at me thoughtfully. "You're right," she said. "I'll keep it."

I leaned back and smiled. Inwardly, some darker part of my mind complained I was an idiot. Why didn't I just hand her my sunglasses as well, along with every dime in my pocket as a tip? I told myself to shut up. Sure, I could use some luck. But the ring hadn't brought Jenna luck in love, and that was what she really cared about. Winning at cards wasn't all there was to life.

At some point while we were talking, I put my hands into my pockets. I frowned, finding something hard in there. Something unexpected. I jerked my hand out in alarm when I realized what it was.

"What's wrong?" Jenna asked.

I clenched my teeth and looked pained. How did you tell a woman you had a dead man's finger in your pocket? And indeed, that's just what I'd found. I had kept the Gray Man's finger in there since I'd walked out on the cultists and had my little talk with Gilling. It felt odd to the touch—like a pen in my pocket. Only this pen flexed when I walked around, now that I was thinking about it, I could feel the joints move. I felt a little sick, and couldn't hide the fact from Jenna.

"I've had a hard night," I said, standing up. "Can I use your bathroom?"

"Of course," she said. "The eggs Benedict probably didn't help."

I nodded, wishing she was right. I went into the bathroom, which was more or less equivalent to a million other hotel bathrooms. I pushed the door shut with my foot and looked at myself in the mirror. I could see the outline of the finger in my pocket.

"Do you have any tissues out there in the room? I don't see—" I began, but then I found the box. It was hidden under the bathroom counter. I pulled out a tissue—then ripped out a half dozen more. I wadded them up and reached into my pocket, using them like a glove. I could barely feel the shape of it, and that was just fine with me.

I had worked it halfway out of my pocket when a pretty nose poked into the restroom with me. She had a tissue in her hand. I realized I hadn't locked the door.

"Are you OK?" Jenna asked.

I jumped. It was a natural reaction. I must have felt guilty at some level. The finger, which I was wrapping in a fresh layer of paper, sprang seemingly of its own accord onto the bathroom counter. The counter was polished to look like a granite slab. The finger stood out as a pale curled object, unmistakably alien on the slate-gray surface.

The finger thumped down, and Jenna craned her neck to look at it. I thought about pushing her out, but it was already too late.

"What is that—" she began, then she cut off in a strangled scream. She disappeared and I walked after her.

"Sorry you had to see that," I told her.

"What's wrong with you?" she demanded. She sat on the bed now, beside the phone. She had put one hand on the receiver, but she hadn't picked it up and dialed the police yet. Instead, she'd grabbed a pillow with her other hand and hugged it to her chest.

"I never told you about what McKesson and I found," I said, "about the Gray Men."

"What Gray Men? Are you some kind of weirdo? I really can pick them. Mom always said that, you know. She said if there were six football players and a freak in a line, I would choose the lucky number seven every time."

I ran my fingers through my hair. I wasn't quite sure how to talk her through this one. In the end, I decided just to dive into it. I told her about McKesson, about the Gray Men in their city of cubes, and about shooting them as they came through into our world. I urged her to remember she'd seen her husband step away into an impossible rip in space. Before I was finished, she was staring at me in disbelief.

"That's how my story must have sounded to the cops," she said. "No wonder they looked at me the way they did."

27

After I'd talked Jenna into a relative state of calm, she finally came to believe what I was saying—with reservations. At least she'd taken her hand away from the phone. She still had a death grip on her pillow. After a few minutes more, during which I explained how I'd come into possession of this unusual trophy, she was willing to look at the finger again. I noticed, however, that when she followed me toward the bathroom, she didn't follow closely.

What finally convinced her I was telling the truth wasn't the grayish color of the finger's skin. That seemed normal enough, given that it had been dead for some time. What did it was the pearl-colored spur on the knuckle. Once examined closely, it seemed distinctly inhuman.

"So, you killed some kind of mutant?" she asked, leaning around the corner of the doorway.

"I don't think so. In his world, he was perfectly normal. There were quite a number of these Gray Men in evidence."

"How did you walk around all day with that in your pocket and not think about it?" she demanded.

I thought of alcohol, of Holly, and the resulting long night of distractions. But I decided to leave Holly out of my explanation.

"I had a few drinks," I said. "And I was overwhelmed with other things, such as surviving."

Jenna was willing to accept that. She peeked at the finger with big eyes. "What are we going to do with it?" she asked, her voice hushed.

I wasn't so impressed by it now. I had originally thought I could use it to get McKesson's attention. Maybe I could threaten to take it to medical people and blow this whole thing into a big news story. After all, he'd said it was his job to cover up details like this. But I realized now that the newspeople weren't going to be terribly interested. Unsubstantiated sightings of aliens, bigfoot, and the like went on every day. They always turned out to be hoaxes. That indicated to me that they were either being covered up, or they really were hoaxes. In either case, no one was going to take me seriously. Still, I didn't want to give up on a piece of real evidence. I supposed that part of my personality wanted to investigate the darkest of secrets.

"Have you got something to keep it in?" I asked Jenna.

She looked at me and winced. "Do we *have* to keep it? Won't it start to rot or something?"

"I don't know," I said, "but I'm not dropping it in the hotel room trash."

"Maybe you could sneak into a room across the hall and dump it there."

"How rude," I said, laughing. "But seriously, do you have something?"

In the end, she produced a small plastic bottle filled with shampoo. "Here," she said. "But I'm not touching it."

I dumped the shampoo into the sink. I washed out the bottle and dried it with the hotel hair dryer. Then I used a plastic key card to scoot and nudge the finger into the bottle and screwed on the cap. I could see it through the orange plastic. I shook it, and the spur rattled.

"That is the most disgusting thing ever," Jenna said.

"You should never enroll in medical school."

"Don't worry."

I frowned at the finger in the bottle. It did look exactly like it had when I'd found it. There had been no discoloration. Even the bloody end, where it had been severed, looked…fresh.

Still frowning, I unscrewed the bottle again.

"What are you doing?" Jenna asked.

I tipped it upside down over the counter. The finger didn't fall out right away; I had to shake it. The spur on the back of the knuckle had gotten caught on the opening.

"I am not going to watch this," she said, leaving.

I finally managed to shake it out upon the countertop. I used the plastic key card again, scooting it around so the severed end faced me. I saw the flesh was red and looked like raw meat. Yes, it was disgusting, but it was also bizarre. Why hadn't the blood dried up? Why did it still look wet and freshly severed? I tapped at it again and examined it, my face inches from the countertop.

Jenna had returned to the doorway. "You have to tell me why you are playing with that thing, or you have to leave."

I glanced at her. "It's strange," I said. "But don't you think it should have dried up by now? I mean, it looks like it was just cut off. So disgusting."

"You said it was from some alien. Maybe their blood stays wet longer."

I thought about what McKesson had said about these other places—that in other worlds the rules were sometimes different. I wondered if that could be the case here. It didn't sound right, however. This was our world. Wouldn't this finger have to play by our physical laws? Evaporation dried things, turning liquids into solids.

I picked up the bottle and looked inside. There was no trace of the blood that I could see. I turned my pocket inside out next. There were no stains there. Not the slightest trace of blood.

"I think we really have something here," I said. "Do you have a lighter?"

"I don't smoke."

I picked up the wad of tissues I'd used to take the finger from my pocket. I carefully leafed through them. There was no blood on any of them.

"Have you got a knife?" I asked.

Jenna stared at me. "You've got to be kidding. Don't you think it's dead already?"

"Anything will do. A nail file?"

Sighing, she left and rummaged in her makeup kit. She came back and handed me a pair of nail clippers. "I don't want them back when you're done," she said, and left the bathroom.

I couldn't cut the nail—or the flesh. I tried the tip of the pearly spur—it was like steel. I tried the delicate strips of torn skin next, but couldn't dent them. It was as if the finger was made of soft, flexible titanium. I couldn't mark any part of it. And yet, it had been cut free of a Gray Man recently. Therefore, it must have undergone some kind of change to its nature.

Finally, the clippers broke in my hand. I tried soaking the finger in the sink, then toweling it off. There were no changes in its appearance. I left the finger on the counter and walked back into the room.

"Well?" Jenna asked. "Are you going to tell me why you've turned into a ghoul?"

"I think it's an object," I said, frowning.

She looked at me, shaking her head in confusion.

"Like your ring or my sunglasses. I can't change or damage it. Even though it's a piece of dead flesh, it won't rot, and the blood in it won't exit. The skin can't be cut."

"How could that happen?"

"It's *frozen* somehow," I said. "Like the other objects. It's impervious."

"Are you going to use it as a bulletproof shield? It's a little on the small side."

I shook my head. "If it is an object, it has a power."

"What power?"

"I don't know," I said. "But I mean to find out."

I put the finger back in the small plastic bottle. "I need some help," I told Jenna.

"As long as I don't have to touch it—or look at it much," she said.

"I want to hang it around my neck. I need some kind of strong, stringlike material."

Jenna stared at me for a second or two. "You're going to make a necklace out of it?"

I nodded. "A talisman, I suppose."

"That's crazy."

After a bit more polite urging, I got Jenna to help me drill two holes through the bottle's cap with her nail file. She donated a tiny black purse she didn't really need, and we removed the strap. I promised to buy her a new one.

Within a few minutes, I had the finger hanging securely around my neck. I stuffed it under my shirt.

"How does it look?" I asked her.

"I almost can't see it," she said, examining me. "But even if it was invisible, I'd know it was there. And that's not attractive. Do you really have to carry it around?"

"If it's an object, it has a power," I said. "All the objects I've seen have to be worn by the user in order to work."

"What if it has the power to cook eggs or switch channels on the TV?"

"Mildly useful," I said. "But I think it's more than that. I told you about the cultists, remember? They tried to use their powers on me, but somehow missed."

"You think this alien body part protected you? Like some kind of lucky rabbit's foot?"

"Gilling said I had *objects*—not just one. Maybe he knew, somehow."

"He sounds crazier than you are," she said.

I beamed. "I'll take that as a compliment."

"What are we going to do now?" she asked.

"We're not going to do anything. I'm going to test it."

"You mean—you're going to see if it protects you?"

"Yes, and since I'm pretty sure it will only protect the wearer, I'm going alone."

She took off her ring again and put it into my hand. "I really want you to use this," she said, clearly expecting an argument. "Consider it a loan if that helps. I can't find out what happened to Robert with it. But I bet you'll be glad to have a little luck now and then."

This time, after a moment of hesitation, I took the ring. Her logic persuaded me—OK, and a little touch of greed. I eyed the golden circle, trying not to feel excited about it. Somehow, these objects captivated my mind. I put the ring on my thinnest finger and twisted it so the diamond was on the inside. It looked like a simple gold band.

"I'm going to give this back when I return," I said.

"I know."

I tried out the ring, using it to cheat at Keno in the lobby restaurant. I was careful, only winning every tenth game or so. Jenna had told me she didn't feel good about using her ring anywhere other than the Lucky Seven. She still held a grudge against that place. I wasn't interested in money—I only needed enough to survive. But I wanted to know how to use my objects.

Half an hour later, I left Jenna and headed for the Lucky Seven. I wanted to have another talk with Rostok. I figured Jenna was probably safer without the ring than she was with it, anyway. These objects seemed to attract trouble.

28

I didn't get to Rostok right away. Someone had just been found dead in the Lucky Seven, under less-than-ideal circumstances, and that changed things.

The hotel was less imposing in the dying daylight. It was also less attractive without the twinkling green lights. The casino resembled two square towers of gray concrete—which was exactly what it was. I approached the building in the shade of the west tower and walked up the red-carpeted steps. I felt numerous eyes on me the moment I passed through the polished glass doors. Undoubtedly, a dozen cameras and eyeballs were checking me out. As I crossed the hotel lobby, a man in a khaki uniform with a mustache that covered his upper lip in red-pepper bristles tapped me on the shoulder. After some initial confusion, I realized first off that someone was dead; McKesson had been called but hadn't gotten there yet; and that rather than being about to give me the boot, they wanted me up to the room where the murder had occurred right away. As they put it, "You work with McKesson, right?" And who was I to say I didn't? After all, we often wound up appearing together at unpleasant events. McKesson would be mad I'd pretended to be his partner, but I'd deal with him later.

In the bowels of the hotel, we passed through a door with a combination lock, like the one I'd encountered on my first trip to visit Rostok. I wondered if I would be meeting the hotel's owner and his pet named Ezzie again today. I rather hoped I wouldn't, even though they were the most probable sources of hard information in this place.

"The body is right inside," the security guy told me. He stopped and tapped on the combination lock. It beeped five times then clicked open.

I must have had a funny look on my face, because he frowned at me as I hesitantly stepped into the room. I tried to force myself to act calm and in charge. I straightened my shoulders and walked confidently into the dimly lit room.

The first thing that hit me was the smell. It was an awful mix of barbeque and burnt plastic. The lights were on automatic, and they flickered into full brilliance at about the same time the security guys let the door click behind me.

What I saw next stopped me in my tracks. Bernie, the pit boss that Jenna and I had just spoken with a day ago, was dead.

He was lying on his back on what appeared to be a conference table. He hadn't passed away in his sleep either. He had a foot-wide burn mark over his body—a long streak of charcoal, as if someone had run him over with a steam iron. Blackened flesh and melted clothes had fused together. His one remaining eye was open, staring sightlessly at the fluorescent lights directly overhead.

I took an unsteady step forward, with my hand over my nose. Getting closer to the corpse wasn't making the smell any better. I walked around the conference table, looking for evidence. The carpet was burned at the foot of the table, where something hot had first gotten hold of the man. That streak of melted carpet fibers could only have been caused by intense heat. It led from a spot on the floor about six feet from the corpse. The trail was straight and purposeful. Whatever had caused it had rolled right up and right over Bernie. But the trail ended abruptly after that. There was no sign of a burned path leading into or out of the room. The conference table itself was barely scorched. There were even a few paper cups and a stray pen sitting undisturbed on the table itself.

I checked Bernie's wrists next. His hands had been burned away to bone and ash. I assumed this might be considered a defensive wound. He'd burned away his hands trying to defend himself. But his wrists were intact, and there were lines of blood and flaked skin around each of them. I nodded, still holding my nose. Someone had cuffed him and let him die helplessly.

My immediate suspicion, of course, was that it had been Ezzie, or one of her type. It almost certainly had been a creature like the lava slug I'd found in the middle of my burnt house. What else could it be? The evidence pointed toward an organized effort, however. The only way such a creature could get into and out of a building without burning it down was via a rip in space. Could the cultists be involved? Gilling might have brought it in, rolled it over him, and then popped it home again. Or maybe that was Rostok's power, here inside the Lucky Seven. Maybe that's why he had Ezzie, because he could move things into and out of his domain.

Frowning, I straightened up. I knew I didn't have much time left. I was surprised, in fact, that McKesson hadn't shown up yet. He was the master when it came to finding freaky crimes.

I opened the door and stepped out between the two security men, both of whom were waiting nervously in the hall. I noticed that they took pains not to look inside the conference room.

"This is quite a mess you have here," I said.

"You got that right," Mr. Red Mustache said. "How are you going to do it? A big black body bag and an ambulance around the back? We'll wheel the gurney out ourselves. The less the paramedics see, the better."

"I'm afraid we have a problem," I said.

They looked instantly worried.

"News has leaked out about this—accident," I said. "Do either of you have cell phones on your persons?"

Sagging jaws. They blinked and looked confused.

"We didn't call anyone, Mr. Draith."

I nodded as if I didn't believe a word they said. "I see. Well, it doesn't really matter. The call records are all there in the system, aren't they? We'll find out in the end. In any case, I need to talk to Mr. Rostok."

"That's not possible—"

"It's not only possible, it needs to happen *now*. If you don't want a news wagon out there in the valet parking with a satellite uplink to Los Angeles, I'd suggest you cooperate and quit trying to cover your tracks."

"We aren't covering up anything," Mr. Mustache said. "We didn't call anyone—did you, Nate?"

Nate shook his head. His eyes were big and scared.

"If corpses can't be neatly disposed of, a guilty party must be found. Can either of you two gentlemen guess who that might turn out to be in this situation?"

Confusion on their faces was replaced by panic. "Right this way, Mr. Draith."

They put me on a private elevator to the top floor. After crossing an empty lobby, I found myself in front of a familiar door. It opened at my approach. As before, no one greeted me at first. I took a confident step forward into the darkened room and stood calmly.

"Can I sit down while my eyes adjust, Mr. Rostok?"

"You may indeed, Mr. Draith," came the rumbling response. "You've changed, haven't you? Death stalks you, and it has built character where there was none before."

Not quite sure what he was getting at, I felt in front of me until I found the chair I'd sat in previously. I put my butt in the seat and peered into the gloom. The LED lights were there, I could see them faintly all around me. I thought to myself I should bring a flashlight next time I came to visit this reclusive man.

"I'm through with riddles, if that's what you mean," I said. "Let's cut the crap, shall we? Ezzie killed Bernie. The evidence is clear. You called McKesson to clean up the mess. Must be nice to have the police so terrified of unexplainable deaths they are willing to clean up your messes for you."

"It is convenient." Rostok chuckled. "But Ezzie didn't kill anyone. She's old now, you see. Her kind become larger and cooler as they age. You would have smelled burnt carpet the first time you met her in this room if she'd been hot enough to hurt anyone."

"Hmm. I suppose you have a point there. But it was definitely one of her kind. Are you denying involvement?"

"Tell me, is this Bernie person your golfing partner? Or perhaps a friend you get drunk with? Have you two exchanged your most private sorrows?"

"Far from it."

"Then why are you so interested in how he died? It's not your job. You're not really a detective."

I snorted. "I think I'm a better investigator than McKesson. He is the opposite of a detective. Rather than seeking truth, he's a master of deceit. But I'll tell you why I'm interested. Because everyone I seem to get close to—dies. They all die in bizarre, usually horrible ways. Wouldn't you want to know who was behind such murders?"

Rostok moved, standing up and walking past me. I saw his hulking shadow and heard his footsteps upon the carpet. Then I heard ice cubes falling into a glass. "Would you like a drink?" he asked.

"Sure."

"I suppose I would want to understand what was happening to me in your situation," he said. "But the answers aren't here for you. In fact, your arrival here a second time might endanger my life as well."

"More riddles? Is that all you have for me?"

Liquids filled a glass I couldn't see. Ice tinkled and clicked.

"Reach out your hand," he said.

I did so, and a glass was pressed into my palm. I brought it to my nose to identify the beverage. It was vodka with some cream flavorings. I sipped it and found it pleasant. Unsurprisingly, Rostok drank the pricey stuff.

"Have you ever heard of Indian Springs?" he asked.

"No. Have you ever heard of Howard Hughes?"

Rostok laughed at that, the first real laugh I'd heard from him. "Say what you will, but my paranoia has served me well," he said.

"Tell me about Indian Springs, then."

"It's a small town less than a hundred kilometers north of here. Just beyond that, they set off more nuclear tests than anywhere else in the world. There have been about two thousand such tests in all history, and nine hundred and fifty-one of them were performed very near Las Vegas. Did you know that?"

I thought about it. "I suppose that I did. But it's not something that I think about every day. Are you saying that Ezzie and her kind are some sort of mutants? Because I'm not buying that."

"No, not at all. I'm saying that they performed a lot of strange tests in the last century—playing with physics, you understand. It is my belief that they did more than split atoms under this desert. I think they fractured something bigger."

"Fractured what?"

"I don't know. A membrane between two coexistent places, maybe. Our world appears solid to us, but really it is more like a liquid. These rips in space—I think they are akin to splashing raindrops. They cause a disruption in the otherwise flat, featureless surface of our reality."

I shook my head and gulped my drink. His theories were interesting, but I knew they were only theories. I also knew they weren't helping me. "Can we get back to what happened to Bernie?"

"You said it yourself. *You* happened to Bernie. Everyone you get close to dies."

I stared at the man's dark shape. I didn't like his answer. I thought of Jenna, Holly, even McKesson—I didn't want any of them to die. They were the only people I knew. Well…I guess I wouldn't miss McKesson all that much…

"How do I stop this?" I asked. "What should I do?"

"I think I'm getting old." Rostok sighed. "I shouldn't be talking to you so much. I think these matters are best left alone, Draith. So forget them and live your life. It's time for you to leave now."

I wanted to rage at him in frustration. I decided to give it one last try. "What does your object do in this place, sir? What power do you have over this domain that makes you so strong?"

Rostok chuckled in the darkness. "Pray you never learn the truth about that."

"You want to get rid of me to protect yourself," I said. "Even if I leave now, are you sure you'll be safe from my curse? I've been here to see you twice in the span of a few days. Several events have occurred around the Lucky Seven that needed—cleaning up."

Rostok was silent for a second. "Tell me," he said. "What's the first thing you remember?"

I paused. I'd expected him to become angry. I'd hoped that by poking at his obvious paranoia, I would get more out of him. Instead, he'd switched topics on me and ignored my bait. I almost told him that I could barely remember anything. The accident had eaten up my past. Thinking about it now, I felt more empty than ever. I'd lost all my belongings. If I had a family, I hadn't been able to find them. The only thing I had was the picture that had survived the accident. Two smiling parents and a baby who might or might not be me. No other clues.

"I don't remember much," I admitted.

"Well, work with what you have, then. That's all any of us can do."

After that, he shooed me away. I left even more determined to learn the truth.

When I stepped out of the elevator and into the hallway, I encountered the opposition. There stood McKesson and two red-faced security men. None of them was smiling.

"You've been in there to see the old man?" McKesson asked me. "You've got more balls than brains, you know that, Draith?"

"I've heard that," I said. I looked past the two security guys. They had a gurney with them. A large, lumpy mass filled the body bag on the gurney. "Bernie, I presume?"

McKesson gestured furiously for the security men to take the body down the hallway. They did so, and I had no doubt there was a waiting ambulance outside in the alley. I felt sure the paramedics didn't have their flashers on, and I doubted they would take the body to the city morgue.

"What do you do in cases like this, Jay?" I asked McKesson. "I mean, do you have a big hole full of bones in the desert somewhere? Or do you have a one-way garbage chute set up to dump your waste into the world of the Gray Men? Is that why they are so pissed off?"

McKesson laughed unpleasantly. "That would be pretty cool, actually."

"So, what do you want to do next?" I asked.

McKesson's hand slipped down to his gun. He did it in a natural motion, as if he were adjusting his clothing. He smiled at me confidently.

"It's time to take you in, Draith. You're interfering with my job. Sorry, it's nothing personal."

I didn't plan to turn around and let him snap cuffs on me. He read my eyes, and gave a tiny nod. Neither of us said anything. He made his move, and I did the same. Both of us pulled our pistols out and had the barrel in the other guy's face.

"No plans to come along quietly, eh?" McKesson asked. He jerked his head toward the elevator. Is Rostok dead up there? Did you manage to take out the old man too?"

I glared at him. "We had this argument when we first met. I'm not an assassin."

"All I know is that people keep dying around you, Draith. Important people."

I decided to take a chance. Probably, in retrospect, it was a foolish chance. I grabbed his gun hand with my left and pushed it aside. At the same time, I pushed my weapon into his throat.

There were two dry clicks. McKesson had pulled the trigger. I'm not sure if the gun would have taken part of my face off, if it had fired. It was being pushed off target—but he had fired pretty fast. McKesson must have figured he had to shoot.

"What the hell?" he gasped. For perhaps the first time since I'd met him, I saw real fear in his eyes.

"Your gun misfired," I said. "Happens all the time. I guess I just got lucky. You should buy the good ammo next time, not that cheap South American crap." I knew, naturally, that luck had been with me. I'd grabbed his gun with my left hand—with the very finger that wore Jenna's ring. The ring was, in fact, in direct contact with the metal of his weapon.

He stared at me for a second, baffled. "You're so crazy. I could have taken your head off."

"But you didn't. Now drop it."

The gun thumped down. Apparently, he was in no mood to try his luck against my weapon. I turned him around and cuffed him with his own cuffs. I tucked his gun into the front pocket of his jacket where he couldn't reach it. I walked him to a door marked *trash room* a hundred steps down the hall. It was locked, but my sunglasses opened it, and after that the rolling steel doors that let out onto the parking lot.

"Where's your car?" I asked.

"They're watching us on camera by now. They know."

I thought about that. Maybe he was right. "I know they're watching. But I'm working for Rostok now."

He jerked his head to look at me. I ignored him. It was hard to bluff a cop, especially this one. Whatever the case, we made it to his car unmolested. I let him sit in the passenger seat with his cuffs on while I drove. He wasn't happy.

"They are going to fry you for this, you know that, don't you?" he asked me.

"There's nothing here to fry," I said. "I'm empty. I'm a ghost without a past."

"What are you talking about now?"

I gave him my story, telling him about my missing memories. He stared at me with growing apprehension. Clearly, he figured I belonged in a straitjacket.

"Where are we going?" he asked.

I didn't answer. I headed south, turned east on Sunset, and pulled over at Sunset Park. It was dark now, and there were only a few kids and weirdos around. I dug in the glove compartment.

"What the hell are you doing?" he asked.

I had figured him for a habitual quitter. I found his pack of emergency smokes and a lighter in the glove box. I took out the lighter. McKesson fell quiet as he watched me. It was as if he suspected I was going to singe his eyebrows with the lighter. I remembered him pulling the trigger of his pistol, and thought to myself he'd look pretty funny without eyebrows.

I took the picture of my parents out of its case. There it was: a baby in a bounce chair. My smiling parents clustered close around me, my dad's arm extended to full length to get the shot. If that baby was me, I'd never looked happier.

I flicked the lighter. It took three tries to get it to catch. These cheap safety lighters always hurt your thumb. I sat there behind the steering wheel, breathing hard. This was more difficult than I'd thought it would be. I told myself the flame would only mar one tiny corner.

I held the picture in my left hand and the lighter in my right. I didn't put the flame *under* the picture, but instead brought it down from above to a corner. It took an effort of will, but I touched the flame down to the least interesting corner of the photo. There was no one there, I told myself. The lighter would only blacken what looked like a refrigerator in the background. It would give the picture a bit of character, that's all.

The flame touched the picture for a half second, then I pulled it away. I was sweating.

"Your family?" McKesson said.

"I think so," I said, flicking the lighter again. It had gone out.

"Nice-looking couple. You don't have to do this, you know."

"Do what?"

"Throw it all away. Burn your past."

I studied the photo. Was it a little browner in that corner? It was hard to tell. I turned on the car's dome light and inspected it.

"You know, you've been through a lot lately," McKesson was saying. "People often give up when under heavy stress. I know some people you can talk to."

I let my hands drop to my lap. "Would you shut up?" I asked. "This is hard to do."

McKesson's soft-guy voice vanished as quickly as it had appeared. "All right, asshole. Just tell me straight, are you going to do yourself, me, or the both of us?"

I stared at him for a second. "I'm not shooting anyone. I'm trying to see if this picture will burn."

Again, he gave me that wary stare. I could tell he still thought I was crazy, but this time, he was certain. I flicked the lighter and held it under the picture again. I touched it there, then pulled away, then did it again. Finally, I held it there for ten long seconds, then I let the lighter go out. I held the picture under McKesson's nose.

"There," I said, "see? It's an object. That's why it survived the wreck, my burned house—everything."

McKesson's eyes traveled from me to the picture and back again. "Maybe it has a coating, or something."

"No, no, man," I said. I grabbed the picture again and tried to rip it in half. This act was relatively easy now, as I no longer believed I could damage the picture. The paper flexed and folded, but didn't tear. It was like the strongest plastic I'd ever tried to rip.

"You see?" I asked him. "It's an object. Like your watch. They can't be destroyed."

"Who told you that?" he asked. He stared at me like I was some kind of homeless junkie talking about my secret invisible friends. Was it possible he didn't know all that much about the objects in general?

"Let me show you," I said coldly, putting the picture against his shoulder. I was tired of people telling me I was crazy. I knew what I knew. I aimed my gun at the picture and made sure there were no organs behind the spot.

"What the fuck are you—" he began.

I pulled the trigger. Inside the enclosed car, the bang was deafening, followed instantly by the sound of the bullet ricocheting and a weird cracking noise. I'd angled the gun so the ricochet wouldn't hit me, but the moment after I did it, I realized it had been a dumb, impulsive move.

McKesson roared in pain, twisting around.

"You shot me. I can't believe it. You shot me."

"Calm down. You're not hit, and the bullet could've just as easily hit me. And look…"

I held the picture up. It was perfect. There wasn't even a crease. McKesson stared. He looked down at his shoulder. There was no hole—no blood.

"Where'd the bullet go?"

I pointed to the windshield. There was a new star of shattered glass there, right in front of his face.

"It bounced off the picture then punched through the glass. You'll have a bruise, but you'll be fine."

McKesson stared at me, fear battling with anger. Then, finally, he broke into laughter. It was the laughter of a man reprieved. "You're crazy," he said, but there was a look almost like admiration on his face.

I shrugged. "I just have nothing left to lose."

"You know how much a windshield costs?" McKesson asked, shaking his head and nursing his shoulder.

"So you believe me now?" I said.

"Yeah, but you didn't have to shoot me."

"Remember those two dry clicks?" I asked him. "Now we're even."

We glared at each other quietly for a second.

"Those dry clicks were a cop's reflex," he said finally.

"I've felt the same urge. But now we have to work together."

"So how many damned objects do you have?"

"One too many. I don't know what this picture does, but I know it was the one I started with."

McKesson eyed me. "I'll give you some new information about these things."

"What?"

"Uncuff me, and I'll tell you."

I thought about it, and then nodded. "Truce, though, right? No more guns?"

"OK, Scout's honor."

I didn't trust him worth a damn, and I didn't think he'd ever been a Scout, but I figured we were even now. I put my gun in my pocket and released him. I watched him warily, expecting to get punched. He rubbed his wrists and his bruised shoulder.

"No wonder the perps hate cuffs," he muttered.

"Do you have something to tell me, or was that bullshit?" I asked.

"I don't know that much. I only have one, and I know how to use it. Most of the time, I try to avoid them, or eliminate them, or return them to their powerful owners. That's my job. I'm a peacekeeper and for that, the Community likes me and gives me—special considerations."

"Go on."

"The objects are all trouble. Every one of them will give you bad luck in the end, and using them is like bad karma. The main reason for this is they tend to attract one another. Power draws power to itself—no one I've talked to knows why. That's one reason why you'll tend to meet people with only one object. The more objects you have, the more bad things tend to be attracted to you. Like gravity."

"I don't follow," I said, although it sounded a lot like what Jenna had told me before. "You should still run into people with more than one object. I mean, if they attract one another, then someone is bound to mug someone else and have two objects."

"Right. But the thing is, those people usually end up dead—really fast."

30

We cruised for a time, but McKesson's watch ticked away normally, showing the proper time rather than indicating a new rip in space. Deciding to call it a night, I talked McKesson into dropping me off on the Strip. It was getting late, but I knew I wouldn't sleep for hours. I thought about visiting Holly and Jenna, but I figured they were probably safer on their own than hanging around with me and my load of objects. Besides, I wasn't quite sure what to do next.

The gaudy lights were still on, but the Strip was relatively quiet. During the day, all six lanes were buzzing with tourists. After 2:00 a.m., the sparse traffic consisted largely of cabs and cop cars. Walking north, I passed the Miracle Mile shopping mall and continued on to the mini Eiffel Tower, where construction projects were underway. They always seemed to be building something new along the Strip. Besides the cabs, tourists, and cops, there was a significant population of...unusual people. I passed a man wearing a well-used backpack. He had a bushman's beard that was shot with gray-white stripes. His glasses were shaded green, but appeared to be prescription. Despite the cool night sky, his face was leathery from a thousand sunburns and he wore a cap with a visor like a duck's bill. Like so many before him, he sized me up as I approached the lamppost where he'd stationed himself. I could almost see the gears working. I looked like I had more money than he did, but he could tell I wasn't likely to give it to him. Out of habit or sheer stubbornness, he tried to talk to me. The unintelligible words came out as a wheeze.

"No money," I said.

He shook his head, indicating that wasn't what he was asking for. I had no idea what was on his mind, but I stopped and rummaged in my pockets. I found McKesson's cigarette pack and lighter. I must have shoved them away automatically. I wasn't sure if I was a smoker or not, but either way I didn't want to try one. I might be kick-starting a dead habit. I handed them over.

They were received with an appreciative cough. "Thanks, buddy," I heard.

I kept walking. A cluster of businessmen approached next. Their conversation was loud and alcohol-fueled, punctuated by laughter. I thought to myself that here, at least, were some people enjoying themselves. When we drew close and passed by, my one body to their four, they stepped aside and quieted. They gave me as much space on the sidewalk as they could.

Why was that? I asked myself. How did they *know* I was different? What instinct or facial expression had tipped them off? Sure, I had a gun in my pocket that probably still stank of gunpowder from being recently fired. But they had no way of knowing that. I wore fresh clothes, including a

hoodie, but I wasn't bug-eyed and scowling. Still, they somehow knew to be wary.

The encounter disturbed me more than others I'd had
because I'd already begun to suspect I was a walking dis-
aster. The more I learned of my life, past and present, the
more it involved danger for anyone who came near.

What had Rostok said about my past? To work with what
I had. That meant the photo, I'd supposed at first. I had
studied it, and come up blank. There was no date on the
back. The picture looked new, even though it had obviously
been taken many years earlier. I suspected that was due to
the fact that it was an object. If they couldn't be burned,
they were probably immune to the effects of time as well.

What else had he said? He'd asked me about my earliest memories. He seemed unsurprised I'd lost my memory.
There were no questions about that. Was amnesia so common a thing that it would go unremarked upon? I didn't
think it was. Where did that leave me? I thought hard for a
while, and there was only one person I could come up with:
Dr. Meng. She'd let me go and asked me to keep doing what
I was doing, to get at the bottom of the deaths. I certainly
hadn't found many answers, but I knew enough to make a
report. I decided I would return to the sanatorium in the
morning and talk to Meng again. Maybe, with the new information I had, she could fit more pieces into this puzzle, and
we could help each other.

At the next corner, I paused for a red light near a bus
stop. Two Asian girls leaned sleepily together on the bus
stop bench. Their heads touched to form a pyramid for
mutual support. One wore a spray of magenta spikes, while
the other's hair was a tropical blue. They both sported
nose rings and clusters of what looked like staples punched
through their ears. Flame-shaped tattoos grew up out of

both their blouses to lick their necks. They were young and pretty, despite their best attempts to the contrary. I could tell they were tired, rather than destitute. The pair caused me to smile faintly. They were only travelers, far from home. I suspected the dyes could be washed out and some of the metal bits were just clip-ons. Maybe the matching tattoos were spray-ons as well. In any case, they were clearly up past their bedtime.

Something about the two girls on the bench made me dig out my cell and call Holly. I figured she'd probably gone home by now. I'd avoided it up until now, not wanting to explain Jenna or apologize for meeting her. There had been a waiting game going on between us, I realized. Neither of us had called the other all day. I had to admit, there had been a lot going on and I hadn't really thought about it much. But I figured she probably had been thinking about us. I wasn't sure how my call would be received. Had she grown angrier, or cooled off? There was only one way to find out.

"Hello?" a familiar voice said.

She had answered on the second ring at 2:00 a.m. I figured that was a good sign.

"Hi," I said, trying to sound neutral, as if all was well. "I'm out on the Strip—"

"Looking for another place to stay the night, is that it?" she snapped.

"I was the one who took you in last time."

"Still, you're looking for a bed, aren't you? What happened? Did she have to go home to take care of her kids?"

"Holly, you're jumping to conclusions." I was going to continue, but hesitated. I'd been about to say that Jenna and I had never slept together—but we actually had slept in the same bed. Then I was going to say we hadn't had sex—but we *had* kissed. And I'd have been lying if I said there wasn't something going on between the two of us. I felt a little hot, despite the cool evening breezes.

"What were you going to say?" Holly asked.

"Look, Jenna isn't my girlfriend. I've been helping her find her husband, who stepped into one of those rips and never came out again."

"Oh," she said. "That's different. So there's nothing between you two?"

"There have been some emotional moments. I've hugged her—you know, to comfort her."

"I see," Holly said. Her voice had turned cooler again, but not angry, not icy. Wary. Finally, she sighed. "I'm sorry then. I'm just tired of players, you know? I've been messed with too many times."

I wanted to tell her I'd been under the impression we'd had some casual fun the night before, and I hadn't figured we'd gotten engaged yet. But none of those words would help me, so I didn't bother. Instead, I told her a heavily edited story about my day. I left out unpleasant details like shooting McKesson in the shoulder.

"I could use your help," she said when I was finished. "I need to go back to the apartment and get my stuff. Just a few things."

"You mean the money, right?"

"Yeah."

"Haven't you slipped back inside and gathered all that hidden cash up yet?"

"I tried, but they put up a new door and the cops have it taped up. My key didn't work. But I know you can get in."

"Yeah, OK," I said. "Come pick me up."

I gave her the address and ten minutes later we were driving in her car. She was quiet at first and I thought she was still angry. I thought about giving her an apology, but I didn't think I'd done anything wrong. We drove quietly through town in sparse traffic.

Holly let out a heavy sigh. "I'm sorry," she said.

"It's all right," I said, thinking she meant her tirade concerning Jenna. "I understand the confusion."

"No, not about—whoever."

"What then?"

She paused for a moment, as if struggling with words. "You've been very nice, Quentin," she said at last. "You don't deserve someone like me in your life, that's the truth."

I glanced at her. I didn't know what to say, so I kept quiet.

"Remember when we first met?" she asked.

"Sure, at Tony's."

"I didn't show up there by accident. I was sent there."

Alarm bells went off in my head. I recalled thinking Holly's appearance was a big coincidence at the time, but I'd somehow forgotten about that. I began to worry. Maybe I wasn't paranoid enough.

"Who sent you?"

"Gilling."

Slowly, I nodded my head. "Why'd he send you?"

"To find and steal the sunglasses. To find Tony's stuff—whatever he had. Instead, I found you."

My head began to pound. She'd been working for the cultists. "That's why I found you in his basement, then? Because you failed to rip me off?"

"I didn't plan to rip you off. I didn't know it was going to be *you* I met at Tony's place."

"Why did Gilling chain you in his cellar?"

"I think he was trying scare me into giving his money back. But I'd already spent it by that time, even though I didn't bring him what he wanted."

"Let me get this straight, you took money to snuggle up to me and take my objects?"

Holly shook her head and reached out a hand to touch my arm. "No. It wasn't like that. I went down there to look around for the sunglasses. You had them, so I followed you around for a while. But I never tried to take them. I guess you kind of grew on me. Anyway, Gilling became tired of waiting and grabbed me."

"Why didn't you tell me any of this when I found you in the basement?"

She shrugged and looked embarrassed. "I don't know. I liked you. I didn't want you to dump me."

I wasn't sure what I felt about Holly now. I fumed all the way to her apartment door.

"Are we still friends?" she asked me quietly, standing there in the dark.

I nodded after a moment. "Yeah."

I worked my magic on the door and it popped open. I had time to give Holly a smug smile. She kissed me on the cheek and pushed her way through a mile of yellow tape and stepped inside.

I should have been on my guard. I should have gone in with my gun in my hand—but I didn't. I was too busy thinking about Holly and impressing her with my little sunglasses trick.

The Gray Men were waiting for us.

The door had been sealed, but of course that didn't matter to them. They could go anywhere they wanted. The first Gray Man was standing right there in front of the coffee table as we stepped inside and snapped on the lights. Only, it was a Gray Woman this time. She was the first alien female I'd encountered—unless Ezzie counted. I was surprised, even though I shouldn't have been. She wore a hood, as had others I'd seen. I noticed her hands didn't have spurs on the backs of them. Perhaps the females of the species didn't get spurs.

In the split second before I fumbled in my pocket for my gun, I realized the alien was examining objects on the coffee table. She had Holly's TV remote in her hands, holding it high. She ran some kind of cube-shaped, metallic device over it. The metal seemed to shine and twist in her hand as she scanned the TV remote with it. I had no doubt it was some kind of scientific instrument.

"Hey, that's mine," Holly said, reaching for the remote. I came in behind her, and I had my gun out now, but no clear shot with Holly in the way.

The alien glanced at us, and Holly froze. I think she hadn't realized the stranger wasn't human until that moment. She hadn't seen the gray fingers and understood what they meant. The eyes were particularly strange—they were gray as well, but looked more like silver due to being wet. The hood slipped away from the head, and I got a good look at her. There was no hair on her head. None at all. A smooth gray skin covered everything except those eyes.

I took aim. But that's when something touched my head from behind. It touched me just behind the ear. A blinding jolt of pain and numbness filled me. I tumbled forward, passing out. I stayed conscious long enough to see the second alien step over me and grab Holly, applying his weapon to her skull as well.

I wanted to rise. I wanted to pull out my gun and shoot them both—but everything went black before I could do anything further.

31

When I woke up, I could barely breathe and couldn't move my limbs. For a good minute, my arms wouldn't obey me. I figured I'd been shocked—or something like it. My nerves weren't operating properly. I dragged myself up with legs that flopped and stung like they'd been bloodless for several minutes. Slowly, with a great deal of unpleasant tingling, my body began to function again. I sat down on the couch, rubbing my head. I didn't see any sign of the Gray Men or Holly.

As soon as my mind was working again, I located my possessions. They were all there: the photo, the sunglasses, the ring, and the finger around my neck. They hadn't even taken my gun. I found that strange, but I didn't have time to puzzle it out now.

When I could stand, I stumbled through the apartment calling for Holly. There was only one bedroom, and I found the rip there. It was shrinking already, the colors those of a dying flame. I could see through the rip this time—which was good. Unlike with Gilling's failures, I at least had some warning as to what I was going to find at the other end. I also assumed that I would be able to return—if I moved quickly enough.

I opened up my cell and called McKesson.

"Jay here," he answered.

"Detective? It's Draith."

"Talk fast."

"They've got Holly. The Gray Men were in her apartment—two of them at least."

"Oh, so that's where I'm headed," he said. "Thanks for the tip."

I realized he must be coming here already, having followed the directions of his watch. "They knocked me out and stepped back out," I said. "They must have taken her with them."

"But not you, eh? How come nothing ever happens to you? Are you sure you aren't the one on the wrong side, Draith?"

"Screw you."

"Just a question. Stay there. I'll arrive in one minute flat."

"No chance," I said. "I'm stepping out after her."

I closed the cell phone and never heard if he liked the idea or not. I didn't care. I only hesitated for one second further before I stepped into the rip. It was like cliff-diving— the best approach was not to think about the craziness of what you were doing. Once inside the blurred region of air, which hovered directly over Holly's bed, I was able to keep moving forward. My shoes soon crunched on desert sand.

The scene that appeared to me was both familiar and strange. As before, it greatly resembled the open desert of southern Nevada, but without the structures of man. Instead, a building stood nearby built all of randomly stacked cubes. Windowless and opaque, the structure loomed perhaps a hundred feet high. Off to my left—possibly to the east, was another, much larger structure. That was the city I'd seen before. A stack of cubes so huge it matched the mountains in the region for size and height.

None of that mattered to me, however, because Holly lay on the ground at my feet. She had been stripped to her skin, and all of her belongings were missing. Even her earrings had been ripped out. Both her earlobes trickled blood.

I knelt beside her, cradled her head, and spoke to her, but I already knew the truth. There was more blood pooled under her body, caking up the sands. They had shot her through the heart several times.

My eyes stung, but I couldn't seem to shed a tear. I wasn't just sad, I was angry, furious. Holly had shared the only life I knew and now she was dead, and I didn't know the reason for it. What if there wasn't a reason for it?

"Why you and not me?" I asked no one.

I gazed toward the cubical stack. They had to have gone there. It was less than a mile away. I didn't see a vehicle, but there were footprints and a single, wide swath in the sand. The strange track led away from this place back toward the smaller pile of cubes. It looked like the sort of track a bull-dozer would leave behind.

I tried to think clearly, to plan my next move, but it was difficult. We hadn't known one another long, but I definitely felt something for Holly.

They'd stripped her, presumably to figure out whether any of her possessions were objects, and then shot her and dumped her here. They'd taken everything from her, looking for objects, but left mine alone. Why?

For the first time, I wondered if my amnesia had been induced by trauma. Had I lost too many friends in just such a manner? Had it broken my mind and left me unable to recall any of it after the accident? I couldn't be sure.

I wanted revenge, of course. I burned for it. Not just for Holly, but for all the rest of them. For people I couldn't remember and for those I didn't know well. For future victims, of which I was sure there would be many.

Did I have a chance, given the odds? No, but I stepped onto the path toward the cubes anyway.

"Don't do it, Draith," called a familiar voice. "It's not the right time."

I glanced back to see McKesson. He'd stepped through the rip and stood on the sands behind me.

"That's a murder victim," I said. "You're a detective. I could use your help."

For once, McKesson didn't have his usual sarcastic swagger. "We can't win," he said. "Not here, not now. This is their territory. They outnumber us a billion to one."

McKesson knelt beside Holly, checking her pulse. His hand fell away.

"A sad waste," he said. "She's the hooker who found you the night of the accident, right?"

"Holly wasn't a hooker," I said angrily.

"Yeah, OK. Be cool."

"Let's do something about it," I said. I lifted my .32 auto and looked at him seriously.

"Two pistols against a building full of armed aliens?" he asked. "Like I said, I fight when the odds are in my favor, Draith. Come back home with me. This rip is going to fade soon."

"I'm not letting them get away with this."

McKesson suddenly grew angry. "All right, fine. Go on. March over there and die. They're watching us right now, you know. They aren't fools."

"They'd have shot us by now if they could."

"Maybe. Or maybe we're part of their plan. They could have killed us by now."

"You don't even care? You just cover their tracks and let more people die? Why not expose them, set up an army of cops to blow them away the next time they step through?"

McKesson rubbed his face. "It might turn out that way, someday. I'm getting tired of these Gray Men, same as you are. But for now, I've got my orders."

It always came down to that. No matter how many times we teamed up, McKesson could never get out from under his mysterious bosses.

"Who gives them?"

He shook his head, refusing to answer.

"I should shoot you again," I said.

"I've still got a bruise the size of Delaware from the last time you did."

I glanced at his right shoulder. He seemed to be favoring it. I hoped it hurt a lot.

"Are you at least going to help me carry her body home?" I asked.

"Yeah," he said, glancing back toward the rip, which was turning orange now and seemed to be moving more slowly. "But let's hurry. This thing is about to die."

We carried Holly back home together, and as I felt her cooling skin against my palms, I swore I would have my pound of flesh. I supposed that was the way all wars escalated, but I didn't care. She looked very young and as if she were just sleeping. Which made it worse.

McKesson insisted on dressing her in a robe before we called the cops. "It already looks enough like a sex crime," he explained.

This just seemed to add insult to injury and made me madder. "So the hell what?"

"You are a boyfriend. Even with me helping out, you might spend a few days being sweated by the guys downtown. I don't run the whole department. Which way do you want it?"

I shook my head and went to the closet to search. Everything Holly owned in the way of bed wear was sexy. There were silk pieces and satin pieces—I took a short robe of lavender satin because at least it wasn't see-through. Even though the point was not just to help me, but to give her some dignity, it all felt wrong. Here I was, helping a detective alter evidence at the scene of a crime. I wondered how many things like this happened every day. I hoped the count was low. I brought him the satin robe and held it out to him.

"You put it on her," he said. "I'm not touching anything in this place. They'll have to dust her for prints. You have an excuse as the boyfriend."

I couldn't believe I was having this conversation, with Holly dead less than an hour.

"This isn't going to work," I said. "There are no bullet holes in the robe."

"Doesn't matter," he said.

"Yeah, it *does*. How can you not know that? Any coroner will know the body was moved."

McKesson stepped close to me and lowered his voice to a conspiratorial whisper. "You have to trust me," he said. "That's not how it's going to happen. All I need is good photos of her with some clothes on."

I stared at him, hating what he was implying—that more people were in on this. I realized that he had to be right. It couldn't be just McKesson cleaning things up by himself. He had to have help within the department to get away with these cover-ups. Still, I didn't think he was behind any of these events; he was caught up in them as much as I was.

"What do they pay you to do all this?" I asked him.

"Not enough."

In the end, I couldn't do it. I couldn't push Holly's dead arms into the robe. Instead, I pulled a sheet from the bed and draped it over her.

"This is going to make it harder to clear you," McKesson complained.

"You'll manage," I said, heading for the door.

"Hold on a second. I need a statement."

"Make it up."

"C'mon, Draith, give me something."

"OK, you want a statement? Here's a statement. Holly wasn't a hooker. She was a friend of mine. And now she's dead, and I don't know why."

I walked out the door and slammed it behind me.

32

Maybe it wasn't right to take Holly's car to visit Jenna, but I needed to see a familiar face, someone who I thought understood me, at least a little. I also just couldn't bring myself to hail another cab. I wanted to be alone for a while, trying hard not to think of Holly. As I drove, something McKesson had said came back to me. He'd said these objects never brought you happiness. They attracted trouble and each other. And people who carried more than one of them generally ended up dead—really fast. I had to admit, of all the bullshit I'd heard out of him, that part was certainly true.

I found Jenna's room at the hotel and let myself in. It was more than rude of me, I knew, but I was starting to get lost again, seeing in memory Holly's dead body in the desert. I knew there was no escaping the impact of that, but perhaps talking to Jenna would distract me for a while.

Maybe it was selfish of me to come see Jenna. It had occurred to me that I should stay away from her, that I was possibly endangering her life by coming back to her. But I also knew that friends died when I wasn't there to protect them too.

I stood in the half-light coming in from the bathroom, watching her sleep. She was pretty—in a different way than Holly had been. She was sexy too, but had a certain innocence about her. I thought about waking her up, or taking a shower, or simply lying down beside her and falling asleep. In the end, the minibar captured my attention. I opened it and built myself a water glass full of clear and tan liquids.

Jenna came awake with a gasp.

"Who's there?" she said.

"It's just me, Jenna," I said. "I'm sorry."

"Dammit, Draith, you shouldn't *do* that! I know you have the power, but you can't just wander into a woman's room at midnight."

"It's more like four in the morning."

"No wonder I feel like I'm having a heart attack," she said. "Don't you ever sleep at night?"

I thought about it. "No," I said. "I don't seem to. Not often, at least."

I told her why I'd come. I told her about Holly. There was no one else to tell, really. I told her and sipped my alcohol. It was warm and mixed with clashing flavors. I didn't care. It tasted like gasoline, but I still drank it.

Jenna tried to comfort me, but it didn't work. After I finished my drink, I took a shower, then I passed out on her bed. The last memory I had was of dawn gleaming under the heavy hotel curtains and of Jenna gently pulling a sheet over me.

At about noon, I got up to find she had ordered room service. She sat at the small, round table with me and ate it.

"What are you going to do next?" she asked.

"Put you on a plane home while I go back to where it all started for me: Dr. Meng's sanatorium," I said.

Jenna blinked at me for a moment. "No, I don't think so."

"Well, I do. I'm not losing you too." I couldn't get Holly's face out of my mind—the way she'd looked as I pulled the sheet over her.

"You forget, I want revenge as much as you do. I'm in this with you. I might not have quite as good a reason to be pissed off as you do, but that remains to be seen."

"Revenge? You mean against Robert?"

"I mean against whoever it was that changed him. He wasn't the same man when he stepped out on me. I think this place changed him, and he might still be alive somewhere, needing my help."

"You're still not going with me."

"How are you going to stop me?" Jenna was giving me a look that didn't brook interference.

I nodded, chewing bacon. I figured Jenna was one of those women who made up lists of excuses for husbands that cheated on them. But she did have spine. She had some good points too. Maybe something *had* happened to Robert to change him. With all the strange things going on, it was very possible. I kept going back and forth about whether I should let Jenna have her way, while she waited patiently, arms folded as she leaned back in her chair.

"OK," I said when we'd finished breakfast and I felt human again. "You can come with me to Meng's, but only because you might be safer with me than staying here. And you have to do what I say. It might get dangerous." The truth was, I needed company, and I really didn't know what would be more or less dangerous for her. At least with her by my side, I knew where she was at all times.

"Yes, boss," she replied, but somehow it didn't sound all that respectful.

We reached the sanatorium in the early afternoon. Jenna clearly knew it was Holly's car, but didn't say a word. We didn't park out front, but pulled to the curb a block or so away.

"What are you planning, exactly?" Jenna asked me.

I shrugged. "Nothing special. We'll walk up to the door and ask to see the good doctor."

"What if she doesn't want to see you?"

"Then we'll insist."

I adjusted the talisman around my neck. The purse strap was uncomfortable. The finger in the small, narrow bottle rolled around inside at times—I could feel it fall over with a tiny thumping movement when I walked fast. I tried not to think about it, or the three other objects on my person. If McKesson was right about objects attracting one another, I had to be akin to a giant cartoon magnet about now.

The sanatorium was built of heavy cement bricks. Other than sheer gray walls, the institution had only one distinguishing characteristic: a tower that loomed over the front entrance. I'd read up on the place online. The building had once served the neighborhood as a chapel. The tower looked unoccupied, but I now suspected Meng lived up there. I was quite certain she never left the premises, as this was her seat of power.

I put my hand on the worn brass door handle and pulled. It didn't budge. There was a buzzer to my left and a camera lens above that. I pressed the button for several seconds before letting up.

After a pause, I heard a female voice come over the intercom. "I'm sorry, sir, visiting hours are over for the day."

The intercom was scratchy, but I thought I recognized the voice of the nurse I'd met some days earlier under unpleasant circumstances. What was her name? Miranda, as I recalled. Her tone was professional, but I could tell that Miranda didn't want to meet me again.

I looked into the camera, but I didn't smile. I hadn't shaved for a while, and my eyes weren't welcoming. All I could think of was Holly and other friends, most of whom I'd apparently forgotten about. Someone was going to have to do a lot of explaining, and possibly pay a price.

"Open the door, Miranda," I said.

Another pause. "I'm sorry, Mr. Draith, but you'll have to—"

"I'm coming in, one way or the other. Tell Dr. Meng I've got a lot of things to report."

Five seconds later, the door buzzed. I pulled it open and Jenna followed me inside. She looked worried. There was something about mental institutions that made people nervous.

There was a waiting room inside, but it was empty. Nothing but dusty, green-upholstered furniture and a few well-worn magazines. A TV mounted high in one corner played a video loop of health ads. Maybe visiting hours really were over. I didn't care.

There was only one set of doors, so I pushed through them. They led into a hallway that looked vaguely familiar. My earliest memories were of this place. These walls didn't fill me with a homey feeling, however. Quite the opposite.

When we reached the nurses' station, there was no one there. A phone blinked on hold. Another TV was tuned to security cameras, showing the exterior of the building. A cup of coffee, half-empty, sat next to a keyboard. Closed doors lined the hallways beyond the station. Each door was built with thick steel and had a small glass window above the handle. The windows were crisscrossed with silvery wire.

"Miranda?" I called.

No response came back, not even an echo. I looked around and realized the entire floor was quiet. Since when was a building full of crazy people as silent as a morgue? I frowned. When I'd been here before, I'd figured it was around 5:00 a.m. so the other patients were asleep. But that excuse wasn't working for me now.

"Where is everyone?" Jenna whispered to me. She was standing close to me now, almost leaning up against me.

All I could hear was the buzz of fluorescent lights overhead. I glanced at Jenna, and wondered for the hundredth time since entering whether it was a colossal mistake for her to be here.

"This place is really creepy," she said. "Should we ring the bell or call someone?"

I looked at her. "Why don't you go back outside and wait?"

I could see in her face she liked the idea. She seriously considered it. She'd faced a few security guys before, and had seen the air shimmer and open up to other places. But this was different, somehow. We were invading a dangerous place and we had no backup plan to escape.

Jenna's face tightened and she shook her head. "No. I'm in this with you."

I didn't have time to argue with her, so I nodded and led her down the hallway to Dr. Meng's office. I didn't bother to tap on the door; I just tried to open it. The door was locked, so I used my sunglasses and let myself in, Jenna behind me. If they could be rude, so could I.

Dr. Meng was inside. She didn't look at all surprised to see me. She wore a welcoming smile. When she saw Jenna following me, however, she paused and raised her eyebrows.

"Hello, Quentin," she said. "Who's your friend?"

Jenna spoke up before I could tell her not to identify herself. "I'm Jenna Townsend," she said.

"Oh," Meng said, nodding. "The bride, of course. Please come in and make yourselves comfortable."

We walked in, but we didn't sit down. Jenna walked closer to the doctor's desk and stared at her. "You know who I am? You know what happened to Robert, don't you?"

"I know of him, yes," Dr. Meng said. "Please sit down."

"No, I don't think so," Jenna said. "Not until you tell me—"

Jenna broke off then. Her face had gone blank. Frowning, I stared from her to Dr. Meng, who had something in her hand now. I recognized it. A metal object of old bronze. It was the hood ornament. She lifted it up and placed it on the desk between us. I eyed the small figure of a woman in a gown with wings upraised.

"I know you're doing something to Jenna," I said, digging in my pocket for my pistol. "Let her go."

"This is my place, Mr. Draith. I make the rules here. Don't be rude and upset me."

I wasn't entirely sure what she could do, but I recalled the time she'd somehow thrown me out of her building. Maybe my talisman would protect me from such things— but maybe it wouldn't. It was untested. I decided to play it as coolly as I could.

"OK," I said, sitting down. "Is that thing supposed to be an angel?"

Dr. Meng ignored me, turning to Jenna. "Now, my dear, for the third time, *sit down*."

Jenna immediately did as she was told. If the chair hadn't been right there, she would flopped onto the floor. I saw the wooden way she moved.

Jenna stared expressionlessly. Her anger was gone. She just stared at Dr. Meng.

"An odd thing to witness, isn't it?" Dr. Meng asked. "At first, I found it disturbing. But now I like the effect. It makes life more orderly. And much quieter."

I thought, in a rush, of the dozens of silent rooms that lined the halls. Who was inside them? Were they empty, or filled with staring zombies like Jenna? I was horrified by the idea. My hand squeezed around the pistol in my jacket pocket, and my thoughts turned dark. If I simply kept it out of sight in my pocket and tilted up the barrel, I could fire without warning. I could shoot Dr. Meng and free Jenna. I could shoot her before she could turn me into a zombie and put me in one of her cells with the rest of them.

I sucked in a deep breath and tried to relax, thinking of the several objects I wore. I was a technomancer now— maybe as dangerous an individual as the good doctor herself. Her complete confidence was disturbing, however.

"So that's your power?" I asked. "To blank people's minds?"

"It's more than that," Meng said. "I can write new thoughts upon the walls of a blank mind."

"Did you damage my brain?" I asked. "Is that why my memory is incomplete?"

"You were in such a state. Really, it was a mercy. We had to repair your body *and* your mind, you see. What do you do with a computer when it will not operate, Mr. Draith? Why, you turn it off and restart it. Please try to understand and don't upset yourself."

"But when I left, I was transported out of here. You dropped me from this place onto a stairway in front of the exit."

Dr. Meng smiled and slowly shook her head. "No. That's not what happened. I simply ordered you to leave, and when you reached the limits of my domain, my grip on you faded. I'm not surprised you fell down the stairs. That's a common side effect when my grip suddenly lets go."

I gazed at her with growing alarm. I had been in her grasp from the beginning. "Why don't you just blank me right now?" I asked.

"I'm hoping you have information for me. You always do."

Those last words burned into my mind. *You always do.* I'd been here before, I thought. Maybe many times. Somehow, I knew that was true. My heart raced in my chest. I felt fearful and sick.

"Aren't you a little worried?" I asked. "Why don't you order me to put my gun on the table, at least? You know I'm armed, don't you?"

"Of course you are. Your work is inherently dangerous. You often find a weapon and use it. But to answer your question, I can tell you I conditioned you long ago not to harm me. I was never in any danger from you. Not this time, or any other time you've been in my office."

I wanted, more than anything else at that moment, to kill her. Maybe I wouldn't be able to do it, but I should at least try to free myself and Jenna. I looked at Jenna. I couldn't stand seeing her that way. Meng was a monster.

I stood up and pulled out my pistol.

"What are you doing?" Meng asked.

Was there the slightest tinge of worry in that voice? I hoped so. I hoped I made her nervous.

"Testing your theories, and mine," I said. I aimed the gun at her—or rather, I tried to. I couldn't do it. My arm refused to obey. I recalled the last time I'd invaded her office. I'd flashed the pistol and aimed it confidently at the ceiling. I'd thought at the time I was in charge. But I never had been. I hadn't aimed it at Meng because I couldn't do it.

It was a very strange thing to order your hand to obey you and have it steadfastly refuse. It wasn't as if it were numb, or as if another mind controlled it. My arm simply didn't get the message I was sending. The muscles didn't contract or loosen. Nothing happened.

I turned back to Meng, my face white. "I can't do it."

"No, you can't. Now, give me your report."

My eyes narrowed.

Meng frowned. "I said, give me your report," she repeated. This time, I thought I saw the metal statuette glitter—but it could have been my imagination.

I caught on then. She was trying to exert her dominance over me. But I didn't feel it. I didn't feel any urge to obey her at all. My mind raced. What had she said? That she was able to write new thoughts into a person's mind. Right now, it wasn't working.

I sat down then and forced my face not to grin. It was difficult.

"After I left, I wandered the streets…" I began, recounting my adventures for her.

While I spoke, she relaxed again. Everything was as it should be—but it wasn't. I was free to do anything but harm her. I paused now and then while I told my tale to think about my situation. Soon, I had a plan.

I bided my time, talking for about half an hour. There was a lot to tell. I learned a little from her by the questions Dr. Meng asked—what interested her and what didn't. She was particularly interested in the cultists. She didn't know much about them. I told her all about Gilling and his crew. I left out, naturally, everything about the finger that was hanging around my neck. She didn't need to know I could resist her magic.

The part she liked best, oddly enough, was when I told her about placing the photo against McKesson's shoulder and firing a bullet into it. She laughed aloud, saying that she wished she could have been there to see that. I gathered that the Community members all relied on McKesson—he was something like a shared Igor for them all—but none of them liked him.

At one point she turned and poured herself a fresh cup of coffee. I paused.

"Continue," she said, glancing back at me.

That imperious order left me with a flash of anger. I don't know why that particular moment caused me to feel such rage. Maybe it was the arrogance, the automatic assumption I was her plaything, her puppet.

I struggled to continue my story in an even tone of voice. While I did so, I reached up and ripped loose my talisman. The strap didn't break, but the weak metal clasp we'd attached to the bottle did. I slipped the thing down into my lap and held it there in my fist.

Next, I quietly popped the magazine out of my .32 automatic, letting it clatter onto the floor. Before she could turn around, I quickly took the photo of my supposed family and threw it on the desk between us. When she turned back, she noticed it. Her eyes slid up to me, and once again she was frowning.

"Where did this come from?" she asked.

"From my pocket," I said.

Dr. Meng stared. "I didn't tell you to put it here. Is it part of your report?"

Finally, at long last, I allowed myself to smile. In fact, I grinned broadly. The grin turned into something feral, the kind of grin the wolf must have had when it ate good old Granny.

"No, it's not," I said. I slowly lifted my gun and aimed it right at her. The look on her face was worth a year's pay to me. "I'm sorry, but I have a confession to make. I'm not in your power. I haven't been since I walked in."

She stared at the gun in absolute horror. That single expression made my day. I could aim the gun at her now because it was unloaded—but she didn't know that.

"But how?" she said.

I shrugged. "New objects," I explained.

"Why would you pretend?"

"To see what you asked about. How much you knew."

"So, your stories were real?"

"With a few omissions, yes. Now I want to know some things. Let's call it *your* report."

"I'll grant you one question for initiative," she said.

I eyed her. She still sounded self-confident, but that could have been an act. I decided to ask my question regardless. "Why did you send me out there to wander around?"

"I thought that was obvious. To locate rogues with objects and mark them for death."

"Death," I said, somehow surprised to hear her admit that was the mission. I felt hot and mildly sick. I really had been an assassin of sorts. The hound leading the hunters. "So you fed this information to the Gray Men? They weren't trying to kill me all this time, they were trying to kill the people I located?"

Meng shrugged. She eased herself into her chair across from me. I let her do it. I reached out to her desk and tapped the picture.

"Is this my family?" I asked her.

"I honestly don't know. You had it with you when we picked you up. It was your sole object, your qualification as a rogue."

"What does the photograph do?" I asked.

She smirked at me. "Haven't figured that out yet?" she asked. She reached toward it, slowly stretching her arm across the table. As if by chance, she brushed against her bronze statuette. My empty gun tracked her movements. I realized she was about to give mind control another try. I didn't blame her.

"Go ahead and make your move," I said confidently. "If it will help you accept this reversal, I'll allow it. Try to give me another command."

Meng grabbed the statuette with desperate fingers. This time I was sure I saw a tiny white flash. But I didn't feel any effects.

"Jenna, kill him," Meng said, her voice low like cat's growl.

I realized, in shock, that she'd never intended to influence my mind again. She had failed with me, but Jenna was still in her power. I felt small hands reaching for me. I pushed Jenna away, but she kept coming, so I shoved her down. She bounced back up, making strange sounds deep in her throat. Her face was—insane.

I turned back toward Meng and realized she was in the act of leaving. She had opened a door I hadn't realized was there. I wouldn't call it a secret door, but it was covered by a bulletin board and the door handle was unusually low. It swung open to reveal a dark space beyond.

"Don't make me kill you," I said to Meng.

Meng froze in the doorway, and looked back in real fear now. I had my hand out, pushing against Jenna's chest to keep her off me. Fortunately, Jenna wasn't very large or strong. She tore at my wrists with her broken nails, and we were both bleeding. Soon, she was going to get the idea to bite me, and I didn't want that.

"Release Jenna, or I'll put a round into your legs right now," I said. I lowered my aim and paused.

"Jenna," Meng said, "be yourself."

Jenna stumbled and grabbed on to me for support. She looked down at her hands and my palm against her chest. There was blood on both of us.

"What did you do?" Jenna asked me breathlessly.

"She did it," I said, gesturing toward Meng. "She blanked your mind then ordered you to attack me."

Jenna stared, disbelieving and upset. She looked down at the finger that rolled around in the bottle in my hand. I was pressing it against her, so she could hardly miss it.

"Meng, step over here," I said. "Come back to the desk. We'll try to talk civilly again."

Slowly, the doctor complied. She didn't look happy about it.

"The talisman worked?" Jenna asked me.

"What talisman?" Meng asked, but we ignored her.

"That's what you did to Robert, isn't it?" Jenna asked her suddenly. She held out her hand in my direction. "Give it to me, Quentin."

"Hold on, Jenna," I told her.

"I don't know what you're talking about—" Meng began.

I felt a stabbing pain in my hand as Jenna suddenly bit me, blood welling up. I roared in pain and surprise, dropping the talisman. Jenna caught it. She had that wild look in her eyes again.

I realized Meng was using her powers again—and then I knew no more.

33

When I woke up, I was lying on the floor of Meng's office. The first thing I noticed was the noise. The entire sanatorium had come alive at last. It was filled with wild sounds: banging, screeches, and warbling noises like the cries of the distant birds. The inmates had awakened.

Jenna stood over me, aiming my pistol over toward Meng's chair and dry-clicking it. She was breathing hard. Her eyes were wide and her lips were curled back. Her hair hung over her face unheeded, exaggerating her wild expression. I knew then what she had done. I struggled to my feet, feeling dizzy. I looked over the desk—there was Meng, sprawled on the floor. There was blood on Meng's chair, on the floor, and a growing circle of it stained her white lab coat. It looked like wine spilled upon a tablecloth.

"You shot her," I said.

"Yeah," she said in a hollow voice. "We have to get out of here."

I picked up the .32 auto's magazine from the floor, staring at it. "There must have been a round in the chamber."

The bizarre sounds coming from the hallway behind me increased in volume. As my mind grew clearer, I realized Jenna had released everyone in this place who was under Meng's control. The doctor had a bullet in her chest, and as a result, we were all off the leash. Jenna had cut the strings of every puppet at once.

I took the gun from Jenna's rubbery fingers. I reloaded the weapon and pulled back the slider to chamber another round. We went to the office door, and after a momentary hesitation, I threw open the door and leaned out into the hallway.

In the hallway, the noise was a hundred times worse. People howled, cackled, and sang at the tops of their lungs. I had no doubt some of them had been brought here for good reasons originally, their mental health far from stable, but none of that could explain the madness I heard roaring from dozens of combined throats.

I was at a loss to understand it, but I imagined they'd been imprisoned here, silent and motionless in their cells for years. Countless quiet hours had been imposed upon unbalanced minds. Now that they'd finally been released, they had gone completely mad.

Doors shook with powerful blows. Wired windows cracked, spitting flecks of glass. Door handles rattled under furious hands. From somewhere, wisps of smoke had crept into the hallway. I wondered if one of the upper floors was ablaze.

A pair of people rounded the corner at the nurse's station, heading our way. Nurse Miranda was in the lead and right behind her was the orderly I'd beaten down to escape this hellhole a week ago.

"You!" Miranda screamed.

There was a light in her eyes I didn't like. I was glad I had her pistol, because right then I was sure she would have emptied the gun in our direction. I lifted the gun and found that I either had no compulsion against harming her, or Dr. Meng's state had freed me. The two slowed as they saw the gun in my steady hand.

"Put it down, Draith," Miranda said.

"No," I said. "I'm free. Just like the rest of them."

They both advanced, their hands up with open palms. They wore expressions akin to people approaching a strange growling dog in their living room. *There's a good doggie.*

I took a step back, but my gun didn't waver. Miranda turned toward the orderly, her eyes were wide. "He must have killed her," she said.

"No, I did it," Jenna said. "She told me what she did to my Robert, so I shot her."

I glanced at Jenna, recalling the fierce, determined rage I'd seen in her the night I'd met her in the casino. I reminded myself never to get onto this woman's bad side. She looked cute and sounded innocent, but she was a killer.

"You don't understand what you've done," Miranda said. She walked closer, peering into the office. "Where is the doctor?"

"On the floor behind her desk," I said.

"Will you allow me to help her?" she asked.

I nodded and backed up two more steps.

"Go get the emergency cart," the nurse told the orderly.

He hastened to obey, disappearing for a moment. He came back at a run, wheeling a white-clothed cart full of medical supplies. I wasn't sure how I felt about that. If they succeeded in reviving the good doctor, would that mean she would again hold sway over me and all the others in this building?

The howling had subsided. We could still hear the noise coming from the upper floors, but the nearest inmates were watching us. In a dozen dimly lit little windows, faces and staring eyes were pressed hard, straining to see. They fogged the windows with their panting breaths and their cheeks left residues of sweat and blood. Why were they quiet now? What were they thinking, this audience of crazies? I had no idea, but their scrutiny was unnerving.

"Let's get out of here," Jenna whispered to me, tugging on my arm. "This is her place. If she awakens, she might be able to turn us against each other."

I thought about her words, and I also thought of giving her the gun to shoot Dr. Meng again—just to make sure. If I left now and the doctor recovered, would I regret it?

In the end, it was the crazies who decided matters for us. They'd been waiting for something and we learned what it was very suddenly. An alarm went off, a keening sound. It was a smoke alarm. I knew that annoying, piercing blast well.

Then I heard another sound—a much more frightening one. The doors all clicked open. When the fire alarm went off, the doors were built to automatically unlock themselves to allow the inmates to escape.

A dozen doors opened; many were thrown wide with a bang. From each dim room came a shambling person with slack lips and haunted eyes. Old women, teenage boys, balding men in glasses. There were fat ones, but most I would describe as thin, even gaunt. They all came out of their rooms, where they'd been held for so long.

I aimed my gun at them, but they took no notice. They didn't even look at me or my weapon. Ignoring us, they surged forward and caught the orderly. They knew him well, it seemed, and they clearly did not have a favorable opinion of him. He managed to stay on his feet at first, shoving them back, shouting and threatening. But more came. He bashed two to the floor, where they bled and crawled. He broke free and reached the door of Meng's office. Inside, nurse Miranda worked to save Meng's life.

Somehow, the door had swung closed and locked. This lock, among all of them, seemed immune to the fire system. Perhaps Meng had had the wisdom and foresight to disable the unlocking mechanism on her own office door. Whatever the case, Miranda had locked the orderly out.

The inmates rushed close. He used his stun gun liberally. It crackled and flashed while the reaching inmates shrieked. But in the end, they took the man down. I backed away from them down the hallway with Jenna doing her best to drag me. I was left with a choice: I could shoot the enraged inmates, or I could run.

I decided to run. What right did I have to kill these people? Who was I to say his life was more valuable than theirs? He had most assuredly abused them. He was part of this place—part of an institution meant to help people, but which had gone bad and stolen what little they had left of their own minds.

We reached the emergency exit at the far end of the building. I recognized it once I was inside the concrete stairway. A few people wandered the steps above us, lost. I hit the panic bar on the outside door and threw it open.

Fresh, cool air washed over me. Holding Jenna's hand, I led her outside into the streets. I had escaped the sanatorium again. Part of me wondered just how many times I'd done so before. Would this be the last time? I hoped so.

We hustled to the car, trying to cover our faces from security cameras. We were two fugitives on the run now, it seemed. If Meng lived, she'd probably send the police after us. If she didn't, the Community might send their minions. I didn't like my odds in either case. I probably didn't have much freedom left.

I took out my cheap cell and tapped in McKesson's number. He answered, yawning. I nodded to myself—an afternoon sleeper. Like me, he seemed to be on the go all night. I supposed that when you were dealing with aliens and rips in space, you had to expect to work nights.

"What do you want, Draith?" he answered.

I nodded to myself. He had my number traced and identified by now. So much for my precautions. I had to ditch this phone soon in case the rest of the police force was tracing calls every time I used it.

"I just paid Dr. Meng a visit," I said.

"Really? In that case, I'm surprised you still know who I am."

"So you do know what her power is. You could have warned me."

"I warned you not to go there."

I set my irritation aside. "In any case, you might want to send some emergency units down to the sanatorium," I said.

"What did you do?"

"I shot her," I said.

Jenna frowned at me. I waved for her to stay quiet.

McKesson didn't say anything for a few seconds. I think he was in shock. "You sure know how to stir up shit, don't you?" he asked finally.

"She tried to pull some mind-control trick on me. It was self-defense."

"Self-defense?" McKesson laughed unpleasantly. "You think that will hold up in a court of law? Or with the rest of the Community? They hate each other, you know, but they hate a killer rogue even more."

"I'm not even sure she's dead," I said.

"You better hope she is. She's got friends. But I'm not one of them. Let me bring you in, Quentin."

"No."

I heard sounds of rustling. I figured he was getting out of bed and pulling on clothes.

"Where do I find you?" he asked.

"I'm hoping you won't. Listen, do you want to stop these murders? These attacks by the Gray Men and others?"

"Yeah," he said warily, "but it depends on what you want to do."

"Keep the cops off me for a few days. I'm going back to those cubes. I'm going to do some convincing of my own."

"We've got a truce with them—"

"No we don't," I snapped. "You keep saying that, and I keep telling you we don't have anything. You told me yourself they grow bolder every day. They've been using me to find others. Meng seemed to be in on that, maybe picking up an object now and then and keeping them busy killing rogues. But I'm stronger now. I'm strong enough to make my move."

"You're crazy, Draith. You're just one rogue with a couple of tricks in his pocket."

"Gilling has a new term for powerful rogues: technomancers."

McKesson snorted at that. "Gilling belongs in one of Meng's cells. You know you can't possibly take out more than a few Gray Men alone. Not on their home turf."

"Who said I was going alone?" I asked him.

After I hung up on McKesson, I asked Jenna to drive to Henderson. Even though I had a plan I was still feeling woozy and didn't want to risk blacking out with my foot on the pedal. She agreed. I could tell something was on her mind, but I didn't feel like prying it out of her. I leaned back in my seat and closed my eyes. When she was ready to talk, I would listen.

"Meng told me about Robert while you were blank," she finally said in a small voice. "You sat there like a zombie. It was very strange."

"You did the same thing while I talked to her."

"Such an *evil* woman," she said. "Seeing you like that—understanding her power over people's lives—it made it much easier to shoot her. She was a monster. All those peo-ple...she locked them up and made them sit there for so long..."

"What did she do to your husband?"

"Apparently, he was a rogue, like you. He had the ring, a minor power. He went to see her, to try to sell her his services, I guess. She took his mind for her own instead. She told him to find others. She used him, just the way she used you."

"I don't see how that adds up with the rip appearing in your room and with his disappearance."

"She said he knew about the cultists and Rostok too. I think Gilling opened that rip in our room. He went to the cultists and then vanished. Meng said she didn't know where he went. But she could have been lying."

"A distinct possibility," I said. "But yeah, the cultists. Their involvement makes sense. They tried to enter that same room again later, while McKesson and I were there. Gilling summoned a rip into that room and then Robert stepped out. Maybe that's how his shoe ended up in their cellar. Gilling indicated he knew who Robert was."

We merged onto Interstate 515. It was rush hour and traffic was heavy.

"Did Meng say anything that explains the way Robert treated you? Why he might have run out on you?"

"Yes. She said she told him to leave me, because I would get in the way. She said something about difficult commands causing bizarre behavior. If she commanded a person to cut off their own toes, for example, they might laugh hysterically while they did it."

"Nice lady," I said.

"It wasn't as hard to pull the trigger as I thought it would be."

"Why would she provoke you when you had a gun on her?"

"I think she believed she had the upper hand. Do you remember biting my leg?"

I shook my head.

"Well, you did. When she blanked your mind, you fell to the ground. I had the talisman, which kept me safe, but it left your mind open to her. While I was talking to her, you grabbed me hard and bit my calf. I knew I was going to lose, so I shot her."

"Sorry," I said, remembering none of it.

"Don't be. It gave me the strength to fire."

I thought of the bite Jenna had given me. I rubbed a bloody spot in the meat of my palm. "That woman was a real live witch," I said.

"Can she come after us?" Jenna asked. "If she's still alive, that is?"

"I don't think so. Her power is strong, but localized. She must stay in the sanatorium to use it."

"I see. She's a prisoner there just like her inmates. I wonder how many years she's gone without leaving those walls."

We'd probably never know the truth. My other thoughts were much more disturbing. I didn't tell Jenna, but I was worried Meng would send assassins after us. She might not be able to leave the sanatorium safely, but she'd shown she could use people like me to do her work for her.

When we arrived in Henderson, we stopped at a gas station. I washed my hands in the public bathroom. The blood had finally stopped flowing from my gouged palm and wrists. Jenna really had done her worst. My face, reflected by the scratched mirrors, was drawn and pale. I thought to myself I was almost as gray as a Gray Man.

I had the feeling Meng was still alive. I wondered if I would come to regret not having finished the job when I had the chance. But I couldn't have murdered a helpless woman while she bled on the floor, even after what she had done to me. That kind of coldness wasn't in me, and I hoped it never would be.

It was dark by the time we reached the abandoned mansion at the top of the hill. I smirked at the thought, knowing it was far from abandoned. The cultists had made it their gathering place. I wondered if they would return tonight.

Jenna pulled up at the curb and left the car's engine idling. "What's the plan?" she asked.

She'd asked that before, but I'd avoided the question. I'd done so partly because I didn't have a clear plan, and partly because whatever I was about to do, she wasn't going to be coming with me.

"I'll check the place out and call you when I learn anything interesting," I said.

Jenna narrowed her eyes at me. "You think you are going to get away with ditching me? Now?"

I took off her wedding ring—or rather Robert's ring—and handed it to her. "You'll need it if I don't come back," I said.

She shook her head and refused to take it. "No way," she said.

"Really," I said, trying to press the ring into her hand. "It's yours."

She pulled her hands back and placed them in her lap. "I don't want it. My memories of Robert are all painful now. The last thing I want to do is wear his ring. Just let me come with you. We did well as a team at the sanatorium."

"Sort of," I said, putting the ring back onto my hand. "But if there had been only one of us, we couldn't have been turned against one another."

I felt her eyes on me. I took the time to reload my pistol and to dig out the extra magazines I'd bought for it. I dropped more bullets into my pockets when the magazines were full. After all, there were a lot of Gray Men in those cubes.

Jenna blinked away tears. She leaned close and hugged me. It was an angry, dismissive hug.

"Just go then," she said.

"I'll call you. Find a safe place for us to hide when this is over. You can take the car, I won't need it," I said as I climbed out.

"Why would we need to hide if it's over?"

"I guess I mean—if I fail."

Jenna nodded and drove off. I stood there, watching her. When her brake lights flashed and she turned the corner, I remembered sending Holly away from this place. I hadn't managed to keep her alive, but I tried not to think about that.

I walked onto the property, following the fence, and stayed behind overgrown brush. The grounds had really gone to hell. It must have been nearly a year since the land had been properly cared for. I'd seen this kind of neglect before in abandoned, repossessed properties. The bank would make sure the lawn was watered, but they never put any money into trimming anything. Plants of every variety grew in wild profusion. Wasps' nests buzzed everywhere and broken pipes had formed muddy spots on the lawn.

Eventually, I reached the side door that led down into the cellar. I knew that route in, and hoped I would encounter less trouble that way. I quietly twisted the door handle. It was locked.

I slipped on my sunglasses, but then the door swung open silently. It hung there ajar, and I couldn't see past it into the dark interior. I put away my sunglasses and pulled out my gun instead.

"Come in, Mr. Draith," said a familiar voice. It was Gilling.

"You expected me?" I asked, still standing outside. I gripped my pistol in both hands.

"Not really, but we do have security cameras."

I looked around and saw a few plastic bubbles. They didn't look like much, but they were big enough to hide an infrared camera. I knew this could be a trap. The cultists could be in there, all waiting for me. I was armed, but they might be armed as well. Their little tricks wouldn't work on me, but if there were enough of them, that wouldn't matter. A significant part of me wanted to retreat, to jump the nearest fence and call the mission a failure.

"Come, come, Mr. Draith." Gilling laughed. "Do you have so little faith? I will unilaterally declare a truce. Tell me why you've come to visit. Don't be rude and leave me bursting with curiosity."

Taking in a deep breath, I leaned forward and nudged the door open the rest of the way. So much for my plans to stealthily investigate the place.

I stepped inside and waited for my eyes to adjust to the deep gloom of the interior. Outside there were lights from neighboring houses, stars and streetlamps, but inside there was only a single candle in the middle of the room. Gilling stood near the candle, leaning against what appeared to be a bookshelf. I peered at the shadowy corners of the room, trying to see if any of his accomplices were about.

"Could you put that thing away?" Gilling asked. "You're making me nervous."

I flicked my eyes to him, then eyed the surroundings again. I didn't see anything upsetting, so I slipped the gun into my coat pocket. My hand still held onto the grip, however.

"Slightly better," Gilling said. "As you can see, I'm alone. The rest aren't here yet."

"So you knew I was coming?"

He shook his head. With a faint smile playing over his lips, he pushed open the door that led through into the wine cellar. There, I could see the shimmer of a rip he'd apparently created. Finally, I caught on.

"You saw me on the cameras and stepped over here to meet me?"

"Exactly. I was at my residence."

"Which is—where?"

He made a dismissive gesture. "My home is at the other end of these security cameras."

I knew the cameras fed into the web, and his home could be anywhere. I could see the advantage of his system. Using his power to create portals, he could watch places such as the mansion and arrive when he felt like it.

I stared at the shimmering, twisting region of space that hung there in the wine cellar. Such a power. It dwarfed anything I could do. What would it be like, I wondered, to be able to open a path to any other place one wished to go? What would I do if I had such an ability? Travel the world? Empty bank vaults? I wasn't sure. Clearly, Gilling had bigger ideas. He was trying to use his power to gain even *more* power.

"I really did come to see you," I said.

"Why?"

"To ask for your help." I then briefly explained my encounter with Dr. Meng. I left out any mention of Jenna. Even though I needed them, I had little trust for Gilling and his bizarre crew. I didn't want anyone to get funny ideas about using Jenna as a lever against me.

Gilling's eyes lit up with excitement as I spoke. He picked up his burning candle and stepped closer to me as

I continued. His eyes reflected the tiny yellow flame, and I could see he was entranced with my story.

"This is simply amazing!" he said when I'd finished. "You are a hero for all rogues...do you know that?"

"Not really. Why?"

"Because you've bested an experienced member of the Community in her own domain. That is almost unheard of. You are a rogue among rogues. You will be remembered as our champion. A man to be feared. Unfortunately, they will come for you now—but how many will they have to send to take you down? They can only send their beasts, their simple minions. You've shown time and again you are the stronger."

Gilling spoke with hope in his voice. His every word made me feel the opposite. Each syllable confirmed my deepest fears and hammered another nail in my coffin. How could I fend off an army of goons from the Community?

"I don't even know most of them. How many are there?"

"How many what?"

"Members of the Community. People with powerful domains. Technomancers."

"Nine—or eleven, depending on who does the counting," Gilling said. "You, my good man, have lowered that count by one."

"She might not be dead."

"A pity. When taking on a throng, it's best not to miss with your first strike."

I straightened up, coming to a decision. I would join this man's strange, disturbing gang. I would do it to protect Jenna. Perhaps, with enough rogues banded together and my collection of objects, I could defeat those who came for us, or at least enough of them to force them to leave us alone.

"Gilling, do you remember your offer to me? Last time we met?"

"Hmm?"

"To join you," I said. "I think I'll take you up on that. I'm offering you a temporary alliance, please understand. I'm not cutting up any meat."

Gilling stared at me for a second with wide, glittering eyes. "Ha!" he shouted after a moment, then stepped back, putting a fine-boned hand to his chin. "Why, I do think you are serious. Can that be? Have I not made myself clear, fellow rogue?"

"What do you mean?"

"I mean, my crazy friend, I can no longer allow your presence here. I have a great deal of problems of my own. Any and all of our associations are herewith at a permanent end. You are a great danger to me and everyone in my cabal. If you really wish to help me and prolong your own existence, you should flee the desert now. Take your girlfriend with you and run to the far side of the globe. Perhaps that will be far enough…"

I nodded. "That's what I thought you meant." I wasn't thrilled to learn he knew about Jenna.

Gilling pushed wide the door leading into the wine cellar. "Don't try to follow me," he called over his shoulder. "I mean you no harm, but my home is well guarded. You might not survive the trip."

A sense of desperation set in. I needed him more than ever now. What could I offer this man for help?

"Gilling?"

Gilling paused at the edge of the burning rip he'd formed. Already, it had diminished somewhat, becoming orange in color. It looked smaller and colder. I wondered where it led. He had one foot in the wine cellar and the other—someplace else. The foot that had moved forward was darker, indistinct. It was as if half of him were a painting that had been blurred by an artist's hand.

"What, my doomed champion?"

"What if I did it under the direction of another member of the Community?" I asked.

"Who?"

"Rostok."

I could see he no longer wanted to listen to me, that he wanted to step away into the safe nothingness that lay ahead of him.

"Rostok told you to kill Dr. Meng?"

"No," I said. "Not exactly. But he did send me to her. He knew what she was, and what she had done. He knew what I am as well. I only acted in self-defense."

Gilling shook his head. "A series of intriguing technicalities. No doubt you might convince a member or two Rostok was behind the matter, but they will want you dead still. If Rostok has a powerful assassin on the board, the rest will want to stomp the spider down all the more."

"What if I give you an object, then?" I asked. "What if I hire your help?"

"You call me a mercenary?"

"I've got a ring I can spare," I said, knowing he liked rings. I realized it was Jenna's and not mine to give, but I also figured she would be dead if I didn't get help fast.

"A ring?" Gilling asked.

It could have been my imagination, but his voice seemed to rise up a half octave when he said those two words.

"Yeah," I said. "It gives the wearer luck."

Gilling laughed, stepping back out of the glimmering space that was his exit. I stepped toward him, closing the distance between us slowly.

"Luck?" he cried. "Again with the jokes, Draith! You must stop, really! You have to be the unluckiest man I've ever had the misfortune to encounter. Do you know that three of my followers have died since I first met you?"

I explained briefly how it worked. He cocked his head while I spoke, staring at my hands. "That's Robert's ring. I had wondered—never mind."

I watched him closely. He'd been about to confess more knowledge of Robert's disappearance. But right now, I didn't care about that. I cared only about Jenna and me.

"What exactly is the nature of your proposal?" Gilling asked.

I told him I intended to go to the cubes of the Gray Men and find the source of their power to open paths into our world from theirs. I planned to close those pathways, if I could.

Gilling surprised me by walking closer as I spoke. He studied me intently with those odd eyes of his. As I finished, he reached up slowly and plucked the ring from my fingers.

"They will probably kill us all," Gilling said. "You know that, don't you?"

I nodded.

Gilling held the ring up and admired it. He twisted it this way and that, letting his burning candle reflect from the curved gold loop. The diamond glittered.

"The Gray Men have killed members of my cabal. I understand that better now. You cursed us by visiting us, you know. First, sweet old Caroline died when Rheinman slew her with his hammer. The blow was meant for you, but flew right past and punctured her brain. After that, the Gray Men started coming. You marked us with your mere presence."

"Everyone I meet dies eventually, it seems."

Gilling nodded slowly. "So, your proposal is to have us die *faster*?"

It was my turn to chuckle. "Possibly. Or possibly, we'll stop the Gray Men. We will shut them down and stop the assassinations. We'll become heroes for our side. Hopefully, the rest of the Community will forgive me for Meng's—accident."

Gilling began to pace, still eyeing the ring. "We can claim that Rostok sponsored the whole effort. That Meng was in league with the Gray Men."

"It's possible," I said. "Why else would they keep coming and letting me go?"

Gilling stopped pacing and smiled at me. "You are charming me, aren't you?"

I started to deny his odd statement, but he shushed me with fluttering hands.

"No, no, it is very clear," he said. "First you bring these killers to me—unwittingly, perhaps. Then you request my help to stop them. You create a crisis and then require more blood from me as the only solution. And to think that we considered *you* as a source of blood at one time! Ironic."

"Are you in or not?" I asked. "Because I'm going to move on them one way or the other. They won't leave me in peace, so I might as well end it. I'd rather die than have them kill every interesting person I meet."

Thin fingers waved away my words as if they stunk up the air.

"No more bravado, please," Gilling said. "I've had all I can stomach. But I will join you anyway. I will march my fledgling army against the Gray Men. It will be glorious—or tragic. At least it will be better than sitting in this hole awaiting a fate decided by others."

35

Over the next several hours, Gilling made a number of quiet cell phone calls. Soon thereafter, his people began to arrive. I watched the security cameras as the driveway filled up and they kept filing in. Gilling and I had moved up from the cellar into the main living area. I got the feeling there would be a lot of people coming.

They were a motley crew. Most were disheveled and a few appeared homeless. I supposed that the introduction into one's life of high technology—or magic, take your pick—was always disruptive. How could you keep your mind on a retail job when the inexplicable object in your pocket begged to be used?

I was surprised by one familiar face. It belonged to the bearded, homeless-looking fellow I'd met on the Strip late last night. He nodded to me and pulled out the pack of McKesson's cigarettes I'd given him. He rattled the empty package at me hopefully.

"More smokes?" he asked.

I shook my head. "What's your trick?"

He slowly removed his hat in response. He reached up and plucked a penny from the top of his bald head. He handed it to me. I snorted.

"Your hat makes pennies?" I asked. "That's it?"

"No," he said. "Usually it makes paperclips, nails, or nickels. Always something metal. Sometimes, I get lucky and find a quarter."

I peered at his hat. It looked normal enough. It was a hunter's cap with a long visor. It could have been old or new. It was hard to tell with objects, as they didn't age.

"Where does the stuff come from?" I asked.

The man shrugged, putting his hat back on his head. I got the feeling he didn't like the way my eyes were crawling all over his prized possession. He needn't have worried. I was intrigued by it, but it had to be the most pathetic power I'd encountered yet.

"I don't know where the stuff comes from," he said. "But it seems to come from nearby."

I smiled at him suddenly. "The casinos," I said. "That's why you walk up and down the Strip, isn't it? You pull coins out of the slots."

The man shrugged shyly. "They won't even let me into those places to go to the bathroom. I figure it's payback."

"Quentin's the name," I said, shaking hands with him.

"I'm Old Red," he said. "My hair's not really red any-more, but it used to be."

I nodded and began to turn away. He reached up under his cap again, and this time he frowned at me. He stared oddly at an object in his hand and then slowly handed it over.

"Is this yours?" he asked.

It was a .32 caliber bullet. I realized with a start that he had pulled it out of my pocket—or my magazine. I was instantly glad I didn't have a surgical pin in my knee or a pacemaker in my chest.

"Um, thanks," I said, pocketing the ammo.

Old Red steered clear of me after that. Maybe the fact I was armed worried him. To me, he looked like a bystander rather than a combatant.

The one who disliked me the most was obvious from the start. It was the mechanic with the ball-peen hammer, Rheinman. I could tell he was still upset about missing me and killing the woman named Caroline who'd shaken her doll at me. I ignored Rheinman's sidelong glares.

I half expected McKesson to show up and join the crowd, drawn by the twitching hands on his watch, but he didn't. People had brought food and folding chairs. It was like a strange, subdued block party. I had to wonder what the neighbors thought of the affair. The party was quiet, but I wondered if they might call the police. After all, the house was supposedly abandoned. I asked Gilling about the possibility we would be reported and he'd told me not to worry, he had it covered. Maybe one of his team had somehow made us all invisible, or unnoticeable. I wasn't sure, so I worried anyway.

It was after ten o'clock when Gilling called the meeting to order. There were more people here tonight than there had been when I'd met up with them the first time. I counted about twenty members. Gilling threw his arms high and everyone quieted. There was no doubt he was in charge.

"There is a stranger in our midst," he said. "A new man, a rogue who may be my equal in power."

Everyone was staring at me by this time. They had no doubt who the outsider was. Some of them had already tried to kill me once.

"This man is a both a blessing and a curse to us," Gilling continued. "He's powerful, yes. So powerful he faced one of the Community in her domain, fought with her and won."

There was a susurration of crowd noises at that. They murmured and stared. I slouched against a wall and kept my eyes on Gilling.

"He has come to us to ask our help and to give us his strength. Recently, several of our members have been killed. Others have abandoned us. We know the source of these attacks—those creatures from the shadows known as the Gray Men. It is my belief they see us as competitors."

I straightened and took a step away from the wall I'd been leaning against. "In what way are you competitors?" I asked.

Gilling turned toward me. "We can move at will to their existence. They can do the same. I'm sure there are others, but I don't know who they are."

"How do they do it?" I asked. "Do you think they have an object like your ring?"

Gilling flashed me a look of annoyance. I took that as confirmation that his object was indeed a ring. Apparently, he didn't like that detail to be advertised.

"No," he said. "I don't think they use objects. They might not even be aware of their existence. They have advanced technology that performs these miracles of physics."

I thought to myself that they were certainly aware of them. I recalled the female of their species and how she had been carefully examining objects in Holly's apartment. She'd obviously been looking for something. I decided not to argue with Gilling about it.

"You mean they have some kind of machine that lets them invade our world?" I asked.

"Yes."

"Where is this machine?"

"Inside the cubes," he said.

"The smaller stack or the larger one?"

He blinked at me. "You know their place well," he said. "The smaller one."

"How do we get there?"

The group members were now talking openly among themselves. Apparently, the implications of our discussion were freaking them out. Gilling raised his arms for quiet.

"That's right, my brothers and sisters. Draith wants us to help him against the Gray Men who plague all of us. He wants us to step into their world and stop them."

I walked slowly through the crowd toward Gilling. I kept my hands in my pockets. The crowd parted for me, moving away from me as I approached.

"From the sound of it, there's only one way we can stop them," I said.

Gilling nodded. "That's correct. We must step through and break into their small stack of cubes. We must destroy their machine to break their power."

I nodded. It occurred to me that I now better understood the Gray Men. They'd been one step ahead of us. They'd reasoned it through and come to the logical conclusion that they wanted to be the only force that could step through whatever barrier separated our worlds. Perhaps all this time, they'd been trying to kill Gilling. Maybe they didn't know who he was, but they knew someone on our side had the power to travel to their world at will.

The conversation and the planning continued. Some of the members loved the idea; others were fearful and opposed it. They wrangled on into the night. I was no longer listening. Instead, I was thinking of the balance of power between the two sides. Between the Gray Men and these cultists. In the final analysis, I had to give the Gray Men the advantage. They were obviously advanced and more organized. Still, I thought the Gray Men must have felt *some* fear every time they came to our world, but they kept doing it. They came and carried out their missions, or died trying. What if they were just as afraid of us as we were of them?

Gilling ended the night by passing out weapons and spare objects. I saw the doll Caroline had used to attack me—a doll that produced a gush of heat. Gilling gave it to the homeless fellow, Old Red. I winced at that. I could have been wrong, but I thought he was as likely to burn some of our own members down as the nearest Gray Man.

By midnight, the fever of war ran through the group. I was struck by their emotional nature. Was there more here at work than just natural anger toward invaders? I came to think that either someone in the group was heating their collective emotions with an object—or that the objects themselves tended to unbalance people who possessed them too long. One theory was as good as the other. Whichever was correct, they'd built themselves up into a frenzy bent on revenge by midnight.

I watched with growing detachment as they formed into groups and made plans. Their powers were quite varied and diverse. One old woman had the power to make others float in the air—but not herself. A middle-aged man with a banker's paunch was a healer of sorts, and was put on duty as the medic. We were a vigilante group in this dark struggle. Earth's own militia.

As Gilling had said, it could only end in triumph or tragedy. I was convinced that the effort was necessary. Whoever had the power to choose the time and place of any battle had all the power. In this case, if we broke their machine, they could no longer visit us. But if they killed Gilling or stole his object, we could no longer visit them. At that point, we would be unable to attack, we could only defend.

Of one thing I was almost certain: whichever side lost this struggle would lose its power to cross the barrier between the worlds, and would therefore be at the mercy of its enemies.

36

Gilling led us out front to where the driveway circled around a large fountain. I saw most of the cars had been parked on the lawn. Overlapping tire tracks there on the grass made it obvious they did this often. No wonder the sprinkler pipes were broken and leaking.

He organized us into two groups and named them squads.

"My group is the support squad," he explained. "Draith will lead the combat squad, just as we practiced during our defensive drills. The combat squad will go in first, then the support squad will go in when it is safe to do so and set up our defenses."

These statements caused me to raise my eyebrows. I waved to him.

"I have a few questions," I said.

He took me aside while the others busied themselves. They rolled up two black SUVs and opened the backs of them. Each had several large plastic bags. They opened the bags and began dumping them into the empty fountain. A dusty plume quickly arose to fill the yard.

"What is that?" I asked.

"A mixture of grass seed and rice," he explained. "It will serve as the organic fuel to open a large rip. These materials are harder to work with than blood, but they are long-lasting and easier to obtain in quantity."

I shook my head. This was indeed a strange business. I was left wondering if the witches of Salem had been up to something all those centuries in the past. This was beginning to look like a spell and a ritual to me. The only difference was our greater understanding of the process.

"How can we get away with this? Are you paying the police off? Or the neighbors?"

Gilling laughed lightly. "No. See that woman over there?"

I followed his finger toward a drooping, unkempt palm tree. I peered, and saw the outline of a thin woman under the low-hanging fronds. "Who is it?" I asked.

"Her name is Abigail," he said. "She is one of my best. She covers our tracks. She makes this place quiet, dark, and—uninteresting."

"Yes, I've met her before. She controls minds? Like Meng?"

Gilling's hand fluttered. "Not exactly. Abigail changes the air, I think. It becomes more dense and harder to see and hear through. Look up at the stars."

I did as he asked, and frowned. They were normally dim near the city due to light pollution, but the stars here were blurred almost to the point of invisibility.

"That is very odd," I said. "It reminds me of the way the other side of a rip looks. All smeared and wavering."

"Yes. I think it is a similar effect. She increases the density of the air, I believe. She makes it thicker."

"Why is she under that palm?"

"To concentrate. She needs to focus to maintain the effect."

"Now," I said, "tell me who is on my combat squad and why."

He pointed out each of my team members. There were six of them. They included Old Red with his new dolly that threw blasts of heat around and Rheinman with his hammer, who obviously still hated me. In addition were three men who carried hunting rifles and grim expressions. Gilling explained to me they possessed objects of minor power, but two had been in the military and one was an ex-cop.

The last member of my team I knew at a glance. She was young and wild-looking. She had a knife in her hand that I'd been introduced to when I'd first met these cultists. She had slashed the back of my leg with it.

"That's Fiona," he said. "Her object is the knife. She can slash with it at a distance of ten paces—more if she is angry."

"That's how she got me the night I walked past her," I said, nodding.

Gilling disagreed. "I don't think so. Her knife touched you without help. If you had not been protected, she would have cut your throat while sitting on the floor a good distance away."

I stared at the wild-eyed girl. She couldn't be more than fourteen. Her hair floated around her head like a wispy cloud. Her arms were thin and pale, but I knew they were deadly. No wonder the cultists hadn't cowered when I had waved my gun at them that night.

"Once I set the fire, Abigail will be the first to step through," Gilling told me. "She will thicken the air and make us hard to sense. I will move in more support people, my entire team. Your combat team will come next."

"How far will we be from the cubes?" I asked.

"A few miles."

I stared at him. "You plan to walk across the desert to the cubes? With fifteen people?"

Gilling crossed his arms. "You have a better plan?"

I didn't like marching in the open for so long. I thought of several possible options. "Can't you open the rip closer to our destination?"

"Not when stepping out to another place. In our own existence, I can connect two points as I did when invading your hotel room from here. But to go to the lands of the Gray Men, I can only tear through the membrane between a spot here and a corresponding spot on the other side."

"Let's pack up, then," I said. "We can drive close to the enemy cubes and come out closer to our goal."

Gilling's fingers ran over his face thoughtfully. "We operate from the mansion usually—we are familiar with it. I'm not sure where to go. It's not like we have a map, you know."

"All right," I said. "I'll scout. Just Abigail for cover and maybe Fiona for backup."

"You make me curious. Out of all of them, why Fiona?"

"Because she won't hesitate to strike when things go wrong. And add Old Red to the group. I want to see if he can handle that heat-blast effectively."

In the end, he agreed to my plan for a scouting mission. Ten minutes after that, the three of us stepped through into the world of the Gray Men through a rip we'd opened for that purpose. This rip seemed higher and stronger than those I'd seen before. Perhaps it was the large amount of fuel Gilling had put down in the bed of the fountain. It was a bonfire in comparison to previous rips. I hoped that wouldn't make us stand out more to the enemy.

I felt the thrill that must run through every warrior when he first steps out of his village to raid his neighbor on the far side the forest. It was exhilarating and terrifying at the same time. My heart pounded in my ears and I kept swallowing. Would they be waiting for us? What kind of automated defenses did they have planted out there in the seemingly featureless sands? I feared we might be fooling ourselves, pitting our own amateur wits against an organized military force. But it was too late to turn back.

I had second thoughts as the rip loomed up under Gilling's nurturing hands. I thought about calling the army or the marines. Surely, a pack of trained government agents could do a better job than I, with or without objects. But I knew just convincing them I wasn't a lunatic would take weeks, if it could be done at all. And I didn't have weeks. The Gray Men would not stop coming. They were hunting us down one by one.

When we were on pure sand again on the far side, I immediately checked out our position. My pistol was in my hand, even though I knew it didn't have much range. Luckily, we seemed to have made it across unobserved. I gazed toward the cube city and the smaller, closer stack of cubes to the east. It was the smaller stack that interested me more. It was little more than a geometric shadow in the night. How far was it? It was hard to tell in the open desert, but it had to be several miles. A second moon peeped over a distant rocky set of mountains behind the cube city.

Abigail had her eyes closed and her palms aimed up toward the sky. I knew she was using her air-thickening trick to hide us. Fiona prowled around ahead of me, her knife twitching in her hand. She was more than a little mental,

Gilling had told me quietly while the rest gathered. When he'd found her, she'd killed her own parents by accident, slashing at the air. He'd taken her in and taught her to control her object. I thought it was a clear testament to the power of these objects upon the human mind that she had refused to give it up even after the knife had brought her so much grief.

As Abigail's shield began to take hold, Old Red finally stepped out of the rip. He was a cagey one; I had to give him that. He had held back inside the safe zone to see if we all died first. He stepped up to my side, his head swiveling this way and that. His hunter's cap remained firmly planted on his head.

"Don't pull anything out of your hat," I told him. "I might need every bullet."

Old Red gave a raspy chuckle. "Don't worry, bud."

"Someone's coming," Fiona said.

My head whipped around. Behind us, a single light shone. The light was bluish in color and very bright. It was moving toward us—moving fast.

"They saw us," Old Red said. "Let's go home."

I hesitated, staring at the approaching light. It was like the brilliant eye of a cyclops. Some army we were. The first time a Gray Man even poked a nose in our direction, my "combat team" wanted to run for it. The worst of it was I wanted to run too.

"We can take them," Fiona said.

"How did they see us? Abigail? Is your little trick working?"

She didn't look at me, but pointed upward. I did and saw the wavering stars. It was the same effect I'd seen back home.

"I bet they saw the rip when it first flared up," Old Red said. "Gilling made it a big one."

"They're slowing down," Fiona said. "They can't see us now. If we wait, they'll probably drive right by."

I thought about it. "Can we close up this rip if we go to the far side and tell Gilling to turn it off?"

"Doesn't work that way," Old Red said. "Takes time to die. You've seen them, haven't you?"

I had indeed seen more than my fair share. I decided to wait around. We were supposed to be scouts, after all. "Let's see what they do. We can always step back out to safety. We have an army on the far side to back us up."

The others were nervous, but willing to go with my plan. We waited. The enemy vehicle did not make a straight path toward us. Instead, it drifted westward as it drew near.

"See?" Old Red crowed. "They can't see us. They're going to sail right by."

I could tell he wanted very much for that to happen. But it didn't. When they got close, they suddenly slowed and began to circle. They drove in a full loop around us. I glanced back and saw Old Red was about one foot from backing into the rip. I couldn't really blame him. He was an old homeless guy who stole coins with his trick hat. He hadn't signed on for a fight to the death with aliens in a strange desert. He'd probably joined Gilling's group for the free food.

"Can you thicken the air up enough to stop them?" I asked Abigail.

She shook her head, concentrating on her task. She was doing a good job. The Gray Men clearly didn't know where we were. But they knew they'd seen something out here. It occurred to me that we couldn't retreat easily now. Abigail's barrier would vanish if we ran, and then they would see the big rip. They would come through right into the mansion, and not in the wine cellar this time. The cultists would be in even more danger after that. This was exactly the kind of thing the enemy seemed to be looking for.

"Just hold on, everyone," I said. "They haven't spotted us yet."

I shouldn't have said those words. The vehicle turned away, then swung around and plowed right into the region of space we were in. The blinding headlight swiveled and bathed us in light.

I could have ordered everyone to step back right then, to retreat. Maybe I should have done it. But I wanted to let these gray bastards know they were in a fight first. I was tired of running like a rat. When leading the living, it's probably best to think of them rather than the dead, but I couldn't help it. I thought of Holly, and I wanted revenge.

"Fire!" I ordered. "Knock out that light!"

Everyone opened up. I felt a gush of heat go by me and the van-shaped vehicle rocked with the impact. Here and there the smooth metal vehicle puffed flame and white sparks.

I squeezed off rounds one at time. Fiona worked her knife in the air like a Japanese chef, and Old Red loosed more blasts. The light did go out, and I was never sure afterward which of us nailed it. If I had to guess, I would give the honor to Old Red. Whatever the case, we were cast into gloom again. Several shapes piled out of the vehicle. They were Gray Men, I was sure of that. They didn't talk or shout. I'd never heard one utter a word up until now, and this occasion wasn't any different.

They were carrying those big beam weapons of theirs, but they didn't have a chance to freeze us. Old Red let go first and his next puff caught three of them. They were staggering, burning. Like inhuman torches, they clawed at the sky and fell into the sands, thrashing.

"Circle around to the left, Fiona," I said. I didn't want them to take cover on the far side of the vehicle and shoot under it. We had to stop them quickly.

Fiona did as I asked without hesitation, scuttling sideways like a crab over the desert floor, staying low and keeping her eyes on the vehicle. She *wanted* to fight. I could see that clearly. Could these objects, depending on their natures, alter the mental outlook of their users? I felt it had to be the case, watching Fiona. No normal young girl would act like that. She was a like some kind of barbarian.

"Keep up our shield, Abigail," I shouted back over my shoulder. I glanced and saw she still stood with her hands held high. To stop her, they were going to have to cut her down. I didn't want to see that happen, so I kept flanking them.

In the end, a Gray Man hiding on the other side of the vehicle edged around it, shooting. He didn't see me immediately in the dark. The only source of light was the big rip itself, slowly spinning in the sand. Unfortunately, the Gray Man got off a shot before I could take him down with my pistol. A blue-white blaze of plasma fired toward the rip. I put five rounds into him and he went down. I kept going around the vehicle. There was only one other Gray Man, and he was dead in the desert. Fiona stood over him with her knife in her twitching hand. She panted and stared at the body.

We'd won.

37

Victory had come at a price. The Gray Man who'd gotten off a shot had killed Old Red. His cap and the dolly had survived, of course, but the rest of his upper body was a block of ice. The ice had cracked when he'd hit the sand. You could see frozen organs and shattered ribs inside.

Abigail stood still, eyes closed, concentrating.

Fiona came up beside me and stared at Old Red's remains. "What do we do now?" she asked.

I had been scanning the horizon, but didn't see further signs of the enemy. I figured they had to be coming, though. The group we'd ambushed must have reported our position. After losing contact, the next time they sent a force they would come in strength. I imagined Gray Men quietly scrambling and loading their weapons into more trucks out there somewhere.

"We're scouts, so let's scout. We check out their truck, learn as much about their technology as we can," I said, with more confidence than I felt.

The design of the truck was odd—there were no curves to it. There were slanted, diagonal lines, but no rounded edges. The corners of the vehicle were so sharp they couldn't have been molded metal; they had to be flat sheets of steel that met at precise points. Was this an example of advanced engineering or their chosen style? I wasn't sure.

The cockpit had very simple controls. A bar of metal shaped like a delta wing seemed to serve as both the throttle and the steering mechanism, depending on how you manipulated it. The system reminded me of a joystick. There didn't seem to be an ignition or even a start button. Experimentally, I touched the power bar. The engine thrummed into life. I nodded; it had sensed my contact. My physiology must have been similar enough to a Gray Man's to fool it. I gave the bar a tiny nudge forward, and the vehicle surged a few feet in response.

"Anyone could drive this," I said to Fiona. She stood outside in the sand, watching me with big eyes.

"Are we going to steal this machine and ride to their base?" she asked. The next words she blurted out in a rush: "I want to kill more of them."

I glanced at her, trying not to appear disturbed. She stood there with dead Gray Men all around her feet. Old Red lay farther away, turned half to ice behind her. The smell of burnt alien flesh alone was cloying and difficult to take. But all Fiona could think of was her next kill. That knife she gripped and regripped in her hand had a hold over her mind I didn't fully understand. Maybe only certain objects generated such emotions. I had several objects and didn't feel any urge to kill.

"I don't think so," I told her, climbing down out of the cockpit. "They'll all come to this spot. We can't be so obvious. I'm going to go back and talk to Gilling. Stay here and cover Abigail."

As I walked to the rip and stepped within its embrace, Abigail spoke to me. Her voice was just above a whisper. I could tell all her concentration was required to keep up our shielding.

"Can't we all go home?" she asked.

Abigail was so peaceful compared to Fiona, the contrast was shocking. Her curly black locks hung around her neck. Her upraised hands were tipped with blood-red nails. She was as peaceful and calm as Fiona was bloodthirsty. She only wanted to go home to our existence, and I felt bad turning her down, but I didn't want to give up yet. We'd proven we could fight with them and win on their turf. We were the aggressors for once. I wasn't ready to run yet.

"Just give me a few minutes more, Abigail. If you drop the shield, they will see the rip clearly and come right here. They will know everything then."

Abigail nodded slowly, sadly, accepting my instructions. Fiona had no difficulties with my instructions. She stood near Abigail and slashed at the alien truck. It was odd, seeing her cut the air and hearing scraping sounds coming from the metal of the vehicle that stood about fifty feet away. I wondered vaguely if slashing something metal could dull the edge of her knife—even though she wasn't actually touching it.

Feeling like a bastard, I stepped back home and left them in the hostile desert. A half dozen hands with tightly held objects rose up to confront me when I stepped into view. They lowered their objects when I stepped out of the blurring rip and they realized who I was.

"Where are the rest?" Gilling asked. His voice sounded confident, almost disinterested, but I could tell he had been waiting nervously like the rest of them.

"The Gray Men saw us before we could get the shielding up. A truck came out to investigate."

A dozen glittering eyes stared at me. No one spoke. I could see they thought I might be the last survivor. Rheinman, the mechanic with the ball-peen hammer, tapped his palm with the head of his object. His cheeks twitched. He probably figured I'd ditched the rest—or killed them.

"We won the fight, and we captured their truck," I said.

A murmur went through the group. They were relieved and fearful all at once. I understood what they were thinking as they exchanged worried glances. They'd officially announced war upon the Gray Men now.

"Where are the rest?" Gilling asked again.

"Abigail is maintaining her shield. Fiona is protecting her. But Old Red died in the fighting. He was hit by one of those big projection guns of theirs."

"It's a failure, then," said the rifleman named Souza. "We've alerted them. We have to abort the mission."

Everyone started talking at once. Everyone except for Gilling and me. Instead, Gilling eyed me curiously. Maybe he didn't believe my story. I barely cared. While they argued about what to do next, I reloaded my .32 auto.

I let them talk for a minute or so, shouting that our cover was blown, that this was supposed to be a quiet mission, not a pitched battle. The consensus was that we couldn't face their organized army on their own ground.

I listened, but not too closely. My mind was made up. I was going to press ahead.

Gilling raised his bejeweled fingers and the group quieted. "Let's hear what our scout suggests."

"I want to open a new rip to the east, much closer to the cubes. Who's coming with me?"

People shuffled their feet. A siren rose and fell in the distance. They looked this way and that, studying the streets that wound down the hillside. I knew they were getting nervous. Without Abigail to cover them, someone might have called the cops and sent them up here by now.

"If nothing else, we must retrieve the body of Old Red," Gilling said. "Show us where he is."

I stepped through and a dozen people followed me, most of them reluctantly. I was relieved to find Abigail and Fiona as I had left them. The only change was the rising of a second small moon on the horizon. It was yellow and sickly looking in comparison to our own luna. The surrounding desert was dark and quiet. But maybe the trucks were out there, full of angry Gray Men with their deadly weapons. Maybe they'd grown smarter and this time kept their lights off to surprise us. Thoughts like these caused the skin on the back of my neck to crawl.

They hauled Old Red's remains home and experimented with the beam rifles the Gray Men had dropped. No one could figure out how to make them operate, however. Perhaps they were linked somehow to their users.

"Are you going to go out into the desert with me and open a new rip?" I asked Gilling.

He shook his head slowly. He didn't bother looking at me. He was too busy staring out into the darkness. I could tell he was wondering what was stalking us out there. I followed his gaze and wondered the same thing.

"Lost your nerve already?" I asked.

"It wasn't supposed to go like this. We signed on for a quiet raid. We can't fight an army."

"I don't care," I told him. "I'll take that alien truck to the cubes alone if I have to."

Gilling stared at me as if I were crazy. "They know we are here now."

"Maybe. But they don't know what we're planning. They don't know who we are. I doubt they will suspect a serious raid. I want to hit them now, while we still have a shred of surprise left."

Gilling shook his head. "We aren't an army. Not even the scouting mission went right. More are sure to die—maybe all of us. I can't order them to do this."

"All right," I said, turning away from him and facing the ragtag crowd.

They were wandering around in the sand, looking like house cats who'd slipped out the front door for the first time. I didn't think any of them had ever left their home existence before.

"I'm taking that truck and using it to sneak into the Gray Men's cube base. With luck, they'll think we're their kind. Who's coming with me?"

Any idea of combat squads and support squads had been cast aside. Now it was down to who had the guts to keep going when death was a clear possibility. Most of them wouldn't even meet my eyes. A few looked positively terrified.

Fiona volunteered immediately. "I'm in," she said.

I was surprised when Rheinman stepped forward next. "Just don't get in my way again," he said. He held his hammer in his hand with tight knuckles.

I nodded, letting his bad attitude go without comment. "Who else?" I asked.

In the end, most of them abandoned us. I had high hopes for Abigail, but she refused with a shake of her head. Among the riflemen, only Souza stepped forward.

"Can I have Old Red's stuff?" Souza asked Gilling.

Gilling nodded once. The man pulled on the red cap and grabbed up the heat-blasting rag doll with a tight smile. So that was how you moved up in this outfit, I thought to myself.

"What about you, Gilling?" I asked.

Gilling put up his hands. "Very well," he said. "I'll open your new rip for you. Let's go back home now before we all get killed in this strange land."

I tried not to smile, but I failed. That was what I had been hoping for. I jumped out of the cockpit and headed for the shimmering rip. The others followed me hastily, with many worried glances over their shoulders.

Abigail was the last to come through. I knew at that point the rip would be exposed to the Gray Men. They seemed to have some way of sensing these phenomena, even if it was only by spotting them visually. It wouldn't be long now before Gray Men came to investigate.

"That's all of us," I told Gilling. "Close the rip fast."

He shook his head. "I can't. It's like a fire. It has to burn itself out."

I looked down at the various foodstuffs they'd poured into the bowl of the big fountain. It looked like this rip was going to last for days if we didn't do something.

"Shovels, everyone!" I shouted. "Empty out this material or the Gray Men will come for us."

People hastened to do as I asked. But the rifleman named Souza stepped forward. "Let me handle it," he said.

I nodded.

"Everyone step back!" Souza roared.

We did as he asked and he lifted the rag doll. I'd seen two people die who handled it now, and I'd begun to think that if I'd ever seen a cursed object, this was it.

With a broad grin on his face, teeth clenching, Souza released gouts of heat into the bowl of the fountain. It wasn't quite like a flamethrower—the heat wasn't visible flame. I suspected this was because the projection of heat wasn't done by spraying out gas or flaming liquid. Instead, it was more as if pure energy gushed out of Souza and his upraised toy. Maybe it caused an infrared beam to lance out and set every molecule it touched into rapid motion—the very essence of heat.

The stuff in the fountain hissed, steamed, and then finally burst into lively flames. Everyone backed several steps farther away. Only Abigail stood close, shielding us from detection in this world now, as she had in the last. I appreciated her focus and reliability. If any of us were owed a medal when this was over, it would be her.

Before Souza was done, I saw blurry figures stepping through the rip. The Gray Men!

"They're coming through!" I shouted.

Everyone who had a weapon raised it. Souza sent more heat toward them, causing the blaze to leap higher. The four man-shapes I could see standing in the midst of the inferno hesitated.

"Will it burn through to them?" I asked Gilling.

He shook his head. "I don't think so. There are three existences here, our world, theirs, and the in-between of the rip. If they stay inside the rip, bullets, fire, explosions—nothing will affect them.

They stood there as the rip began to slowly die. It was being starved for fuel now. It was in competition with the flames Souza had created.

Souza himself ran with sweat and his teeth gleamed wetly. He was wild with excitement. Using his object so thoroughly, so successfully, had brought him a rush of joy. I knew the feeling, but could tell the sensation he was experiencing was infinitely more intense.

Finally, Souza stepped back and unslung his rifle. "Let 'em come now," he said. "I'll shoot them as they burn."

Rheinman stepped up with his hammer and I held my pistol at the ready. We all stared at the shimmering shapes in the rip. I wondered what they were thinking. They had to have seen what we'd done to the men in the truck.

After another minute, the Gray Men moved away as one. They retreated, stepping back into their own existence. The fires and the rip died together. Soon, there was nothing there in the bowl of the fountain but drifting ash and hot embers. The PVC pipes at the bottom of the fountain had burnt away to nothing. The blue tiles had cracked and been scorched black.

"They won't suspect our next move," I told Gilling. "This will help us. We've just created a diversion."

Gilling looked less than pleased. "They will circle around this spot in the desert on their side. Soon they will create their own rip near here and come for revenge."

"Maybe. But they won't get any satisfaction if we leave right now."

The rest of the cultists didn't need any further urging. They were already climbing into their vehicles.

"Whoever's with me, we're taking Gilling's SUV," I said. "Come on, Gilling."

"What if I've changed my mind?"

"Then you are a liar and a coward. Did you really think this was going to go perfectly?"

Gilling rubbed his face. After a moment's inner debate, he threw me a jingling set of keys. "You drive," he said.

We both climbed into the SUV along with Fiona, Abigail, Rheinman, and the sweating Souza who still gripped his dolly as if it were a bag of cash. We followed the rush of cars out of the grounds and rolled down dark streets. As we reached the bottom of the hill, a fire engine passed us going up the lane. I chuckled. Someone had called the fire department. If they met up with the Gray Men, everyone was in for a shock.

We headed northeast, out of Henderson. I turned onto Pabco road, which led up into the Frenchman Mountain area. This was where I'd estimated the enemy base was located now that I'd seen it from two different angles. My triangulation was very crude, but in both our existences this region was rocky and barren.

Frenchman Mountain itself was a geographical oddity. Standing on the eastern border of Las Vegas, north of Henderson, the mountain was formed of the most ancient rock to be found anywhere on the North American continent. The peaks and ridges had been pushed up from an ancient seabed of a nameless ocean. The stones here were thick with fossils of strange creatures that had been extinct for eons. Trilobite fossils were common, things that resembled lobsters stripped of their claws. They had once crawled here in great numbers.

I didn't really understand the relationship between our existence and that of the Gray Men, but if we shared a history, this spot was more likely than most to be comparable. I'd done a little thinking about the parallel places we both lived in. Maybe our earth was the same as this place, but there had been a single twist of fate in the distant past of both worlds that had set them apart. Perhaps they represented one possibility, one fork in the road of time, while we represented another. If that were the case, then Frenchman Mountain might be a shared ancestor of history, since every stone here was over a billion years old.

I was peering ahead through the windshield, trying to estimate our distance from Henderson, when something caught my eye off to the north.

"What the hell is that?" I asked, pointing off to the right. Everyone stared.

"That is someone trying to signal us," Gilling said with certainty.

"Who…? Could it be the Gray Men?"

"Maybe. But this is unusual behavior. They've never crossed to our world and attempted communication. In fact, they've never spoken or attempted any form of communication whatsoever."

"Well, it might only be someone with engine trouble, but I'm going to see who that is. If it is the Gray Men, we are as ready for them now as we're ever going to be."

"Madness," Gilling said. "Why invite trouble? We are quite close to the planned point of departure. Let's cross over into the world of the Gray Men right now."

"I can't ignore this. What if we could establish some kind of dialogue?"

"Who is leading this expedition?" Gilling asked.

"I'm combat, you're support, remember? So start supporting me."

I left the road and rolled into the desert. At that moment, the people in the backseat became alarmed.

"Where the hell are you going?" Souza asked.

"As close as I can figure, this is the spot," I said. "Whoever is out there seems to agree with me."

"Let's just stop and form the rip if this is close enough," suggested Rheinman.

"I want to see who is signaling and why," I said.

"What if it's the Gray Men?"

"Then they are smarter than I thought."

"All right, but we're off-roading," Rheinman said in my ear. "What if you run into a rock or fly into a gully and flip us over? At least slow down."

I had to admit he had a point. I slowed down and everyone seemed relieved, with the possible exception of Fiona. She was impatient to get closer to anyone she could legitimately slice up with her knife.

I gently rolled toward the light, which flashed three times, disappeared, then flashed three more times. I eased back on the accelerator, as the terrain was getting rougher. Desert plants scraped the bottom of the SUV and cut lines in the paint of our fenders. I slowed down further, bouncing over rocks and scrubby brush.

As we drew near, the flashing signals ceased. I wondered what we'd been led into. Looking around at the pitch-dark desert surrounding us, I had to admit it was a perfect spot for a private massacre.

38

We were all worried by the time we were close to the area where the flashing signals had come from before they'd stopped. I kept looking for a building, a car, or even a man standing out there. But there was nothing.

I finally hit the brakes and we stopped with a long squeal. The engine thrummed and we all stared through the dusty windshield.

"We've got a few bags of fuel in the back," Gilling said. "This is as good a spot as any to make our rip and finish this."

I shook my head. "Someone is out here. We have to know who. Souza, Rheinman, I want you two to walk on patrol along on either side of the truck while we creep forward."

Souza climbed out with his rifle in his hand, but Rheinman hesitated. "Why are you driving while I walk?"

Fiona made a disgusted sound in her throat and unbuckled herself. "Chicken," she said. "I'll do it."

"All right," Rheinman grumbled. "I'm going."

I rolled the truck forward slowly. On either side, my two patrolling men looked everywhere at once, nervously. Finally, I saw the flashing again. Three quick flashes. They seemed impatient. I turned the wheel and came to the top of a low rise. Down below was a shallow depression surrounded by large rocks. Out of the hollowed-out area rose a vapor of some kind.

"Is that smoke?" asked Fiona, rolling down her window and leaning outside.

"I'm not sure," I said.

"It might be steam," Gilling said. "Maybe a vehicle has overheated out here and needs help."

I nodded. We all climbed out of the truck. There were a dozen boulders clustered around the spot. In the middle of them was a scorched area. Had there been a fire? I didn't see much out here that could burn.

A voice spoke up from the shadows surrounding one of the largest rocks. "You took your sweet time getting here," it complained.

We all aimed our weapons at the stranger. He was tall, with a long face and close-together eyes. Walking in a crouch, I saw Souza and Rheinman circling around behind him. I could have called them off, but I didn't. I didn't like running into a stranger by surprise out here any more than they did.

"You've got some explaining to do, Robert," Gilling said.

I glanced at Gilling sharply, then back to the man he'd called Robert. I remembered the wedding pictures Jenna had shown me once. Yes, this could be the man. I felt an odd mixture of emotions—but mostly, I was angry.

"You are Robert Townsend?" I asked.

He shrugged. "To some parties, yes."

"You ditched Jenna on purpose, then, didn't you?"

"Regrettable," Robert said. He sounded bored. He walked forward into the glare of the SUV headlights. Moths had gathered in the blue-white cones of light, circling and tapping at the lenses. We all had weapons, but Robert appeared unconcerned.

"So, you've thrown in with these cultists, have you, Draith?" he asked. "Not the safest move."

"We've decided to do something about the Gray Men," I said.

"Yeah, about that—"

I shook my head. "Don't even try to get in our way, Robert, or whoever you are. Go home and tell your masters we're tired of being hunted by aliens."

"Being hunted is one thing, getting yourself slaughtered is another."

I looked him up and down now that I could see him clearly. I frowned at his legs, which looked like they were both in white plaster casts. The bottom region of each cast was scorched black and brown. My eyes flicked back to the blackened area in the center of the stones.

"You've been somewhere hot, haven't you?" I asked.

Robert gestured to his makeshift boots. "Asbestos," he said. "Nothing works better."

I licked my lips. I didn't like this at all. His presence indicated others knew we were out here and probably what we were up to. Could they have alerted the Gray Men? A terrible thought occurred to me. What if the Gray Men were working with the Community to clean out the riffraff rogues such as myself?

I put away my pistol and waved for the others, who now surrounded him, to do the same. We needed answers more than we needed blood. Fiona was the last to lower her knife. Her eyes were big—and hungry.

"We should kill this one," Gilling said, speaking up at last. "He's a traitor."

"Yeah," said Fiona. "No one will know. Time to die."

Robert tried to look unconcerned. "Don't you people even want to know why I came out to this rock pile?"

"Why?" I asked.

"To stop you from making a big mistake. You must stay away from the Gray Men. Abort your juvenile mission."

"*You* made the mistake by showing up again," Fiona said. "He used to be one of us, Quentin. But he took off with a good object." She had her knife out now. I saw her raise it with a mischievous smile. She made a tiny sawing motion on the air.

Robert threw his hand to his cheek. It came away running with blood. "Keep these freaks off me, Draith," he said.

"Tell me things," I said, waving for Fiona to knock it off. "I don't understand how we're making a mistake. Explain it to me."

Robert wiped away more blood as it oozed from his cheek. "Step down into this crater with me. I've got something to show you."

None of us moved. Instead of following him to the center, we clustered close to the various boulders. They were the only cover out here. I looked around the dark desert. We were all expecting there might be others lurking nearby. Perhaps gunmen.

"You need to speak clearly," Gilling said softly. "My companions are liable to become nervous and kill you, Robert."

"We know you are out here to agitate the Gray Men," he said.

"We?" I asked.

"The Community," Robert replied.

I nodded. "Who among them sent you?"

Robert's eyes flicked over us.

Fiona held up her knife again. "Can I?"

I held up a flat hand to stop her. "Who sent you?" I asked again.

"Every time, Draith," Robert said, shaking his head. "Every time there is a shit storm, I can bet my bottom dollar you are in the middle of it, can't I?"

"I've never met you before," I said.

Robert laughed. "Did Meng scrub your brain clean again? We've met many times. We've worked together. Trust me."

Fiona apparently didn't find his response helpful. She gave him a tiny little jab this time. He made a sound like a dog that had been kicked and reached for his right thigh. Fiona giggled.

"Stop that, you little witch!" he shouted.

"He's avoiding the question," she said to me.

I nodded. "Who sent you?"

"Rostok sent me," Robert said, rubbing at his leg and glaring toward Fiona.

"How'd you get here?" I asked.

Robert waved at the smoldering spot in the midst of the boulders. "How do you think? I had to walk past fifty lava pits full of slugs to get here and pop into this forgotten hole."

"How the hell could anyone know we would be at this precise spot?"

Robert rolled his eyes at me. "You haven't seen many of the big powers yet, have you, Draith? Don't be a fool. You are just a small-time wizard in this game. Think big."

"Help me out," I said.

"Think time distortion. Think clairvoyance. Think rips that are instant and invisible. I don't know. I don't understand everything the Community can do."

I nodded. I glanced at Gilling. He shrugged back. I took this to mean he didn't know what they were capable of either. I marked this experience down on my long list of reasons to be cautious with the Community.

"You are an agent of the Community," I said. "I get that. But why did you leave your ring with Jenna?"

"Objects are trouble. The more you have the more you get."

I had to agree with him on that point. "So, Jenna was safekeeping for the ring, is that it? You figured you could always go back and take it from her?"

Robert shrugged. "The ring is small time. It wasn't worth the trouble it brought."

I thought about that. I didn't believe he would leave the ring with Jenna forever. Maybe he would go back for it later and take it from her. Of course, he wouldn't want to tell me that now. Whatever his intentions were concerning Jenna's ring, he clearly had another object. Something that allowed him to travel out here. Was it the asbestos booties? I doubted it. They looked damaged and makeshift.

Robert was looking at each of us, as if gauging our positions. Did he think he could take us all? His attitude worried me. He was concerned, but not terrified. I decided to keep asking questions. If there was going to be a fight, I might as well get everything out of him that I could, first.

"Let's forget about Jenna and the ring," I said. "Tell me about Bernie from the Lucky Seven, and my house. Both were burned by lava slugs."

"Bernard was my doing," he admitted. "But your house was an accident. Sometimes when you step in and out, things follow you."

"What about Tony Montoro and the others? Who has been killing these people?"

"The Gray Men have been behind most of the attacks."

"Exactly," I said. "That's why we are planning to hit the Gray Men at their base."

"Right. Total insanity."

"Why?"

"Because they will slaughter you, for one thing. And even if they don't, they will take your action as a formal declaration of war. It may be too late already, due to your prior actions."

I frowned at him.

Gilling spoke up suddenly, angrily. "I think I understand," he said. "Only we rogues are suffering, so screw us? Is that it? We are beetles in the dirt as far as your masters are concerned. Well, we're not interested in dying for the comfort of the Gray Men or the Community any longer."

I glanced at Gilling in surprise. Robert's warning had put steel in his spine. At the same time Robert was getting through to me. I hated to admit it, but he was right about one thing. I had no real idea what I was getting myself into by attacking the Gray Men openly.

"Do you understand we have a cold war here, Draith?" Robert asked.

"I've heard that."

"It's a delicate balance of power. But, have you considered the possibility that the balance *isn't* in our favor? What if they are *stronger* than we are? Wouldn't it be a bad idea to piss them off in that case?"

"You're saying we could touch off a war that our world would lose."

"I'm saying you are a know-nothing vigilante. A terrorist. An assassin who might ignite an interworld war."

"You don't even know what we are trying to do," I said.

Robert gave an ugly laugh. "Of course I do. You want revenge. You want blood. You want bodies, because they've killed your kind. Maybe you think you can burn down a stack of their cubes or at least gun down a busload of civilians."

I shook my head and walked up to him. "How little you think of us," I said. "We aren't fools. We want to strike a strategic blow."

"What are you after, then?"

"Their machine," I said. "We mean to destroy the system that allows them to walk on our soil."

Robert looked thoughtful.

"You see the possibilities, don't you?"

"How do you know they don't have a thousand machines?"

"Because they only seem to come through about once a day at most. I think they have a device, and it is in the cubes very near here. I think it takes a lot of preparation or power, and it doesn't work perfectly. If we take that machine out, we can set them back."

"OK," he said, "I'll admit, that doesn't sound as crazy as I thought your plan would be. Ballsy, but rational. But I still can't allow it."

"Allow it?" I asked. "Why not?"

"We all have our masters, Draith," he said. His eyes were almost apologetic.

Alarmed, I raised my pistol. I shouted a warning to everyone, but it was too late. I heard someone scream nearby. The scream turned into a hissing, gargling sound. It was Souza.

The light was bad and the scene was horrific. My mind couldn't quite grasp what my eyes were seeing at first. Then I realized what it had to be. One of the boulders we'd all been maneuvering around was—*eating* Souza. It had already rolled over his feet and now slid upward to complete the process by slowly consuming his legs. I knew it would soon burn his whole body to ash.

Souza was still conscious, still game. He held his dolly up and I felt a gush of heat wash all around me. The heat wave rolled outward in every direction. One of the SUV's tires popped and the headlights dimmed. Fiona fell, howling, beating at her clothes. Here and there in the desert, dry brush sparked and bloomed into flame.

"So *warm*," said a familiar, alien voice. "But Ezzie is still cold. Do it again!"

I realized two things at that moment. First off, *all* the boulders were moving around us, advancing on my cultist allies. Second, Robert was gone, having run off into the dark desert in the confusion. I would deal with Robert, but first I had to help my friends.

We had one critical advantage over Ezzie and her creeping brethren: we were faster. Souza wasn't able to escape, however. I grabbed his arms, and with Rheinman's help tried to drag him away from the moving boulders. The sifting sands helped. If the ground had been a hard surface, I don't think we could have pulled him free; Ezzie was too heavy. As it was, there was blood everywhere. The sands were black with it, and his legs didn't look good. His clothes were smoldering, having gotten some of the backlash of heat when he'd unleashed his object at Ezzie. He still had the rag doll in his hand, his fingers squeezing in a death grip.

We dragged him out into the desert behind the SUV. Rheinman was beating at the stone slugs from a distance with his hammer. Each strike caused a spark and a ringing report from the stone surface of the target. Tiny fountains of dust and rock chips flew where he struck them. Ezzie and her siblings finally retreated, complaining bitterly about the abuse.

Fiona, Gilling, and I tried to tie tourniquets just above the knee on both of Souza's ruined legs. He was losing a lot of blood. Before we could finish, he went limp and stopped breathing.

Robert was going to pay for this. "Rheinman, keep the stones away from the SUV," I said. "Fiona, you come with me. Gilling—stay here and help the others. I'll be back."

Gilling nodded and I headed out into the desert with the bloodthirsty girl at my side. We had a flashlight and found tracks to follow, but they were sketchy. I wasn't even sure they were Robert's. A hundred yards out, I stopped. We'd lost him.

"There," Fiona said, panting.

I followed her gesture. Something glimmered and twisted nearby. I ran to it, seeing a figure standing in front of a rip as it opened up. It was a small, dim whirlwind. But I was sure it led to another place.

"Stick him," I told Fiona. "Aim for his legs. We need to slow him down."

With an infernal grin on her face, she did as I asked. I heard a shout echo back to us. Then Robert stepped out. I ran faster. The rip, unlike those I'd seen Gilling or the Gray Men create, faded quickly. I ran to the spot and stepped out of my existence, blindly walking into another place.

Fiona hadn't followed me. I figured she hadn't been able to run fast enough. I was alone in a new place.

39

Crossing into another existence didn't happen all at once. It was rather like tuning in an old analog radio signal. It didn't come in without some fine-tuning. At first, some elements were hazy while others sharpened. As I stepped out of the dying rip into this new place, the first thing I noticed was the ground. It wasn't sand and spiky plants. Instead, it was comprised of hot, shifting mounds of slag and ash.

Heat. That was the next sensation I felt. All the sweat on my brow began to evaporate. It was dark, just as it had been back home, but there was a dim red glow coming from the ground here and there. I looked at the hottest spots and my mind knew what they had to be: lakes of lava.

My mind panicked for a second. I had fully expected, for some silly reason, to step into the place of the Gray Men. Compared to this strange environment, stacks of alien cubes and multiple moons would have been comforting.

I spotted Robert then, and my mind thawed. I realized with a shock that the rip behind me had faded and the way ahead was full of obstacles. If he vanished again, I might be stuck here until one of the hot little slugs swimming about found me and turned me to ash.

I ran for him as I'd never run in my life. My footing was uneven, and I stumbled over loose stones. I went down at one point, sinking my knees into a black ridge of ash between two smoldering pools. I howled as my knees and hands burned.

I was close enough now for Robert to hear me. He whirled and lifted a gun. The muzzle flashed orange. I threw myself down on the painfully hot ground and fired back with scorched fingers. At a range of around a hundred feet, our pistols were not terribly accurate. I had the advantage of hugging the ground. My arms were steadied by the ridge of hot ash. Unfortunately, I was also in pain, and the ash made my eyes blur.

Two of his rounds came uncomfortably close. He fired a spray of bullets, emptying his pistol fast. Stones jumped behind me and then a block of obsidian sparked and split apart in front of my face. I returned fire. We both missed. I heard him dry-click then drop the gun with a curse. He turned back to his growing rip, but it wasn't ready yet. He couldn't step out.

I stood up and charged after him, reloading and holding my fire until I got closer. I'd made it halfway when he tried to enter the rip again. It was ready now, brighter and stronger. His fingers pushed against the surface of it like a giant bubble. Soon, I knew the bubble would pop and allow him through.

I fired. I couldn't take the chance he would get away and leave me here. I snapped off round after round. This time, as I got closer, I hit him.

He went down on one knee. He crawled into the rip, but before he could make it all the way inside, I grabbed him and pulled him back. I threw him down on the ground and stood over him.

He was a mess. Two rounds in the chest, one in the leg. His breath whistled in his lungs. Blood was already frothing in his mouth. I lowered my pistol to my side.

"You shouldn't have ambushed us," I said.

"You should have left well enough alone. Why couldn't you be happy winning at the slots with my wife?"

I felt a sting of guilt, even though I knew I shouldn't. This guy had abandoned Jenna. He'd been part of a number of murders. But it was still hard to watch him die at my feet.

"I'm hurting," he said. "Take me out of here before the slugs come. You can fix me up."

I shook my head. "Give me some quick answers first."

"OK, just heal me enough to breathe."

I blinked at him. "Heal you?"

"Yeah, you idiot. Use the picture."

I stared, then rummaged in my pockets. I pulled out the photo I'd been carrying since awakening in the sanatorium.

"This?" I asked.

Nodding and coughing, Robert reached for it. Reluctantly, I let him take it. I figured if it was a trick, if he could use it as a weapon against me, my talisman should stop the attack.

He grabbed it and held it to his chest in relief. He rubbed it on the bloody holes in his shirt. The blood didn't stick to the photo. It was impossible to stain it. The sight was an odd one.

"Better," he said, breathing less shallowly.

I shook my head. "The photo has the power of healing? Does it dissolve bullets or what?"

"No," he said. "Don't you know what your own stuff does? God, what a number Meng did on your head. That's your trademark object, Draith. Fast healing. Remember now?"

I did, in a way. I recalled being known for fast healing. I'd been sure I could leave the hospital despite all my injuries. I'd confidently removed my cast. I nodded.

"It doesn't exactly *heal* you, it's more that it stabilizes you—moving you to what you once were," Robert explained. He sounded hurt and tired, but no longer on death's door.

"What if I shoot you in the head?" I asked. "Will it heal that?"

Robert looked up at me with narrowed eyes. "I'd rather not find out," he said.

"Then tell me who you work for."

"Already did. Rostok—the Community."

"Maybe we should go have a chat with him then," I said.

Robert laughed, but the laughter quickly shifted into a nasty coughing fit. "You're as crazy as ever," he said. "Help me up and into the rip. It goes back to the Lucky Seven."

I didn't move. "What is this place, exactly?"

"I don't know that. I'm not sure anyone does. But it is an existence that connects others. You can go through it to other places, if you live. Some worlds are like that. Small, but tightly interconnected. Our world is bigger."

"And the world of the Gray Men?"

"Big, like ours."

I nodded, believing what he said. It added up with what McKesson had told me days ago. He'd talked about getting lost in a place full of bright light and radiation. He'd talked about getting into and out of that world of white glare. Maybe this place was similar.

I helped Robert get to his feet, not knowing what else to ask. I figured that even with my photo, he wasn't immortal.

He was still bleeding and turning paler as the seconds ticked by.

More importantly, the rip looked like it was going to fade soon. I didn't want to be left here hoping I could figure out how to create a new one. I took my photo back from his rubbery fingers, and we stepped into the rip.

We appeared on rich carpets of burgundy framed with green. It had to be the Lucky Seven. I looked around and recognized the lobby area outside Rostok's office. Apparently not everything Robert had told me was a lie. I let him flop in a chair, barely conscious.

I tapped on Rostok's door. The door swung quietly open, just as it had before. The interior was dark, as always. A dim light ran along the bottom of every piece of furniture, limning it with a ghostly nimbus. I entered, leaving Robert in the chair outside. The door swung shut behind me.

40

"Your boy Robert is in pretty bad shape."

"He'll be…taken care of," Rostok said.

I glanced toward the shadow I knew was Rostok. He sat like a hulking cave bear in his overstuffed, leather-upholstered chair. I got up and poured myself a drink at his bar, dropping in three cubes of ice.

"Such impudence," Rostok said behind me.

"Sorry. I'm hot and thirsty. It's been a long day."

Rostok laughed. "Apparently! I'm more than impressed, Draith. You bring me back my chief agent, unarmed and barely alive. Not only have you defeated my best, but you have the balls to come here and flaunt it. I'm beginning to like you."

"Wish I could say the same," I said, swigging my drink. "Do you want one?"

"I'll get my own, if you don't mind."

"Suit yourself," I said, taking a chair and sighing as I sat back and took another big swallow. The best part of these visits was the smooth alcohol. This man spared no expense when it came to booze.

"You must tell me why you've come here...yet again."

I told him then of my adventures in the desert and my struggles with Robert and the Gray Men. I finished by describing my plans to take out whatever means the enemy used to step through into our territory with such impunity.

"And if I don't approve of your plans?"

"I don't know why you wouldn't. We are on the same side, here. Humanity must unite, if only to fight off an inhuman invader."

"Quaint thoughts."

"You don't agree?"

"I do, to some extent. Always, it has been postulated that all men would stand together given the need. Unfortunately, this has not been my experience."

I sipped my drink in the dark. I didn't like the way that sounded. "So, the Community is divided on what to do about the Gray Men?"

"Absolutely. They are also divided concerning your fate."

I swirled the ice cubes around my glass. It was disappointingly empty. "Mind if I freshen this?"

"Be my guest."

I hauled myself up and reloaded. The second glass tasted even smoother than the first.

"I'm going to offer you something, Mr. Draith, but I want you to understand the stakes first."

"I'm listening."

"You have bested more than one of my people. I do not tolerate such failures in field agents. I find I'm in need of talented help. What you have to understand is that taking a position with me is permanent and irreversible. There are many perks, however."

My mind was slightly hazy, in a good way. I realized he was offering me a job. I also realized he was threatening my life.

"You had Bernie killed, didn't you?" I asked.

"He failed me."

I nodded. "Are you firing Robert Townsend also?"

"He's been taken care of."

I felt a tiny chill, despite the alcohol in my blood. "I need some answers before I commit," I said. "How are these objects made?"

Rostok didn't answer right away. He heaved himself up, hulked past me, and began to assemble a drink for himself. When he was back in his chair, he sighed. "You ask too much."

"I've got a guess," I said.

He chuckled. "Tell me this guess."

I'd done a lot of thinking about the Gray Man's finger I kept against my chest even now. The blood was still fresh, unwilling to flow out of the flesh. I knew that was impossible—but there it was. It had to have become an object in the cellar beneath the mansion, and the only strange processes that had occurred there were a number of rips.

"One way the objects are made is when vortexes are formed," I said, voicing my theory. "If they are stuck in between two places for a long time, a normal item might transform somehow into an object."

Rostok didn't answer right away. "Who told you this theory?" he asked finally.

His response indicated to me I was on the right track. I shifted in my chair, throwing one leg over the arm of it.

"Meng," I lied.

"She is not usually so loose with information."

"So, she lives?" I asked, trying to sound unconcerned. Whether Rostok meant to do so or not, he'd confirmed my suspicions about the creation of these objects. They were forged by being caught between two existences.

Rostok huffed. "You believed you had slaughtered one of the Community so easily?"

"Of course not, I just wanted to make sure she was all right. Send her my apologies for the misunderstanding."

"Audacity and lies," Rostok chuckled. "You are full of both, Draith! But as you guessed, objects can be made in this fashion. The process is random, however. They are like diamonds, you see. Rare and valuable. We usually find them buried somewhere, identifiable only by their pristine state. But occasionally a new one is made."

"Why don't you manufacture a thousand objects by creating rips in space over and over until you get one?"

"The process is far from certain. We've tried to do it deliberately, but it never seems to work that way."

"So any rip can create one by accident?" I asked.

"Actually, when the Gray Men create a vortex they do it differently. The odds an object is made seem far greater."

I thought about his words, and a dark suspicion began to take root in my mind. The idea grew there like an evil fungus. Finally, I had to voice what I was thinking.

"I get it now," I said. "Your motivations have suddenly become clear. All along, I've wondered why the Community hadn't formed a coherent defense against the Gray Men. Why let these attacks go unchallenged? The only effort I've seen is from one guy, Detective McKesson, running around picking up the pieces. He covers up the messes, but doesn't seek to stop them from happening."

"Does this list of complaints have a point, Mr. Draith?"

"Yes. Rogues such as I, people you despise, we are doing more to battle the Gray Men than the entire Community. That's because you aren't interested in stopping them at all, are you? No, the Community sees this as some kind of gold rush. Objects are popping up at a much greater rate. You, Meng, and the rest don't care what the Gray Men do as long as they keep finding more objects. If they come here and perform an anal probe or two, what does it matter? You're like fishermen with a big net. All you have to do is let the Gray Men keep coming. If they want to kill rogues, so be it. Just let us run around and die, and then collect the fresh objects, tossing them in your vault afterward."

Rostok cleared his throat and shifted his bulk in his chair. "It is nowhere near as cold a process as you describe. We've gained a few items here and there, yes. But it seems you have gained more than I. You, a clueless rogue, have gathered a powerful set of objects. Enough to defeat Meng and give me pause. I don't like that development. Perhaps we've looked at this the wrong way. Perhaps a scarcity of objects is what we want, in order to retain our relative positions."

"What do you do with all these objects? Just lock them away?"

"No," he rumbled. "We use them. Let rogues check them out for missions—even trade with them. Once you are involved in this game, smaller matters such as money have little value. Barter is everything among the members of the Community. And there is only one currency that we all value."

I sipped my drink as we paused for several long seconds. I thought of all the people who'd died. The Community had the strength and the knowledge to face the Gray Men, but they'd seen fit to sit back and collect scraps. From their perspective, they were becoming rich even as lesser people died. I wouldn't soon forget that.

"What do you know about *me*, Mr. Rostok?" I asked, breaking the silence. "Do you know my past? Do you know if Quentin Draith is even my real name?"

"Worthless information. I don't trouble myself with what people did before they gained an object. It does not matter. What matters is how a man plays the game once he has begun."

I was disappointed. My history was still a blank to me, an empty void I'd like to fill some day.

"One more thing—" I began.

"No. You have milked me like a cow, and I must put a stop to it. Now you will answer *my* question. I have only one. Will you join my house or not?"

I looked at his bulky outline in the darkness. "I will not, at this time. I would prefer to remain like McKesson. Helpful, but independent."

Rostok generated a rumbling laugh. "Independent? There's no such thing. You've been working for Meng all this time, whether you knew it or not. You've been bird-dogging fellow rogues for her for years."

For years. I let that thought sink in, and I didn't like the feel of it.

"McKesson isn't independent," the old man continued. "He works for all of us collectively."

"All right," I said. "I'll take that route. Just as long as we are all on the same side."

Rostok hawked and spat. "You can't play me like this, Draith. You must be more careful when you are in my domain."

I stood up, setting my glass on the coffee table. It gleamed a soft, eldritch blue, lit by some source of light that wasn't immediately obvious to the eye. I calmly walked to the door.

"I'm sorry if I disappointed you, but I really must be going now."

I felt something then, as my back was turned to him. A gush of force. It was an odd sensation, but one that I was familiar with. The wall in front of me shook, as if someone had thrown an invisible couch at it. Perhaps that was exactly what had happened. The force didn't hit me, however. I was immune.

"Some kind of shield, is that it?" Rostok fumed behind me. "I can't be stopped so easily. I have a dozen objects in my vault, Draith. You can't insult me like this—"

"Rostok," I said, turning around with my pistol in my hand. It was at my side, aimed down at the carpet. But it was there, and my finger was on the trigger. "Let's not have any unpleasantness. Please accept my apologies, but I don't trust you. Don't forget, you just sent Robert Townsend to the desert to meddle in my affairs, and he killed a man named Souza, one of my friends."

"Friends? Are you talking about those crazy cultist rogues? Is that what this is about? You might as well call things crawling under rocks in the desert your friends, Draith. They have many similar qualities."

I slipped on my shades and forced the office door open. It had been locked, of course. I gave it an extra hard twist so the tumblers would never go back together properly. They would have to replace the entire mechanism.

"We'll meet again," I said, intending to step out of his office.

Rostok didn't shout, nor did he send any of his minions after me. Instead, he spoke calmly.

"All right, Draith," Rostok said behind me in the gloom. "I respect a man who can turn his back on me and live. What do you want to come work for me?"

"To work for the entire Community, you mean?" I asked. I glanced back, but I could no longer see him. I wondered what he must look like with the lights on.

"If you want it that way. But you'll take your missions from me."

I turned toward him. Standing in the office doorway, I was silhouetted by the relative glare coming in from the lobby area.

"I want peace between the rogues and the Community. Stop kicking us around. And I want war between the Community and the Gray Men."

"Is that all?" Rostok asked incredulously.

"Well, that might be overstating it. What I want is to strike the Gray Men and take out the machine that allows them to come to our version of this universe. I want your help and your blessing to perform this mission. That's my price."

Rostok questioned me about the Gray Men and I explained what I'd seen and where I'd been. It was his turn to get valuable information from me. I only held back the nature of the objects I had and what they could do. Those were secrets I'd decided to keep.

Rostok thought it over when I'd finished laying out my case. "What you are proposing is indeed a declaration of war."

"Let the blame ride on the rogues, then."

"Pretend I'm not involved, eh? The Gray Men, as you call them, are not fools, Draith. They have been probing for some time now, attempting to estimate our strength and determine how we operate. I suspect they don't have objects and don't understand them. They proceed with caution, but if we hit them, they might move against us more directly."

I knew that by "move against us" he meant "move against the Community," which was still the only group he cared about. I decided not to argue further about his abusive treatment of rogues such as myself. I'd given up on arguing for the greater good. I needed him to see a benefit for himself in my actions to gain his cooperation.

"Or," I said, "they might grow bolder as each day passes and we don't respond to their attacks. We should stop thinking as disconnected individuals. We should include Earth's governments as well."

Rostok gave a rumbling laugh at that. "Who do you think makes up much of our Community? We do have government people, plus billionaires and the like. At any rate, I accept your proposal. In return for your service, I will allow this mission to proceed and I will send aid. But don't push me like this again."

I nodded, suddenly regretting I had broken his lock. We were allies now—I hoped. I decided it was best to exit before the damage was discovered. I mumbled my good-byes and pushed the door shut behind me. It didn't quite latch, but it did stay closed long enough for me to leave.

In the lobby area, I found Robert Townsend had vanished. There were bloodstains on the chair where he'd been and a few droplets led to the elevator. I got the impression he'd been dragged away. I wondered if he was still alive. From Rostok's hints, I doubted it. In my mind, I was already editing what I was going to tell Jenna about all this.

I took the stairs down.

41

Things went slowly for a while after that, compared to how fast they'd been going. But a few days later, I once again found myself standing in the desert east of Las Vegas. Under the cover of the falling dusk, McKesson, Rheinman, and Gilling joined me. McKesson was apparently working for Rostok today.

When the rich old man who lived on top of the eastern tower of the Lucky Seven had promised me support, I had envisioned a private army. Instead, I'd received one half-interested detective. I gathered that Rostok still didn't want anything about this action directly traceable to him.

We'd come in two separate vehicles. Gilling drove the SUV this time, while McKesson followed us, bumping along in his sedan. It had taken us better than an hour to find the shallow depression with the scorched region in its midst. I'd been looking for the cluster of boulders, but of course, those had all come to life and crawled away. When we finally found the spot in the red light of the dying sun, McKesson climbed out of his car and began complaining.

"I thought you knew where the hell you were going," he said. "It was sheer luck that I didn't break an axle."

"Sorry," I said without a hint of regret. "This spot doesn't look the same today."

We left Rheinman as lookout and guard at the top of the rise, standing with the two vehicles. We walked down into the pit of the depression, which still felt hot under my shoes. The lava slugs had left hot zones here, which still sent up wisps of vapor when we kicked at the sands that covered them. The creatures had applied enough heat to the land to form trails of slag. Underneath the blowing top layer of grit, spikes of glass were everywhere.

"This is just like the blasted desert up north," McKesson said, toeing the crunchy ground with his black leather shoes.

"The testing sites?" I asked.

"Yeah. Some of the atomic tests were above ground, you know. About a hundred of them. There were big patches of desert turned to glass and slag."

"All right," Gilling said, clasping his hands. "Now that we are all here, Detective, please enlighten us."

"About what?"

"Why did they send you? What have you brought to this—party?"

We both stared at him. I wanted to know the answer too.

McKesson shrugged. "I was asked to help."

"Excuse me, but we're not impressed," Gilling said. "We expected more from Rostok than one mercenary of questionable loyalty."

McKesson snorted. "Look who's talking. A couple of rookie rogues with big ideas. By all logic, I should shoot you both in the back now, bury your corpses, then run back to the Community claiming the Gray Men did it."

"And why would that be a good idea?" I asked, my eyes narrowing.

"Because this is a suicide mission."

I gave him a cold smile. "We aren't turning our backs on you now; you realize that, don't you?"

"Yeah, well, I kinda figured I'd blown that easy out when I told you about it. So, it's time to answer your question, Gilling." McKesson walked to the back of his dusty sedan and popped open the trunk. He lifted something heavy from the back.

I shoved my hand into my jacket pocket and gripped my gun. I realized I'd lost the last shreds of my trusting nature at some point over the preceding days, if I'd ever had such a nature to begin with. By the standards of a normal person, I was paranoid. But as I kept telling myself, I had good cause.

McKesson came back lugging a large metal case. It was about four feet long and made with ugly, green-painted metal. It was unmistakably military in appearance. He put it down at our feet and snapped open the latches. As we watched, he opened it. An even uglier piece of equipment was inside. It consisted of black metal tubes and green conical tips.

"This is what I brought to the party," McKesson said.

I detected a hint of pride in his voice. For the first time today, I was impressed with him. "Some kind of rocket launcher?" I asked.

"Yeah. An RPG-seven with optical sights and an armor-piercing head. Soviet-made. It's a bit out of date, but it'll do the job."

"What job is that?" Gilling asked.

McKesson looked at him with his eyebrows riding high. "What if we can't get inside those cubes with Draith's burglar routine?" he asked. "Or what if this imaginary machine of yours is really big? How were you planning to damage something the size of a house?"

Gilling pursed his lips and nodded. Now we were both impressed.

"Where the hell did you get such a thing?" I asked him.

He shrugged. "Drug dealers have big budgets for toys these days. And sometimes evidence sits around inside a cage in the station basement for a long time."

I shook my head. "You really like to bend the rules don't you, Detective?"

"I like to get the job done," he said. He sealed the case back up again. "We've only got three shots. We have to make them count."

Gilling and I set up the next part of the mission while darkness fell around us. We'd decided to work at night to attract less attention from the road, which was about a mile south of us. Creating the rip down in the depression where we'd met Robert and the slugs seemed as good a spot as any. The glimmer and flash of the rip itself would be invisible from the road down there.

While Gilling was paging through his book, looking for an inspiring bit of poetry to chant, McKesson came close.

"I've got something else," he said quietly.

I looked at him expectantly. He eyed Gilling, then lifted his hand, cupping something within it. I was reminded of a drug deal pass-off. I took the object and examined it. Whatever it was, it was about the size of a doughnut and wrapped in aluminum foil.

"What's with the wrapper?" I said, beginning to peel it open.

"Don't," he said suddenly.

"Why not?"

"It's an object. Rostok said it's dangerous."

"How dangerous?"

"Very. He said not to use it until you wanted to destroy something big."

I nodded. Another bomb. I carefully crushed the aluminum foil over the object and slipped it into my pocket. I'd never handled an object that was directly destructive before. I had respect for such tools, however. I thought of the rag doll that fired gusts of intense heat. That thing seemed to kill anyone who used it. I wasn't sure what Gilling had done with the doll, and I didn't care as long as he didn't give it to me.

"Did you add the foil?" I asked.

McKesson shrugged. "It used to wrap my lunch. I don't like touching objects I don't know how to handle. It's your baby now, but you have to give it back to Rostok when we complete this mission."

"What if I don't want to?"

"Rostok said you will."

I thought about that while we watched Gilling make his final preparations. He used five buckets of organic material to fuel his rip. Each bucket contained a gallon of lard. He'd proclaimed it was almost as good as blood—which was still the best, apparently. Gilling explained the fuel would burn quickly and brightly, but wouldn't last long. I hoped we wouldn't need much time, and I liked the idea of our trail closing quickly behind us. With luck, it would be the last chance the Gray Men had to come after us.

Gilling did his chanting and read from his book of Charles Baudelaire's French poetry. McKesson rolled his eyes.

Quand la Vengeance bat son infernal rappel,
Et de nos facultés se fait le capitaine?
Ange plein de bonté connaissez-vous la haine?…

I listened, catching a few words. The passage was something about angels, armies, and hate. I'd taken the time to look up Baudelaire's work on the Internet. It had been outlawed in France two centuries ago. Gilling sure could pick an uplifting piece.

Somehow, Gilling's chant made the entire experience more otherworldly. I felt disconnected from my surroundings. Maybe it was the stark insanity of what I was about to attempt. We were going to assault unknown beings in their lair and try to damage equipment we'd never seen, but knew they must hold dear. My respect for these Gray Men increased as I embarked on the kind of mission they had performed against us many times. They had real courage to come to our existence and make daring strikes. But when I thought of Holly, Tony, and an unknown number of others, I hated them anyway.

When the rip opened enough to step out, we didn't waste any time. I went first, and then McKesson came right behind me, lugging his RPG box. We left Gilling and Rheinman behind in the desert. Their job was to keep the rip burning until our return and to kill any Gray Men who tried to flank us by coming through to our side.

I could see a blur of walls around us. Where were we? My first thought was that we had made a mistake. Gilling had screwed up, reading the wrong poem, perhaps. With my luck, we'd find ourselves in the Lucky Seven again, or maybe in the middle of a shopping mall. That was going to require quite a bit of explaining.

I pressed ahead and stepped out of the active region of the rip. Reality shifted and rippled around me, but at last my senses operated properly and I saw where I was.

Walls. Flat, square, and boring. They weren't gray, but rather a dull golden color like that of molten tin. I twisted this way and that, looking for armed enemies. There weren't any. The walls were featureless for the most part. The cubical nature of them was unmistakable.

"Bull's-eye," I whispered over my shoulder. "We're inside the cubes!"

I glanced back, expecting to see McKesson standing there with his box. But he still stood in the rip. I could see his outline blurring and whipping about like a dark sheet in a stiff wind. When seen inside a rip, a man looked like a painting done by a half-blind impressionist.

I snorted. McKesson was waiting to see if I died on the spot. I waved both my arms, beckoning him forward. The room was essentially empty, about the size of a standard living room with a high ceiling, and there was only a single corridor against the far wall that led in and out. The corridor had nothing that could block it; there were no doors to close.

McKesson finally inched forward out of the rip.

"All clear?" he asked me quietly.

"Get out here and cover me."

He did so, with many reluctant glances. I felt cautious too, but decided bold action was a better policy. For all I knew, alarms were sounding in other cubes, and armed Gray Men were racing to this spot. We had no idea if they had cameras on us or not.

"Every second we stand around we are losing our element of surprise," I told him.

"Yeah, but the longer they don't know we're here, the longer we have to find this mystery machine of yours."

"You can't carry that box everywhere," I said.

"I suppose you're right. I thought we would have to blast down a wall. I can't believe we're already inside."

I gestured for him to hurry. I watched as he snapped open the box and quickly assembled the RPG. He loaded the weapon and stood up.

"I'll lead," I said. "Don't shoot me in the back."

McKesson shouldered his RPG, which now looked like a large rifle with a pointed rocket on the nose. In his other hand, he carried another charge. We were down to two, and I hoped that would be enough.

We walked for what seemed like a long time, passing more cubical rooms. Each was identical to the one we'd first entered. We passed eight of them, most of which had a truck parked inside. I realized we were in a garage, of sorts. I didn't see how the trucks were supposed to get out of these cubes, since the walls they faced were blank, flat sheets of metal. I didn't see a door or a button to push to open one.

Feeling like a rat sniffing at a trap too complex to comprehend, I pressed ahead. The first cube hadn't had a truck in it and I counted this as a further stroke of good luck. We'd appeared in a relatively quiet region of their garage at night, and that was much better than popping into their mess hall in the middle of dinner. It was almost as if we'd planned it.

A negative thought nagged at me, however. *Nine garages?* Having that many garages indicated they might have a lot of personnel who needed transporting. That news wasn't so good.

We came to the end of the line of garages and the corridor turned to the right. I turned with it, leaning around a corner with my gun in my hand. There was no one there, but new sounds assaulted me. Loud sounds of heavy machinery.

A buzzing hum came through strongest of all, a sound that set my teeth on edge.

"What's wrong?" McKesson hissed at my back.

"Something new up ahead," I said.

I led the way, creeping ahead. I wanted to move faster, but it was nearly impossible. I expected one of those big bolts of energy to burn me down any second.

The next room was different. A dozen times the size of the garages, this region was a massive area filled with hot pipes that sweated thick liquids. I felt the heat on my face the moment I came through.

"What the hell?" asked McKesson.

I shared the thought but didn't say anything. I walked along the empty, safer side. We were in the open now. Thinking about the building layout, I figured we must have seen the entire first floor by now. One side was a row of garages. Logically, these had to be located on the ground level so the trucks could drive out into the desert. Now we had entered the second half of the building, the one dominated by this strange machinery.

"Is this it?" asked McKesson. "This has to be it. Let's blow it up and run."

I shook my head. "For all we know, we'll be destroying their sewage plant. I don't see any projectors or computers. This looks more like a generator for power or hot water."

"What the hell are we going to do, then?" McKesson demanded. "Keep prowling around until they find us?"

"Let's see what's at the far end."

Grumbling behind me, McKesson followed. I picked up the pace to a trot. We were exposed, and the only thing I could think to do was move faster.

We found our first Gray Man then. He was wearing something like a wet suit. He had his back to us and was in the midst of the pipes, checking them or repairing them. The machinery was making so much noise he didn't even notice us pass by.

I felt even more nervous, but also exhilarated. The building wasn't empty, but the Gray Men didn't seem to know we were here. All that changed in the next few seconds.

I heard three sharp pops behind me. I stopped, frowning, and looked back. McKesson wasn't there. I walked with my gun in sweating hands back the way I'd come. He soon reappeared. I knew in an instant what he'd done.

"What the hell?" I demanded.

"What? I eliminated a threat. Are you in love with these guys now too?"

"You didn't have to shoot him!"

"Yeah, I did," he said. "I'm not leaving one of them behind us. Any second he could have seen us in that long, straight hallway. We wouldn't even know, and he'd sound the alarm. Don't forget, Draith, you wanted to come here."

Annoyed and uncertain whether he was right or wrong, I turned and pressed ahead. We finally reached the far end of the building. What we found was a corridor leading back to the other side of the building. Ahead I saw the back of one of their trucks. I understood the building layout now. This ramp led down to the garages again on the other side. We'd taken the long way around the entire bottom floor of the building.

"Something's wrong," McKesson said. "Look at the lighting."

I did, and I saw what he meant. It was bluish now and pulsating slightly. There was no change to the deafening sounds of the place, but the lighting had indeed shifted. I wondered if the Gray Men really were deaf and they used subtle lighting variations to communicate.

"I bet that's a Gray Man alarm signal," McKesson said.

"Yeah, because you executed one of them."

"We've got to take our shot and leave."

I breathed hard, trying to think. We were amateurs, all right. McKesson wasn't even willing to follow my leadership. Now that he'd blown our cover, we didn't have much time.

"Wait here for a second," I said. "I'll check down this corridor."

"That goes back to the garages, back to where we came in."

"Probably, but I'm going to check. If there's no better target, we'll blow up this system. Even if it's full of sewage."

"Hurry," he said.

I ran down the corridor and found a T intersection. A ramp led upward to my right. I had expected stairs or an elevator, but apparently stairs weren't in style for Gray Men. They connected levels with ramps.

That moment of staring and thinking almost cost me my life. A jolt of freezing plasma flashed down from the ramp. I think I survived only because they'd tried for a head shot. Fortunately, they missed. My hair was frosted white, however, and a searing pain lanced the back of my skull. I lurched forward past the intersection with the ramp. Without looking, I pointed my gun up the ramp toward them. Only my gun and my hand were exposed. I fired again and again, blindly. My first empty magazine clattered on the ramp at my feet. I reloaded the gun with a fresh magazine.

Two more beams lanced down at me. They iced over a spot on the floor. The metal crackled and smoked. I fired three return shots, still without looking. I realized there was no way I was going to win this fight. There were several of them, and they were probably already moving to flank me.

I heard more sounds then. Distant booms. I had no idea what they might mean. Almost immediately after these sounds, the lighting shifted again from blue to a subtle lavender. Another, deeper level of alert? What were those booms? The urge to run became overwhelming. This mission was over.

Behind me was the corridor leading to the garages. Ahead, across a deadly kill zone, was the path that led back to where I'd left McKesson. I couldn't see him now. I realized my best move would be to run to the vortex we'd used to come here and step out. I could go home to my own peaceful desert in less than one minute.

But I hesitated. Another snap and boom sounded. More bolts of cold came down the ramp. They weren't advancing, I could tell. They were pinning me down here and probably sending more troops around to get me from behind. Once they had me in a crossfire, I had no hope of survival. But I didn't want to run and leave McKesson behind.

Cursing the day I'd met the man, I fired a last spray of bullets around the corner and up the ramp to make them duck, then I jumped across the open passage. I barely made it. The sole of my right shoe was frozen into a lumpy, misshapen mass. I was never sure afterward if I'd stepped in one of those cold spots or if one of the bolts had clipped my foot. In any case, I was running slightly off balance as I reached end of the corridor.

When I got there, I stared in disbelief. I instantly understood what I had been hearing. McKesson had fired his weapon and run. Hot, goopy fluid like oily blood gushed over the floor. McKesson himself was nowhere to be seen. His RPG, minus the charges, lay on the floor. Immediately next to that was a rip in space.

The rip was a small one, and it was guttering already. It would soon go out and vanish.

I reached into my pocket and pulled out the object McKesson had so thoughtfully wrapped in aluminum foil. I ripped off the foil. If I'd ever needed some firepower, this was the moment.

The object was...an alarm clock. It was small and old-fashioned. Painted a bright yellow, it had two bells on top for ears and a smiling face with closed eyes on the dial. I squinted at the antique child's clock. What was I supposed to do with this? I tried twisting the knobs in back, and the hands spun and the bells on top dinged once. I winced, but there was no reverberating boom. Did one simply set it down and let it go off like a bomb? I wasn't sure. I felt a tickle of sweat.

Rostok had set me up, I thought. He'd given me something that would kill me and the Gray Men together, planning to take great pleasure in the reports afterward. Maybe McKesson was in on it, and that was why he'd fled. Together, the two of them would sip fine booze in the dark tonight, having a laugh at my expense. Perhaps I'd warrant a toast for a job well done.

Running feet. I heard no shouting, but the Gray Men never shouted. They were charging down the corridors after me. In moments, they would come into the area where I was standing and freeze me into a block of ice. When I hit the floor, I would shatter into a dozen shards of icy meat. I could see Old Red's split-open body in my mind.

I almost put the clock down and left, but I couldn't quite do it. The thought that gave me courage was the knowledge that Rostok didn't like losing objects. No one did. That lowered the odds he'd sent me here on a suicide mission.

I decided to give the clock one more try the moment the Gray Men arrived. Maybe it needed a specific target to operate. I didn't have to wait long. Gray Men came jogging into sight.

I held the clock out in front of me and willed it to operate, to fire, to *destroy*. For a fraction of a second, nothing happened. Then the twin, yellow-painted bells on the top of the clock began to rattle. The rattle quickly turned into a high-pitched, irritating ring.

The Gray Men spotted me and raised their weapons. But they didn't fire immediately. Perhaps they were too shocked by the monstrous blob of rock that swelled up between us as fast as a wave crests and breaks. Something huge bubbled up out of the floor in front of the clock. It ballooned higher until it was the size of a car, then grew bigger still, becoming the size of a small bus. The growth slowed at that point, but it seemed to me it was still puffing up and up.

I saw the Gray Men for only a moment. They were on the far side of this massive, rocklike lump. When I saw them, I noted shock in their faces. I heard their guns unleashing frozen beams. The monster I'd created grated with a voice that shook the metal beneath me. It extended two eyes on stone stalks and I knew then what I was seeing. It was a lava creature, one as big as a school bus now. It turned and lurched toward the things that had hurt it with rays of splashing frost. Cold…the sensation it hated above all else.

If there's one thing I'm good at, it's knowing when to run. I turned around and bolted for the small rip McKesson had left behind and dove into it. Behind me the monster's back rippled against the roof, shaking the cubes that could no longer contain it.

I was inside the circle of the rip now, and all sensation of the Gray Men and the monster I'd unleashed upon them ceased as if it had never been. I could no longer hear, see, or smell their world. It was relief, but it was short-lived.

I'd never experienced a passage like this one. I think it was different because the rip was so close to vanishing. The edges weren't stable anymore. They had turned into knives with perfect edges.

I was reminded of a time I'd once picked up a length of sheet metal, freshly cut and curled on the floor. I'd been building something—I couldn't recall what it was. But the memory was a true one from my past, that much I was sure of. I had cut my palms back then, so perfectly I didn't feel it at first. I had taken my hand away, dropping the sheet metal, but my hands had looked fine. A second later, the blood had begun to flow. The illusion of wholeness had vanished. I had sliced both my hands open in long lines.

Stepping through the rip was like that. Its edges cut my legs and shoulders. My head was down; otherwise, I might have cut it cleanly off my neck. As it was, my shirt was slashed open on my back. My left shin got the worst of it. A long gash ran around my bone and a half inch deep into the meat of my calf.

I tumbled and rolled, knowing I was hurt. The ground was hot under me, and rougher than the desert should have been. The feeling of heat became increasingly intense as the rip faded, and I was left lying on a slanted region of smoking black ash.

I recognized the sulfurous smell of the place. Brimstone and fantastic heat. I had to be in the world of the lava slugs. I opened my eyes, gritting my teeth against the pain. I looked around and saw a figure retreating in the distance. He was walking away from me, upslope.

"McKesson!" I roared after him.

The figure paused, then slowly turned around. In front of him, a new rip glimmered. He had been about to step through to some other, better place. He stood there, gazing back at me. I couldn't get up. My leg was too badly cut. My clothes were burning away too. I could feel blood running down my neck and back from a number of serious injuries. I struggled up onto one elbow.

"McKesson, *dammit*! You said you owed me!"

He walked back slowly. "Oh yeah, I owe you all right. You shot me back home in my car, Draith. You remember that?"

"I shot an object," I said. "You just happened to be on the other side of it."

"I still have a bruise, you know."

"You ditched me. You fired the RPG and took off. I could have run for the other rip, but instead I came back down the ramp to find you."

McKesson sighed and crouched next to me. "Can you get up?" he asked.

I shook my head. It was humiliating and painful. "Rostok gave you Robert's object, didn't he?" I asked.

"Robert didn't need it anymore," McKesson said, smiling tightly. He showed me his wrist, but not the one with the watch strapped to it. A dirty white sleeve hung there, clipped by a gold cufflink. I noticed there wasn't another cufflink on the other side. I figured the cufflink must be Robert's object.

"Both his objects were jewelry?" I asked.

"No, the cufflink isn't the object. I just lost the other one."

I looked at his hand again. He had something in his palm. Staring at his hand, I realized he was holding something. A coin. It looked like an ordinary quarter.

"This is it," McKesson said, hefting the quarter. "It's one of the old ones from the nineteen fifties. All silver."

"That's wonderful. Now, get me out of here. I think my pants are burning off."

"First, let me give you a pointer," he said, sounding like a veteran talking to a rookie.

I stared at him, wondering why he wasn't hauling me to my feet. Vaguely, I wondered who in this day and age still wore cufflinks on a regular basis. Maybe that was another of his objects. I didn't know. McKesson was so full of crap, even if he told me everything, I could never be sure what parts he had invented.

"See this ash?" he asked me. "This shit is valuable—sometimes. Dig in it like this."

He demonstrated by kicking at a large hump of ash. "You want to find a good hard spot down in one of the craters. It has to be close to the lava, see? But not too close. Sometimes a big nodule of ash really delivers."

I had no idea what he was talking about, but I watched because I had no choice. McKesson kicked at a blackened lump five or six times until it split open. A mass of crystalline chips sprayed out.

"Now usually, you get crap. Quartz, ebony, glass. But sometimes you get lucky. Sometimes, you get emeralds, peridots, diamonds. Really, it's hard to tell until you take a mess of these to a jeweler."

"Man," I said, teeth clenched in pain. "I really appreciate this, but I'd appreciate a trip home even more."

McKesson chuckled. "Yeah. You wouldn't want to get trapped here. See that slug out there in the pool? He's out in the lava now, but you can tell he's coming. He's smelled you, or something. They sense flesh and blood. They are quicker in the lava, aren't they? Not like on land. Heat makes them move faster."

I craned my neck and stared out into the crater. I couldn't help it.

McKesson squatted nearby. He put out his hand.

"What now?"

"Give me the clock."

I looked at him, hating him. I put the clock in his hand. I found that, just as Rostok had said, I didn't want to keep the thing. How often did I need to destroy a town?

McKesson palmed the alarm clock and pointed at the monster in the lava. "See him?" he asked, his voice husky and urgent. "Right there, about a dozen yards out. That hump isn't a normal bubble. Normal bubbles don't swim in one direction like a cockroach under a napkin."

Did McKesson want to make me rich, save me, torment me, or was he just having fun? I couldn't tell. But I did see the hump in the lava, and it was definitely swimming my way. I wished I wasn't out of ammo—I would have drawn my gun on the detective and ordered him to drag me out of here.

But when I looked back toward McKesson, he was gone. A rip stood in his place. I dragged myself uphill by my elbows, sending up plumes of hot ash. I cursed the day McKesson had been whelped by an inhuman mother. I understood now that he'd wanted me to experience a little pain and fear, because I'd once done the same to him. But he'd made me rich as well. As I passed the broken nodule of black ash on my way to the rip, I scooped up the gemstones that had spilled out. I shoved them in my pockets, where they burned against my thighs and stomach. After all, who knew how long it would be before I returned here? I wasn't the kind of man who passed up easy money.

43

It was nearly two months later when we officially closed the case of the Gray Men. Their murderous rampage had ended—for now. Most parties speculated that the structure of oily pipes we'd blown up had been some kind of a power source. Maybe the monster I'd released in the midst of the building had done the trick. In any case, the machine that allowed them to open rips into our world seemed to have been rendered inoperable.

In truth, we really weren't sure why the raids ended. Maybe it was the shock of being counterattacked successfully. Maybe the Gray Men had their own regiment of government accountants and budget jockeys running their daily lives, just as we did. When the costs grew too high, the risks too great, perhaps someone on their side pulled the plug on the project. Whatever the reason, they had stopped coming, and I received the majority of the credit for stopping them.

Jenna drove out to see me soon after I picked up the keys to my new home. She was impressed, as she'd never seen the mini-mansion before. Standing in the golden afternoon light on the north terrace, the view was breathtaking. We looked down together over a yard full of freshly planted palm trees. Downtown Las Vegas sprawled in the distance, filling the flatlands encircled by stark moonscape mountains.

"Isn't it a little creepy out here—at night, I mean?" Jenna asked me.

I smiled, refilling her glass with fresh chardonnay. "The cultists don't hold their little meetings here anymore," I said.

"But people have died here."

"A few," I admitted. "But I haven't seen their ghosts yet."

"Well, you know what I mean."

"Yeah, you're wondering how I can sleep in a place that attracted the Gray Men more than most. They liked coming here. They did it multiple times."

Jenna and I were friends again. She'd taken the news of Robert's death hard, despite the fact he'd run out on her. I'd learned their whirlwind romance had been a brief, intense thing. Just the sort of relationship that Las Vegas weddings were famous for consummating. But in some ways, I think the brevity of her love affair with Robert helped her get over him faster. She'd been with him a few months, married, and then had it officially annulled on the basis of his disappearance. It was nothing to be proud of, but they were scars that would heal in time.

We sipped from our glasses and gazed down on the metropolis together. From this vantage point, I better understood why rich people liked to build houses on hillsides. It felt as if you owned the world.

"Did Rostok buy the house for you?" she asked me.

I shook my head. "No, I did that on my own."

"You could afford *this?*"

"I had a bit of money, but not enough for this place. One thing that helped—it was a foreclosure and I got it at auction."

"What else helped?" she pressed.

"Well, Rostok's bank held the paper on the mortgage."

"*Rostok* sold the place to you?" she asked, laughing. "I get it. He wants you to stay here and play watchdog. In case they come back."

I grimaced slightly. I had come to a similar conclusion, but didn't want to think about it in those terms. I preferred to call the house a trophy, a prize in return for a job well done—and also as payment for the house Robert had destroyed with his lava slugs. I shrugged, not wanting to dwell on my status with the Community and Rostok in particular. They saw me as both useful and annoying. An irritant that would be tolerated only as long as was necessary. I sensed they wouldn't move against me for now, but I knew Meng still smoldered.

A few other things lingered in my mind. I could not stop thinking about Holly and all the others who had suffered. The Community wanted to blame the Gray Men—but many of the recent deaths could not be attributed to them. Tony, for instance, had died with his innards full of sand. As far as I knew, a weapon that could perform such an odd trick wasn't in the Gray Man arsenal.

I didn't know much about myself either. My prior life was still a hole in my mind, but I'd decided to forge new memories and get along with what I had. Something must have showed on my face, because Jenna stopped talking and eyed me curiously. I smiled and hoped she hadn't just asked me anything important. She smiled back, and I knew I'd lucked out.

There were still mysteries unsolved. I still had work to do, but I didn't want to spoil this moment with Jenna. I turned the conversation to Jenna herself and her plans for the future.

"Are you going home?" I asked her quietly. She'd come fully packed. Her rental car was bursting with suitcases. She'd been on many shopping sprees with the money she'd won from the casinos.

"I have to leave soon. But I could be convinced to stay a few days longer."

I smiled slowly. I reached out and touched her elbow. She didn't pull away, so I touched her shoulder lightly. She still hadn't met my gaze, so I lifted her chin and kissed her.

Soon, I was doing my best to convince her. I had fresh hopes for the rest of the evening.

End of *Technomancer*

ABOUT THE AUTHOR

B. V. Larson is the bestselling author of over twenty novels, spanning genres from military science fiction to epic fantasy to paranormal romance. He lives with his wife and children in the western United States, where he also teaches college.